The Stand-In

The Stand-In

LILY CHU

Published by Sourcebooks Casablanca, an imprint of Sourcebooks
P.O. Box 4410, Naperville, Illinois 60567-4410
(630) 961-3900
sourcebooks.com

Originally published in 2021 as an audiobook by Audible Originals.

Library of Congress Cataloging-in-Publication Data is on file with the publisher.

Printed and bound in United States of America.
WOZ 10 9 8 7 6 5 4 3 2 1

For Auntie Bernie

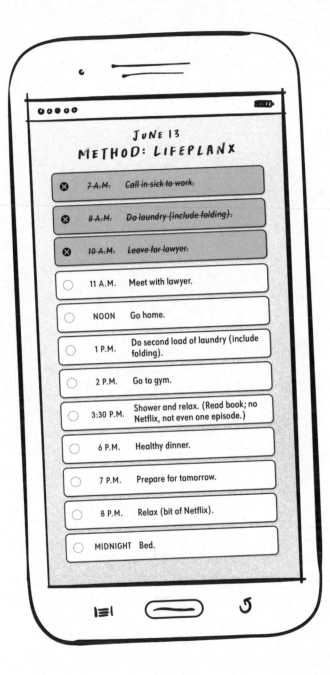

One

My day is tidily laid out on my new LifePlanX app. It's a work of art, to be honest. Here, the Life of Gracie Reed is beautifully organized and color-coded in neat little rows, a guarantee against indecision and inaction.

This Gracie has it together. This Gracie is a boss. Totally unlike the real, pathetic Gracie who just stepped out of the lawyer's office and promptly started blubbering like a spineless wuss. *You waited until you were outside,* I congratulate myself. *You didn't cry in front of him. Small wins are still wins.*

I tap my phone screen so that **meet with lawyer** is emphatically crossed out, which makes me feel a teeny bit better even though nothing's actually changed. But according to my latest self-help read, just saying the word *done* is supposed to deliver a shot of that sweet drug dopamine, and I'll take all the satisfaction I can get.

It's not yet noon so I decide to sneak in a coffee break, which is not on my schedule and is therefore verboten by the LifePlanX app people. Their whole premise is that each minute of your day should be allocated to predetermined tasks without any wavering or add-ons. **You only do what you log** admonishes the tagline. In an effort to keep me on my path to success, the app sends me chipper reminders of where I should be at particular points of the day—and usually am not.

Screw it. I deserve sugar and caffeine. I toss the phone into my bag, jam a baseball cap on my head, and head over to my favorite café.

"Looking glum, friend." Cheri looks up when I enter to the discordant accompaniment of bells. "Want your usual?"

I could actually go for something special as a pick-me-up—maybe one of those bougie frappes with fancy flavors like salted honey or sage caramel—but since she's already started making the latte, I nod before leaning over to inspect the shelf of muffins. "I need chocolate, too."

"Oh, we're at chocolate levels of glumness." She wrinkles her nose. "Sorry, babe. Loni took the last one for her kid."

When Loni sees me look over, she gives a friendly wave, so I hastily attempt to morph my involuntary death stare into a matching reciprocal smile. I don't succeed in time. Her eyes widen and she unconsciously leans against her wife as if seeking protection against my disproportionate muffin wrath. Her wife wraps a loving arm around Loni's shoulders, and I suddenly feel stupid for thinking that baked goods would make me feel better.

"Can't be that bad," says Cheri, cleaning the espresso machine with a cloth. Then she frowns. "I have to stop saying that," she scolds herself. "It can totally be that bad. You might have a broken heart. You might have received a terrible diagnosis. You might have been catfished or lost your true love or witnessed an accident." She pauses as if considering the vast opportunities for sadness the world has to offer, then shakes her head.

It's none of those things, but it's still pretty awful. Thirty-eight minutes ago, I took my courage in hand and gave Fred the Employment Lawyer several hundred dollars to tell me exactly what I suspected: I didn't have any proof my boss, Todd, was a fucking sexual predator, and without proof, I had no case.

"Have you gone to your HR department?" he asked after I'd outlined the situation.

"No." Why would I have bothered when I already knew they wouldn't believe me?

Fred looked at me over his bifocals. "That's usually the first step unless you fear retaliation."

"I did. I do." Todd is malicious, and I don't want to take the risk of having more of his nastiness and spite focused on me.

"Did you tell anyone at all?"

"No."

He nodded. "Then we need proof. Emails. Voice recordings. Witnesses."

"He's smart about it." I sat stiffly in the chair, humiliated at having to tell another human being about how I'd let this level of harassment happen to me. I'd had so much on my plate that at first it was easier to simply ignore Todd's behavior and tell myself it wasn't that big of a deal.

"Then you need to be smarter."

"That's not fair."

"No," he agreed. "It's how the law works. Once you get me that proof, we can nail his sorry ass to the wall. Can you quit?"

Not an option, not right now. I can't jeopardize my employment, and so far I haven't been able to find a new job. I let out a long sigh. Definitely not problems that can be solved by a chocolate muffin.

"I'll take the Bluebell Blueberry Bomberama," I tell Cheri, directing my attention to a decision I can control. It's vegan and bran, more of a refueling puck than sweet treat, but thanks to Loni's selfish toddler, it's the only muffin left except for cardamom squash. Which is also bran.

As I mentally resign myself to a healthy dose of insoluble fiber, a blinding flash of light explodes to my left. Stars dance in my eyes for several seconds and then slowly fade away to reveal a small man wearing a Pink Panther-esque trench coat and trilby hat. "Smile, beautiful."

I automatically obey with a reflexive grin that falls off right away, because what the fuck? He takes another picture, then a tsunami of clicks wash over me as his camera snaps and the flash pings in rapid succession. I squeeze my eyes shut and throw up my arms, holding the muffin in front of my face as protection.

Cheri chucks her dirty dishcloth at the photographer, who yelps indignantly when it lands smack on his chest, covering his raincoat with coffee grounds.

"Yo, Ansel Adams. Get the hell out of my store and stop hounding my customers. You're trespassing."

He opens his mouth to argue, but she threateningly grabs a pot of freshly brewed coffee and leans over the counter as if daring him to mouth off. With an angry shrug, he blows me a kiss and saunters out.

I turn to Cheri. "Ansel Adams?"

She puts down the pot and hands over my latte with a half-turned smile. "Couldn't think of another photographer."

"Ansel Adams did landscapes, didn't he? Not people?"

"Like I said. Couldn't think of another one. Also, that's very judgmental talk coming from a woman who used a muffin as a shield."

I bristle. "He surprised me."

"Right." Safe in her victory, Cheri complacently pats her magenta curls. "What was that even about? You caught up in some naughty scandal?"

Deeply skeptical, I check my phone. The only alert is a notification from LifePlanX about the second load of laundry I should be doing. "Nope."

"Huh. Must have mistaken you for someone else. Makes sense—there's always a lot of filming going on in Toronto. Oh, speaking of, did I tell you I saw Keanu Reeves last week?" She wipes the counter with passionate strokes. "What a god. There's no one else as gorgeous as him around here."

"Uh, Cheri?" It's Loni, who is packing Little Loniette into her stroller as her wife tidies the table. "Outside." She points.

We look out the front window. "Shit," I say. "There are two of them." Inspector-turned-paparazzo Clouseau now has a buddy standing with him outside the café. They're both sporting seriously intense cameras around their necks and gesturing wildly.

"Quick. Go out the back way," Cheri advises in a hiss.

This is bizarre and not on my to-do list. I hesitate, wondering who on earth they think I am, before I duck into the hall and sneak out, feeling pleasantly important. The buzz of acting like a celebrity lasts until I step right into an oil-slicked puddle that smells like raccoon pee. *Damn it.* There's a patch of grass at the end of the alley, so I walk over and wipe my shoe. Once reasonably clean, I sip my latte as I decide what to do. I faked being sick to get out of work so I could meet the lawyer, which means there's no need to go to the office. That I'm Todd-free the rest of the day lightens my mood.

I tap through my phone to the LifePlanX app. According to my schedule, I'm due to go home and spend some time doing chores. Plan the work and work the plan, that's the saying. I wish it were always that easy, though.

I think I've tried every system available to humanity that's supposed to get your life under control, but none of them have helped. My bullet journal bit the dust last winter, when I finally accepted Mom's dementia was too bad for her to live alone. It was a beautiful notebook full of carefully hand-drawn calendars and lists, which slowly devolved into roughly scribbled pages of names and phone numbers in different color inks, a written microcosm of my resentful journey through the healthcare system.

Once Mom had been moved to Glen Lake, I put that notebook aside and turned to an award-winning, minimalist online tasker. That was abandoned five months ago, when checking through the previous weeks, I finally realized that my to-do lists confirmed what I had only dimly suspected up until then—that I was getting assigned my own projects less and less in favor of taking on tasks for others...or for one other person in particular. Todd, my marketing department manager, was blocking my advancement by giving my projects to his slimy protégé, Brent.

I turned to journaling as a release, diligently recording my feelings every day until Todd grabbed my arm during a company event and held on a little too long, while his other hand grazed my hip. No big deal, right? It was a crowded room. Just a mistake, no need to make a fuss, so I tried to laugh it off. I did the same thing the next week when he backed me into a table after I gave him the projections I'd printed out, joking that his bad eyesight meant he had to lean in close. I said nothing when he spent an entire meeting staring at me before saying he liked exotic-looking girls. That's when I put the journal away. I had no desire to relive my days with a written record.

"Stop it," I say softly to my phone. "Stop."

I never say those words to Todd. When it first started happening, I convinced myself this was my issue, not his—I was overreacting or being too sensitive. I'd been too self-conscious to do anything but laugh, not wanting to cause a fuss and embarrass him or needlessly put my job at risk.

The decision to see Fred the Lawyer came to me as I curled up in bed one morning fighting nausea because of another job rejection. It wasn't normal to cry myself to sleep every night. Something had to give.

My phone dings with yet another LifePlanX notification, triggering a Pavlovian instinct to accomplish something, anything. The message flashes on my screen. **Not on track? Sit with that, said the coyote to the bear.**

What the hell does that even mean?

I decide I don't need the additional pressure of a phone that constantly reminds me of my failures. "Coyote this," I whisper as I press the little shaky X in the app's corner.

Yet the moment it disappears from the screen, I feel lost. I'm not proud of my dependence on these kinds of things to maintain focus ("It's like you need a corset for your brain," my über-organized friend Anjali said), but I do. I admit it. I love lists. I *crave* them. I draw visceral pleasure from anything I can put a line through, a check beside, or delete as a declaration that I have **Completed a Task** and am therefore a worthy, functioning human.

But until I download a new, shinier list maker, it looks like I'm on my own.

I walk to the nearest subway stop and briefly hesitate on the platform. Without the restrictions of my app-planned day, I can either go home and wallow in self-pity or visit my mom. Actually, going home isn't even a real option, because Mom takes priority over pretty much everything.

Thirty minutes later, I've reached my stop and am walking the three blocks to Glen Lake. It's a muggy June afternoon and layers of nasty, sweaty stickiness form on my skin, perfectly mirroring my internal state (level: trash goblin). I take a moment to breathe in deeply and force the negative energy away. Seeing Mom is hard enough without going in already dejected.

"You can do this." I give myself a mini pep talk before pressing the intercom button at the main entrance. After all, it's not like I'm the one who has to live here. I only have two jobs: to pay for Agatha Wu Reed's single room and to look cheerful when I visit.

The door opens, but I linger at the threshold like a vampire waiting for an invitation. An older woman walks out and I step out of her way with a quick apology, immediately regretting it because I did nothing to be sorry for. It's a bad habit that has become an automatic reflex. She's followed by an elderly gentleman who reaches for her hand and lovingly tucks it up against his chest. I try to suppress the hungry look I know comes into my eyes as I stare at their intertwined fingers, because no one wants to broadcast their loneliness to others.

It's not like I'm lonesome all the time or pining for a Prince Charming, but sometimes there's a part of me—maybe twenty percent—that wants that kind of connection so badly it hurts. The other eighty percent is more sensible. I have too much on my plate to be thinking about relationships right now, and it's much easier to only have my mom to care about. Putting another person's concerns and needs into the mix would only make things harder.

Covering my sigh, I catch the edge of the door before it closes and step inside.

The woman at the nurses' station looks up as I approach. We're both familiar with each other at this point.

"How is she?" I ask.

"Eating well," she answers in a brisk tone.

I wait, but that's all the information that seems to be forthcoming. "How about her mental state?" I nudge politely, not wanting to nag or ask too many questions.

"Any word on the new home?" The nurse's neat sidestep is answer enough. The entire floor knows I'm trying to get Mom into the Xin Guang private care home on the other side of town.

I shake my head. "Nothing open yet." It could take another year for a room to open, which would at least give me more time to save. Private care is expensive.

The nurse nods with practiced sympathy, a gesture I've become intimately familiar with since Mom entered Glen Lake. "Something will come up," she assures me. "It always does."

That something will come up I have no doubt, but it means I need to have the money to pay for it, which means I need my job, which means putting up with Todd and the hell he's making of my life. I finish signing in and head down the hall.

Glen Lake is clean, reputable, close to my apartment, and the staff are kind. Logically, I know I'm lucky to have found Mom a room here. I don't feel lucky. All I feel is hate. I hate the omnipresent sickly smell of bleach and soup that permeates the rooms, no matter what's served for lunch. I hate the colors—a faded mix of salmon and seafoam I'm sure someone thought was a soothing combination but instead gives the impression of a 1970s bathroom in desperate need of renovation. While I'm hovering above my pit of hostility, let me also drop in the bland, silver-framed art prints on the walls. They're all still-lifes of snapdragons and landscapes or cutesy animal posters. In fact, there's one by my mother's room of an adorable little white kitten sitting next to a pink carnation that I see each time before I go in, and you know what? I hate that, too.

Most of all, I hate the lost expression I see on Mom's face whenever I open her door.

I pause and put all of it—work, Todd, money, the lawyer—out of my mind and arrange a pleasant smile before I push open the door and see Mom sitting on a beige vinyl chair near the window, staring at nothing as soft classical music plays from the television. I watch her for a moment, my jaw clenching so hard my teeth start to ache. She used to be a woman who knit and sewed and painted. She made her own yogurt and bread. She did aerobics back when people unironically wore leotards with little elastic belts and matching leg warmers. It hurts to see her so inactive.

She turns to me, the light from the window hiding her expression. "Ni hao?"

That Mandarin greeting means she's not with me in the present but back in the past where I can't follow her. I do my best to keep bright. I only know a few words but they're enough to answer her. "Hen hao, ni ne?"

My mom has been in Canada for over thirty years but still speaks English with an accent. When I was younger, I didn't notice—it was Mom's voice, no more and no less—but how she speaks, the up and down of her tones, has become more pronounced over the last year. The doctor says it's my imagination, but I think it's because she's back in China so often in her thoughts. Her earlier life there is a mystery to me. She rarely spoke of it, wanting always to look to the now and the future. She even refused to speak Mandarin to me at home, insisting it was better to fit in and accept where we are rather than where we'd been.

"The past is dead," she would tell me when I asked. "It can't be changed. Leave it in memory."

I'm prepared for another frustrating visit where I do my best to pretend I understand what she's saying, but then Mom switches to English. I'm wrong. She's having a good day.

"You changed your hair," she says.

I've had the same short hair for years but I touch my head like it's a new style I'm unsure about. "Do you like it?"

Mom reaches out a gnarled hand and gestures for me to come closer. When I do, she runs her palm over my head with a disapproving snort. "You look like a boy. Why stand out like this?"

Standing out is one of Mom's bugbears, probably from when she first came to Canada and had to assimilate. Her modus operandi was always to choose the middle way. Being too different and not blending in with the crowd makes you an outsider, which draws negative attention and its close companion, criticism. She hammered this into me all my life. I was a solid B-plus student all through school.

"I always had long hair when I was younger," she says. "Everyone did and it was also the style your father liked best."

Even though he's been dead for a decade, hearing about Dad still brings tears to my eyes. "That's how you met." Apparently there were so few women with black hair long enough to stream out in a banner that it stopped my dad dead in his tracks. "Then she smiled at me," he'd say, telling the story. "That's all it took. I was a goner."

"Asked me for a date, right there on Bloor Street," Mom continues.

When I was younger, at this point in the story, Dad would interrupt, faux-aggrieved, to point out that Mom hadn't told him she lived an hour outside the city. "I never would have offered to drive her home had I known," he'd say jokingly, scooping her up in a bear hug that made her squeal and laugh every time. I haven't heard her laugh like that since his death.

I'm feeling fragile and decide that self-care means not having to hear about my parents' perfect, fairy-tale love. I treasure the story, I do, but right now, I can't.

Instead, I turn the conversation to what she had for lunch (ham sandwiches) and how she's sleeping (better now that she has that lavender sachet I brought last time).

Eventually she starts looking out the window and I can tell from her face she's drifting from me, so I pick up the Asian celebrity magazine on her coffee table. It's something I brought her a couple weeks ago, with one of China's top action-movie stars, Sam Yao, in a tuxedo on the cover, flaunting his admirable bone structure and perfectly tousled black hair. His smoldering eyes taunt me with promises of passion and adventure that will never come true for someone as ordinary as me.

A glutton for punishment, I flip to the feature story, a fluff piece about how he enjoys, *oh my gosh, stop the presses,* travel and his work. I scan the article, each mention of unimaginable luxury and public adoration pricking like a thorn, then toss the magazine away, sitting in silence with Mom until it's time for me to go.

DATE: JUNE 14

THREE TASKS A DAY:

☐ GO TO WORK (CHECK WORK TO DOS)

☐ LAUNDRY

☐ GYM

DATE:

THREE TASKS A DAY:

☐ _____

☐ _____

☐ _____

Two

The next day is terrible. Nope. Harrowing, hideous, horrid, and hateful.

My, there are a lot of negative H words. I wonder why that is? It's heinously horrendous.

Here's another: You better *hold* it together and *handle* your shit because you need the money. A two for one.

Todd punishes me for calling in sick yesterday by ripping my proposal to shreds in front of the rest of the team, then tells Brent to take it over and do it right. The other men don't seem to notice but Kathy, the admin assistant, gives me a pitying pout.

I ignore her look, put on a neutral face, and pretend it doesn't bother me. It's better to keep my head down than to protest; experience has taught me the only consequence of reminding Todd he signed off on that proposal two days ago will be negative. For me.

The day drags and I finally leave at seven after the office empties. According to my new task list—I've gone back to basics with a pen and paper—I should go to the gym and do the laundry I didn't do yesterday. Instead I drop off my bag, pull out my sneakers, and start an aimless walk around the neighborhood. The summer sun hasn't yet dropped behind the horizon, so I decide it's safe enough to go on the running trail built along the train tracks near my place. It's busy and I wind around a kid learning to inline skate and dodge a group of Serious Cyclist Dudes in bright jerseys and black shorts. Apparently the Tour de France has made a detour through Toronto—how nice.

I try to relax but the toxic mess in my brain infiltrates my body and I stare hard at a man strolling by with gigantic silver earphones. His face is so punchable that my hand curls into a fist.

The lawyer told me I need to get proof about Todd's behavior, but how? Even if I could outwit him, not only is he a vice president, but his dad is golf buddies with the CEO. And Garnet Brothers Investments isn't the most feminist organization out there. I bet even a dick pic would only get a "Boys will be boys," and Todd's smart enough to not say or do anything that I can call out specifically. Standing too close? Feeling uncomfortable? I was reading into the situation, end of story. The pay is also better than anywhere else I've looked so I'm stuck. Between Mom's private room and saving for the new home, I've burned through all the cash I'd managed to put away.

I stop abruptly, causing a runner to shout "Hey" and shoot me a dirty look as they swerve to miss me. The walk should have calmed me—nature, outside, exercise, all that—but I want to scream. I'll go to bed. A solid night's sleep will get rid of this itchiness inside my skin.

By the time I reach my street, I'm almost in a daze as worry circulates through my brain. Mom. Work. Mom. Money. Work. Todd.

As I wonder what it would be like to walk and walk and keep walking forever, a glossy black SUV pulls up close enough to make me jump to the side. This is not the kind of car that usually comes by my street, which tops out at a Lexus owned by the dentist five doors down. I automatically take three safe steps back to put me out of snatching range and am off the sidewalk and on the grass staring warily when the car door opens.

"Grace Reed?" A very familiar face peers out and I gawk.

It's familiar because, except for her long, lustrous tresses—like a shampoo ad or Agatha Wu strolling down Bloor Street on her way to meet her romantic destiny—this woman is my doppelgänger. We have the same face shape with a pointy chin and similar rounded dark eyes, except I know mine are shadowed with fatigue and hers are simply elegantly shadowed. Her skin is dewy and fresh. I may look dewy, but I certainly do not look fresh.

"Wow," I say, peering at her. "I have to know, are you a bartender on the Danforth? People are always telling me my double works in some bar in the East End."

The woman gazes at me with utter astonishment.

I talk on because my mouth won't stop. "Duh, of course you're not. Otherwise you wouldn't be driving around in that fancy car. Hold on. How do you know who I am?" The surprise of seeing someone who so resembles me knocked that first and very pertinent question clear out of my head. I take another step back.

"You are Grace Reed?" says the woman again.

"Gracie," I correct before my voice trails off. I know that face because—it suddenly clicks—this is Wei Fangli.

Wei Fangli, Chinese A-list movie star, is in my neighborhood. I should have recognized her except it's so shocking she would be here, talking to me on my street, that I didn't connect this woman with the celebrity at all.

Wait, Wei Fangli is here and knows my name?

She glances up and down the street. "Will you get in the car?" she asks. "I want to speak with you."

"No, I don't think so." I take a last step back until the branches of a pine tree brush my head. Why would Wei Fangli be in a residential Toronto neighborhood? I look around and confirm it's not a reality show and there are no cameras filming this interaction.

"Please."

"How about you come out here?" A compromise, because I'm a little curious.

She's considering this when a hand shoots out to touch her

elbow. The hand is attached to a black-blazered arm connected to a man leaning forward.

Even in sunglasses, he is so incandescently beautiful that he shorts out my brain. He's Asian, with jet-black hair falling over his forehead, a narrow nose, and a jawline with an angle sharp enough to measure with a protractor. Although he's sitting, I can tell he's lean with broad shoulders. His handsomeness renders me literally unable to speak, and I get a bit panicked before resentment sets in. How dare he look so good? Someone that attractive should have a little horn they toot to prepare normals like me for their arrival. Despite the shades, he's also unnervingly familiar, but where would I have met a man like this? Nowhere but dreams.

He ducks back into the car before I can place him, and the two talk in low voices. Fangli finally stretches one leg to the ground, foot shod in a delicate high-heeled sandal that might snap under her weight. That shoe probably cost a month in rent.

How could I ever think she was my doppelgänger? Wei Fangli is flawless. She moves like a dancer and her posture is so perfect I feel my own chin lift in response as I try to straighten my back.

"As I said, I have a proposal for you," she says, hovering in the car door. "I'd prefer privacy. Please get into the car. This will only take a few minutes."

Why do I follow her into the car? Do I have a death wish? I might, but right now I'm also very sick of being Gracie Reed and doing normal, safe Gracie Reed things. Whatever happens now will at least be different, and after today, I want that desperately.

When I climb in, the car's interior blows my mind. Two sets of pale leather seats face each other, separated by a shelf with bottles of water and a minibar. A breath of Chanel No. 5 lingers but I can't tell if it's from Fangli or the car itself. Beside me is the man, and after I sit down, I take a good look at his face, trying to keep my composure as I do. He recedes back into the shadows of the car as if removing himself from the conversation.

Like, this man is unreal and his lips are...wow. Despite the improbability of this entire situation, I'm laser-focused on them. They're the Platonic ideal of lips and match the high cheekbones and jet eyebrows that form perfect straight slashes. Then he takes off the sunglasses. Dark eyes taper to lines at the corners and those lips turn down in a frown as he glances at me. There's a feeling akin to the moment when the roller coaster finally dips after teetering at the top of the hill as I tumble from familiarity to recognition.

Sam Yao, the Sexiest Man in the World (officially, as named by *Celebrity* magazine last year), is sitting dourly in the seat next to me.

I'm in a car with Wei Fangli and Sam Yao. Even I know—through Mom's magazines but whatever—that this is Chinese cinema's golden dyad. And they want something from me.

"Why am I here?" I ask. I should probably be scared at this point, but there's something about sitting in a luxurious SUV that takes off some of the edge. If I'd been stuffed into a white van or something, I'd be way more stressed.

"You know who we are?" Fangli asks.

"I know who you look like," I say.

"I really am Wei Fangli." She has an unexpected North American accent. "Would you like to make some money?"

I scoot back against the car seat. "Oh, wow. Right, this was not what I expected. I'm flattered and I am very pro–sex work but that's not really my bag."

Sam snorts. "You think we want to have sex with you?"

He's clearly mocking me, but hearing him say the words *sex with you* is enough to send my imagination into overdrive.

"No?" When I manage to speak, I don't even know the right answer. My work angst has been replaced by a new and unusual torment—being stupidly tongue-tied in the presence of fame.

Why did Fangli want me to get into the car?

Then she flashes me a photo on her phone and I see the reason. "This is you," she says. It's not a question.

The phone screen shows me ducking behind a muffin. "Possibly," I say cautiously. I don't know where this is going.

"This, too."

This time I'm peeking from around the muffin and under the brim of my hat like I'm checking for ghosts, and there's no point denying it. "Some guy took a bunch of photos."

She points to the photo credit. "I know. They thought you were me, and social media is now wondering about my new bran diet. At least your hair is covered by the hat so I don't have to worry about explaining a pixie cut."

"I'm sorry." Why am I apologizing for my own hair? "I mean, I was getting coffee. I didn't tell him I was you." Hopefully this reassures her that it wasn't my intention to impersonate her.

Fangli laughs. "Of course not. His name is Mikey and he specializes in trying to get candid but embarrassing photos. The other paparazzi don't respect him, but he makes a lot of money doing what he does and it got me thinking."

Sam interrupts. "This is confidential and if you sell this to the media, you *will* regret it."

I stare at him, totally nonplussed. "Is this an improv scene? Are you playing the over-the-top villain?"

"Think of how quickly we found you."

Hot or not, he's being a dick and I don't like it. Not-Starstruck Gracie roars back and hip checks Nice Gracie out of the way. I glare at him with the pent-up anger I haven't been able to release all day. "Screw you, buddy. I'm not the one asking for favors here, in case you haven't noticed."

This sparks a spirited argument between Fangli and Sam. I don't speak Mandarin so the fight is indecipherable to me, and I take a moment to get my bearings. I am in a luxury vehicle with two actors, one of whom looks enough like me to be a little freaky.

Here I admit my secret shame. You know how there's always a celebrity that you'll blushingly deny you look like, but you secretly

think you *do* look like, at least after a couple drinks when you're looking in the bathroom mirror in dim light with your hair a certain way?

Once in a while, someone who knows Chinese cinema will
mention that I resemble Wei Fangli, and on my supergood days, my
spectacular days, from specific angles, I think maybe I do. It's nice to
get some external validation.

Fangli delivers what must be a devastating verbal blow because
Sam slams back in the seat and crosses his arms as he very melo-
dramatically gazes out the window. She stares at him and then turns
to me.

"Sam is protective," she explains.

What does that have to do with me? Suddenly suspicious, I
examine the interior of the car. Maybe it's not a reality show but
some new humiliating game show where celebrities pick putzes off
the street and offer them a hundred bucks to run around naked or
drink slime.

"I want you to pretend to be me for two months." She smiles as
if this is an incredibly normal thing to request of a stranger.

"Me be you? You want me to act in a movie?" I try to keep
cool, remembering the exhilaration of inhabiting a character when
I acted in school plays. But it's been a long time and I assume there
are significant differences between acting in a college version of *The
Crucible* and starring in a high-budget film.

"No, no," she assures me. "I'm in a theater production and my
team insists I be seen around the city, but I want to focus on my
work. I'm too tired to do the additional publicity so I want you to be
my double for events."

When I look at her closely, I see the paleness of her skin isn't
only makeup as I'd assumed. Up close, she looks gaunt, almost
haunted.

"I don't think we look enough like each other for that," I say.

She waves the phone at me. "I beg to differ, especially with
makeup. I can reimburse you well for your time."

"How much?" I'm not going to do it, but I want to know. Beside me, Sam mutters under his breath and I take Fangli's lead and ignore him.

"We know you have a job. Most but not all the events are at night or on weekends. I think a hundred thousand is fair." Her voice is calm.

"Are you shitting me?"

Sam exhales. "Fangli never swears."

"I'm not Fangli."

Fangli's look stops him before he can retort, and he settles back into the seat.

I turn back to her. "How do you know so much about me anyway?"

"I hired a private detective after I saw the photo." She says it casually, like how else would she do it?

Now I laugh out loud. A private detective. This is too much.

"We think it's a fair amount for the job," she says.

A hundred thousand dollars means I can say yes to a room at Xin Guang if Mom gets in. It means I don't have to worry about Mom being put in a shared room if I can't meet the payments at Glen Lake. Tempting, but even though I'm sick of my current life, I don't want to be played by a couple of rich movie stars who look at people like me as toys to be used. Mom's voice whispers in my head. *Don't do anything too crazy.*

"I'm not sure." It's always easier to avoid giving a definite no.

"Please." Her face creases. "A hundred and fifty."

That escalated fast. "I'll think about it," I amend. Fangli's pleading face and that amount of money are hard to ignore.

She hands me a card. "Thank you."

Unable to think of a polite way to refuse it, I accept the card.

"I'd like to hear from you within two days," Fangli adds. "It's vital we start right away."

"Right." That's an ambiguous enough answer. I don't want to do this. Do I? No, of course not. I might have wished for an escape ear-lier, but not like this. I want sustainable moneymaking and a reason-able exit strategy. Something stable and safe. This is anything but.

Sam doesn't say anything as I leave.

JUNE 15

FINISH IT

(deal with the most unpalatable thing first)

○ Avoid Todd (unpalatable thing)

○ Go to work (refer to work to-do list)

○ Laundry

○ Gym

○ Check Xin Guang wait list

○ Read 30 minutes

Three

When I wake up the next morning, the first thing I do is check my task list for work. It has about twenty more items than I can hope to accomplish and I put my phone down, discouraged even before my feet hit the ground. I need a list that motivates me to do things instead of one that makes me feel I'll never catch up. I slot the idea in the mental file I've been gathering over the last couple of years, my dream list for the ultimate, and elusive, organizer.

The card lying beside my phone reads *Wei Fangli* in English and Chinese with a phone number and no email. I turn it over in my fingers, pressing the corners into my skin. A hundred and fifty thousand dollars. There's no way her offer can be on the up-and-up, because who in their right mind would try to hire a body double, a stranger, off the street? Out of curiosity, I google "Wei Fangli net worth."

Well. She could definitely afford it.

There's a picture of Fangli with the story, and I take my phone to the mirror to hold it beside my face. Our bone structure is close enough that we could be sisters. I lower the phone and check one of the open browsers on my laptop for the photo from the coffee shop, which I found last night after coming home. With my face partially covered by my muffin and hat, I can see the resemblance to Fangli.

I'm not saying this means I'm gorgeous. The image's caption reads: "Wei Fangli's unique features have a power beyond typical beauty," which is courteous phrasing for "She's sort of strange-looking but it works for her."

Ditto, except my face never seems to work for me unless it's as a gateway for people to stare and ask where I'm from. Or, my personal favorite, what I am. Whenever I was with Dad, people's eyes would jump from his face to mine as they tried to determine where my features came from, because they definitely weren't from western Europe. I didn't look like them and they knew it, but they didn't like not knowing why.

It's all moot. Even for that money, there's no way I could pull off pretending to be a movie star for two months. I don't speak Mandarin, number one, nor do I have the…confidence…Wei Fangli has. Fangli is used to being in the public eye; she's had years of training. When she walks in the room, she doesn't trip on a rug and wonder what to do with her hands. There's a whole series on "Doing Stairs like Wei Fangli" that analyzes how she floats down without looking where she's stepping—and with an occasional scarf toss for good measure. I'm not clumsy, but I'm self-conscious enough that I would freeze. I couldn't even handle a single paparazzo taking photos. What would it be like with a bank of them?

I toss the phone on my bed and get ready for the day. There's a boxy black suit that's my go-to, and I pair it with a thick camel turtleneck that makes the blazer tight under the arms. It's too hot an outfit for June, but the office is always freezing. I stopped wearing my usual red lipstick but I'm expected to look polished, so I apply an unflattering neutral beige I picked out of the drugstore cheap bin. One swipe of mascara. Nothing else. I don't bother to open the cabinet where I store my perfume collection, all those glass bottles filled with flowers and spice. I don't wear any to work, not anymore.

A mirror check confirms I look like an upholstered couch. No wonder Sam Yao thinks it's ridiculous for me to impersonate Fangli. He's right.

Although I leave early, a delay on the subway means I arrive three minutes late. Brent raises his wrist to look at his watch as I walk in to make it clear he notices. I don't make eye contact, but the incident adds to the tight ball in my gut as I turn on my computer. The only sound in the office is the tap of typing, and of course Brent is a heavy but shitty typist, so every few seconds, I hear the backspace key. *Dat-dat-dat-dat-dat. Click. Click click. Dat-dat-dat.*

Garnet Brothers is an investment firm, and the marketing department, where I work as a project coordinator, keeps moderately busy trying to find ways to subtly remind people that only idiots manage their own money. It's a boring but well-established company, which is why I took this job over a more exciting yet riskier role with a tech start-up. The first hour of every morning is spent answering emails I didn't want to deal with on my phone, and about half are other people's problems that have been dumped on me to solve. Most are routine but two or three are complicated enough that I'll need to check with Todd before responding. I decide I can get away with asking about them over email instead of booking a meeting. My gift to me.

"Gracie." Todd's smooth voice comes over my cubicle wall. When I turn, he's standing too close behind me and his blue eyes glint with a cold light. "Come to my office. Now."

He leaves and assumes I'll follow. I do, Brent's gaze boring into my back as I fantasize about reaching behind and giving him the finger. Todd waits until I enter his office and then closes the door. I curse myself for leaving my phone at my desk.

"Bit of a frumpy look for you," he observes. "I liked you better in the black dress with that red lipstick you used to wear. It was hot."

"Ha, thanks." My own response makes me sick. I'm an independent adult woman. I should tell him where to go and I can't. I just... can't. My need for this job is a noose around my neck, a gag in my mouth.

"You'd be quite an attractive girl if you smiled more," he says, sitting on the edge of the desk and adjusting his belt. "I think we could have some good times."

I think of Sam and find a bit of the courage I had last night. "I don't think so." My voice comes out like I've swallowed it.

"No?" He sounds sharp.

I shake my head.

"Too bad. Gracie, we're terminating you as of today."

"*What?*"

He slaps a printout down on the desk. "You called in sick yesterday. Does this look like a girl who's ill?"

It's the same paparazzi photo Fangli had shown me. I try to brazen it out because I can't lose my job.

"That's Wei Fangli. The photo says so."

"Why is Wei Fangli holding the purse that's beside your desk right now?" he asks. It's like listening to a snake speak. "Even under that hat I can tell it's Gracie Reed. Admit it and I'll be easy on you."

Then he licks his lips again, and although my gut clenches so hard I have to stop myself from doubling over, I keep my voice level and stare at a spot between his eyes. "It's not me."

"Human Resources agrees you are no longer an asset to this department," he says. "This is the final nail in your coffin. Unless you want to reconsider?" His eyes shift down and my skin creeps.

I know what he's saying. Not out loud, he's too smart to give me any ammo, but the implication is clear. So is the fact that if I challenge him on this, I'll be told that I should get over myself. This appalling realization crashes down on me, and whatever he sees in my face makes his harden. He shoves a paper toward me. "Your termination agreement. Sign it before the end of the week. Security will see you out."

That's it. He goes back behind his desk, ignoring me. I'm too shocked to react, and when the door opens and two security guards come in, I can only follow them. Luckily, most of my coworkers are out at meetings and I don't see anyone but Brent, grinning openly at my flanking guards, and Kathy, the admin assistant, who hands me my purse and says she'll set up a time for me to come clear my desk. She doesn't look me in the face.

Then I'm out and jobless. My phone beeps to remind me of a meeting in fifteen minutes, and when I delete it, I look at my work task list.

I delete that, too.

Then I go home.

Four

The first day after I get fired, I lie in bed and stare at the ceiling.

The second day after I get fired, I brush my teeth and very carefully, without looking at it, tuck the termination letter face-down under a pile of laundry. Then I call a bomb threat in to Todd's office.

I wish. Instead I go back to bed, pull the covers up, and watch Netflix until my eyes burn. I don't remember which shows.

The third day after I get fired, I text my friend Anjali and ask her to come over. I don't have a lot of friends, probably because I never manage to put in the time and effort necessary to maintain them. Anjali has always been different. I can drift in and out of her life, and each time we start talking, it's as if we never left off. She says she's too busy at work to deal with high-maintenance friends and I know I never have to worry about her yelling that she loves me when we say goodbye, forcing me to say it back. But I depend on her, or at least I depend on knowing she'll be there.

When she gets to my place, she has a bag of chips, two bottles of wine, and an acid expression. "That asshole," she says as she brushes by me. "Did you talk to a lawyer?"

"Before I got fired."

"Did you sign the letter yet?" She kicks her sandals off at the door without me asking. Both of us find wearing outdoor shoes in the house disgusting. "Hold up, did you say *before* you got fired? Did you see this coming?"

I take the wine from her and stay silent.

"Don't sign until you give it to the lawyer to look at," she advises. "You can probably get more severance out of them."

"Enough to cover the lawyer's fees?"

She shrugs and heads to the kitchen. "Five bucks ahead is still ahead," she calls over her shoulder. "Plus it shows Garnet you're no pushover."

That's an Anjali thing to say because her zodiac sign is Leo and her Chinese zodiac is monkey, meaning she's smart and tricky and belligerent. I'm an Aries and a monkey and I'm supposed to be those things, too, instead of a Pisces rabbit: ducking confrontation and never pushing back.

Anjali doesn't know the whole of the Todd story. I only told her that he's a terrible boss. I couldn't tell her about the way he made me feel because it's too humiliating to admit I didn't stop him when I know I should have. I should have reported him to Human Resources. I should have kneed him in the balls. I should have said screw my job and stood up for myself. I should have... I shouldn't have...

She hands me a glass of wine and pours the chips into one of my mixing bowls. "Sit, eat, and drink," she says. "How are you feeling?"

"Numb?"

Anjali swirls the wine. "To be expected. Would you like some advice or to figure it out yourself?"

She's being good, asking before piling in, and it's not her usual approach. I laugh and my throat feels rusty. "How hard was that to do?"

"So fucking hard." She grins. "I'm getting better. The life coach is helping me be more intentional and think before I act because apparently not everyone wants me butting into their business."

I don't want Anjali to help me with a list—I'd prefer to talk—but helping makes her happy so I push over my sheet. "This is what I have so far."

She pulls her black hair behind her shoulders. "You have two things on this list."

"Yep."

"Brush teeth," she reads. "Find job."

"I can check off the first one." I brushed my teeth before she came over, and now the wine tastes terrible. "I should change the second to 'find money.' I could win the lottery."

"Not a viable option." She sighs. "Let's talk for a bit before we tackle your nonlist."

"Fine."

"Tell me exactly what happened."

I don't have the energy to keep it secret anymore and tell her the story. Anjali's eyes narrow until they almost close. "Why didn't you tell me it was this bad?"

"What do you mean?" I'd glossed over the grosser stuff, unwilling to linger on it long enough to even say the words or to bother her with the details.

"You said he was a bad boss," she says gently. "This is far beyond some insecure micromanager, Gracie."

"I know."

She frowns and moves her glass from hand to hand. "Again, why didn't you tell me earlier?"

"You would have told me to quit."

"Right, and?"

"I need that job. Needed. I've been looking for months and there's nothing out there. You would have kept asking me about my job search."

"I'm not that bad," says Anjali. She grimaces at the look I shoot her. "Sorry, maybe I am. But I'm upset you didn't want to talk about it with me."

"I didn't want to talk to anyone about it. Ever. At all."

"Problems don't go away because you ignore them. We could have thought of a plan together."

"Like what, a sting?" It's easier to turn this into a joke.

"We'd mic you up in the bathroom before sending you into the boardroom." She cranes her head left to pretend-whisper into the fake mic in her lapel. "We have eyes on Walrus."

"Subtle."

"Thanks." She sips her wine. "Seriously, tell me next time. It's better to talk it out."

"Next time I get sexually harassed by my boss and fired? Definitely I will call you."

"Good." Anjali nods, satisfied, but then her expression changes. "That's not what I meant."

I start laughing and she hits me with a pillow.

"There won't be a next time," she bellows. "That's the fucking point."

We calm down and I sigh. "I don't want to talk about work anymore."

"Okay. How's your mom?" Anjali only met her a couple of times back when we were in university but she knows the story. Part of the reason our friendship rekindled is that I saw her social media post on helping an aunt with Alzheimer's.

"Good."

Anjali glares at me. "Are we about to have the same talk about your mom as we did about your boss? The trust-your-friends talk I gave twenty seconds ago?"

She's right. "She lives in the past more often. Her Alzheimer's is slow but it's progressing."

"I'm sorry."

"Yeah, me, too." That's the best I can expect now, and I don't want to go into the mess of feelings I have about Mom because I'm not even sure about them myself. I've been dealing with the situation rather than analyzing it, and I'm happy with that. Anjali senses this and turns the conversation to a workplace drama that we happily dissect as we assign outlandish ulterior motivations to all players.

We drink another glass of wine and finish the chips and talk about my new skincare routine (now including double cleansing, toner, and a shitload of moisturizer that guarantees smooth skin into my crone years) and Anjali's crush on the guy at the gym that she decided she's never going to pursue. "If it's a mess, I'd have to find a new gym and this one's cheap as hell," she says.

Anjali slops more wine into our glasses, then grabs a notepad and a pen. "Enough of this. I came here to drink wine and organize your life, and it looks like we're almost out of wine."

I snuggle back into velvety pillows that were specifically bought for the purpose of snuggling. "What's first?"

She taps the pen on the paper. "We can go about this two ways. Practical or blue sky."

"Practical."

"Boring but okay."

I tip my glass back and frown at the ceiling.

"You need money," Anjali prods. "How much fuck-you money do you have?"

Fuck-you money is the money you save for whenever you need to tell your boss or your partner where to go as you blow out the door. Except I used my fuck-you money to pay the extra fees for Mom's private room at Glen Lake. The government only pays the cost for shared rooms and Mom would hate that. We once visited my grandfather in a shared room—he liked the company—and she came out and whispered to me that she'd rather be left in a forest to be eaten by animals than have to deal with a stranger's noises all day. Mom needs quiet.

"Enough for one month and they offered three months of severance."

"Get the lawyer to boost that. Not bad, though. You have time." She writes FIND NEW JOB on the list and then under that, without asking my opinion, four things I need to do to achieve it. She looks up.

"Aren't you obsessed with those to-do list apps? Seems like a good time to bust one out."

"I decided I don't like any of them." None of them do exactly what I want, but what ever does?

"Make your own, then." She tosses this off like it's no big thing and bends down to write:

CLEAN APARTMENT.
GET TODD CURSED.
CALL FRED ABOUT TERMINATION.
EXERCISE EVERY DAY.
ASSASSINATE TODD.
VISIT MOM.

The last makes me catch my breath. What if Xin Guang has a room available soon? It's impossible to know when a room will come free, as it depends on...well, someone dying, which is awfully morbid. They only give you six hours to accept before it goes to the next person on the list. I need to have money ready for a deposit, and I won't have it without a job.

Anjali taps the pen against her leg. "Do you do a monthly budget?"

"Of course." I meant to do one, at least.

She stops tapping. "If I asked, could you provide it in paper or digital format?"

"It's more of a mental tracking."

She doesn't bother to answer. Her pen flies over the paper as she lists out my expected monthly expenses. With each line, my breathing gets a little shallower. Rent. Food. Phone, utilities, Mom's private room. Transit. Clothes. She purses her lips and crosses that out. "Better get used to shopping your closet," she says.

I have no job. No income. No recruiters banging on my digital door to hire a woman who can only offer an average skill set and termination letter instead of a glowing reference.

Suddenly Fangli's offer seems more appealing. I empty my glass and open my mouth to ask Anjali her opinion, then shut it fast because I don't want her answer. I know what it will be.

Instead, I take the paper she hands to me and look it over before adding an invisible task.

CALL WEI FANGLI.

Anjali leaves an hour later, and with the daring of almost a bottle of wine in me, I text the number on the card.

I'm interested in learning more.

I don't even hesitate before I hit Send. This isn't like me but, again, wine.

I pose in the bathroom mirror, trying to imitate Fangli's serene smile and confidence. Both are unsuccessful.

We'll see what tomorrow brings. Probably more failure.

———

The hangxiety hits at exactly four in the morning. I jerk out of sleep, heart hammering and dread breaking over me. I had a few drinks and my entire body knows I fucked up and humiliated myself. What? What? What did I say? I curl up and bury my head under the covers. Anjali came over. We drank wine, made my list. I emailed Fred to set up an appointment about my termination agreement. Anjali read it over, so I know that was fine. When she left, I texted Wei Fangli and very proudly put a thick, black mental line through that task.

I *texted* Wei Fangli.

My body instinctively coils up tighter as I pinpoint my tragic error. Why didn't I wait until the morning and sober reflection?

It's too late now. I reach out and find my water bottle empty so I stumble through the dark apartment to fill it up. In the kitchen, I drink deeply, then refill the bottle and return to bed. My phone is lying facedown on the night table, and I grab it. Maybe my mind is playing tricks on me; I only *thought* I sent the text.

Hotel Xanadu, Room 1573. Noon tomorrow. Wear a hat and sunglasses.

The text had been sent. The text has been answered. I'd put this in motion with wine courage. It's only for more information, I argue with myself. I don't have to take the deal. I can walk out at any time.

Right, that's so like me.

I put the phone down and start an interior conversation I know will take me to dawn. It's not so much a dialogue as it is my brain on a carousel circling through the same thoughts.

You don't want to do this.

You must have wanted it if you sent the text.

You can say no. It's not a blood contract.

Maybe it will be worth it. It's a lot of money.

This is a bad idea. You don't want this. This is a huge risk. Too many things can go wrong.

It's not like things are going right at the moment.

What if you mess up? Everyone will know you're an idiot. They'll make fun of you and you'll go viral and there's no one you can turn to for help. You'll never be able to go outside again, and every time you apply for a job and they search your name, they'll find out and think you're some desperate narcissistic poseur. Mom would be appalled if she knew you were contemplating sticking your head up like this. Who do you think you are?

The thoughts keep hammering me. In the end, it's not dawn before I fall asleep. I don't get back to sleep at all.

TASK BATCHING

batch one
HOUSEHOLD + ORGANIZATION TASKS

- LAUNDRY
- TIDY APARTMENT

batch two
INTERPERSONAL TASKS

- MEETING WITH WEI FANGLI

batch three
MENTAL WELL-BEING TASKS

- GYM
- START JOURNALING
- GET A RELAXING HOBBY LIKE COBRA FIGHTING

Five

At 11:50 a.m. the next day I do my best to swing into the Xanadu like I own the place. Although I know the hotel is one of the most exclusive in the city, I'm a little disappointed there's no Olivia Newton-John memorabilia. The lobby is decorated with sleek black vases on spotless glass tables, each holding a single white poppy with a hot-pink stem. The faint, light smell of green tea and fig wafts through the space as an olfactory welcome.

As my heart thumps, I remind myself it's only a hotel. I've been to a lot of hotels, including a honeymoon suite in Niagara Falls (not on a honeymoon) that had a heart-shaped red hot tub with short, curly hairs decorating the taps. But there's no denying if I had to place the Xanadu and that tourist trap on a map, they would occupy diametric spaces.

I try to look like I belong as I search for the elevators, which I can't find because the lobby has apparently been carved from a single slab of black marble traced with golden veins. I tilt down my sunglasses—I obeyed the disguise instructions, grateful because this wouldn't have occurred to me at all—and assess the situation. A woman in a black suit, so slender she's barely wider than her stilettoes, comes near me and I stop her.

"Sorry, can you tell me where the elevators are?"

She looks down her medically sculpted nose. "Do I look like the help?" Her voice is high and weedy.

Normally I'd crawl away and die after being given that look, but this time her attitude is like chewing on tinfoil. "Yes." I glance at her projecting chest as though searching for a name tag. "Aren't you Tracy? From the front desk." Then I sidestep her and walk away, rejoicing in my single hit at the one percent. Eat the rich.

I eventually find the elevators at the back of the lobby near the recessed concierge desk. The elevators are black marble as well, and I spend the time going up to the fifteenth floor wondering if some poor sap spends their time polishing every square inch of this design nightmare. The walls shine like mirrors, reflective enough that I can take off my hat and give my hair a final fix.

The elevator doors silently open onto a monochrome-gray corridor with bronze sconces on the walls. My hand tightens on my purse, and I force my breath out through the lump in my chest. *You don't need to take any deals. This is an informational interview only.*

I check the directions painted in script on the wall and find Room 1573 seven doors down to the left. My hand hovers near the peephole: I can knock or I can run.

The choice is taken from me when the door swings open to reveal a woman I don't recognize. Her black hair is cut into a sleek bob that parts precisely in the middle to frame her face and swings forward when she nods at me. "Ms. Reed?"

"Yes." I pull off my shades, and her eyes widen slightly as she gestures me in. I try to pretend this is nothing out of my ordinary, but this is no standard room. Every other place I've stayed has the closet to one side of the door, the bathroom on the other, and the bed in the room beyond placed on slightly stained industrial carpet, possibly with a faint pattern picked out in maroon. Here I stand on a thick, ivory-toned Persian rug laid over dark hardwood floors in a room larger than my whole apartment. A conversation zone of deep white-leather couches surrounds a large, glossy black coffee table. Floor-to-ceiling windows reveal the lake, and I can see the green trees of the Toronto Islands. The air is slightly perfumed with cedar from a line of flickering black-jarred candles lining the side table.

I do my best to not look flustered but I know the red is creeping up my neck from nerves.

Fangli stands as I enter, and I'm not surprised to see her watchdog Sam there. I *am* surprised when my heart skips a beat. He stands in a puddle of morning sun that lights him up. In all black with his hair tumbling down over his eyes, Sam Yao is so hot and so cool that he should explode from the contrast.

"I can't believe you're going through with this," he tells Fangli, in English so it's obvious he wants me to hear. He doesn't look at me.

Bam! There we go! He was a jerk in the car and he's a jerk now. He was obviously posing in the perfect light because he's a movie star and that's what they do. I feel him becoming less attractive in my mind. The idea slowly comes to me that this man is going to be out of my life in a minute and I don't have to like him or impress him; it's a revelation for my usual people-pleasing self.

Fangli comes over, tailored gray pantsuit flowing around her, and leans in to deliver not one but three air-kisses. I stand straight, not wanting to move accidentally to the wrong side and mess up her perfectly applied red lipstick. Up close, her makeup can't cover the dark shadows under her eyes or the anxiety pinching her face. Despite the fatigue, her skin is smooth and luminous. The more I look at her, the more I can feel my every imperfection, including the freckles on my nose that never bothered me before. I'm the country mouse next to the city mouse.

"I'm grateful you came," she says, taking my hands and drawing me over to the couch. When I realize how pleased I am to follow her, I make sure to keep some distance between us. My internet search this morning made it clear she's been expertly trained to charm. I couldn't find a single negative article about her. She's never stepped wrong in her public or personal life, has never been a drunken mess or said an unkind word. In fact, the phrase "consummate professional" came up multiple times.

I ruffle up my hair as we sit down. Like a fish senses a shark, I feel Sam moving to the couches behind me, but I don't look. "I'm not sure this is the right thing for me," I say cautiously. I should tell her flat out that I made a mistake when I texted her but it's hard when faced with Fangli in person. I decided in the elevator to have a quick conversation, give a noncommittal answer, and then leave the country, which is obviously the best and most reasonable way to deal with this situation with minimal awkwardness. Maybe I should have ghosted on this entire meeting.

"Before we begin, you need to sign this." Sam slides a paper in front of me.

I read it over. *This nondisclosure agreement (the "Agreement") dated on this 19th day of June...* "An NDA?"

"We need to protect ourselves."

"It's the usual process," Fangli assures me. "It protects both of us."

To irritate Sam, I read the Agreement with exaggerated slowness. It's a reasonable request for someone who assumes I'm untrustworthy and can be summarized as *Gracie will keep her mouth shut under pain of death or at least protracted and expensive legal proceedings.* I sign it and Fangli does as well, with Sam as the witness.

"Now we can speak freely," says Fangli, looking at the signatures with satisfaction.

"Right. As I said, I'm not sure about this," I say.

"You lost your job this week," Sam says, coming into my field of vision.

I don't reply and Fangli speaks as if he hasn't said a word. "It's as I discussed in the car. I'm here for two months and I need a double for public appearances. You would live next door in a room that adjoins this suite."

Live here in a luxury hotel. Okay, there's that. "Who would know?"

"Only the three of us and my assistant. My manager would not approve." She smiles tightly.

"Why not?"

Behind me, Sam sighs. "Because this is an outrageous idea. That's why he wouldn't approve and why Fangli isn't telling him." I glance over, surprised. He doesn't sound harsh, only worn out, like a man who's done his heroic best and failed mightily.

"My manager is what you would call a workaholic," Fangli says, not looking at Sam. "He doesn't understand exhaustion but I'm tired out."

Having experienced burnout, this makes sense, although my solution was not to hire a body double. Well, it takes all kinds. An idea occurs to me. "Are you using me to lure a stalker?"

"No."

No stalkers, that's good. "What kind of events are we talking about?" Why am I asking when I don't want to do it? It's like a job interview where you know the moment you walk in that the place isn't for you, but you feel obliged to go through the motions so as to not be rude. I don't have the courage to cut this short, not after saying I would come.

Maybe I'm a little intrigued. After all, movie stars don't approach me every day.

The assistant brings tea as Fangli talks. Sam lurks behind the couch, close enough for me to know he's there but not to feel actively threatened. He's silent but his disapproval is like a whisper in my ear. Even though I know it's not about me per se but rather about Fangli's whole plan, it bothers me and I almost want to agree just to spite him. *Take that, Sam Yao. Being gorgeous doesn't mean you get everything you want. Welcome to life.*

"I'm not sure this will work," I say finally. "We look a bit alike, but we're very different people."

She gives me a wry, weary look. "I've been misidentified often enough to know most people in North America won't see those differences."

"Photos can be seen around the world," I point out.

She shrugs. "You've already been mistaken for me in a photo without even trying."

The whole thing is fairly straightforward as she lays it out. I would spend a few days learning Fangli 101 and Famous Actor Basics like grooming, smiling into cameras, and avoiding deep conversations. Then I'd go to two or three events a week. Sometimes openings or special events, sometimes simply being seen in restaurants or around the city because her management insists she build her image in North America while she's here. "Only my assistant is with me now, though," she says. "The rest of the team returned home after I was settled in so we don't have to worry about them noticing you."

She would personally take care of any event that involved people she knew well.

"What about your fans?" I ask. "Won't they be disappointed if they find out that I'm not you?"

Fangli's smile looks a bit crooked. "They don't want me," she says. "They want the beautiful, perfect Wei Fangli they see on their screens, and I can't match her either. Think of it like a stunt actor or a body double. Are fans less excited during an action scene when another woman jumps out of a car instead of me?"

I see her point and don't have an answer besides a slight discomfort that I repress.

"That doesn't sound like a lot," I say. "You really can't handle it?"

Sam's voice crashes over my shoulder. "Do you think you'd be here if this wasn't her last resort?"

"No one asked you," I snap defensively, feeling my cheeks flush. I should have thought before I spoke.

Fangli presses her hands low for us to calm down. "It's a reasonable question. I love the stage but it's draining. This way, I can do my best but keep my team and my fans happy."

Sam's phone rings, and when he leaves the room, my eyes automatically follow him. He obviously never skips leg day because his thick thighs curve out with pure muscle, a pleasant sight accentuated by the tight black jeans.

Once he's out of the room, I think of Mom and her room at Xin

Guang. I think of the way my savings are going to dwindle. Then, like a shallow bitch, I remember how much I liked the sound of the audience cheering after those university plays, of not blending in for those few moments.

"I'm so grateful you're doing this." Fangli's voice is flat, and when she raises her eyes to me, they're glinting with tears. "I'm at my wits' end trying to please everyone."

I'm defeated. I let her believe I'd do it and I can't say no now. My vision tunnels slightly and I feel trapped, even with the lure of potential applause. "Okay." I hear my mouth say the word before I know I'm saying it. But the second I do, my shoulders straighten because—be honest—I want this escape, this new experience. Otherwise, I would have tossed that card in the garbage right away.

"Yes," I say more firmly. "I'm in."

Mom would kill me if she knew but for once I want to take a chance on living my life in a lane that's not the dead middle—and by living my life, I guess I mean impersonating Fangli's.

She beams. "I know your mother is Chinese. Do you speak Mandarin? Cantonese?"

"Neither."

Her face falls but she rallies. "We can work around it. I'll say I want to work on my English, and I'll only speak it here in honor of being in Canada." She nods as if this is a fine, workable solution. I marvel at how she makes the decision without agonizing about what others would think or if it was the best course of action. "I'm very glad you decided to accept."

We have a moment of communal silence and I almost forget she's a famous movie star. She feels comfortable, like we might have been friends in much different circumstances. It must be that vaunted Fangli charm. Then she says, "Sam doesn't agree with what I'm doing, but he'll be fine."

I shrug. Now that the decision has been made I'm better, more controlled. "I can't imagine seeing him much."

Fangli widens her brown eyes. "Didn't I cover that?"

My heart sinks. "Don't tell me."

"Oh." She's silent and I realize she took me literally.

"Sorry. Tell me. Sam's part of this?"

"He's my usual escort. He'll be yours." She waves her hands. "No touching. No hugging, kissing, or holding hands. He was very firm on that."

"He was, was he?" Although I should be pleased about the clear boundaries, I'm a little unsettled they had this talk in advance. Did they work through scenarios such as *what if the body double is so uncontrollably attracted to me she tries to jump me*? Does he have a script? Do I need to sign another contract?

Sam comes back in the room and I stand, not wanting to give him the advantage of height. He's still about six inches taller than I am, but that's better than looming over me by an extra two feet when I'm seated. He looks at the two of us. "We're doing this?"

"Gracie has agreed."

Sam's lips thin. "Did she?" He doesn't look at me.

"I did." I give him a big fake smile, not wanting him to know how bothered I am by his attitude. "We're a team now."

"We're not a team."

I keep the smile. "We sure are. Remember, you came to me."

He stares me down. "Fangli did."

My courage ebbs. "If this is going to work, don't you need to pretend to enjoy my company, at least?"

Sam gives me a flat look before he reaches down and runs his hand over his shirt, tugging the material enough to outline his chest for a brief and wondrous moment. He lowers his head and seeks my eyes with his. His lips part as if he's seen me for the first time and likes what he sees. I'm mesmerized as he walks over because under his gaze, I'm the only woman in the world. His eyes turn from my eyes to my mouth, and he bites his inner lower lip before looking into my eyes again.

I stop breathing.

Sam stands close enough to lean down and whisper in my ear. "I'm a very good actor."

Then he straightens and I see the cold Sam I'm already used to.

"Sam," says Fangli sharply. "What are you doing?"

I'm too shook to even be embarrassed by my reaction. He's a master.

"Wow," I finally say. "That was serious Academy Award material."

He doesn't smile. "I already have an Oscar, thanks."

This time, Fangli stands up and physically moves between us.

But that walk over to me is a gauntlet he's thrown and I consider the challenge. I'm about to pretend to be Wei Fangli, and if there's a better chance to make some changes in my life, I don't know when it will be. I can remain the go-along-to-get-along Gracie, or I can be the strong Gracie I always wished I was, the Gracie who speaks her mind instead of swallowing her words. An oversize mirror leans against the far wall and I catch sight of the woman reflected there, slumped over and dressed in gray with her arms crossed so tightly across her chest that her shirt wrinkles. I drop my arms to my sides, raise my head, and turn to smile at Sam over Fangli's shoulder. It's a victory when he looks away first.

Six

F angli's assistant, Mei, takes me aside, and by four in the afternoon, I'm exhausted, my hand cramped from writing notes on
little Xanadu notepads with black Xanadu pens. Mei is an unsmil-
ing, infinite encyclopedia of all things Fangli. I have notes on what
the actor refuses to eat, what designers she wears, her favorite
words and phrases. Even more mind-blowing is the knowledge that
all this is necessary because there are enough people in the world
who know Wei Fangli would never, ever touch an orange vegetable
that to eat a carrot would make the news. I'm filled with shock at
how little of Fangli's life is private and awe that I think I can pull
this off.

Eventually Mei excuses herself to take care of some business so
I'm alone as I shake out my hand and watch another plane lift off
from the island airport. My exhilaration of earlier has bottomed out
to stunned disbelief over what I've gotten myself into. I look at the
positives: I'm making money and it's frankly far more interesting
than lying in bed surfing job boards. If life hands you lemons and
all that.

In the afternoon summer light, sailboats swoop over the lake, tip-
ping this way and that with the wind. That's what I thought movie-
star life was: leisure, beach holidays, and shopping. I forgot the work
that got them there. Mei mentioned that Fangli hasn't been on a real

vacation in four years; even when she takes breaks, she appears at events and prepares for roles. Her life sounds stifling and it's no surprise she wants a breather.

Well, it's what she chose, and when I turn from the window to grab an artisanal yuzu-infused sparkling water from the full-size but inconspicuous refrigerator, I decide it has its benefits.

Sipping the water straight from the can, I flip through my notes. There are pages upon pages, and even looking at them depresses me. None of my usual to-do lists are up for this level of organization, but I need one to make this happen. I get stressed without those lists, those checks. I need the perfect system to organize this.

Make your own, then. Anjali's words dance in front of me in bright-pink neon. I put the drink down. I've been creating a planning-system wish list for ages, but it never once occurred to me that instead of trying to make other processes fit my life, I could make my own.

Now that the idea has been planted, I want to try it. What can go wrong, after all? I mess up a to-do list? Even I can deal with that.

"Are you ready to leave?" Mei comes into the room. "Ms. Wei will be too busy to see you again."

"I'm ready."

We decided I'd move over to the Xanadu the day after next. In the meantime, I have notes to go over and a long list of Fangli's English and subtitled Chinese interviews to watch and read. Fangli in news footage. A complete biography of Fangli's life. A full filmography.

I look at the list now and wrinkle my nose. This is a lot of content to consume, even for the most dedicated couch potato. "Do I have to know all of them?"

"I've starred the most important," Mei says. "Those you must watch immediately. People quote lines from the movies at Ms. Wei."

When I get back in two days, Mei will have a schedule for me. We've decided to explain my presence at the hotel by saying I'm a local makeup artist and family friend, and Fangli is doing my auntie a favor by letting me work on her to build my clientele. Until then, I'm free to go home and binge on Wei Fangli trivia, have Anjali come over (twice in a week, which is more than usual but it's been a very strange few days), and think about how I'm going to deal with Sam.

I put on my sunglasses and leave, Mei shutting the door firmly behind me.

Down in the lobby, no one looks twice and the familiar veil of inconspicuousness falls over me. Will that change by next week? I think it will and I feel my chin rise. There's a Gracie there who's tired of being overlooked, even though it's entirely of my own doing. Is that the real reason I took this job?

Disquieted, I get on the subway.

————

When I spill the story to Anjali that night, she has the anticipated response.

"Are you out of your fucking mind, Gracie?"

Maybe it was a mistake to tell Anjali, but I desperately need to tell someone despite Sam's sepulchral warnings of doom and NDA-related lawsuits, and she's the only person I speak to on a regular basis. I tend toward acquaintances over friends, and this is not acquaintance-level information.

"I didn't come here for the judgment." I pour out the wine before ripping open a bag of ketchup chips. Gross combination but I need the fat-salt-alcohol juggernaut hit.

"First, I came to *your* place. Second, consider the judgment to be on the house." She shakes her head so her glossy black hair, nourished by weekly coconut oil masks, sweeps through the air. Anjali using her hair for emphasis is the only time I regret cutting mine short. It used to be past my shoulders but it was never as pretty as Anjali's.

"I've already agreed." I stick my hand into the bag, and Anjali cringes and hands me a bowl.

"Stop being a pig."

I tip a few chips into the bowl, hand it to her, and then go back to eating out of the bag before I pause. "Do you think I shouldn't eat the chips?" I flutter my hand toward my hips.

"Does Wei Fangli look like a woman who eats a lot of chips? Drinks beer? Eats carbs?"

"No." I chew a chip morosely, put the bag aside, and then grab it back and hold it to my chest as I brighten. "Wait. She must since she thinks we look similar."

"Then eat the damn chips." Anjali throws herself on the couch. "Jesus, eating chips is the least of your problems. Have you thought this through?"

"No." I sit across from her. "Obviously not. This is a secret. They made me sign an NDA."

"It's good you told me because at least someone will know the truth when they kill you and pretend your body is hers so she can escape for a new life in Bali."

"That's the plot of a movie." It might even be one of Fangli's.

"If they only wanted your body, then you'd probably already be dead," she agrees. "Honestly, though, how are you going to pull this off? You're only half-Chinese."

I try not to wince at the "only," which implies that half isn't enough. It's not that big a deal. I'm sure Anjali didn't mean it the way it came out, and I don't want to put her on the spot and make her feel bad. "It's bizarre how much alike we look," I say.

Anjali takes out her phone and runs a quick image search. "It is," she agrees, swiping through the photos. "What are you going to do about not speaking Chinese?"

"Fangli's going to say she wants to work on her English, which is already perfect. Thank God she has no accent because I'd be doomed."

"Why no accent?"

"Vocal coach. Plus Sam will be there to help me in tough spots. Mostly it's to be seen out and about."

"Sam?"

"Sam Yao."

She sits bolt upright on the couch, brown eyes eating up her face. "Sam Yao. Sexiest Man? Award-winning actor? Cheekbones that massage your ovaries?"

"I know all this." I'd better watch his movies, too. Meh. I'll read his Wikipedia/IMDb pages and call it a day. My antipathy to Sam, ovary masseuse or not, is strong.

"I can't believe you didn't lead with this." Anjali downs half the wine in her glass and coughs. "You know he's a UN goodwill ambassador for the environment."

"Huh." Didn't know that but it doesn't change my opinion of him.

Anjali leans forward. "Is he hot in real life or weird-looking?"

"Burningly hot. A raging inferno sheathed in ice and smooth muscle." I sigh. "With dimples that come out when he smiles."

She tsks at me. "Seriously."

"I'm being serious. The dimples are really deep." She looks a bit dreamy, and I feel bad for interrupting her Sam fantasy with reality. "I don't like him."

"Why not?"

"He's rude. Brisk. Doesn't like me." I look down in the bag of chips to poke around for the biggest one.

"He's probably worried about this incredibly stupid idea," says the eternal optimist. "Why did he agree to it?"

"Fangli snapped him in line." That's right. I'm on a first-name basis with movie stars. I force back a slightly hysterical giggle before Anjali thinks I've totally lost it.

Her thick and perfectly groomed black eyebrows rise. "Rumors say they're dating."

"Maybe but they act more like good friends." I fish out the last good chip before I'm reduced to tilting the bag up to my mouth to drink down the crumbs.

"'Act' is the key word. They're actors, so how can you tell what's real and what isn't? In any case, be careful. A guy like that would chew you up and spit you out as bones."

I scrunch my nose. "Graphic."

She sighs. "Not that it wouldn't be worth it. Try to get him my number."

"He can barely stand to be in the same room as me."

"You'll handle him," she says with misplaced confidence as she goes to the kitchen and runs the tap. After returning with two glasses of water, she sits down. "For fun, let's go through all the things that can go wrong."

"I've already been through them, multiple times."

"Excellent, then it'll be a nice refresher." She lifts one finger. "We've talked about using your dead body as proof of Fangli's demise to help her escape from a stifling public life."

"That's not going to happen."

"Potentially far-fetched but remains possible." She flips up a second finger. "No time to job hunt."

"I am capable of scanning job sites for ten minutes each day while training to be a body double."

"Number three—and this is the biggie—if this goes wrong, your privacy will be shot." She points at her phone. "Imagine you all over ZZTV and social media, outed as an impersonator. It took you two years to try out red lipstick, for God's sake, and you've even stopped doing that. You only wear two colors, black and boring. How are you going to handle worldwide attention even if it doesn't all go to shit?"

Since I've already worried this to death, I have the answer Fangli gave me, the one I've been consoling myself with. "First, I did wear the lipstick." Until Todd's attention ruined that cosmetic adventure. "Second, it's going to be like playing a part, and I've done that before."

"Are you saying that being in a school play is good preparation for walking a red carpet? You can't be that delusional."

"I'm saying I've done some research and I will inhabit a persona to help me cope, like an actor in a play or a performer onstage."

"You're going to Sasha Fierce this?"

I shrug. "Works for Beyoncé."

She picks up her wine, puts it down, and then picks it up again. "And the part about it all going to hell?"

"They have teams to take care of that," I say. Fangli assured me if her plan went south, she'd call her manager and he'd do what was needed, even though he'd be furious she'd left him in the dark. Sam hadn't disputed this, so I took it as truth.

"The team's solution might be to let you hang," Anjali says.

"The whole point of this is that it doesn't get out," I reason.

She blinks. "Holy smokes, you want to do this. You're finding excuses because you want it."

"It's the money."

"No, it's not. You want to fake being Fangli." She shakes her finger. "Insert the *trust your friend* lecture here."

I throw myself back on the couch. "I'm doing it for the money."

"How many times do these words need to leave my red-wine-stained zombie lips? Trust."

"It's a lot of money," I say. "I don't have a job."

"Your." She leans forward as if daring me.

"Look, I don't have much of a choice."

"*Friend.*" She nearly yells it and gestures at me with her wineglass, almost spilling it on the couch.

I crack. "Fuck. I do. I want to do it. I admit it." I cover my face and feel the skin heat with embarrassment beneath my hands.

"Okay."

Peeking out from my fingers, I see her grinning at me. "What?"

"Yeah, I get it. It's a terrible idea but I get why you want to do it."

"You do?"

"You get to live like a movie star and hang out with Sam Yao for two months. What's not to get?" She sighs. "I'd probably do the same. Life's for living, right?"

That hasn't been my mantra to date, but it's far more affirming than *play it safe*, so I grasp at it. "I'm nervous."

"You should be," she says darkly, nixing any hope for a pep talk.

"But if you're going to do it, you're going to do it. How much money are we talking about, by the way?"

I tell her how much and she frowns.

"Did you negotiate?"

"Should I have?" I didn't even think of it. "She originally offered a hundred grand."

"Then she would have gone higher. When do you get paid?" She sees my face. "You didn't ask, did you?"

"I will," I promise. Chagrin sets in at my poor business sense.

"You need to tell them to give you at least twenty percent up front. Do it tomorrow." I give her a look and she's self-aware enough to laugh. "I'm doing it again, aren't I? Getting in your face exactly like the life coach says I do?"

"You are, but you're right."

"I know. I did your budget for you. I'm going to back off now and promise not to text you about this tomorrow."

I raise my eyebrows.

"Not text you more than once," she amends.

"Thank you."

"Here's to hoping you don't end up dead." She raises her glass.

"Aw, thanks."

We toast.

JUNE 20
KANBAN SYSTEM

To do:

- See Mom
- Watch Fangli video/movies
- Scan Sam: Best of YouTube compilation
- Text Fangli about $$$

In Progress:

- Laundry (need to fold)
- Fred the lawyer re: termination (waiting for reply)

Done:

- ✗ Running (goal: 30 minutes)

Seven

The next morning, I settle myself at my worn and scratched kitchen table with the index cards I spent three hours writing up last night. Fangli drinks her coffee black. I flip over my flash card. Correct. She was born November 10, 19...damn. I check the card and try to commit the year to memory by chanting it five times.

Her first movie was *Along the River*. Check. Released when? I forgot to add that in and ferret around online for the answer.

Fill in the rest of the line: "Forever is..." I pause and drag the pen against the table as I run through cheesy lines from her movies. "Only a day with you." Got it.

This prep work is more intense than I thought. My cozy kitchen feels like it's going to close in on me, and if I stay for much longer, I'll start to see the crumbs I should have cleaned up but didn't and the glass in the sink I ought to wash but won't. There are so many things I should do.

A text comes from Anjali. Get the money.

Me: It's on my list.

Anjali: Do it now. Don't think, do.

She's right.

Before I can psych myself out, I send a text to Fangli. Hey, sorry, we didn't talk about a payment schedule. Would a 20% advance be okay? No worries if not.

I stare at the last line, almost hearing Anjali's disgusted groan. Out comes No worries if not. Instead, I write Thanks and agonize over whether to add an exclamation mark or period before I go with the exclamation.

I send it before I can think twice, then stuff everything I need into a bag and head out the door, careful to wear a floppy hat and sunglasses. I'm both nervous to check my texts and desperate for a response, which results in me pulling my phone halfway out of my pocket several times before stopping dead on the sidewalk to look.

No problem at all, Fangli wrote. Mei will get it to you. Another 30% at six weeks and then the remainder on contract completion.

Oh. That was easier than I thought. I check it off my list with a light heart and send a triumphant text to Anjali.

On my way to Cheri's coffee shop, I hesitate. It might not be safe to go there; if the photographer is waiting, I'll get caught before I begin. I need to think about these celebrity things now and how they'll affect Fangli, so I duck into another place before I hop on the bus. Today I'll work in Mom's room and keep her company. She might enjoy watching one of Fangli's movies with me.

It's a good morning. We get her favorite dim sum delivered and feast on har gao and congee and rice and noodles for lunch. I haven't gone out for dim sum since Mom went into the home. It was something we did together, and to go alone would close a book of memories I'm not prepared to shelve. I offer some to the nurse at the station but she puts her hand out to refuse. "I don't even know what they put in that sort of food," she says.

While I never progressed past North American crowd favorites and refuse to eat phoenix claws (because they're chicken feet), thousand-year eggs (because they're gray), or fish eyes (because they're fish eyes), these are delicious shrimp dumplings, for crying out loud. Sorry they aren't chicken nuggets.

I polish off the dumplings and settle down to work. Getting into character might help and I decide I'm not Gracie Reed, jobless failure, but an ethnographer studying the lives of the rich and famous, trying to parse out and isolate every attitude and gesture. With my collection of note-taking implements in easy grasp, I go to the first URL on Mei's list.

It takes about two hours of dedicated viewing—Fangli has done a lot of media, what the hell have I been doing with my life—before I come across a video montage of Fangli and Sam together. Or Samli, as their fans call them.

This I watch six times. Maybe seven. They move as one unit, and Sam's smile when he turns to Fangli is more real than the one he presents to the cameras. When they hit the red carpet at the 1:56 mark, she stumbles and he catches her, pulling her tight and looking down into her raised face like a love scene from one of their movies before raising his hand to brush her hair off her face.

If I didn't know firsthand what he's like in real life, I would be sighing. Maybe I do a bit because deep down I have a fantasy of him looking at me like that, as if I'm the only person who matters in the middle of all that chaos. I stifle this immediately. I don't like Sam and how he unnerves me. Plus, maybe the gossip is right and they are a couple. Best to assume they are.

Enough of reality, or this manufactured Hollywood version of it. I put in the period drama Mei triple-starred, *The Pearl Lotus*. The plot is straightforward enough: Fangli plays an empress trying to save the emperor from a nefarious plot hatched by an old and jowly evil general. Sam plays the noble and sharp-jawed rival general, returned from some war with his love for the empress burning bright.

Mom dozes beside me and I watch, enthralled, as the film unfolds. As stunning as the sets and costumes are—Fangli wears a gown of embroidered gold so lovely it's a character in its own right—I can't look away from Fangli and Sam. At the pivotal moment, Fangli has to choose between love and duty. If she sends him on a mission, it will save the emperor but ensure certain death for Sam. They both know whatever decision she makes, Sam will do it without hesitation—not out of loyalty to the emperor or China but for her.

They're alone in a garden by a pond that has a pearly-painted gold lotus. Fangli, the empress, doesn't hesitate to order the mission. There's no change in her confident, arrogant demeanor, but her eyes show a devastated woman. Then comes the scene I pause and replay several times. Sam bows but instead of looking down, his eyes never leave her. Fangli stands straight and her face is calm, but the silk sleeves covering her arms tremble as if a wind passes over. Between them, without a word, the two lay out the agony of unrequited love and the pain of duty. The music is a single erhu playing a slow refrain.

The nursing home's vinyl chair creaks under me as I sit back, my sneakers squeaking on the worn linoleum, dingy with years of worn-in grime. I have uncomfortable emotions that I don't want to pull out from the log I've stuffed them under. That a period drama has evoked them almost offends me because I should get upset at the news, not a make-believe story of two fictional people. Fangli and Sam—mostly Sam if I'm going to be honest—make me vulnerable. I have a yearning for...what?

I don't know. More. That's all I can tell. I don't like that Sam can make me feel this deeply without even knowing his power.

After this scene, Mom wakes up from her doze and blinks as if trying to remember who I am. I smile. "Gracie, Mom. I'm Gracie."

She doesn't reply but turns from me to what I'm watching. Thinking to make it easier, I shift the screen so she can see it.

Her hand stretches out faster than I thought she was able, and she says something in Chinese. "It's *The Pearl Lotus*," I say helpfully, checking the screen to see what's happening. "That's Wei Fangli playing the empress. You know her. She's an actor."

She shakes her head desperately and I curse myself. There are rare days when the thought of home spirals Mom into a deep depression instead of making her comfortable. Past experience tells me there's nothing I can do so I turn off the laptop and hold her hand as she rocks back and forth.

JUNE 21

	BILLABLE HOURS TEMPLATE		
DATE	TIME	TASK	HOURS
6/21	9:00 A.M.	WAKE	
6/21	9:15 A.M.	HOW LONG DOES IT TAKE TO BRUSH MY TEETH? HOW DO I SCHEDULE THIS?	
6/21	9:30 A.M.	SCREW THIS.	
		~~PACK~~	
	3:30 P.M.	XANADU	
		???	

Eight

There are days when everything comes together as though part of a well-practiced symphony. Hair wisps stay down. Socks stay up instead of bunching in the toes of shoes. The keys are where you left them, the phone fully charged, and the pantry well stocked with coffee or, at the very least, instant packs.

Today is not that day.

I practice the deep breathing my favorite lifestyle blog insists will change my life—not that I need any help in that department, thanks kindly, I've managed to pull that off in spades this week—and stare at my phone, which I forgot to charge. I will it to reach the magical fifty percent charge point that's the lowest I'm comfortable with leaving the house. Forty percent. Forty-one.

I pick up the book I'm reading and hesitate. I've never not finished a book, and although this one is trying my patience, I'm almost done. I should see it through. It might get better. I toss it in my bag. Then I take it out. New Gracie isn't going to waste her time on a book she doesn't like. I don't owe the book anything.

I put it back in.

Forty-four percent.

I weigh the consequences of an undercharged phone against being late for my meeting with Fangli. Suddenly angry, I grab the phone. Today things are going to change. I'm not going to be limited by a list or a percentage on a phone screen. It's a matter of having a growth mindset, and frankly, I should be embarrassed about a phone keeping me from my destiny.

I take the damn book out again and thump it down on my night table.

Fighting a slight twinge of anxiety, I decide to buy a portable charger and pocket the phone, grab my bag, and run out the door. My neighborhood is the residential equivalent of the golden mean, gentrified enough that I can choose between two hipster coffee shops filled with people tapping seriously on decal-covered laptops but not so slick that the rent is unaffordable for people with small kids or precarious jobs.

Today I don't stop for coffee. Today I go to live a life of exquisite luxury and deceit.

This time, I walk into the Xanadu like I belong. That's right, man wearing an excellent suit and so much plastic surgery your cheekbones puff into your eyes. This is my world now. Out of my way, little woman with head-to-toe Gucci. (I know it is, because every garment is labeled.) Take a hike, incredible-looking man at the elevator staring at me.

Oh, that's Sam. I debate pretending I don't see him because it might be less awkward than making conversation, but he waves me over with an almost imperceptible gesture. With the new Fangliesque gait I practiced in front of the mirror, I stride over, dragging my suitcase behind me, and try not to let him notice my shaking knees.

"Did you hurt your leg?" he asks as he stabs at the number panel.

"I am walking like a movie star."

"You're walking like your shoes are too loose and you're trying to shuffle them on your feet as you move."

"Oh." This is too precise a critique to be taken as an insult so I decide to file it under Potentially Useful and think about it later.

"You're going through with this?" His beautifully accented voice is low. According to his Wikipedia page, he had a British tutor growing up.

"Obviously." I own my decision the same way Anjali or Fangli would.

He blows out his breath. "I'm doing this for Fangli and I want to be honest with you. I don't think you have what it takes. You couldn't manage a single photographer, let alone fifty."

True but no need to point it out. "I was surprised."

"When you screw this up, you can cause more damage than you know. Why are you doing this? Do you want to be famous that bad?" Even though his tone is earnest, the words are rude and that's what I react to.

"She. Asked. *Me*. I didn't go hunting her down and begging to be her second. You were there." I don't want to be famous, which is such a boring and jejune goal for a self-actualized human being that I would be ashamed to admit it. I need the money for my mother—that's why I'm here. Not the applause. Not being seen. Money for Mom's room.

"You should have said no."

"You should have stopped her if it means so much to you."

He grimaces. "You don't know Fangli."

You don't know me either. I ignore him until the elevator doors open, then stalk out. My suitcase turns on its side and I struggle to get it back upright as Sam stands, arms crossed, and watches. His thoughts might as well be on a huge bubble over his head.

She can't handle it.

Sam Yao can get under my skin without even trying, effortlessly pulling out every insecurity by simply being himself—confident, polished. Rich. Feted. All the things I'm not nor will ever be. Well, fuck him. Maybe I am a loser, but at least I'd help someone with their suitcase. I decide right then to exclude Sam from my usual policy of being nice. After I beat the bag into submission and tussle it down to 1573, Mei opens the door and watches as Sam follows me in.

"Ms. Wei will be back soon," she says, keeping her gaze on Sam. "She had a meeting after your early show finished."

"I'll stay." He goes to the window, which lights up his features like a goddamn sculpture, making me angrier, and pulls out his phone.

Mei stares after him, her eyes shining. Then, with a sigh, she turns to much more boring me.

"Your suite is ready."

As promised, it's right next door to Fangli's. Again I try to be cool and again I fail when I rush into the space like I've been living in a camping tent and washing in a ditch for the last year. Living room! King-size bed! Big table and windows looking over the lake and huge mirrors on the closets. My own set of candles. I check the scent; it's called Woods and I decide it's the only smell I want in my nose for the rest of my life. I release my suitcase, which promptly topples over. Mei prods it with her toe. "Your things?"

"Yes."

"They aren't Ms. Wei's style." Interesting, since she hasn't seen anything in the suitcase. She walks over and pulls open the (walk-in!) closet. "You need to wear these. I'll leave you to get settled."

The second she leaves, I step into the closet, suitcase dragging behind me. The walk-in is big enough to comfortably hold a chandelier of interconnected glass tubes, a chaise longue, and a cabinet in the middle. I walk around the chaise and wonder who they expect to lounge around in a closet.

When I turn to the clothes hanging in neat tiers along the walls, I realize that person could be me because I could spend all day here. I tuck my hands in my pockets as I survey my new and very lavish domain. Dresses—color-coded and arranged by length—are on the left beside a row of jackets. To the right are shirts, black shading through to white, and below that pants and skirts. I jiggle the drawers of the cabinet in the middle of the space and realize that must be where the jewelry is and that I'm not to be trusted with it. That's fair. I don't trust me with jewelry either. My last pair of earrings—silver threader chains—fell out of my ears and down a grate before I'd had them on for an hour.

The entire back wall is shoes and bags.

Is that...? I edge closer. It is. It's a Birkin. In fact, there are three Birkins lined in a neat row below what looks like the quilted leather of several Chanel clutches. I don't even recognize the other brands but I assume they are expensive.

I take a photo and send to Anjali.

Show me the rest of that closet, she texts. **Then take the Birkins and run.**

I give in and start touching, letting my fingers run over the rich fabrics and luxurious leathers. I send the occasional photo to Anjali, who only replies with names and numbers.

Balenciaga. $4k

Chanel. $2k

Givenchy. $8k

When I'm done, I stand back. All of the clothes look my size, and in that entire closet there's not one item I would have chosen for myself. No jeans. No flat shoes. Not a single pair of sweatpants. Am I expected to loaf around in clothes with non-stretchy waistbands like some sort of animal?

These are clothes you wear to be seen. I pull out a dress so elegantly cut it looks like art and turn to the three-way mirror while holding it against my body. This is not a dress you wear when binge-watching TV and eating pizza. I don't even think it permits sitting positions. It gives me another peek into Fangli's life and a premonition of what I can expect from the next two months.

Sam appears in the doorway of the closet. "Not wasting any time, I see."

"Yes. I uprooted my life for a designer dress. Why are you here?"

Sam speaks to my reflection in the mirror. "I want to appeal to your better nature. You can see Fangli is desperate. Is that what you want, fame without putting in the work? To prey on someone like her?"

"It's hardly fame when people think I'm another woman." There's a quaver in my voice as that little maggot that wanted to seek out the photographers squirms. Sam hears it and steps closer.

"You got fired." His voice is low. "Why?"

"None of your business." He's the last person I would tell about Todd.

"Did you think this was a shortcut? That a woman as pretty as you could reach higher than working at an investment company? You saw a way to get your foot in the door and took it?"

I keep my eyes on him in the mirror. My shame at him reading me so well has turned to anger, and I pull it over me like chain mail. "You want me to leave?"

He hesitates. "Fangli wants you to stay."

"Then knock it off," I say to his reflection. "Otherwise I go out that door and she's left on her own."

His perfect lips thin but we hear Fangli greeting Mei in the other room.

"Your choice, movie star," I say, channeling the new Gracie. "Also, you're a dick for thinking that working at a regular job is reaching lower than being an actor."

The tension between us rises, and I think he's going to call my bluff. I drop the dress and reach out for the handle of my suitcase as Fangli comes in. "You came," she says with relief.

That tone of utter exhausted gratitude must be what changes Sam's opinion because he leans in to me. "We're getting to know each other."

Fangli looks from his warm face to my confused one. Because I'm not an actor, I haven't been able to adjust to the new Sam in seconds.

"Let me change and we'll talk," she says.

When she leaves the room, Sam moves away and we face off

again. "Be civil," I say. It's hard to not try to keep the peace, even after a fight. "We need to work together."

There's another long silence and then Sam simply turns and leaves. I watch him go, wondering if I've won this round. I think I did and I get back a tiny bit of the pride Todd whittled away.

I go back to the closet before a thought stops me dead.

Did Sam Yao, *the* Sam Yao, call me pretty?

True to her promise, Fangli is soon back in my room. Her face is scrubbed clean and she wears a huge bathrobe that drags behind her like the train on a gown. She could attend the Met Gala as is. I've sorted through the clothes again and noticed they come in several categories: Major Event, Very Fancy, and Regular Fancy.

"Do you like them?" She points at the wardrobe.

"You must like shopping. Is that one of the things I'll need to do?"

She looks honestly shocked. "I don't go to stores. They send people to me."

We stare at each other. "How do they know what you want?" I ask.

Fangli shrugs. "They bring the collection. I like to pick my own garments. Otherwise a stylist would create my looks."

"Right."

She comes over and picks up the same dress I'd been holding when Sam came in. "This is my favorite."

"Me, too." We smile at each other.

"Claudie at Chanel designed it for me after I signed on as their brand ambassador. It's one of a kind." She sounds utterly guileless, and despite myself, I burst out laughing. I think I like Fangli.

She sits down on a chair and crosses her legs in a manner I know I'm going to have to replicate and will find difficult. "I thought we'd chat tonight, get to know each other. I ordered dinner."

"Thanks. Umm, how was your day?" I pause. "I don't know much about what you're doing in Toronto besides acting in a play."

"All things you should know." She settles into the chair and I groan inwardly. She's so fucking graceful, goddammit.

Fangli talks for about an hour as I make notes and nibble on the smoked salmon salad that arrives. It has distractingly good deep-fried capers. She's here in a play that's showing on King Street. *Operation Oblivion* is a World War Two historical drama, and as she talks, I can't believe I've never heard this story before. Apparently there was a group of Chinese-Canadian volunteers called Force 136 recruited for dangerous special missions in Asia.

"This was *not* covered in my history class," I say. I think through the dates. "Chinese weren't even allowed to vote in Canada then."

"As part of their training, they had to swim with fifty-pound packs," says Fangli. "Very few of them knew how to swim because they were banned from most Canadian pools."

Although Force 136's recruitment happened on the other side of the country, the story follows Sam's character as he finds one of the first recruits, who is dying in Toronto, and falls in love with Fangli, who works in a Chinatown restaurant.

"Don't you usually do movies?" I ask. "And shouldn't those roles go to Canadian actors?"

"Yes, they should and we're only here for part of the run because Sam is friends with the director and he thought it would be good publicity. We both started in theater back in China." She recrosses her legs. "I love being on the stage, so it was a nice break. Being in front of an audience is a different experience."

"I can see that."

"Do you act?"

"I did in school." I shrug. "It was only for fun."

"You enjoyed it?"

"Loved it."

Her smile lights up her face. "Then you understand why I'm here. How is your practice coming along?"

I take a deep breath. "Take a look."

Grabbing a pair of heels out of the closet, I pop them on and take a few steps before I stop, smile, and wave. Fangli's eyes open wide.

"Do it again." It's Sam, from the door. I do it again, a little more self-conscious now that he's here. A lot more.

"It looks strange." He frowns. "Not like it needs practice but wrong."

"I practiced in front of the mirror."

His eyes narrow. "Practiced how, exactly?"

This is embarrassing. "Ah. You know. Like *practice*."

He folds his arms and waits for me to answer.

I try to wait him out and fail. He can stand like that for hours, I bet, stubbornly refusing to give in. Fangli watches with those leaf-like eyebrows delicately raised.

I admit defeat. "I propped the tablet near the mirror and copied what I saw."

"You're a human uncanny valley." He and Fangli share a look. "Unbelievable."

Uncanny valley? "What? I'm not an android."

He sighs, grabs the tablet, and leads me to the mirror. "Watch." He taps for a second, finds a video of Fangli smiling and waving, and then plays it.

"I've seen this." I'm insulted. I did my homework.

"You're not watching." His voice is the perfect degree of smoky deep. Sam looks in the mirror and our eyes meet in the glass. Then I shift my gaze to his right hand, which waves the same as Fangli does in the video.

"Very elegant," I say, trying to regain myself.

"Like the Queen," Fangli interjects. She does the wave in person.

"Except totally wrong." He turns. "Fangli's right-handed and that's how she waves. You're looking in the mirror and copying it, but that means you've been waving your left hand. Everything is backward because her wave was filmed."

I stare at my hand, astounded. "Are you putting me on? That's why it felt so weird?"

"Yes." He gives Fangli an eloquent look that I read as saying what an idiot I am.

"Shit." I deflate. All that work and I did it backward. I bury my head in my hands.

"A fixable problem," declares Fangli. "You and Mei can work on it in the morning."

She leaves and Sam hesitates. Then he shakes his head. "Right-handed," he says.

He calls out after Fangli and I wish I knew what they were saying.

Wow, if there was only some way to learn Mandarin, maybe with a handheld device that's conveniently attached to my hand for about eighteen hours a day and can provide access to a thing like language lessons given at my own speed for $2.99 or less.

I whip out my phone.

In six minutes, a Scottish gent and a lady from Beijing cheerily work me through how to say where I'm from in perfect Mandarin. I freeze as they shift into telling me how to ask where others are from and pause the app. I could have done this years ago when Mom started getting bad. I could have been speaking to her all this time. I put that thought aside. I did the best I could.

Then I'm alone in my luxury room waving in the mirror at myself and practicing my new language skills by telling my reflection I'm a Canadian in poorly accented Mandarin.

Good times.

Nine

I'm strolling into a Rodeo Drive boutique wearing a huge black hat and shoulder pads big enough to block traffic when the bright summer sun pierces through my closed eyelids. Burrowing in the soft, fluffy bed, I try to go back to sleep but can't because Mei is standing by the foot of my bed barking my name.

"It's time to get up."

I throw the covers off and squint out the window. The sun's up but it feels suspiciously early. "What time is it?"

"Seven."

I groan. "One more hour." I was up late, alternating between deciding which clothes matched best with the multiple Louis Vuitton bags and learning how to ask people their names in Chinese.

"Ms. Wei is an early riser. She's already at a meeting." Mei might not mean to sound smugly virtuous on Fangli's behalf, but that's what I hear.

I haul myself up and shuffle off to brush my teeth. When I get back, I examine the outfit Mei has laid on the bed. "Are we going out?"

"No."

Yet she's chosen pants with ironed creases. "Can't I wear yoga pants since it's only us?"

"No."

She leaves and I realize my clothes from home are gone. That's a later problem, though, so I pull on the outfit. The white linen pants wrinkle on contact with my skin, and I immediately stain the black silk top with deodorant and have to change. In the mirror I practice my Fangli wave again, this time with the correct hand. The shoes are adorable sling-backs that I put on to check the full effect.

Huh. I turn around. I hadn't realized the difference expensive tailoring made because I now have outstanding posture. Do I look like Fangli? The spacious closet makes finding what I need so much easier than trying to sort through a bunch of shirts crammed tight enough to wrinkle, and I quickly locate a high-necked black shirt. I pull it on like a headband, the collar framing my face and the rest of the material flowing down my back, and toss my head. It's not the perfect facsimile of long hair but I get the idea, albeit with a nunnish feel.

"I came to see if you were dressed." Mei, who apparently has no concept of privacy, is at the door, staring at my turtleneck wig. I snatch it off and run a hand through my hair.

"Uh, yeah. Thanks."

She backs out of the room, and I toss the shirt on the bed and follow.

Fueled by coffee and fear of failure, I'm the ideal Fangli student that day. Apparently she does her own makeup except for big events, so Mei shows me the Fangli Standard Face, which necessitates a raft of expensive products to achieve the correct smooth skin and pretty smoky eye. Mei picks up the lipstick, a vibrant red that glides on like a dream, then goes over the edges with a lip pencil before blotting and painting me again.

I stare in the mirror at my lips. It's been a long time since I've had that much color, and I'd forgotten how bright it is. It makes my mouth the glossy focus of my face. No wonder Todd liked it. I shiver.

"Is this Fangli's usual color?" I ask.

"Chanel Rouge Allure in Pirate," says Mei. "It's all she wears in public."

I stay silent as Mei scrutinizes my face from the side. The makeup is part of a disguise. It's Fangli's face being created in the mirror, and when people see it, they won't see me. I relax slightly.

"Sun damage." Mei clucks and makes a note on her phone, disrupting my chain of thought. I focus on what we're doing. "I'll get better concealer." She takes a closer look. "And a waxing kit." Then she reaches over and drags out a mannequin head. "Here."

On the head is a wig. I haven't worn one since Halloween, and that was a blue flapper bob. I poke it. "Is this real hair?"

She slaps it on my head like a hat and it is the Lamborghini of hair accessories. It's definitely all real, and probably the kind to receive regular conditioning. The hair swings as if it's my own, far better than my turtleneck stand-in, and when I shake my head, it doesn't budge. It's been so long since I had long hair that I forgot how fun it was; I whip my head around like I'm about to star in *Showgirls* until I get a little dizzy. I need to take a photo of this for Mom because she'll love it.

This time when I go to the mirror, Mei stands beside me with a critical eye before pulling out her phone to show a photo of Fangli in a similar outfit. I arrange my pose like hers—one foot out and slightly twisted in a move my mom also taught me as a teenager—and turn my face slightly up and to the left with that little smile, then scrupulously check the pose and lower my shoulders a fraction. Mei takes a photo and when we look at it, I think *maybe* this will work.

"Terrible." Mei taps on her phone.

"What?" Deflated, I move my legs back to my usual slightly hunched stance and pull off the wig. It's hot.

There's a knock on the door and Mei opens it to reveal Sam. They whisper together, looking at me, and I try to decide if my better course of action is to pretend I don't know they are very obviously talking about me or to break into their conversation.

Take the bull by the horns.

"Hey. I'm right here."

Sam doesn't look at me. "We know." He gives Mei an instruction that causes her to disappear out the side door to Fangli's suite, leaving the two of us alone. Sam walks by to stand near the window, and when he turns to regard me, I swear the light shifts to pool around him. I've always wondered about charisma, if it really exists, and with Sam I can feel an excess of energy that simply makes him more attractive. Fangli has it, too, a vitality that draws attention no matter what she's doing.

I hope to God that's something that can be learned, because I sure as hell don't have it.

Beyond that, I can't decide what bothers me about Sam. I've seen him often enough in media that he's familiar, but when he stands here in person, it's a whole new ball game.

"You look different from your movies," I say finally. He's sharper, icier than he is in the photos. More unreal looking and far more striking.

"I know," he says dismissively. "Mei says you're hopeless."

I object to this. "'Hopeless' is a little strong."

"You are no judge. Walk for me."

"Why?" I stand my ground.

When he turns, the sun lights one part of his face and shadows the rest like a perfume ad. I groan. "Do you do that on purpose? Pose in the light?" I mimic his stance.

"Of course I do." He pulls his chin up slightly and that's it. I burst out laughing. He's so perfectly arrogant that I begin to see him more as a comedic character than a man. He brings his brows together. "Something funny?"

"Not at all."

"Really. Because you're laughing."

"Well, you," I admit. "You're funny. Who does that?"

The knit brows are joined by pursed lips. "Is there a problem in putting your best self forward?"

"I guess not." I clear my throat to change the subject. "Are you honestly here to watch me walk?"

Sam comes over from the window and stands in front of me. I'd say he was trying to intimidate me because of how he looks down his nose, but it reminds me of one of his roles—he was a lowly delivery guy who also fought crime—and I can feel my lips twitch. He glares at me as if he knows what I'm thinking. "Fangli refuses to let go of this," he says. He looks over my shoulder and chooses his words. "I said I would help."

"If you're looking for ideas, you can help by not being an asshole," I suggest.

"I can help by making sure you don't tarnish Fangli's reputation with your ignorance." He leans forward. "I don't like it but I'll do what I can to mitigate the risk to her, even if it means working with you."

"A real professional."

"I work with many people I don't respect. Or like."

"Me, too." We eye each other and I pull back. I'd held out enough of an olive branch. Now it was business time. "Then let's do this."

"Walk around again." He sprawls in a chair and takes up more space than he has a right to.

"Give me a second." I replay one of the clips on my tablet. On the screen, Fangli, dressed in a white satin pantsuit, strolls by like she's walking the runway. I can't do it like that. I throw back my shoulders and decide to simply go. Sam's eyes follow me as I walk across the room, which, hilariously, is long enough that I can really get some steps in.

When I come back to the center, he looks thoughtful, as if I'm a puzzle to be solved rather than an insect to squish. This is a decided improvement. "That was less ghastly than last night," he compliments me. "You have a similar walk to Fangli."

"No, we don't." This I'm sure about.

Sam sighs and takes out his phone, which he taps and shoves under my nose. It shows a dark-haired woman walking away through a lobby, her body language confident and natural.

"This is what you want me to walk like, I know. I'm trying."

"Unbelievable," he says. "That's you. Like I said. When you're being yourself."

I watch it again and realize it's me walking out of the hotel the other day. I didn't know I looked like that. "Why do you have this?"

"I took it when you left to prove to Fangli what a hopeless idea this was." He looks back at the screen. "You moved better than I thought you would," he says grudgingly.

"That is a deeply creepy thing to do." I'm a little awed at his dedication.

"I know." He says it without shame.

I flop down on the chair next to him and he winces. I guess Fangli isn't a flopper either. "The problem is when I know I'm being watched, I forget how to move. My hands are too big and flappy."

Sam motions for me to get up. "It's because you consider your body a flaccid thing you inhabit instead of a tool to be trained. When Fangli walks down the street, it's the same as if she's walking a red carpet or on set. Be conscious of your body, like a dancer. Every muscle has a job. Every gesture has a purpose."

I don't like Sam talking about bodies, but I power through. "How?"

"I can't describe it better than that. Each movement is a decision. You don't simply walk. You decide every step, every tilt of your head. You think of how you want to look and you make that happen. Your awareness has to be external—what are people seeing? What do you *want* them to see?"

I look thoughtfully in the mirror. I overthink things on good days, so this advice could well blast me right out of orbit. Think about things more than I do?

"Go again."

I do.

"That was worse than before." He rubs the back of his hand against his forehead. "How can a woman not walk?"

"I'm not used to an audience."

"There's always an audience," he says dismissively. "You've had the privilege of being able to ignore it."

"What's that mean?"

"You can walk down the street and be seen but not noticed."

Great, now I have Sam Yao stressing my invisibility as a person—exactly what every woman wants to hear.

He keeps talking. "From the moment she leaves her room, every action Fangli takes can be recorded and shared globally. Her public self is a role she plays the same as in a film. Outside these walls, Wei Fangli is a character. She has to think about how she looks all the time because a single unguarded moment can bring international public humiliation and ridicule."

The unspoken threat is there—as Fangli, that large-scale mortification can be all mine if I bungle this. I grit my teeth and try again. Again.

By the sixth time, I grasp the edges of what he's telling me. It's a sense of being conscious of my environment and how I inhabit it. I recall a behind-the-scenes segment of an actor about to walk the red carpet. She's told exactly where the marks are and shown photos of the scene. Standing near the wall, I survey the room as Sam scrolls through his phone, a slight frown on his face and his attention off me. This time I don't see it as a way to get from point A to B. I think of where I want to be within it. The room is my setting, not simply empty space with a few bits of furniture acting as obstacles.

"That's not so bad." Sam looks up from his phone to watch me, and I stumble slightly as I meet his eyes. He shakes his head and goes back to his phone.

Sam is a character. Fangli is a character. I need to be one as well. I'm not Gracie doing laps of the hotel room. I need to be Fangli.

Inhabiting a new persona is liberating, and Sam tilts his head when I walk by again. "Better."

By the time Sam indicates I have passed Module 1: The Art of Walking, I have blisters from the adorable sling-backs. "Good enough," he congratulates me. He checks the time. "Keep practicing. I need to get to the theater."

I collapse on the bed to see a text.

You alive? It's Anjali.

Not fish bait yet, I text back.

Prove it's you.

I send her a photo of me lounging on my closet chair wearing a pair of embroidered heels too high for me to walk in. I don't know the brand—the name is in Japanese—but I assume they're pricey.

I accept that with respect. Hotty Hotterman treating you ok?

Not too bad. Today with Sam could have been worse. He wasn't actively mean.

When's your first event?

Few days from now. I have time.

We text casually back and forth as I try on more of the clothes and try to decide what feels easiest to wear. I send shots to Anjali, who has a bad habit of liking the most uncomfortable outfits best.

Beauty is pain, she writes. Fangli is a fashion icon. She's not schlepping to the store in pj's.

She probably has people to do that for her anyway. Mei had told me Fangli will go straight to her suite after the show, so after some more strolling around the room, I eat and go to bed, legs and feet aching and face slathered with a retinol serum Fangli's dermatologist has apparently recommended for dire cases.

That's the end of my first day. I learned to walk.

JUNE 23

IVY LEE METHOD: TOP 6 TASKS

1. LEARN TO BE FANGLI.

2. CHINESE APP-MINIMUM ONE MODULE.

3. WORK ON MY OWN TASK PLANNER.

4.

5.

6. WEIRD, THOSE ARE ALL THE TASKS.

Ten

"W hy are you here?" I demand. Sam is sitting in my suite's living area when I come out of the bedroom, dress swinging around my legs as I halt. I forgot to shave them and pray he doesn't look down. Mr. Physical Perfection doesn't need to see that stubble.

He doesn't put down his phone as he sips his coffee. "I have some time so I'm here to run your boot camp."

I grab a coffee for myself, yawning. It was another night of fitful sleep as I ran through my many anxieties. My old therapist used to try to get me to have some perspective on my problems. That worked well enough when all I had to understand was that the world would not end if I returned a phone call Tuesday instead of Monday. My coping techniques are markedly less effective when facing a situation where public disgrace at a global level is a real possibility if I screw up.

"Where's Fangli?" I ask.

"Resting."

Although it would be nice to see her, the entire reason I'm here is so she can get a break. "What's on tap today?"

"Conversation." From the flat tone, I can tell he's as thrilled as I am to spend the next several hours making small talk.

I try to rally. "Should we start with an icebreaker?"

He doesn't change expression.

"Icebreaker it is." I try to smile. He's making it hard for me to do what Fangli hired me to do.

"No icebreakers."

"Childhood memories?"

"No."

"Best vacations? Favorite food? Two truths and a lie?"

I'm on the receiving end of an eye roll that would put a sulky teenager to shame and bite my lips together to keep from laughing.

"What?" he demands.

"Nothing." I walk over to the table. "Tell me what you come up with, then."

We sit. Sam's here under duress but it's not my job to make this go smoothly. I blink. That's not something I usually think. Sam brings out the worst in me.

Or maybe the best. This isn't my usual reaction, which would be to fuss and worry and fill the empty silence with whatever came into my head.

To pass the time, I take out my phone and check the news, which is bad. An email from Garnet Brothers gives me such a punch my whole body jerks with sudden coldness. I forward it straight to Fred the Lawyer.

"What happened?" Sam's attention is on me.

"Nothing. Why?" I avoid his eyes.

He frowns. "You were looking at your phone and yelped like a small dog. It's obvious you had a message you didn't like."

"This is what passes for conversation with you?" I ask. I don't want to talk about the email, let alone with Sam.

"It can." He smiles, the slow, predatory grin I remember from binge-watching his movies. It's intriguing to see it in real life. "Do you want to talk about it?"

"I don't think I do," I say. "That's the face you get when you're about to fuck someone over."

"It's what?" The smile disappears. "Fangli doesn't swear."

"Again, I'm not actually Fangli. Your expression. It's the 'you underestimated me and now I'm going to wreak some havoc' look. From your movies. You did it before fighting the Triad guy in *Dragon Claw*, and you did it when you were confronting the man who betrayed you in *Glass House*. Oh, and you did it a bunch of times in *Alley Boom Down*. It was almost a tic."

When his eyes widen, I see they're very dark brown and not the black I thought. "How many of my movies have you watched?"

"Most of them." I make a face because Mei made it clear skimming the web for plot summaries wasn't an option and the man's been busy. "Why is this a problem? Don't you make them to be watched?"

Sam angles his head up to the ceiling, lost in thought. Then, God help me, he runs his thumb across his lower lip. In the hierarchy of unconsciously sizzling things hot men do, that has to be tops. The incomplete list, as compiled by me on behalf of all people who find men attractive, is:

1.   THUMB ON LOWER LIP (MENTIONED).
2.   LOOK UP FROM BENEATH EYELASHES; ONLY FOR SOME MEN.
3.   HOLD A KITTEN. BONUS POINTS IF FACE IS BURIED IN FUR AND HE SMILES/ADDRESSES THE KITTEN DIRECTLY AS IF THE KITTEN CARES. PUPPIES WILL DO.
4.   THAT SIDEWAYS GLANCE OVER THE SHOULDER.
5.   LOOSEN TIE.
6.   RUN HAND THROUGH HAIR.
7.   LOOK IN YOUR EYES AS HE TAKES HIS THUMB OFF HIS LIP AND ASKS WHAT YOU'RE STARING AT.

"What?" I shake out of my musing state.

Sam tilts his head slightly. I add that as number eight to the list. "I asked what you're staring at," he repeats.

Mei comes into the room before I have to answer but my

Mandarin language app has only gotten me to letting people know I'm feeling happy today so I have no hope of following their conversation. I check the rest of my in-box as they talk. It's been a couple of days since I've seen Mom, but I email her every day and the nursing staff tell me they print out the messages. Occasionally one of the nicer nurses or a volunteer sends me an update. I get antsy if I don't see her at least once a week in person but I have a couple more days before that becomes a problem.

I put the phone away, dropping my head to the side to try to roll out the faint tightness of a tension headache inching up my neck. If this is how I feel after only two days living as a pseudo celebrity, I can't imagine the level of stress that is Fangli's everyday experience.

"Hao." Sam ends the conversation and Mei glides out the door in the crisp white shirt and black skirt I've started to think of as her uniform.

"What?" I stretch and he shuts his eyes as if physically pained when my shoulders pop. I do it again.

"Change of plans," he says, in the same tone as a general readying himself for an unplanned battle. "We need to go out tonight."

"Whoa, what?" I'm not prepared for this.

Neither is Sam, by the looks of it. "After the show, we have a dinner reservation."

"Why?"

He spins his phone over. There's a photo of Fangli looking tired with Chinese on the bottom.

"Can you translate?" I ask.

"There's speculation over Fangli's state of health. Her management doesn't like it." He takes the phone back. "Fangli has an image to protect."

There's no way I can blow eating food. I've been doing it for years. I cheer up a bit. "Where are we going?"

"It's called Ala."

I immediately start googling. "Fancy."

"It's an appropriate place for us to be seen."

Out of curiosity, I click on their online reservation system and see the next available table is two months away and at five in the evening. "How do you plan to get a table?"

Sam gives me an unfathomable look. "I can always get a table."

I let that pass. There's no menu on their website because the chef only uses the freshest ingredients from the morning markets. *Plated with exquisite detail* enthuses a Yelp reviewer.

Sam's phone dings and he picks it up. "I've got to deal with this and don't have time to eat lunch. I expect you to be ready for nine thirty."

He disappears right as room service arrives. Once he's gone, I page through my Fangli notes as I wolf down the pasta and then pop a Tylenol. At the top of my to-do list is one overwhelming task: Pretend to be Wei Fangli.

That's a big action item. But if there's one thing my thorough examination of productivity plans has taught me, it's to break big tasks into smaller actions. Humming happily to myself, I check for any new apps that might meet my needs. I'm multitasking, as this is good research for Eppy as well. I decided last night Eppy—secret acronym for Easy Planning Per Year—would be the name of my task planner.

"Wo ke le. I am thirsty." I absentmindedly repeat the language lesson that has become the background music of my life. Hopefully it will subliminally enter my brain. There's nothing new to try out in the world of productivity planning so I grab a pen and some paper.

"Wo chi mifan. I eat rice." Do I need to find footage of Fangli eating? I ponder this for a minute before discarding it as unnecessary.

"Wo he shui. I drink water." An outfit. Won't be a problem, I can wear the dress I have on. I tap the pen against my teeth and write "shave legs."

I add a few more tasks but then remember that outside of being Fangli, I need to check the wait list at Xin Guang, call the lawyer about Garnet Brothers, and pay my rent. I add them and make a face for not thinking of my own life earlier.

Finally, I check my bank account to see if the payment to Mom's home went through.

Then I look again because I am a lot of zeros richer than I was yesterday. It's Fangli's first payment. My situation is suddenly more real than it had been six minutes ago. Money has officially changed hands, which means I now owe her. My head is aching too much to think about it so I shut down the app and suck in deep breaths.

Taking my notepad and phone into the bedroom, I toss them onto the rumpled duvet and climb up beside them. (Mei has told housekeeping we'll call if we need anyone to come make up the room or bring fresh towels in order to head off any inadvertent missteps by yours truly, so I'm in charge of making my own bed.) My eyes droop and I set my alarm for an hour. A quick nap and I'll be as good as new.

———

I wake slowly and bury my face back into the fluffy puffball of a pillow the Xanadu has decided is the most appropriately extravagant of sleeping options. A few more minutes, I promise myself, even though I'm more rested than I've been in days. I yawn and stretch, thinking how calm the room feels in the dusk. Relaxing.

Dusk?

I fumble for my phone. It's almost nine and Sam's coming in thirty minutes for dinner.

"No. Damn, no." Fully awake, I leap out of bed, get tangled in the bedsheets, and fall over in a cloudy white lump before I stumble to the bathroom, trailing the sheets behind me like the most inelegant of wedding dresses. It's too late for the refreshing shower I had planned, so I splash water on my face and do my best to brush my hair and teeth at the same time. The face. I groan as I mentally review the multistep Fangli Face process. I screw up the eyeliner twice and then poke myself in the eye with the mascara wand. This is not a good start.

At least the lipstick goes on without a problem, and I suck on my finger to make sure I don't get any on my teeth, a tip from Mom back when I first started wearing lipstick. It worked for my first neutral corals and even better once I worked up to my ruby reds.

Since I slept in the dress I was going to wear—and in my bra, which I peel off for the relief of unsticking it and wiping my under-boob with a towel—I need to find a new outfit.

"Are you ready?" Sam's impatient voice comes from the living room. He's early.

"Don't look. I'm getting dressed. How did you get in here?" I yell back as I yank another dress out. This one's black, so there's no way it can't be stylish, at least not in Toronto. "Do you have a key card?"

"Yes."

I don't like that. I'll get it back over dinner. Dress zipped, I stuff my feet into the lowest heels I can find and launch myself through the bedroom door before Sam comes to pull me out.

Then I freeze. He's all in black as well, with a collared shirt tucked into tailored black slacks and a black blazer. One hand is placed casually in his pocket and his hair is artfully tumbled. My eyes widen in appreciation.

This appreciation is not reciprocated when he looks me up and down. "You can't be serious."

"What?" I check the mirror. One eye is pink from where I introduced the mascara wand, and I guess I sneezed because black dappled lines decorate the skin under both eyes. I have marks from where I was sleeping on my cheek, and when I smile, I see Mom's tried and tested lipstick trick has not worked because I look like a postprandial vampire. Also, I forgot the wig.

"Right." I lick my teeth to get rid of the red lipstick as I rub under my eyes and dash back into the room to adjust my foundation to cover the sleep creases. I pull out the wig and arrange it on my head before I come back out with a little more Fangli attitude.

This time Sam gives me a long, appraising look. I smile Fangli's smile and he nods reluctantly. "I guess it'll do," he says. "Perfume. She only wears Chanel because she's their brand ambassador."

"Good. I like No. 19 Poudre." I don't wear it all the time, though. I never liked the idea of a signature fragrance, not when there are so many options.

"What?" He's startled I would know an actual perfume. "Mei says the fragrance collection is in the drawer under the mirror."

Fragrance collection? How did I miss that? I go back in and gasp with delight at the lines of bottles. It's like being in the Chanel store. "She has Les Exclusifs!"

"Les what?" He comes in and leans against the door like a black-clad demon as I rummage through the long, rectangular bottles labeled with that inimitable square Chanel font. There it is, Bois des Iles, which I bought once and couldn't justify the expense to buy again. I spray it and start coughing from the droplets in the air. I breathed too soon. Sam looks tired as he watches me choke.

"It's a special collection of fragrances." I don't know much about clothes but perfume has always been my thing. I have over three hundred samples logged on a spreadsheet with my ratings. Pathetic, I know, but scent is the sense that I've always reacted to most intensely. Even as a kid, I would have a fit if my parents changed their laundry detergent. Sam smells good, a faint fresh spice mixed with the fragrance of chipped stone. Sounds weird, but it's appealing.

"You like that?" He sniffs the air with more caution than I did. "I smell sandalwood."

"You're right." I recap the bottle. It gives a little magnetic click in the very satisfying Chanel way. "Sandalwood is my mother's favorite perfume."

"My mother's as well," he says, as if shocked we could have anything in common. "Can we go now?"

We walk to the elevator, and I have the pleasure of a steady stream of advice and criticism battering my ear. "Shoulders back," Sam says.

I push back my shoulders.

"Not that far back. Smile more."

Forward come the shoulders as I smile and hiss at him through clenched teeth. "Can you lay off? It's an empty corridor."

"With security cameras that record sellable video, housecleaning staff and people behind those peepholes." He eyes me with pretend fondness. "You are *never* not watched."

The elevator opens as I consider this. It's like he and Fangli live in a surveillance state gone amok. We don't talk in the elevator, and when we get out, he steers me away from the main door.

"We're not walking?" The restaurant's only about twenty minutes away and the summer evening is perfect for strolling.

"Too public."

I guess it's a good call because even the low heels I chose hurt my feet. I've been focusing so hard on my walking that I don't notice the people in the lobby until we're halfway through. Even in the Xanadu, temporary home of the rich and famous, Sam causes a ripple of interest. Eyes move to me and I realize it's not only Sam, it's Sam and me together. A brief silence falls over the lobby as we walk through, and I stumble slightly with the weight of their attention. Sam snaps his arm out and gathers me close in a single move that I know looks sexily protective, like the faithful bodyguard he played in one of his movies.

I think I hear a woman moan.

Gathering my wits, I flutter my eyelashes at him. I swear his mouth twitches but I must be wrong because he steadies me and then tucks my hand under his arm.

"Walk," he mutters.

I make it to the car, which is not a car but an SUV that should have little flags fluttering on the front motorcade-style. Sam helps me in, which has the advantage of preventing people from seeing me sprawl sideways when I catch my foot.

He climbs in after me and closes his eyes.

"That wasn't so bad," I congratulate myself.

Sam opens one eye. "I hate to see your version of bad."

"We made it." I feel confident as I fix up my wig. Then I straighten up. "Is it like that wherever you go?"

"What?"

"People looking."

"I told you it was." He doesn't sound impatient, only resigned.

I think about it. It was exhilarating, but I don't want to tell Sam this. The little worm in my brain expands slightly as I realize I liked it. I liked being seen. Being admired.

It wasn't you. That was for Fangli. No one would have turned for Gracie, not even a Gracie with a designer dress and long hair.

Good to remember.

Eleven

When we arrive at the restaurant, it's hard to not be seduced. I smooth out the front of my dress as I get out of the car to the stares of passersby. They might not recognize us, but the sleek car and the manager who rushes out to meet us when the valet opens the door are visual signifiers that here be people with money and influence.

How would Fangli act? She's used to fancy places, so she would resist trailing her fingers along the side of the staircase to see if that was real velvet covering the walls. When she reached the top of the stairs, she would check the room casually for acquaintances and wouldn't squeak with glee when spotting Margaret Atwood.

So I don't do those things either. Instead, I keep my expression schooled and focus on Sam's shoulders as the manager leads us to a back table, the most private option the room offers. A silence washes over the restaurant, followed by a hum as people recognize us. This is a fancy place and its patrons are too cool to do anything so gauche as take photos or come up to us so the buzz is all we get.

I wonder if Margaret Atwood got the same attention.

The manager deftly slides the chair forward as I sit down and I give myself a silent high five for smiling in thanks, as a woman used to this would, instead of erupting into a flurry of "it's okay" and "I got it, no worries" mumbles. The manager nods and leaves us alone with the menus. Too bad the table is turned so we're on display to the rest of the room. I would much prefer to face the wall and have only my back visible.

I pick up the heavy card-stock menu that lies in front of me. Instead of long-winded descriptions or lists of ingredients, there are only five words typed in a row:

Fish

Meat

Bird

Vegetable

Sweet

I check the back but that's it. There are no prices and I peek over at Sam's paper. No prices there either.

"What is it now?" he asks, not lifting his eyes from the world's most uninformative menu.

"You don't think it's strange to order 'bird' and leave the rest up to chance?"

He shrugs. "I trust the chef."

We order when the server comes (Meat for Sam and Fish for me), and I proudly remember to tell them no carrots in my best Fangli voice—low, confident, and warm. Sam gets into a spirited discussion of the best vintages on offer that will match our mystery food.

"I should have known you're a wine guy," I say when the server goes to get the drinks.

"A what?"

"You know, one of those guys who holds up the whole table to wax eloquent about viscosity and bouquet or whatever it is."

"I hardly think I was holding up the whole table—which is you— to give the server an idea of what we want and to show respect to the sommelier's cellar. It's a pity she's not in today."

Then he starts speaking in Mandarin. I understand why when the server reappears; obviously it would be suspicious to be speaking English with only the two of us and I'm impressed Sam thought of this detail. I smile and nod as if I have a clue of what he's saying.

The server shows us the bottle and uncorks the wine before pouring a bit into Sam's glass with a neat flick of his wrist. He gives the bottle a quick swipe with the white cloth in his other hand and waits for Sam to swirl and taste and give his approving nod. I try to look interested.

The server leaves and I drink the wine down in a gulp before Sam's narrowed eyes tell me I've made a tactical error. "I was thirsty," I excuse myself.

He looks away for a moment as if gathering strength. "Fangli doesn't drink."

I forgot. "Then why did you pour me the glass?" I ask, incensed. Am I expected to sit there with a full glass and not drink it? In a stressful situation? Does he think I'm made of steel?

Apparently he does. "Imagine this is poison," he suggests as he refills my glass a measly centimeter. "Also, wine is for sipping, not guzzling."

"Why bother, then?"

Sam appears pained as he traces his finger down the stem of his glass. "Because you should take your time to appreciate good wine?"

"No, why have the wine if she can't drink it?"

He sighs. "People expect there to be wine at dinner, so Fangli would have it visible."

I gape at him. "Does she do anything without a motive?"

Those dimples flash. "Does anyone?"

"Why doesn't she come out and say she doesn't drink?"

"Because then she would cut out all branding opportunities for alcohol companies. They pay well." Sam glances at his watch. "This should take an hour and then we'll be done." He doesn't bother to disguise his relief.

"Great."

There's a long silence as Sam regards me. "I don't think this will work," he says softly. "You're not Fangli."

I've never been into the idea of being rescued by a knight in shining armor, but seeing Sam so unequivocally on Team Fangli stings. I ignore it; I've been on my own too long for this to matter much. "Then maybe you should step up your helping game," I say.

"Why are you even doing this?" Sam tilts his head to the side.

I shrug. "It's a lot of money, and as you so kindly pointed out, I'm out of work." I don't trust him enough to go into Mom's situation and what I want the money for.

"I knew it." Sam sounds satisfied. "I'm never wrong."

"I know you did. You've been rabbiting on about it since this all came about." I reach for the wine but Sam's face causes me to veer over into water-glass territory. "It doesn't change what's going on. You lost and we're doing this."

He wrinkles his nose but still looks like a sex god.

"Stop that," I say.

"What?"

"You keep trying to trip me up by showing me how attractive you are. I know, okay? Everyone knows. *Celebrity* magazine knows. This entire restaurant knows. So knock it off." Then for good measure, I add, "At least the looks make up for your personality."

He stiffens. That apparently hit home and I celebrate. Call me Peppermint Petty. "I have a good personality," he says.

"Do you hate the people who do your makeup?"

"No." He's confused.

"The guy bringing the food? The person who cooked it?"

"Of course not."

I take a deep breath to calm my nerves and say what I think. "Then lay off me. Fangli and I made a deal and I'm doing a job. I'm sorry you got roped into it but you didn't have to play along. You have a problem, take it out on Fangli, because it was *her fucking idea*."

Because I'm a quick learner, despite what Sam thinks, I know there's a good chance that at least one person in the restaurant is watching us at any given moment so I deliver this with a sweet sunny smile while leaning forward as if telling Sam an amusing story.

There's a long silence as Sam runs his thumb over his lip. Number one from the list again. The action forces me to look away and I beam vaguely at the wall behind him, making sure my posture is straight and doing my best to resist checking that my wig isn't crooked. It's hard work, being Fangli.

"Fine," he says.

"Fine, what?"

"You're right. I will treat you with..." He struggles for a word.

"Respect?"

He looks up at the ceiling.

"Warmth? Affability? Gregariousness?"

His gaze comes back down to my face. "Sociability."

What does that mean? I suppose anything is better than active disdain. My heart rate slows now that the confrontation is over and I have at least a partial victory, but my brain gerbils rouse themselves to start doing their laps on the wheel around my head. Why couldn't I have said the same to Todd? Told him to treat me with respect? Stood up for myself?

I look at Sam, who's checking his phone as if he doesn't have a care in the world. Is it because Sam, acting or not, prickly or not, seems like a fundamentally good human being who, although misguidedly, is behaving in what he thinks is the best interest of a friend or possibly girlfriend? That Todd defeated me because I knew he was at his core a deeply terrible person?

Thank God the food comes quickly because Sam's newly professed sociability does not extend to cheerful conversation. Wo zai chi fan (*I am eating*; finally I have a phrase that matches what I'm doing) but the food's so good I slow down to savor it. I was initially worried that it would be one of those platter-sized dishes with a thimbleful of food and a drizzle of some pomegranate–pine needle reduction, but I was wrong. The poached fish with ginger reminds me of my childhood.

"What do you think?" Sam looks up from what looks like a steak but it's almost round like a baseball.

"Incredible." I take another bite. "My mom used to make something like this but with way more garlic."

"Lucky. I don't think either of my parents have even made their own tea for the last forty years."

"Did you eat out a lot?"

"Sometimes. Usually the amahs would cook for me but we had a chef for my parents."

As if regretting sharing this information, Sam turns back to his food and we don't speak for the rest of the meal. After the plates are cleared and we're waiting for tea, I decide I enjoy the silence. I've been on enough dates to know I no longer have the desire to pretend a man is interesting, and with Sam I'm free of the need to bother. He's not making an effort either, which gives me time to think about how much I've already adapted to people watching me, especially now that Margaret Atwood has left and there's no one else to stare at.

None of them are obvious about it, but the occasional glances are like the flutter of butterfly wings on my skin. Individually it's nothing, but collectively, it turns heavy. Sam picks up his tea when it arrives.

"We should talk so it doesn't look like we're fighting." He delivers this in a dismal tone, like he's going in for a disagreeable but necessary dental procedure.

I give him a go-right-ahead gesture and he stares at me, at a loss for words.

I rock the cup in the saucer. "Do you hire people to talk for you the same way you hire them to make your dinner reservations?"

"It's been a long time since I've talked to someone outside of work," he says.

If that's true, it's sad. Not enough to make me reassess his attitude but enough to make me continue the conversation. "What about your friends?"

"They're all in the industry."

Definitely sad. Too insular. I'm curious about this life they live. "Your Wikipedia page says you started as a stage actor."

"We both did, Fangli and I, for a few years after drama school. Our teachers recommended it and they were right."

"Why?"

He leans forward. "There's an energy you get from a live audience that hones your craft. Their reactions can change the entire meaning of a performance and you need to adapt."

I nod. "I remember once in university I said a line that was meant to be poignant. It worked in rehearsals but then the audience laughed. They thought it was funny."

Sam taps the table. "Exactly. You need to react in the moment. There's no scene to cut and try again. You have one shot with that audience and then it's over. You can't redo it."

"Do you ever have regrets about a way you played a role on the stage?"

"Many. All the time." He pushes his cup to the side. "My first roles were overacted and my gestures stiff."

"Inexperience?"

He looks at me. "In part. It's easier to act a part than to feel it. It was a battle to open up onstage."

A flash comes from over my shoulder, and when Sam's face smooths out from his previous animation, I realize that he's been speaking to me not as Public Sam but as himself. "Someone took a photo," he murmurs.

I had forgotten that I was there to play a role. I fold up my napkin with what I hope is elegance. "What do I do?"

"Keep talking. Fangli wouldn't notice a single photo. It's expected."

"Why did you get into movies if you like the stage so much?"

He gives me a big smile. "You'll like this answer: money." He changes the topic. "You'll be with Mei tomorrow," he says. "Final prep."

"For what?"

He raises his eyebrows. "Your new life as Fangli, of course."

Twelve

Fangli's in her room when we arrive back at the hotel, but she comes into mine when she hears us. From her reddened eyes, I know she's been crying but I don't feel comfortable enough to ask her what's wrong, so I take my cue from Sam, who pretends not to notice. Maybe this is normal for her. He goes to his own suite down the hall, leaving us alone with Mei, who is in the kitchen making tea.

Fangli shakes her head, her hair bouncing. "I can't get over how much we look alike," she says. "How was dinner?"

I take off the wig and toss it on the table, where it spreads like an octopus. "It wasn't what I expected," I say as I scratch my head. Gross, but the wig makes me itchy.

"How so?" Fangli accepts the tea Mei brings out and I breathe in the delicate flowery aroma. It's not jasmine or chrysanthemum so I sniff again. Maybe chamomile. Mei reminds Fangli of her personal trainer appointment in the morning, picks up my abandoned wig without comment, and leaves.

I sit cautiously on a chair, not wanting to tear a seam in my dress. "I was worried people would come talk to me," I say.

"That happens occasionally, but most people are respectful, particularly in your country."

"Some aren't?"

She looks at me over the cup before she places it back on the table. "I'm not a person to them. I'm an object, a product. Commodities don't have feelings or emotions."

"Ah." I don't know what to say. My last boyfriend had a verbal code for these situations, where you have to acknowledge the issue but don't have a productive comment. I dust it off and deploy. "That's rough. How do you feel about that?"

"It's upsetting." Fangli smiles. "Thank you."

"For what?"

"Asking. Understanding. Not telling me I should be grateful, that it's my duty to be seen and let fans come to me. That it comes with the territory of being rich and famous and I knew what I signed up for when I started acting."

I think about this. Even for a movie star, it's not right. "You need space to be yourself."

"I wonder who that is at times," she says softly. Then she shakes her shoulders like a wet dog and puts her tea down. "Tell me about your day."

"Well, I mostly slept." I grimace. "Sorry, didn't mean to rub that in."

"I'm only a bit jealous. The dinner?"

"Oh, incredible." I describe the food in excruciating detail until I notice her confused expression. "What?"

"I meant with Sam. Was he..." She searches for a word.

"I can handle it."

Fangli eyes me sympathetically. "I'm sorry he's being difficult," she says. "I'll talk to him."

"No, we've figured it out. It wasn't as bad as I thought it would be."

She nods. "Thank you." When she closes her eyes, her entire face draws in and grows tight.

"Tired?" I ask. I go to the fridge and grab two cans of seltzer. According to Mei, Fangli only drinks out of glass, so I open the cabinet.

"The can is fine." She reaches out and plucks it from my hand.

"Mei said glass only."

Fangli holds the can to the side of her throat to enjoy the cold before opening it. It leaves a faint red mark on her skin. "I don't care, to be honest. The image consultant said it was better because it was more sophisticated."

"Image consultant?" I can guess the point from the name but it seems utterly unnecessary.

She grins at me. "I see her every six months. She was trained as a futurist."

This is intriguing. "What does she tell you?"

Fangli tilts the can to drink in gulps. "It's quite an experience. I enjoy it."

"She dresses you?"

"Not for that money." Fangli laughs. "She comes in for half a day, and we talk about world events and trends she sees. She works with CEOs mostly."

"I don't get it."

"I need to be exactly a little ahead. Not too much and not behind."

"How?" I'm puzzled. "How do you do that?"

"Training." She shrugs. "Plus at this point, I create trends. If I cut my hair like yours, you would see a spike in that look globally in the next three months, beginning with specific demographic segments in Asian urban centers before spreading out to Western and European cities. Advertisers map out my brand reach and potential for market penetration before they sign me to promote their products."

"Whoa." She says that like it's no biggie but it hits me that being Fangli is a multimillion-dollar business. This must be why Sam is so worried; there's a lot of money at stake if I screw up. No pressure.

"I try not to think about it." She beams. "Now tell me about what you'd be doing if you weren't here."

"Like, if I had a real job that wasn't pretending to be you?" I think of Todd and shiver. My fear of him... Wait. Fear? Was I scared of him? It's such a big word, more suited to a life-or-death situation than his kind of garden-variety assholeness, but the word sits right. I'd been scared, but to be honest, it wasn't only Todd's actions but my own reactions that frightened me. I'd freeze when he approached me. What did that say about me that I didn't stop him?

"Or anything."

"I'd go see my mom. She has Alzheimer's and lives in a nursing home." I get that out quickly, not wanting any pity.

Fangli doesn't give me the look I dread. She only nods. "She's lucky to have a devoted daughter since your father passed away."

It must have been noted in the dossier she'd received from the private eye, but she does me the credit of mentioning it straight out instead of pretending she didn't know about Dad. "He died almost ten years ago." Cancer's a bitch. I try not to think about it.

"Ah. I never knew my mother. She died when I was a baby. My father remarried to a nice woman but we have little in common."

"Is he alive?"

"Lives in Beijing. I see him when I go home but he refuses to leave China."

"Why?" There's so much of the world to see.

"He says the world is in China." She rolls her eyes. "I have no idea what it means either."

"He didn't have a problem with you acting?"

Fangli stretches and pulls her mass of hair back into a loose ponytail that she immediately drops down. "I've only ever wanted two things in my life. A pet cat—which he refused when I was a child and now I'm not home enough to take care of even if I had one—and to act."

"How did you know that's what you wanted to do?" I'm intrigued.

"I always knew." She flicks the tab of her can idly with a perfectly manicured finger painted with clear nail polish. "My school was chosen to put on a play in honor of a visit from the General Secretary. One of the directors from the Central Academy of Drama saw me and told my father that I would bring glory to China. It was the only reason my father let me apply. He wanted me to be a scientist."

"Really." I could be wrong, but I don't think many North American actors are encouraged to go into the industry out of patriotism.

"That's where I met Sam," she adds. "We were in the same year at school."

"Did you ever..." I wriggle my eyebrows with meaning as I test the ground. I'm nosy, okay? She doesn't have to answer.

"Never."

"You're not a couple?" I feel lighter, which is weird because it's not as if not dating Fangli means Sam's open to me.

She shudders. "Sam is like my brother, but people find it impossible to believe a man and woman can simply be friends. I could never see him like that. Ever." She makes a kind of hilarious choking face.

"Really?" I lean forward. "Not even when you met?" Because I imagine even in the blundering teenage years Sam would have stood out.

"At the Academy, there was no time for dating, and in any case, I had a crush on his best friend."

"A love triangle?"

"We were young and neither Sam nor I are interested in each other, so more of a one-way love line than a triangle." Fangli laughs. "Poor Chen. He started a technology company and I haven't seen him in ages. He lives in Vancouver." She raises her eyebrows. "The detective said you were single."

"For two years," I say. "Riley was—I mean, is, he's not dead—a nice guy."

"But?"

"I don't know." Talking with Fangli is so comfortable, like talking to the sister I always wanted. Or what I imagine sisterhood to be like. "It was never a raging passion but one day I cooked dinner and we ate and when I was doing the dishes, I knew if I had to do that every night for the rest of my life, I would shrivel to a husk."

"You cooked and did the dishes?" Fangli frowns. "What did he do?"

I blink. "I don't know. I always did them."

"I see. Well, how did he take it?" Fangli leans forward, eyes wide.

"That's the zinger. I agonized for a week before I decided the best way to tell him. I didn't want to hurt him, so I wanted to avoid a restaurant in case the place would have bad memories for him. We lived together, but it seemed cold to sit him down in the living room. In the end, I asked him to go for a walk."

"Why that?"

"I thought it would help distract from the message."

She nods as if filing this away. "The zinger, as you called it?"

"Right. I do all this planning and then I tell him, *Hey, it's not you, it's me but I think this is over.*"

"Did he cry?" She leans further in.

"Nope."

"Yell?"

"Not at all."

Her nose scrunches up. "What did he say?"

Even now, I can't believe it. "He said, 'Okay, cool.'"

Fangli waits. Then she asks, "That's it?"

"That's it. 'Okay, cool.' Nothing else. We turned around and went home. I slept in the spare room and we were very genial roommates for three weeks before he found a new place. He shook my hand when he left."

I hadn't told Anjali that tidbit, too stunned and almost embarrassed when it happened. Fangli's eyes are huge with disbelief.

"A handshake?" she repeats.

"Like this." I give her the single firm and professional shake that Riley gave me before he walked out the door, like I was a new client he was confident was going to sign on because of the solid pitch he'd given.

I can see her try to control it, but Fangli's lip twitches. The more she presses her lips together, the more I can feel my own starting to edge up.

"I'm sorry," she whispers, covering her mouth with her hand. "It's not funny. But a handshake?"

I'll give her this—she makes a valiant attempt to get herself under control. Then I give her a nod, that sharp, imperious, and excessively irritating dip of the head that Riley'd always given me whenever he'd finished explaining in detail why he was right and I was wrong.

That's all it takes. Fangli snorts inelegantly into her hand, which sets me off. This in turn starts her giggling, which gets me cackling. Within seconds, we're both doubled up, laughing until we can't breathe. Riley might have been the trigger, but this is a simple and much-needed stress release.

"How long were you together?" she gasps.

"Two years." I wipe the tears away, but when she hears that, her giggles start up again.

"Two years," she finally whispers to herself as I rub my stomach, which hurts from laughing. She stands up. "What sort of a man does that?"

"Good question," I say, sobering a little.

She looks at me closely. "One that doesn't deserve you."

"He's out of my life," I say. "It was easy to *shake* it off."

That sets Fangli off again and occasional gusts of laughter follow as she waves good night and goes to bed. I can't help but smile. I'd always had lingering feelings about that breakup, wondering how boring I was that "okay" was all the emotion Riley could summon.

I'd felt lacking but Fangli's contagious glee had shifted something in my mind. The humor plucked out the remaining sting. Did Fangli give me the validation that I didn't know I craved, or was it simply relief at telling someone? Regardless, I could put it to rest.

Speaking of rest...I crack a yawn so big it nearly turns my face inside out. Bed for me, too.

— JUNE 25 —

EPPY NOTES

MAYBE NESTED CIRCLES
WILL WORK AS A VISUAL.

CIRCLES ARE DUMB. HOW WOULD YOU
MAKE THAT WORK WITH TASKS?

COLUMNS. YES. COLUMNS AND CIRCLES TO
ADD LONG-TERM AND DAILY TASKS.

NEED TO BE ABLE TO
LOG EXTRAS, LIKE
EMOTIONAL STATE.

FORGET THAT.
NO EMOTIONAL STATE.

DEFINITELY NEED TO BE ABLE TO NOT FEEL
GUILTY FOR WHAT YOU DON'T DO; FOCUS
ON THE POSITIVE. HUH, MAYBE EMOTIONAL
AFTER ALL; CAN FILTER TASKS BY WHAT
MOOD YOU ARE IN — NEEDS MORE THOUGHT.

Thirteen

Now that we've come to our agreement, I prefer being with Sam more than with Mei. She is like the most intimidating executive assistant for the most demanding CEO. She's precise, unflappable, expressionless, and perpetually unamused. Like, I know I'm not funny but isn't it common courtesy to at least fake a smile at bad jokes?

Not if you're Mei.

I should find her easy to deal with, like a robot, but instead I have the dual sense of being judged and anxious. At least with Sam I'm judged and anxious but I have something nice to look at.

Today Mei takes me on a deep dive into Fangli's art collection. My art collection is two framed posters from IKEA in my living room, so there's a lot of information to cover. This is worse than an exam, and I tap out after three hours of art that I have no idea how to interpret.

"Time for a break," I say, slapping the bound booklet on the table and going to the fridge. "Do you want some water?" I drink water. Wo he shui. I better make time to listen to my app today so I can get to good things like talking about the weather.

"Bu yao." Mei doesn't look up.

I get the tone if not the words. It's a hard no.

"I thought I'd go see my mother this afternoon," I say when I return to the table. "After all, I'm not a prisoner." The last is a little too defensive because if I'm a prisoner, it's a pampered one taken out for meals in exorbitantly expensive restaurants.

"There is no time," Mei says. Her voice is smooth. "You have a facial booked and are then going shopping."

"What about the clothes in there?" I point at the huge closet.

"Mr. Yao and Ms. Wei feel you would benefit from picking out some of your own things. I have an appointment set for an acceptable brand."

"Fangli says they come to her."

Mei doesn't change expression. "They are coming here."

It's time for lunch and I think she thaws a bit when I ask her to eat with me. It's sashimi today, and I dig in after cracking open a Diet Coke. "Have you worked with Fangli for long?" I don't know anything about Mei personally.

"Two years." She's a delicate eater and I slow down a bit out of shame.

"What did you do before that?"

"I worked in the studio doing odd jobs."

"Where did you learn English?"

"I taught myself."

I wait for any questions from her side or even a follow-up answer but she's content to eat in silence. Ball's in my court. "Does Sam have an assistant as well?"

She pauses. "Deng is ill and Mr. Yao decided to make do."

"That's too bad. I hope he gets better." The polite words come automatically.

No reply. I decide to get some external confirmation of what Fangli said the night before. "When I was doing research, there were a lot of pieces about Sam and Fangli being a couple."

"Yes." Her voice is wooden. I can't read this chick worth beans.

"Is it true?"

Mei's cheeks pinken. "Mr. Yao and Ms. Wei are good friends. I believe Mr. Yao's attentions are elsewhere."

He has a girlfriend. I stuff some ruby-red tuna into my face. This is disappointing and should not be, not by a long shot. He's rich, famous, and incredibly handsome. He's a UN ambassador. It should be Amal Alamuddin Yao instead of Clooney.

Mei is now fully red and I wonder what gossip she has that she's not sharing. I shouldn't put her on the spot so I change the topic. "Are there plans for tonight?"

"An art exhibit."

That's why I've been crammed full of knowledge today. My heart thumps. "I have to talk?"

"About art." She glances at her watch. "Time for the facial."

———

I know about art now, I text Anjali.

She sends a photo of the *Mona Lisa* smoking a blunt.

It's good to text with Anjali, a bit of normalcy in what is turning out to be a whackadoodle week. She tells me about work; I tell her about how to walk upstairs in a miniskirt. (Apparently the key is to angle your body to the side.) We've been talking more since I've been living at the Xanadu. Anjali says she wants to live like the one percent vicariously through me but it's obvious she's checking in to make sure I'm safe. Her concern touches me more than I thought it would, and I make an effort to text her every day so she knows I'm alive.

Then she's off to a meeting and I prepare to be pampered.

The aesthetician comes to the room and sets up shop with bottles and vials and bright-white towels before inviting me to lie down with a smile filled with teeth so bleached they're blue. Then comes an hour of cosseting, from cold masks to face rollers from the top of my head to the tops of my boobs or, as the aesthetician calls it, my décolletage. There are many creams and smells. My multiple imperfections are poked and prodded and eventually eradicated under the skillful hands and tweezers of the aesthetician. It finishes with a face mask that warms and tightens my skin as ten fingers rub and scratch against my scalp. If I'd been a cat, I would have purred. I think I purr anyway because I am a gooey, limp jellyfish with no visible pores. The aesthetician assures me this is a new process so I can go out right away instead of letting my skin settle. I take her word for it.

I lie there in a blissful daze of relaxation until she starts to pull off the mask, which has cemented itself to my face. At my mewl of protest, the aesthetician pauses. "This shouldn't hurt," she says.

I would have answered had I been able to move my lips, but the mask has glued them in place. The woman tugs at the mask and lifts my head right off the table.

"I haven't seen this before," she says in a thoughtful tone.

There are certain times I don't want to hear that I'm special. The first is from any healthcare professional. A close second is from a woman who's slathered me with goop she can't get off my face. Mei materializes beside me like Porella, the Avenging Angel of Skincare, as the woman slowly peels the mask off. I swivel my eyes to her face and see the droplets of stress sweat on her upper lip as Mei murmurs a stream of low-voiced encouragement that the aesthetician and I both interpret as thinly veiled threats.

I've never been flayed but I have ripped off adhesive bandages. I imagine this experience is somewhere between the two. I'm no yeti but whatever hairs were on my face bid my skin an unwilling farewell as she detaches the mask millimeter by millimeter and I try not to squeal. It's hard.

When she gives a final rip, I screech.

The door bangs open. "What the hell's going on?"

A lot of things happen at once. Sam comes through the door in a dark blur. Shocked, I pop up from the table like a jack-in-the-box, forgetting that I'm only wrapped in a towel that immediately falls off. Sam makes eye contact with me before his eyes dip down to my gigantic heart-polka-dot granny panties and he freezes before he slaps his hands over his face and stumbles back making inarticulate sounds. I scramble to pick up the towel, in the process knocking the portable table with my butt. It slams into the poor aesthetician, who is gawking at the beauty that is Sam Yao. She falls back and then lets out a high keening sound as her hand plunges into the pot of whitish devil goo that has made such a mess of my face.

Mei rises up and gets us organized without a single word. Sam is sent to wait in his room. I'm directed to get back on the table with a finger jab. She gives a look to the aesthetician—a marvel of expressionless eloquence—who wipes her twitching hands with a towel.

All that beautiful relaxation has gone. How could I have forgotten to get the key from Sam? My face, the skin much thinner than it was ten minutes ago, burns with shame. How much did he see? Once I'm not dressed in a towel, we're going to have words, but now I'm a beaten human sprawled across the table with Mei bending over me shaking her head and the aesthetician poking at me with cautious fingers.

"Nothing a cooling mask won't solve," she chirps finally.

I catch Mei's eye and we have a moment of communion as I beg her through an interpretive eyebrow dance to save me.

"We're due for another appointment," she says smoothly.

"Then I'll use a toner and…"

"I'm good!" I swing my feet down and slide on the thin terry cloth slippers. I finally manage to back out, holding the towel around me. Mei follows me into the bedroom, me poking my head around the door to make sure it's Sam-free, and we both look in the mirror to survey the blotchy patches that cover my face like an infectious disease.

I crane my neck to the side and suck in my cheek. There's a patch that resembles Australia. "It's not that bad," I say. "A little sore, maybe. That's the point of exfoliation, right? To get rid of dead layers to get your skin softer?" I've never done more than a crushed-apricot-seed scrub, so this is out of my realm of experience.

I splash cold water on my face to relieve some of the burn and then dampen a towel to press against my cheek. There's no point getting angry at the aesthetician, who probably did the best she could, so I keep my mouth shut and try to look on the bright side. Mei watches me in the mirror. "Did she ask about your skin type? What medications you're on? If you had previous allergies?"

"What does that matter?" I move the towel to the other side.

"It's her job and she failed if she didn't check."

"Well, it's too late now. I'm sure she did her best." I don't want to get her in trouble. I grab a vial of hotel moisturizer and slather my face with the smell of vanilla and nutmeg. I read a study that said that men like women to smell like sweet foods but I don't think this is what they had in mind. I now smell like a bakery prepping for the holidays.

Perfect.

———

I decide to ignore Sam's spectator status in my latest disgrace and pray he'll do the same. There's no need for either of us to relive that moment of grooming chaos, and now that we've called a détente, it would be rude of him to try to lord it over me.

Mei puts the shopping visitors off for an hour as she works over my face with a solid inch of foundation.

"Whoa." I lean over and inspect the space where Australia used to be. Nothing. "You did a fantastic job."

Mei says nothing but packs away the brushes and paints with the grim satisfaction of a woman who has accomplished the impossible. Then she hands me the wig.

"Am I Fangli for this?"

"Yes."

I tuck my short hair in and let the wig fall down my back. Maybe I'll grow my hair out. I wonder if Sam prefers long hair or short.

Nope. No, I do not wonder that, not at all. It is a matter of utter indifference to me what Sam prefers.

Mei takes me back into the main room of the suite where rolling closets have been set up. I stop dead in the door as a man and a woman pop out. They're dressed identically but in opposites, his white shirt and black pants offsetting her black shirt and white pants. Both have long black hair in braids that frame appraising pursed lips and cheekbones that can be seen from the stratosphere. I'm almost certain they're multiracial and I stare without shame because it's such a thrill for me to see people who look a bit like me and who are around my age. If only I had known more people like me growing up. Or even now. Anjali once told me she could go home to her parent's village and be surrounded with people who looked like her, spoke her language, and knew her history for generations back.

Maybe it would be stifling. I'll never know because there will never be a place like that for me, a community of people who share my history and family.

But this isn't the time to dwell on the lived experiences of individuals creating a biracial identity in modern North America, because these clothes are my jam. If Fangli's closet is timeless luxury, these two are also high-end but with an edge. I can tell they run the sort of store that has three shirts hanging on a rod and a DJ. I'm intimidated by their coolness even as I'm panting to see what they have. "Local designers," says Mei. "Trace and Hendon from House of Swing."

I can handle this as long as they don't ask too many questions. We shake hands and then the woman, Trace, jumps in by asking about my design philosophy.

"My design philosophy," I echo.

"Right," she encourages me. "What do you want to accomplish?"

Besides not being naked? I struggle for an answer before I remember one of the artist's statements in Fangli's art summary. "I value the ability of line to arouse the emotive state," I plagiarize.

They contemplate this before Hendon smiles. "Good. Now tell us..."

Before I'm forced to elaborate on whatever the hell I said, Sam comes into the room. I really need to get that key from him, number one, and why is he here, number two?

"When Fangli told me you were coming, I wanted to stop by," he says. "I admire your work." Both Trace and Hendon straighten up and smooth their hair. Sam has that effect on people when he tries, and for some reason, he's trying now. Or is he genuinely interested in fashion design? I think he might be, because in less than a minute, he has them talking about their own philosophy and pulling out clothes that illustrate different factors.

I'm left to my own devices, which is good because I can browse through the racks as they talk. I pull out an elegant dress, a black-and-white sheath that drops straight down from the shoulders, and rub the material between my fingers. It feels like a thick satin but without the shine.

I look over my shoulder to see Sam watching me. He turns from the conversation to pick out a hanger. "Try this," he tells me. He's wearing a short-sleeved shirt and his biceps flex as he hands me the mass of black fabric. Both Trace's and Hendon's eyes are glued to his arm. I tear my gaze away.

"I like this dress," I say.

"You can try on both." Then he directs that smile at me. "This will suit you."

It's an easy request and I really have no reason to not try on the... whatever it is he's holding out...but I balk. I don't want him dressing me and thinking he knows what suits me better than I do myself. But Trace and Hendon nod in approval and I bend. I don't want to embarrass anyone. Plus, Fangli would probably try on the damn thing.

I take them both and a few other items that catch my attention and bring them into the bedroom. The first thing that goes on is the sheath dress I chose. I frown. Although it looked good on the hanger, once on, it hangs and weighs me down, forcing me to wriggle under the heavy material pulling against my shoulders.

Fine, it's a no-go. I pull on high-waisted wide black pants with little buttons on the hips and a black shirt and then, joy of joys, slip into a pair of closed-toe flat slides. So comfortable. No heels. I bite my lip as I wonder whether I'm supposed to go out so they can see. I guess I should? Would Fangli normally? Mei isn't around to ask; she disappeared when Sam arrived.

I'll go out as if I want to match another shirt to the pants. Then they can see me and comment but it's not like I'm seeking suggestions. Fangli wouldn't need advice. She probably legit has a design philosophy.

All three make an identical approving expression when I come out but Sam is the one I focus on. He tilts his head to the side, then reaches out for a pale-pink shirt. I try to not make a face because I never wear pastels. He gives it a shake and I take it back into the room.

Damn Sam, I think when I pull it on. The shirt is perfect. Once on, the color becomes more of a mood. I feel...pretty? Yes. It's a very pretty look. I look at the mirror appraisingly. I've never been pretty. Cute was about as high as I ever rose in the looks hierarchy, which, according to me, goes:

Gorgeous/Stunning

Beautiful

Pretty, and on the other side of the spectrum, Handsome

Striking

Attractive

Cute

[Then, way down]

Unique

Yet this pink is magical. I come out with a little bit of swagger, and Trace and Hendon both say "Yes" in unison. Sam doesn't say anything but the look in his eyes reminds me of that first day when he walked across the room, looking at me like I was the most important woman in the world, the only person who mattered to him. Right now, his attention is focused on me and only me, but unlike last time, it doesn't seem like a challenge.

It's overwhelming. I go back to the room and untangle the black thing Sam gave me, which turns out to be a jumpsuit that's tight around the ankles with a collared top and an open back. No way to wear a bra. Huh. I give a bit of a jump and decide I'll have to find those plastic disks you glue to your boobs to keep them in place.

Since I don't have them now, I'll have to own it. I walk out and the designers both come over to start fussing over the fit. Sam crosses his arms but he looks in my eyes, not at the neckline or the free-flying girls. It's as if he sees me, Gracie, and I wonder if it's truly me and not Fangli, or something between them that could never be.

It puts me off-balance and I drop my eyes first.

Fourteen

I take the pants, the shirts, and the jumpsuit but say no to the dress. Sam lingers until the room is empty, and I try to forget he saw me two hours ago madly searching for my towel with half my face ripped off. When I was mostly naked.

"Art show tonight," he says. "Fangli thinks you're ready."

"Fangli's hardly even seen me as her." I take off the wig to air out my brain for a few minutes. "Where is it?"

"Don't you know?" He adjusts his sleeves.

I shrug. I haven't been keeping track of what events are coming since Mei has been teaching me pretty much on the fly.

"The Museum of Contemporary Art."

"Am I buying some art?"

"No. You're interested in supporting local artists and you're there to admire. It's a private showing of a private collection."

"Will there be media?"

"Possibly. There's not much point in having expensive things and important people admire them if no one knows." He yawns. "I can deal with that."

"I can do it."

He looks like he's going to argue but instead checks his watch. "We leave in an hour."

Then he's gone before I can ask him for his key.

An hour. First I call the nursing home and they reassure me that Mom's fine. Then I check my list, which is getting stressful and daunting again. What if I try sorting the tasks out by the time they will take? I spend a happy twenty minutes sorting and resorting the tasks from least to most time needed before deciding the value of the task was more important. Once they're listed, I realize I'd spent the whole time working on the list instead of doing any tasks. It could be because one of those tasks, *call the lawyer*, makes me so uncomfortable I have trouble seeing the words. My eyes skitter over them.

Not a good start to creating my own productivity method. I add "find a way to deal with disagreeable tasks" on the list.

At least I've left myself enough time to get ready. I stick the plastic disks Mei found to my boobs, impressed at their enhanced perkiness. I should wear these all the time. She left me with instructions about freshening my face, and I dab and shade and line like a soldier applying camouflage paint before battle. The jumpsuit, which Trace and Hendon tailored with expert fingers before they left, slides over my skin like space-age armor, and I begrudge Sam slightly for having such good taste. I adjust the wig.

When I look in the mirror, this time I'm Fangli. Or Fangli in cute but comfortable shoes.

Mei ordered me to wait until Fangli arrives home so there aren't conflicting reports of her being seen twice. I come out when I hear our adjoining door open and nearly exclaim out loud. If she looked beaten down that first day I saw her in the SUV, today she's so drained she's transparent.

"What's wrong?" I ask.

She rubs her forehead. "A bit tired."

This isn't regular physical fatigue. I normally have the emotional sense of a squirrel but Fangli's entire being radiates a feeling I'm very familiar with. She's so tense she can barely move and so lethargic she doesn't want to. I think she's depressed. Not sad. *Depressed*, with all the loaded meaning the term brings.

"Fangli?" My voice is tentative.

She raises her head and tries to smile before her eyes widen. "Incredible. It's like looking at my reflection when you have on makeup. Where did you get that jumpsuit? I want one."

"Thanks."

"You need better jewelry than those little gold hoops, though. Red for some color." She calls to Mei, who appears in a few minutes and puts a pair of earrings and a bracelet into my hand.

"Please tell me these are fake." The heavy cool weight of the bracelet slithers over my fingers when I pick it up.

Fangli shrugs. "It's all insured. Put them on."

The earrings are chandeliers that are surprisingly light for the number of gems in them, and the tennis bracelet of alternating rubies and diamonds soon warms on my wrist.

"Lovely," Fangli approves. "Now you look finished."

She stands up and we look at ourselves in the mirror. "How is it possible we look so alike?" I ask. "Do you have a photo of your parents?" Obviously Brad Reed of Brampton, Ontario, won't look like Fangli's father, but maybe our mothers are long-lost twins.

"Only my father." We both pull out our phones, and when Sam comes in, we're comparing and contrasting nose and eye shape.

Sam shakes his head. "If you weren't only half, I'd think you were a real Chinese."

My breath catches but before I can think of what to say, he turns to Fangli and speaks to her in Mandarin. His casual dismissal makes me... I don't know. I'm sure German, which came up with schadenfreude and kummerspeck, has a word for the unnamable mix of emotions I have, but even as an adult, I don't have the language. Why did it bother me less when Anjali said almost the same thing?

"Ready?" Sam turns to me and I decide it's not worth the fight. What would I say? Tell him half is good enough to be real?

We're both quiet as we descend. I'm not sure what Sam's thinking but despite my choice to not mention what he said, the words keep turning over in my mind. A past therapist had once gently invited me to sit with the idea that I had internalized having less of a claim to call myself white or Chinese because I never felt I belonged to either group. I had ignored that because it's not like I was going around feeling bad when no one gave me one of their Team White or Team Chinese T-shirts. But Sam's comment has stirred up some apparently unresolved feelings.

I push those thoughts back down into the dark hole where they usually lurk. This won't be the last time I hear something like this, and it wasn't the first, but I don't have the capacity to work through it, not when I'm about to go out in public impersonating an international celebrity. I firmly invite myself to sit with the idea that it's time to concentrate on the job at hand.

This time when we go through the lobby, I channel my full Fangli attitude as I sweep through. It's much easier when I don't have to worry about tottering on pencil-thin heels and my boobs look aerodynamic.

The car is waiting and I'm a little horrified at how easily I've adapted to a life of deluxe perks. *Thou art but an impersonator,* I chant to myself. *Two months and you're back to the subway at rush hour, unseen and unknown.*

Sam doesn't comment on my performance, and I go under the assumption that no news is good news. Instead, he starts running through tips on how to handle the upcoming event. I would listen but his collar is slightly open at the neck and I'm distracted by wondering what he looks like with no shirt on. I bet there are images online but I definitely can't check that on my phone here in front of him. Honestly, I wouldn't even if he weren't here. A few weeks ago, I'd have no hesitation about searching shirtless pictures of him, but now it's squicky to even think of looking for them, as if I'd be violating his privacy—even if he'd posed for them.

I'd tucked Mei's art dossier into my purse before I left, and I pull it out to give me something to think about besides Sam's chest. Fangli's favorite theme is rejuvenation and she built her collection around that, although it's bizarre to me that a person my own age has an art collection, let alone a thematic one. I flip through the printouts again, frowning at a photograph of an upside-down face with the lips spread far apart in a pained scream, and try to see how it's at all invigorating.

Sam sees my struggle and points to the artist's statement. I read it twice but it might as well be written in Swedish for all that I understand it. "I'm not going to talk about the art," I say. "I'll furrow my brow and nod as I pace in front of it."

"What if you're asked what you think?"

I role-played this with Mei, so I feel confident. "That I'm fascinated and then ask them what they think."

He pinches the bridge of his nose. "Really?"

"Well, what would you say?"

"I'd pick an element and comment on it before asking them their opinion."

I wave the pain-face picture at him and he plucks it out of my hand. "The placement calls to mind Yong Chen's work on loneliness and juxtaposes the idea of isolation with that of rejuvenation. Is it an individual or communal activity?"

I try to release my clenched fists. "Because I am familiar with the works of Yong Chen."

"Or you could say what you honestly think when you see it. How does it make you feel? What does it evoke?"

Before I answer, he's barreling on to his next point, waving at the dossier. "Once art is out of the artist's hands, it's up to the viewer to determine meaning."

"I disagree."

"You do?" He raises those fine slanted eyebrows.

"Isolationism is passé." I give a theatrical sniff and toss my wealth of fake hair. "You need to consider the context of the work and intent. Art isn't created in a vacuum."

"Yet interpretation is mediated by the experiences and values of the viewer."

I'm getting into this. "Which are in turn affected by knowledge of the artist's intention. Is 'viewer' even the correct word? Viewing implies distance and lack of engagement. Art should move us from viewing to active participation."

"All art?" He leans forward, elbows on his knees. The pose drops his shirt down to reveal the shadowed muscles of his chest.

"Why do you act?" Looking down, I see his chest. Looking up, that face. There is no safe zone.

"I need to tell stories." No hesitation when he answers. "Ones only I can give life to."

"Do you want someone to watch and forget? Or to be changed?"

"The latter, obviously."

I stare at him and he grimaces.

"That might be stretching it. Amused, at a minimum."

"There you go."

"You win." He sits back up.

"We weren't fighting."

"No," he says with surprise. "That won't last." He looks at his very pretty watch. "Almost time."

Dread builds. Dinner the other night was fine since all I had to do was eat. This is going to be me on display, with people who are comfortable approaching me and expecting articulate conversation.

This is why I'm getting the semi-big bucks. Fangli is confident I can do it, and despite his multitude of personality flaws, Sam will have my back if it will help Fangli.

He's getting into quiz mode. "What's your latest art purchase?" he asks.

"A Murat Tekin painting," I say. Triumphant, I scramble through my notes. "Damn. That's the last I sold. Look at that price tag. Is this what art people talk about?"

"Depends on the crowd." He sighs. "Why she can't be interested in more traditional art, I don't know."

"What do you collect?" I ask. "Ming porcelains?"

"Ru ware from the Northern Song dynasty." He glances at me out of the corner of those dark eyes. "My collection is currently touring. It's in Berlin right now."

"Oh." I keep forgetting he comes from money as well as being famous. "That's neat."

He doesn't grace this with a response, and I page through more screaming faces and outstretched hands as my anxiety ratchets up. At least I look right for the occasion and Sam's single nod was a definite step up from his previous expressions when he saw me. The jumpsuit flows around my hips like water. It's simple and perfect and the wig, with its heavy weight of hair, feels natural for the first time. I've even toned down my concerns about losing Fangli's jewelry by about seventy percent.

The car takes us to the west end of town and turns down a residential street that transforms into an industrial zone. I peer out the window. "I know where we are."

"You should. Don't you live nearby?"

"I don't go to a lot of modern art museums."

"It's contemporary art," he corrects me.

I look at the dossier. "Aren't they the same?"

Sam sighs. "Contemporary art is evolving and started around sixty years ago. It's differentiated from modern art in that it's more conceptually rather than aesthetically based."

"Oh. Thus the screaming faces?"

"Thus the screaming faces." He rubs his eyes. "I'm not sure this is a good idea."

"I can do it." I'm confident now in the face of his doubt.

We turn a corner near a warehouse and then another before the car pulls up in front of a multistory building in the middle of what looks like an abandoned field. With a shock, I realize where I am. It's right by the path where I go running. I must have passed this place a dozen times and only ever noticed the microbrewery next to it. This lack of awareness of my own surroundings saps my confidence and I grab Sam's arm.

"You're right. Let's leave."

He puts his hand on mine, I think to comfort me, but instead he shakes me off. "Too late."

The door opens and we're confronted by two strangers. Mei prepped me so I know they aren't Fangli's acquaintances, and I also know at this moment there is no way on earth I'm going to survive tonight.

"Showtime," Sam says over his shoulder and gets out of the car.

I need out of here, now.

Fifteen

The two people from the art gallery introduce themselves, and I don't even catch the names because I'm focused on my new plan. I stroke my throat as I mouth "laryngitis." Sam turns wide eyes on me and I give him my softest and most beseeching Fangli smile, the one she uses when she's apologizing. His return—and much more aggressive—smile says he'll cover for me but we're going to have one hell of a talk in private.

Sam has a gruesomely expressive face.

Our greeters burst out in polite worry, and Sam steps manfully into the breach. "Fangli refused to stay away," he says. "She's thrilled to see the exhibit, but of course you'll have to forgive her for not speaking. She needs to recover her voice for the show tomorrow."

The man darts away and I wonder if he's off to spread the word. There's a photographer on hand and Sam and I pose for some shots before going inside. Mei had given me instructions on Fangli's favored pose, and I point my chin down and to the side with a slight tilt to my lips. The shutter clicks rapid-fire beside us, but unlike the scene with Mikey at the coffee shop, I don't feel under attack. I might not be in control of the situation or have much of a clue what's going on, but being dressed for the part and with someone who knows what he's doing gives me a thin feeling of power.

Sam touches my bare arm to tell me we can stop and leans down to whisper in my ear. "Not bad."

"High praise." Even whispered, nerves give me a snippy tone that he ignores. The photographer was only one of tonight's hurdles.

That familiar hush-and-buzz comes over the room when we enter, and I give my superstar Fangli smile as people come up. The first few minutes pass by in a blur as I refuse a glass of wine with great regret and nod my way through many introductions while immediately forgetting names and faces. I'm almost blinded by the beading on dresses, or more accurately gowns. These people are dressed fancier on a Tuesday night than I've seen at weddings, and one woman is channeling the excesses of the 1980s with sequined shoulder pads big enough for a linebacker and a suffocating dose of Dior's Poison. I can't tell if it's her usual style or an artistic statement.

My jumpsuit seems almost too sedate. Then I see a woman cast a covetous glance at my earrings and feel better. Fangli thought I looked good and Sam considers me acceptable, which means I'm batting a thousand.

Sam hovers beside me to handle conversations, which at first are softballs about how we like the city and the unseasonable chill of the summer night. It's nice to know that even with a well-heeled art crowd, the weather remains a go-to Canadian conversation starter.

As we work through the throng, I notice the many shiny jewels decorating ears, fingers, and throats. With a start, I remember that Fangli once paid a half-million dollars for a canvas of hands in various poses. I am in a room of people who consider it reasonable to buy a photograph that costs the same as a house.

They're only people, I try to remind myself as I'm introduced to a woman with puffy lips and tight skin. She wears only a single jewel, a large pendant that I'm a thousand percent sure is not cubic zirconia. It's only money. Money doesn't make you better or more worthy of respect.

But the attitude is different in the room. Since my convenient laryngitis means I can't talk, I listen in on the conversations. Every single person there has an expectation that they'll be heard. They all take up space. I watch a man adjust his lapels before he moves across the room and how the servers melt out of his way without a word.

This is why Sam's not sure about me. I look like Fangli but I haven't learned how to command a room like she does. Because of her fame, Fangli—even without the diamonds—is the cynosure of most occasions. Mom told me being the center of attention was to be avoided. Now it's my job to make attention my bitch.

Mei didn't address that in particular, but Sam the Master is here to learn from.

Keeping my face friendly but aloof, I watch him and have a tiny epiphany. It's not what he or the rest of the crowd are saying. It's how they act. I'm at the zoo watching the animals jostle for dominance and Sam is at the apex. He decides who to speak to. He never approaches; they come to him.

But they look at me as if waiting for me to move first. When we do get closer, they get a little too in my space. Is it because they sense a lack of strength in me? Would they do the same to the real Fangli?

I can't afford self-doubt right now. Luckily, escape comes in the form of the gentle nudge from Sam that I know is my cue to start actively appreciating art. To my pleasure, what I see is far more accessible than Fangli's collection, and I move to a mannequin surrounded by barbed wire decorated with twinkling shards of mirror. The artist has written "mine" in tiny letters on every centimeter of the mannequin's skin in a hundred different languages. A bloodred poppy rises from her head. I know this isn't Fangli's style—she doesn't do installations—but I walk around so I can see it at all angles and read the statement.

Around me, the collectors are making utterly impenetrable comments. It's like listening to a code designed to weed out the culturally ignorant. Which is me, but only Sam and I know that.

As I lean in to see better, a man across the room squints at me. I do my best to control my breathing but Sam turns swiftly. "What?" he murmurs, eyes trained on my face.

"Nothing." I channel a sloth, moving unhurriedly to avoid the attention of the potential predator. It's hard because almost the entire room has one eye on us as if monitoring our location at all times. The stress of trying to emulate Fangli's poise is in part drowned by a more acute worry: Ex-manager Todd is in the room across from me.

I shouldn't be surprised; I've heard him brag about his father's art collection. He's with a blond woman who wears a smile that never wavers and I wonder if she knows, or cares, what kind of a man he is. I bend in to Sam and he curves down over me like a hero from his period dramas. "How long do we need to stay?" I whisper.

"At least another hour."

"Can we go to a new room? Is this the only one?"

In response, he puts his hand on the bare skin of my back and guides me through a door I hadn't noticed into another exhibit. I'm so disturbed I barely even clock the warm comfort his touch gives me. We might not be friends, but in this moment, he's the one in my corner. To my relief, the new room is a video installation with the light dimmed until it's almost difficult to see. The cave-like ambiance deepens when I stand next to the wall and Sam comes close as if guarding me.

"Gracie," he murmurs. "Tell me what's happening."

He used my name, my real name. When I don't answer, he draws me in and tilts my chin up to analyze my face. "Do you need to leave? We can."

I shake my head and he frowns. "You're sure?"

Simply knowing he's there is enough to calm me since I don't think Todd will try to approach me with another man there.

The truth comes crashing down on me. I'm not Gracie. I'm Wei Fangli right now and Todd has no power over me. He can't touch me. He can't fire me and he can't intimidate me without having Sam or the organizers taking action. I'm protected because I'm now a famous person of value. I'm *seen* here.

I toss my head and Sam shifts away as if giving me space. "I'm good," I say.

He looks at me for a long moment, then nods. "I trust you to tell me if you need out."

Sam follows as I examine the videos, all featuring Anpanman, the Japanese superhero. The artist has put the character, who has a pastry for a head, in food-based situations such as cooking shows and grocery stores. His usually cheerful face looks by turns worried and menacing.

Fascinated, I thumb the controller to bring up the next video.

"You like these?" Sam asks.

I keep facing the screen so no one can see me speaking, thus negating my laryngitis story. "My dad went on a work trip to Japan once and brought me an Anpanman figure that I loved. I never saw the show. I guess they're not like this?" The video we're watching shows Anpanman tearing off part of his head to give to a hungry cat before being viciously attacked by a flock of seagulls at an outdoor food court.

Sam leans in beside me to watch the video. "Much less violent but Anpanman does give parts of his head away to people in need. Then Uncle Jam bakes him a new one."

"Is it selfless if you can get a new head when you need one?"

Sam shrugs, his arm brushing against mine. "I know people who could have ten heads right beside them ready to go and not give a crumb."

So do I, at that. The video ends and we both turn at the same time. His face is so close to mine that if I moved half a step... His eyes dip from my eyes to my lips and a shivery wave rolls through me.

I could move that step. Prickles run down the backs of my thighs from the tension. Sam might move. Might he? Does he come a bit closer? My feet are nailed to the ground but inside I'm whirling like a tornado.

"Mr. Yao?"

Sam stands abruptly when he hears his name and I blink, hard, and turn back to Anpanman with unseeing eyes. This night is giving me the mental equivalent of whiplash as it yanks me between emotional extremes. Impersonating Fangli. Todd. Sam, so close to me.

After Sam's conversation finishes, we leave the room by mutual silent agreement, weaving in and out of the crowd and only pausing for Sam to engage with people every few feet. News of my voicelessness must have spread because I'm spared any chatting besides hopes that I get better soon.

Despite my newfound confidence, I don't want to meet with Todd, so I do my best to steer Sam away. It's nerve-racking to know he's there, and my core tightens so hard I shake. Sam's hand returns to my waist, fortifying me, and the muscles relax enough to let me stop clenching my teeth.

Exactly an hour later, Sam tells the organizer goodbye and we pose for a few more photos which I think I handle like a pro. We're almost out the door when a call comes from a small group near the tiny gift store. It takes me a moment to react since I forgot Wei Fangli is my name tonight.

I turn with my most effervescent smile. They push forward a young woman with long black hair tied in a neat, high ponytail as their spokesperson, and suddenly I know I'm not at all ready for the fresh hell that's about to open below me.

Dear God, she talks to me in Mandarin. The dark pit to the underworld expands exponentially and flames lick the edges.

"An autograph?" Sam jumps in with English.

The flames burst over the edge. Double dear God. I have no idea what Fangli's writing looks like and there is zero, and I mean *zero*, chance I'll be able to manage faking the Chinese characters. Time stops as the young woman holds out a notepad with hopeful eyes.

I automatically take it and then look around for a place to put it down and forge Fangli's signature. Why didn't I fake a broken wrist? Sprained finger? Sam talks to me in Chinese, which, since it is not about being hungry or how to get to the store, I'm at a loss to interpret. My bright smile hurts my cheeks as I trail Sam to a high cocktail table.

He puts the notepad down and then steps behind me, hiding me from view. "Pretend you're writing," he murmurs.

My hand trembles as I do as he says, but now it's not because I'm about to get my cover blown but because he's pressing against me, his hard body against mine. I know it's to hide us from the girls watching but my knees are weak. I curse and hope he doesn't notice because I'll never live it down.

He pretends to hand me the pen but, at the last minute, dips his hand down to quickly scrawl what I assume is Fangli's name. Then he gives me the pen. It takes him milliseconds.

I pick up both and return them to the swooning fan. She bows to me and I automatically bow back before giving the wave—with the right hand because I practiced that—and leave.

Then, once we're in the car, to my shame, I burst into tears.

With an excess of empathy I didn't expect, Sam hands me a tissue and waits until the sobs subside. "You did well," he says.

"Sorry." I snuffle into the tissues and more appear when I reach out my hand. I bury my face.

"Was it that man?"

My head shoots up. "What?"

Sam glances out the window as the shifting streetlights take turns hiding and highlighting his face. "A man with a blue suit escorting a blond woman. He was watching you and you were concentrating on trying to avoid him instead."

"Do you think he noticed?" I'm a bit nonplussed that he read the situation so well.

"No, you were unexpectedly subtle."

Good, because that would be bad. I fight back another wave of sickness. Todd fired me because of the misidentified photo of Fangli. He knows we look alike. What if he says something?

He's got power over me again. I debate telling Sam but decide against it. I'll wait and see.

He twists in the seat and gives me a straight look. "Who is he?"

"My old manager."

"You don't like him."

"Would you like the person who fired you?"

"It's more than that. I could tell." He raises his eyebrows. "I can read you."

This is too true to debate. "He's a jerk and I don't like him."

"Ah." Sam regards me. "Did he recognize you?"

"No. I didn't want to give him the chance to see me up close or speak to me, though."

"Wise."

I dab at my eyes with the tissue. "The art was nice."

Sam exhales. "I think you might be the only person to describe contemporary art as nice."

"Thought-provoking? Evocative? Bleeding-edge?"

"Is that better than cutting-edge?"

"One step beyond." I hum a line from the Madness song and his lips twitch again. That's a definite victory. "Do you ever get used to it?" The pillowy darkness of the car's interior makes it easier to ask. "That attention?"

"I've never not known it." Sam's voice wraps around me. "You know who my parents are."

Sam's august parentage, a movie-star mother and director father, is mentioned in almost every profile. He takes my silence as a yes and continues. "My parents are many wonderful things but they both also crave attention. I've had cameras around my whole life."

I try to imagine that. All the missteps I took documented and commented on, all the terrible hair days and disastrous fashion choices logged for posterity and resurfaced on listicles every few years. "I don't know how you cope."

"I don't know another way to live." He doesn't say it with bitterness but as a fact of life.

"What if you want to be alone?"

"I stay in the house. It's the only place I can be myself."

"Oh." Lonely.

"You're improving." He changes the subject. I parse his tone for an insult, and even though I come up short, I'm suspicious of this seeming goodwill.

I clear my throat. "Thank you. For asking if I wanted to leave earlier."

He loosens his collar. "Seemed like a safer option to get you out of the situation rather than watch you blow it for Fangli."

My insides shrivel. Of course it was because of Fangli. He wasn't watching out for *me*, he was making sure I didn't screw it up for *her*. I hold my expression under control, unwilling to give him the slightest hint that I might have thought otherwise, and keep my tone light.

"Since you thought I was terrible, it doesn't seem like the bar was very high."

"Fangli's been better since you've been here," he says. "She's calmer now that she doesn't have to worry about going out."

"About Fangli." I pause and decide to take the plunge. "She's not okay."

"What do you mean?"

"I don't know her very well." I think about this and amend it. "I don't know her at all but I think she's depressed."

He stiffens. "What would you know about it?"

I push on because if it's true, Fangli needs more help than hiring a body double. "I remember feeling the same way when I was diagnosed. Her expression, it's the same I saw in the mirror."

Sam leans forward to take one of the bottled waters from the holder and cracks it open with a vicious twist. "I've worked with North Americans for a long time, but I continue to marvel at your openness in speaking of such things."

"Not everyone can or does." The world would be a better place if we did.

"It's more than would happen at home." He drinks half the water. "This is not your concern."

"I think that—"

"No. Fangli is tired, that's all." He shuts me down and we ride in silence until the hotel.

Before we get out, I make one last attempt. "You don't think that, Sam. She needs help."

He doesn't say anything, and I fix the smile on my face for the strangers in the lobby before I get out of the car.

Sixteen

S am comes into my suite for a debrief but I ignore him as I take off the new shoes and wiggle my toes with pleasure against the cool wooden floor. Even though they were flat, they pinched. That jumpsuit was a definite winner; I might buy it off Fangli to keep for my own when the two months are done since Mei warned me I wouldn't be able to wear it again while I was here. Fangli doesn't wear the same outfit twice for events.

"You need to practice Fangli's autograph," Sam says when he comes back to the table with water. "That could have been bad, and I don't know how Mei let it slip through the cracks. She's usually so organized and perceptive about what needs to be done."

I have to agree, even though it bugs me to admit he's right. "Do you have a copy of it?"

"Here." He scribbles three characters on a sheet, the strong lines swooping over each other. "Wei, there's her family name. Then Fang, for fragrant, and Li for jasmine."

I took Mandarin in university, and back then my painstaking strokes were like a toddler with a crayon compared to this confident scrawl. No wonder I got a D grade. He rolls up his sleeves (*ding, ding,* add that to the hot man list), then shakes the pen at me. I hitch a chair up to the table and admire his forearms. His wrists are broad and I realize I have never noticed a man's wrists in my life, let alone known

I had a preference for broad ones with very slightly visible veins.

As expected, my first attempts are terrible because I have awful handwriting in any language and even my own name looks like a wiggly line decorated with a dot that hovers between the *c* and the *e* but rarely right over the *i*. Sam looks up from his phone to see my progress.

"That's not very good," he observes.

I hand him the pen. "Do it again," I say. "Slower."

This time, I watch as Sam dips the pen down and writes Fangli's name on the paper. He hands the pen to me and I chew on my lip as I analyze it. Tracing the characters into muscle memory might help, so I try to remember where Sam started the character.

"Here." He takes my hand and guides it to the beginning. His touch is warm but I shiver.

"I have it." I grab my hand back. When I trace the line, I'm ashamed to see it's shaky. I'm reading more into his casual touch than he means, and it makes me react badly.

"I can do this on my own," I say, standing up from the table and whacking my thighs against the edge. *Ow.* Back down I go.

"Clearly not. Sit down and keep trying."

This makes me stiffen and forget the stripe of pain across my legs. "You're not my boss, you know. I can handle this."

"What would you have done on your own? Fake a last-minute broken wrist like you did a sore throat?"

"That was a good solution to the problem." Or...I could have explained that I'm only speaking English while in Canada, like I was supposed to. The pressure made me forget what we had planned for this exact situation.

He shoves back from the table. "Wrong. You were hired to do a job and you didn't do it. Mei spent hours with you, hours she should have been spending doing her goddamn job, and you threw it away."

I never thought that Mei also had work to do full-time for Fangli. "Part of her job is to help me."

That's a jerk thing to say, and I know it the fucking *second* it comes out of my mouth. Embarrassed, I double down, stick my chin out, and go on the offensive. "None of you mentioned autographs. I was unprepared."

He looks at me in honest surprise. "Are you unable to think independently about what might come up and plan for it?"

"Hey, sorry I'm not rich and famous. People don't go around asking for my autograph. You should have told me."

"That people ask for autographs is only common sense."

"Not to me and apparently not to Mei." Digging myself in deeper.

"Don't blame Mei." Sam puts one hand on the table. "You're not even trying. This is more than pulling on a wig. You need to make an effort. Acting is work, and it doesn't matter if you're on the stage or attending that party."

Sam's about a meter from me and I can see the muscle in his jaw twitching. "I *am* trying," I grit out.

"This matters," he snaps. "I told Fangli this was a fucking terrible idea but she was sure you could do it."

I hear the unspoken words loud and clear. *Look at how wrong she was.*

"I can do it."

"Tonight was your chance and you faked losing your voice." He shakes his head in disbelief. "How did you think that was a reasonable solution?"

I look down at the table. "I lost my nerve, okay? I admit it."

He doesn't give me the sympathy I'm fishing for. Sam adjusts his jacket and I have to look up to see his face, which is stern. "There's no room for you to lose your nerve. Do better."

With that, he brushes past me and out the door. I lunge after him and throw all three locks so he can't get back in because I forgot to get the key off him *again*. Right now, though, that's the least of my worries.

I rip off the jumpsuit and throw it into the corner before I pick it up, smoothing out the wrinkles in the fabric with my hand. Sam's right and I hate him for it because it highlights how I failed. I took a risk and I screwed it up. That's all on me, even though I gutlessly tried to pin it on Mei. I was an idiot to think I could do this.

For Fangli and Sam and Mei, this is real and it has an impact. I like Fangli. I'm sorry for her. I'm deep in the throes of the Benjamin Franklin effect—I like her more because she asked me to do her a favor. Even if it was for money.

I throw myself on the bed and start peeling the miserable plastic disks off my chest. It's a bad day for my body hair because much like the face mask earlier, the boob supporters are doing an excellent job of epilating any skin they've been in contact with. After trudging to the bathroom and double cleansing my face, I look in the mirror. My face and chest are covered with red blotches and I sigh.

Ever since I had to put Mom into the home, I've made a pleat here and a crease there to origami my life to become small and manageable. Although I was never as bold as Anjali, who once quit her job and started her own business to see what it was like, I was brave enough to want to live instead of settling for existing. Before Mom got too sick, I sought out experiences. Not like I was going to bungee jump out of a plane or anything, but I took an art class and forced myself to be social. I went for dinner by myself because I wanted to. I joined Anjali on a last-minute trip to Cuba. No big deal for some people but enough for me to feel like I was reaching out of my middle-of-the-road comfort zone. Now I'm as vulnerable as a snail without a shell, an easy mark for the Todds of the world to come by and sprinkle salt on me like an unpleasant child happy to flex what little power they have.

I plod into the bathroom and slather on a variety of creams before I pull on pajamas and climb into bed, pulling the covers high as I give in to the stress of the night. Seeing Todd hit me harder than I thought it would, and now I have the additional worry of hoping he doesn't cop on to what I'm doing for Fangli. My mind automatically goes to the ZZTV interview and Mom getting hounded in the nursing home because of her imposter daughter. Fangli's reputation in tatters. The end of the world, really, because that's the final destination of every journey I take down Anxiety Road.

Sam's comments cut deep, too. I so stupidly thought we had a connection. Now I see how wrong I was, because to him, I'm first and foremost an employee who isn't performing up to expectations. I thought he chose me an outfit because he wanted to see me look good, but it was for Fangli. Escorting me close enough to touch through the art exhibit? Because that's what people expected to see. Taking my hand to guide the pen? Because he wanted me to learn the stupid signature. This is a job to him and I thought I was so fabulous that Sam Yao might be having feelings for me, like some fairy tale. I'd even forgotten that mystery girlfriend Mei alluded to and Sam has never mentioned.

I bury my face in the pillow and hum to try to drown out the remorseless shame that slices through my skin, leaving cold tingles in its wake. We've known each other less than a week; what do I even know about him? I'm a nobody and he hangs out with celebrities because—news flash—he's one of the hottest commodities on the globe. Of course I'm nothing but a temporary person in his life, nothing special. Nobody unique. The only saving grace in this fiasco is that all this only happened in my head. Sam has no idea I was wondering about kissing him at the art gallery, and he's never, ever going to find out. This is a job, a short-term contract, and I'm an utterly delusional fool for thinking the Sam I saw was the real man and not a character.

Plus I haven't seen Mom in days. She must be lonely. I put out my hand for my phone, thinking that maybe I can text Anjali to talk me down, but then I see the time. It's late and I don't want to bother her.

The tears come hot and ugly. I bury my face back into the pillow, my breath gasping as sobs rack my body, forcing me to curl up with my knees close. The heat of my breath combines with the tears to stick the white cotton to my face. It only lasts a few minutes, but by the time I peel the pillow off, hiccupping, I'm drained.

I turn over the pillow to the dry side and pull the covers over my head. Then I go to sleep, tears leaking out from the eyelids I've squeezed shut.

SUG TASK

GET IT TOGETHER, GRACIE

↙ ↓ ↘

SERIOUSNESS LEVEL	URGENCY LEVEL	GROWTH LEVEL
VERY IMPORTANT.	HIGH. DO ASAP, WITHIN DAYS IF NOT HOURS	YES, THE ISSUE WILL GET WORSE IF I DON'T DEAL WITH IT.

Seventeen

The next day, I wake early, right at dawn, and lie for a moment on the sheets debating whether to get up or go back to sleep. After the emotional eruption of the previous night, I'd thought my rest would be wrecked by nightmares but I slept better than I have in a long time. Out of habit, I check my phone. No texts from Sam, the same as always, because *he has never thought about me as anything other than a job.*

Right. Get up.

In the bathroom, I check my skin. As hoped, the blotches are gone. My eyes are lit with a subtle golden light, a nice side effect from the crying, as if I've flooded the impurities out of my eyeballs. I wash up, and after I remove the traces of tears from my cheeks, I'm refreshed in a way that I haven't felt in a while.

Back in the main suite, I make a coffee from the pod machine and pull out my laptop to transcribe and organize all the notes about my new task system. My breakdown last night was an eye-opener and I face the coming day with something approaching zest. Fuck Sam. He thinks I suck? I'll show him. He thinks I'm not trying? Screw him.

Fuck Todd, on principle.

I'm on a roll. *Fuck you, Sam, and you, Todd, and you, Mei, for making conversation hard even though I was an asshole to blame you for my shortcomings. Not you, Fangli. You're okay.*

I might be fueled by negative energy but I tap away with frantic fingers, not even going back to correct my typos because I don't want to break my train of thought. I lose myself in my own words as I write, each idea leading to another and connecting again. I'm so involved that I don't even notice Mei entering the room—since she comes from the adjoining suite, the multiple door locks don't block her—until she sits beside me at the table. Even then it takes me a few seconds to get out of my mind space.

She says nothing but puts her tablet down on the table in front of me. It shows a photo of me from last night, and although I'm initially relieved to see that I look exactly like Fangli because makeup is magic, I can tell from Mei's face the story isn't as positive as it could be. I skim the text.

Chinese megastar Wei Fangli was missing her megawatt smile last night at a private exhibit at the Museum of Contemporary Art. It might have been the sore throat that prevented her from speaking, but sources say there's trouble in paradise in her rumored longtime relationship with superstar Sam Yao. Both are in Toronto starring in Operation Oblivion, *a World War Two drama showing at the Royal Alexandra Theatre.*

"Who are the sources?" I ask. This is bad news because I thought Sam and I had been doing quite well, at least in public.

Mei says nothing, as usual.

Fangli comes in, her eyes wide. "What happened?" she demands. When she sits, her right leg jiggles up and down in a rapid staccato.

"It was my fault," I say. Fangli isn't herself.

"I thought you said you were getting along." Her leg moves faster, and Mei shifts her gaze to the floor.

"We are." I lower my voice to soothe her. Mei meets my eyes but I can't tell what she's thinking so I'm on my own. "Fangli, look at me."

She does with wide eyes that I don't like the look of.

"It was my fault," I repeat slowly. "I'm sorry. I'll do better."

This seems to get through because the leg shaking slows.

"It was an off night," I say. "I was nervous but I know what to expect now. It won't happen again."

As I say the words, I realize I mean them. Despite the dickish way he delivered the message, Sam was right. I've been a half person, just doing the minimum to get by because I haven't had the spirit to do more, not with Todd and my mom and life. I don't want that anymore. I told Fangli I'd do a job and I'm going to do it, but in my own way. I've been too passive, a balloon buffeted by the wind.

Fangli's face doesn't change, but her leg stops moving.

"I need to visit my mom this morning," I say in a firm voice. "I'll be back by noon and then I'm going to practice your autograph for twenty minutes. Fangli, are you here today?"

She looks at Mei, who looks at me.

I soldier on. "If you're free this afternoon, when I'm done, I'll come to you and you can show me the way you'd act if someone approaches you so I know what to do."

"Ms. Wei has several appointments before she has to go to the theater," says Mei.

"We can work around them." I wave my phone at her. "Send me a meeting invitation for any time after noon." If this is a job, I'm going to treat it as a job.

Fangli bends her head and takes a deep breath.

"I'll see you this afternoon," I say. "Unless you want to come visit my mom."

Her face brightens before Mei shakes her head. "Ms. Wei has several meetings this morning," she repeats. "It's not wise to risk photos of you two together."

"Next time, then," I say. "You're always welcome to come. I'll wear a pirate disguise so no one will see the resemblance."

This is a very bad joke but Fangli does me the favor of smiling before Mei ushers her out. I check the time and calculate that leaving in ten minutes will give me plenty of time to get to Mom's, stay for a couple of hours, and head back. In the bathroom, I keep my face bare and decide with my short hair and pale lips, no one will see me as Fangli. I discover my old clothes in the bottom of the chest of drawers and pull on a pair of baggy jeans with a loose tank. Accessorized with sunglasses, I look like me again.

Then I pick up my phone. I have Sam's number because Mei gave it to me for emergencies but I've never used it. I could text him to say...what? I stuff the phone into my purse and head for the door. Finding pathetic excuses to accidentally be in the same place or texting "just to see" is the same technique a teenager with a crush would use and I'm not going to do that. Sam made his stance clear.

I'll respect it. It's time to step up.

———

As I anticipate, no one in the Xanadu lobby looks twice at the messy and unstylish figure who passes through on her way to public transportation. I miss the attention, but only a bit.

The nurse nods at me when I arrive, judging me because it's been a few days since I've been by. I sign in and head down the hall. Mom's routine is structured, and I have the timetable up at home and saved as a photo in my phone. Ten in the morning means free time/social activities but Mom would rather gnaw off her own face than play cards, which is one of the only activities they have, so I peek in her room first. To my surprise, it's empty. I quickly check to make sure she has clean clothes and everything is tidy, then head over to the solarium.

When I reach the room, I stand between the open French doors and search for her. The solarium is busy enough, perhaps ten or twelve people all sitting alone with a newspaper in front of them or looking out the window. There's no music or conversation, and inside my chest, a little hole widens. I need that money from Fangli so I can slap it down on the table when Xin Guang calls. It could be any day now. I've been on that list forever.

I cross the room to Mom, grateful she doesn't need a wheelchair. I've seen some of the other residents, their arms too weak to roll themselves along, waiting for a nurse or volunteer to have a moment to take them where they want to go. Mom remains mobile and that's good news.

I want to bury my face in her shoulder the way I did as a child. Instead I reach out and give her a gentle hug. Her bones are light under my touch but her eyes crinkle when she smiles, the same as they always do, the deep lines radiating out to her temples.

"Hi, sweetie," she says. Then she shakes her head. "Did you cut your hair?"

"Do you like it?"

"Aiya. So short."

She settles me in a chair beside her, and I sit for a moment with her hand on my head. She's always had a very soft energy, and I close my eyes to let it wash away the wretched shame left over from last night. Mom energy, man. When it works, it works good.

I talk to her about the people I saw on the way over. Then I lie about work and tell her it's the same-old, same-old, elaborating a bit on some fake work drama. She bobs her head as she listens to me, but when I ask her questions, she only smiles and strokes her hand down my arm. I chatter on for a few more minutes before I lapse into silence. The other people in the room are so quiet it's like being in a gallery surrounded by sculptures. When a volunteer comes in to ask if anyone wants tea, her voice echoes off the walls.

After fetching some tea for Mom and coffee for myself, I grab a newspaper and start reading out loud. I go slowly but don't pay attention to the words because I'm thinking about building out my planner again. I need to check over what I wrote this morning but I know the idea's there. I know I have it. A warm flush steals over me, a deep satisfaction I haven't felt in a long time.

The two hours pass slowly and I fetch more coffee, more tea, and some cookies. Mom leaves the tea to form a scum on the top as she focuses on the nothing happening outside. Around us, the other residents flow into the room and take positions. That each has their own preferred chair is clear and I wonder what happens when an oblivious resident takes the wrong seat. Probably a cage match.

I get Mom to lunch, then head back to the Xanadu after giving her a kiss. Seeing her has calmed me and put this entire situation in perspective. I know what I need to do and I'm now ready to do it right.

No one is in my suite when I arrive but Fangli's voice comes from next door. Mei sent me a calendar invite for an hour from now so I don't waste time. I have to rummage around to find the paper Sam left me last night, and I spend exactly twenty minutes repeating the signature until I can mimic the smooth strokes without looking. I tuck the paper away with pride. A small achievement but done. A check off my list. Dopamine achieved.

I have forty minutes left so I pull out my laptop to make more sense of my notes. I'm in the middle of sketching out a visual for how my task list could look when a knock comes on the interconnecting door between the suites. Must be Fangli, ready a few minutes early. I leave my laptop up and go to open the door.

Sam stands there, hands placed elegantly in pockets, excellent wrists revealed.

I strive for a neutral expression as I step back and gesture for him to come in. Professional. Polite and distant in the way new colleagues should be. "I thought you were busy today." We don't have an event for a couple of days. Mei sent me a slew of calendar invites while I was with Mom that I read over so I knew what was coming before accepting *rat-a-tat*.

"I finished early and I don't need to be at the theater until later." He runs his hand through his wavy black hair and it falls back into his eyes exactly as it was, covering the thick, straight brows. "Fangli is upset because of our fight last night."

He's here because of Fangli. I try not to resent it. "I told her it was fine."

"Good." He hesitates and then glances over his shoulder. I peek over and see Mei standing alone in the middle of Fangli's suite, watching us.

Sam closes the door and spies my laptop, which I shut down. "What are you working on?"

"Notes on what I'm doing here so I can sell them to the highest bidder when I leave."

He stares at me with wide eyes and I rub the back of my neck.

"Give me a break," I say. "It's a personal project that has nothing to do with you, because you know what? I've had nothing to do with you for most of my life."

There's a brief silence and Sam rocks forward, hands in his pockets. "We might have gotten off on the wrong foot," he says.

"We?" This is an impressively broad statement. "Might?"

He sits down. "I was in the wrong."

"What?" I sit down as well and push my laptop to the side. The usual sharpness is missing from Sam's voice and I think I'm talking to the real man, a creature as elusive as a cryptid.

He's not looking at me but somewhere over my shoulder. "I was angry in the car last night and I took it out on you."

"You were right," I say. I end up looking over his shoulder as well, out toward the lake. "I wasn't taking this seriously, but I will."

"You're not doing badly," he says. "Don't get me wrong, the fake sore throat was an appalling idea, but generally you're trying." Now our eyes meet and his skim away. "It's what you said in the car. About Fangli."

I want to interrupt but it would only be to hear my own voice. Instead I stay quiet because Sam is struggling and I don't want to silence him.

"You're right. Fangli is sick." A light flush goes up from his throat. "Not physically. In her mind."

"What is it?"

"She gets panic attacks. Bad ones, where she can't tell what's real and what's not. She started getting them when we were students." He pauses. "It can make her too anxious to work and she won't talk about it much. Her manager told her to keep it quiet, said no one wants to think that Wei Fangli is crazy. She doesn't either. It frightens her."

The bitterness in his voice confirms the truth. "What has she been doing?"

"Acupuncture. Diet." He sighs. "I talked her into working the show in Canada because I thought a new environment might help ease her into talking to someone and getting help. She can't do that back home. She feels too much shame."

"It's getting worse?"

He drops his hands down between his legs and lowers his head. "She's struggling. She's desperate to hide it from everyone and I'm the only person she can talk to. I'm so used to protecting her secret that to hear you say it made me overreact."

"She needs to talk to a therapist, a doctor. There are medications that help." I hesitate. "I'm on them."

His eyes flash back to me. "What?"

"I have panic, too. Depression. I started taking meds two years ago." It's hard to talk about. I know it happens and I know it's not uncommon, I really do, but part of me still thinks being on medication seems weak, like I can't deal. I know it's wrong, but in my head, it's a willpower issue, not a brain chemical issue.

His grin is wry. "Sounds like you're similar in more ways than appearance."

"How can I help her?"

"I wasn't lying last night when I said you being here was helping her. She's managing better."

I make a decision. I hold out my hand, palm raised. "Let's start over. Instead of you thinking I'm a hopeless failure and me thinking you're an arrogant two-dimensional douchebag, let's be Gracie and Sam, doing a job together."

"I never said you were that," he protests. Then he pauses. "Hold on. That's how you see me?"

I stare pointedly at my hand in answer.

"I'm sorry." He takes my hand briefly and lets it go. "I took my anger out on you because I couldn't stop this plan of Fangli's from happening. It was a dick move, as I think you would call it."

"I would," I agree with equanimity.

"Right, okay. Glad we got that sorted."

"Hi, Sam," I say. "Nice to meet you."

This time, he's the one who reaches out his hand. "Gracie. I look forward to our partnership."

When we shake, I'm not touching Sam Yao, famous movie star. He's only Sam.

A Sam who becomes awkward when our hands release. He looks down, flexing his fingers and frowning. "Where do we go from here?" he asks.

His open uncertainty is comforting in one way—it's nice to see he's only human—but also disturbing in that at least one of us should know how the hell to navigate this situation.

That person will have to be me.

"We keep working but we do it together," I decide. "I'll tell you if I need help instead of avoiding the situation."

"I'll try to listen."

"Sam."

"I *will* listen," he says.

I pull out a paper and he watches as I write. Although I can see him almost vibrating with curiosity, he waits until I'm ready. I hand over the sheet and he reads out loud in his low voice.

"'This agreement (the 'Agreement') dated on this 26th day of June lays out the working arrangement ('Arrangement') of Sam Yao and Gracie Reed.'" Here he looks up. "Is the legal language necessary?"

"Makes it binding."

Sam goes back to the sheet.

"'Both parties solemnly swear to: One. Treat each other with the respect due to a work colleague,'" he reads. "Why did you number it if you only have one rule?"

"You can add more," I say. "Everything else seemed redundant."

He thinks for a while, then shrugs. "You're probably right." He signs with a flourish and hands it over. I sign and fold the paper.

"Now it's official," I say. "We're partners."

He grins, a lopsided expression that soon turns into a boisterous laugh. "You're something else, Gracie Reed."

I can't help but smile back. I think he might be right.

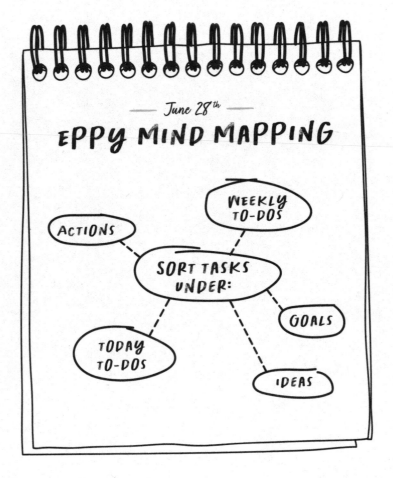

Eighteen

The next two days are an easy schedule I enjoy. I settle my sever-ance with Garnet Brothers and set up an in-box rule so all mes-sages with a garnetbrothers.com email go straight to Fred the Lawyer. I hadn't realized how much I dreaded opening my email and seeing one from Todd.

I devote most of my days to Fangli practice and this time I do it right, listing all the ways she could be approached and my planned responses. If someone comes up to me on the street. In the wash-room. Wants a photo. Wants a selfie, an autograph. I go on a binge of Fangli content until I'm able to parrot her mannerisms to the point that I slip into my Fangli persona even when I'm not in public. Sam assures me it happens to him when he gets deep into a role.

Because Sam, to my utter surprise, has become invaluable. Whenever he's not at the theater, we practice until it feels like second nature to turn to him with a smile and to see his affectionate look. Even if it's not an act, I'm no longer so naive and desperate to see it for anything but what it is: support for a friend. He's doing this for Fangli and her career. I'm only a tool. This hurts less than I thought it would, probably because now that I think about it, the idea of sweeping Sam Yao off his feet with my joblessness and lack of fame is so laughable.

It's too bad that his new friendliness makes him more appealing. Not physically, because you can't improve on perfection, but simply as a person. This Sam isn't cold and distant but goofy and charming. He's addicted to 1990s Brit pop and sang all of Oasis's "Wonderwall" with me one evening to Fangli's great delight, complete with overly emotive air guitar.

His jokes are terrible, like on the level of dad jokes, which is revealed when he sees me jotting down some notes. "Gracie, do you know why you shouldn't write with a broken pencil?"

"What?" What's he talking about?

"Because it's pointless. Have you heard the one about the sheet of paper?"

"Sam, are you okay?"

"Actually, it's pretty tearable." With a beatific smile, he turns away, happy to have delivered two of the worst jokes in the world.

He's a fucking amazing dancer, which I find out by accident one day when I try to figure out how to do a fad dance I saw on social media. He watched it through once and then repeated it flawlessly as I gaped at him.

He shrugged it off. "My mother says I have good bodily kines-thetic intelligence. From her, naturally."

"There's no way I can do that."

"Sure you can. It's all in the hips."

Only after he spends a futile five minutes trying to teach me to do a body roll does he give up. Thank God, because if I had to watch him thrust his hips at me while tracing his hands down his distressingly toned chest one more time I would have exploded. He doesn't notice the impact he's having and sits on the couch. "What were you doing before trying to dance?"

"Watching *The Pearl Lotus* again." I decided that it would be good to have another viewing now that I was a little more used to being Fangli.

"May I join you?" This Sam, too, is scrupulously polite compared to the old one.

"Sure, but you have to tell me the behind-the-scenes gossip." I start the movie, then pause it. "Do you find it strange to watch your-self on-screen?"

"I never used to watch my own movies," he says. "Do you want popcorn?"

"Yes." He gets up to nuke a bag and I wait for him to continue. "Well?"

"Well, what?" Sam bends down to open a cabinet for bowls.

"Acting. Watching yourself. You never used to but you do now?"

"It's an incredibly uncomfortable experience," he says as sharp little pops come from the microwave. "Every scene can be improved but there it is, forever. My idiot expressions. How stupid I look in a costume. I couldn't stand it for ages."

"What changed?"

"My friend Chen pointed out that if I never see my own work, I can never improve. It made sense and it's become easier." The micro-wave dings and he grabs the bag, swearing when he opens it and the steam burns his hand. "That being said, it's hard when I'm sitting with someone taking the mickey."

"Taking the what?"

"It's a term my tutor used. It means to make fun of someone."

"I would never!" I'm affronted he thinks me that mean.

Sam brings over two bowls and hands me one. "A bit of a joke... I know you wouldn't."

We start the movie again, and a few minutes later, he pauses it. "Do you see that?"

I squint at the scene, which takes place in the throne room under a golden dragon with ruby eyes. "Is that a Starbucks cup?"

"No one would admit to leaving it there."

"It was yours, wasn't it?"

When he laughs, his whole face lights up with mischief. "That trended on social media for days. I couldn't tell anyone. Too embar-rassed." Then he pats his pocket and pulls out his vibrating phone. His face hardens and he very decisively rejects the call.

He sees me looking. "My mother," he says.

I do some rough mental calculations. "Isn't it five in the morning or something in Beijing?"

"More like three but my mother is not limited by things such as time zones when it comes to trying to control my life."

Hearing Sam has trouble with his mom hits me the same way it did when I saw my teacher in the grocery store as a kid—almost disconcertingly intimate. "What's up?"

"Nothing."

My nosiness knows no bounds. "I'll tell you about my secret project."

Sam quirks his eyebrow. "I don't believe you."

"It's called Eppy. There's a teaser."

Sam gives in. "You know who my mother is."

"Lu Lili. We used to watch her movies."

"My father."

"Ren Shu, the director."

"Right. My mother is a force." He grimaces. "I've been in twenty-three movies. I've been acting for over fifteen years. I'm one of the highest paid actors in China, and nevertheless, at the age of thirty, I feel the need for her approval."

"Moms," I say.

"Moms," he agrees. "She wants me to quit acting and join my father's entertainment company."

"As an actor?"

"Groomed to be the CEO, like him. It's my duty as a good son."

"That sounds very dynastic."

"It is." He drinks with a closed face. "What Lu Lili wants, she gets. She has enough influence to prevent other companies from hiring me, and she would be confident it's for my own good."

"You don't want to?"

"We're different people," he says with vehemence. "Different ambitions. She doesn't understand that. It's because she loves us, but she also has no boundaries."

I lean back into the couch and pull my legs up. "What are you going to do?"

He points to the phone. "Avoid her calls."

"Not the best long-term plan."

"It's worked so far." He does that head tilt. "What do you suggest?"

"Have you tried telling her how you feel?"

Sam looks legitimately horrified. "We are not feelings people."

"Might be time to start unless you want to keep ignoring your own mother because you're scared to have a conversation. At age thirty."

"I'm not scared."

I throw a pillow at him and then marvel at how at ease I am. "Don't lie."

"You don't know my mother."

"I know my mother."

"You have a lot of heart-to-hearts with her?"

"No," I admit. "I wish I had. Do as I say, not as I do."

"Thanks."

He turns the movie back on and we watch in silence for a few minutes. Then he stops it again. "Tell me about this Eppy."

Why is it so difficult to talk about the things that are important to you? I understand in the grand scheme of life, creating a to-do list that works is not on the same level as fixing climate change, but to me, perfecting this list is a Thing. Sam has turned to me with his whole body and he's leaning forward as if he's interested.

I deflect. "Just something I'm working on."

When I freeze him out, the atmosphere changes between us. He pulls back, and because I'm a fucking people pleaser, I crumble. "It's a to-do list," I blurt out.

A slight line appears between his eyes. "Of tasks you need to do?"

"No, how to organize one. A planning method. None of the ones I've tried work for me so I'm creating my own." This sounds stupid. I pick at the seam of the couch.

The line fades as his eyes widen. "Like bullet journals?"

My turn to get big-eyed. "You like lists?"

In reply, he pulls out his phone and shows me an entire folder of productivity tools. "My assistant, Deng, got me into them but I haven't found the right one."

"Me neither."

"You decided to make your own." He smiles. "Eppy. I like it. I would never have thought of creating my own system."

It's hardly even a compliment but his tone makes me go red. "It's nothing," I mumble. "No big deal."

"Why not? You saw a problem and you're fixing it. Most people would work around it."

"I haven't gotten very far."

The line returns. "There are enough people in the world ready to put you down. Do you need to join them?"

His words hit me in the gut. "Is that your motto?"

Sam picks up the popcorn bowl and looks into it. Because we are having a serious conversation, I try not to notice the sharp angle of his face down from his cheekbone to his chin but man, it's hard. "It has to be. Everything I do is criticized. What I wear. Who I date. Movie roles and how I do in them."

Of course. "How do you cope?"

"I don't read the reviews. Good or bad." He passes me the bowl. "Will you let me beta test it?"

"You want to?" This gives me a huge rush that I can't hide.

He laughs. "A chance to organize my life? You bet." Then he turns the movie on and I sit back, almost too happy.

June 30th

MINDSET SHIFT!

LOVE LIST ♡

THEY'RE NOT TASKS, THEY'RE OPPORTUNITIES!

DO AT LEAST TWO MORE MANDARIN MODULES—IMPROVE MY COMMUNICATION WITH MOM.

LAUNDRY—I WILL HAVE CLEAN CLOTHES.

PRACTICE FANGLI VOICE—LIMIT CHANCES OF PUBLIC HUMILIATION.

READ SCRIPT FROM OPERATION OBLIVION—THIS IS HONESTLY A FUN TASK WITH NO MINDSET SHIFT NEEDED.

Nineteen

I make an effort with Fangli. I'm not comfortable talking to her about her mental health straight on, but one night when she comes over, I mention that I forgot to take my medication and let her see me swallow a pill.

"Are you sick?" she asks with concern.

I try to respond casually. "I have depression and panic. These SSRIs help calm me down because they adjust my brain chemistry."

Her eyes widen. "What?"

"I've had it a long time, but I only started dealing with it a couple of years ago," I say. "It was hard for me to admit I needed help." Try excruciating, but I'm trying to make it sound easier for Fangli, like this is something she can do.

She doesn't reply for a moment, then says, "I'd like to go for a walk."

I take the hint. "You should. Fresh air is good."

"I don't know the city very well. I get driven everywhere."

"Let's go together," I say suddenly. "We'll go to a shitty dive bar where no one will expect you. You can wear my clothes."

She looks torn. "I'm not sure it's a good idea. Someone might get a photo."

I think. "What if we get ready and you take a look at yourself? We won't go unless you're comfortable."

Fangli looks out at the dark night through the window. "It'll be hard to see my face on the street," she says as if convincing herself.

I pull a pair of jeans and a tank top out of my drawer. "Here."

She grins and trots away with the clothes. When she comes back five minutes later, I have to laugh. She's added a belt, tied the shirt with a small knot, and added heels. She looks fantastic.

"Close." I fix the shirt into a messy French tuck and give her a pair of my flat sandals and a hat. "No makeup."

"Not even lipstick?"

"Use this." It's a tinted lip balm.

When we stand side by side, we look almost like sisters, but there's no way an average person will mistake the slight, ponytailed and bare-faced woman in the ball cap for a film star, at least not in Toronto. "Looks good to me," I say.

"Let's do it." She has a pink flush on her cheeks. "We'll wander around with a coffee from the Starbucks."

"I'll go down first and wait for you outside the lobby doors, just in case," I say. "The lobby's the worst part for people watching who's coming in and out."

Fangli nods as she takes the little cross-body bag I give her. With my short hair and minimal makeup I look like no one in particular, so I stroll through the lobby without an issue. Fangli joins me and we hit the streets.

I decide to ditch the dive bar idea and take her up Yonge Street, which is only a few minutes from the hotel. I tap in our coffee orders for the mobile pickup, and soon Fangli is living the dream of sipping a decaf Americano as she walks up a dirty sidewalk. Since it's summer, there are people milling around, and except for a guy who walks in front of us to say, "Hubba-hubba," Fangli is thrilled to discover no one gives a shit who she is.

"What's it like for you back home?" I ask. "Can you walk around like this?"

She shakes her head so hard her hat falls off. "I have a driver and security."

"Even to go to the store?"

Fangli waves her coffee at me. "I don't go to the store. It's not safe for me or people around me. I get mobbed."

"But not here."

She grins. "I'm not as popular here. It's a pleasure."

I try to imagine being this famous. "Do you like it?"

"It's not a matter of like or not. It's what it is. I need to act because I want to be remembered for something, for this life to mean something." She shrugs. "I can do what I love and make money at it. How can I complain that I can't go get coffee whenever I want?"

We pass a drugstore and Fangli pauses to look at a sign promoting a sale on Trident. "Do you need some gum?" I ask.

She shakes her head. "I haven't chewed gum in years. My manager forbade it. It looks inelegant."

Imagine being forbidden a stick of Juicy Fruit. "Tonight's for you," I say. "Go nuts."

We duck in. I leave Fangli deliberating over the candy display—how are there so many gum flavors in the world?—and look around. It's a big store, with a high-end cosmetics counter. I have all I need back at the hotel, but my eyes linger on the lipsticks. The last one I bought was the unflattering neutral I got for Garnet Brothers.

"Can I help you with something?" A sales associate comes over with a practiced smile.

"No, thanks. I'm only browsing."

"Of course. I'm right here if you need me."

She heads over to organize a shelf of concealers. In front of me are a shiny line of Diors in little black and silver cases. They look sleek and chic, and in the last row, on the far left, is a deep oxblood shade. It's darker and edgier than the brighter reds I used to wear and I now wear as Fangli, but I can't take my eyes off it.

"Excuse me." The woman turns back around at my call. "Sorry, can I get that lipstick?"

"Sure." She opens a wide drawer and grabs it. "I'll cash you out."

After I suffer a momentary heart attack because since when has lipstick cost fifty bucks, I join Fangli at the front of the store where it looks like she's buying one of every gum on display. Not quite under-the-radar behavior but she's so happy I don't mention it.

My new purchase is tucked safely in my purse, a secret that gives me as much joy as Fangli seems to be getting from the gum. It's such a small thing, that little tube in my purse, but it's so big at the same time. It's mine.

Fangli finishes scanning her items at the self-checkout. When we leave, she swings her bag like a kid with a new toy.

"Want some?" she asks, digging into the bag.

I hold up my coffee. "Later."

A roar comes from the crowd ahead; there's a concert at Yonge-Dundas Square. "Want to check it out?" I ask. It sounds fun.

Fangli's face is longing but hesitant. "Will it be safe?"

"Sure. We'll stay on the edge so we don't get squished in the crowd."

This eases her concern. The music isn't crazy loud, and on the edges, people are dancing and smoking. Fangli stares around with wide eyes. Most of the people are in their twenties and they cover all styles. "Everyone is different," she marvels. "The crowd is so small."

I try to see it from her perspective. "How many people live in Beijing?" I ask.

"Over twenty million."

About ten times the size of Toronto. I can't even comprehend how big that is. There's a churro truck nearby, so I grab a couple. We get covered in sugar, lick dulce de leche off our fingers, and shout out the chorus to the song, or at least what we think are the words. It's fun until I pull out my phone to check the time and see a row of increasingly frantic texts from Sam.

Where are you?

Are you with Fangli?

Then variations on this for the last hour. He must have come by right after we left. The final message sounds like he's about to call the police so I shoot him a quick reply.

We're on a walk. All good.

The set ends and people cheer. Fangli turns to me with shining eyes, hardly looking a day over twenty. "That was amazing."

Yonge Street's now packed with the dispersing crowd, some yelling out the lyrics in a call-and-response that echoes up the street, so I lead her over to Dundas Street and then down through Nathan Phillips Square, where we walk up the winding concrete path to the green roof. It's locked so we can't go in, but we stand on the city hall balcony and hang our hands over the edge, the concrete rough under our arms. "I'd forgotten what it was like to be around people enjoying their lives," she says.

"What about when you go home?"

She snorts. "My father's life is his work. I might as well be at my own place."

"Surely you have friends." Actors are people, for crying out loud.

"All actors or in the industry." She runs her hands over her arms. "We can't escape each other. All of my friends I made in school... I fell out of touch with them."

"What about Chen, the guy you had a crush on?"

"Only a small crush. Him, too, and it's hard to meet new people. I don't know what they want from me, and I work so much I can't give them the time they deserve." She speaks matter-of-factly and then glances at the dark sky. "We should head back."

I check my phone and see I missed a text from Sam. **Can I join you?**

Damn, he must be really worried about Fangli if he's willing to be seen with both of us. I shove down the wistful thought of him worrying about me one day and type out a response. **We're on our way back now.**

We walk by the fountain pool and are almost at Bay Street when I say, "Why don't you email him?"

"Who?" Fangli is looking curiously at her reflection in the dark window. "I don't look like me at all."

"Chen."

She shrugs. "Why? Another person to ignore for my career?"

I'm no therapist but I power on. "It could be that. Or you might find someone to talk to."

"That doesn't work out for me." She sounds defeated. "I need to be alone too much."

I won't fight her on it, not wanting to wreck the vibe tonight, so I tell her about an epically bad holiday party I endured at a restaurant as we pass it. "No one knew the drinks were doubles and the CEO did a cancan dance on the bar. People were making out all over the place."

Fangli's holding her stomach, wheezing with laughter. "Then what?"

"The CEO slipped in the guacamole and put his back out. Didn't come to work for a week, but the next day, we got an all-staff email about no more alcohol at company parties." I pause. "Two of the couples making out got married, though."

We giggle in intermittent bursts all the way to the hotel. Fangli goes up first as I hit a convenience store to grab some chips. The churro whet my appetite and I want to balance the sweet with salt.

A knock on the door comes after we get in, and I open it to reveal Sam. He looks serious but when he sees Fangli, all the tension melts out of him. He comes in and rummages in the fridge for a beer. "Did you have fun?"

Fangli chatters to him in Mandarin as I open the chips and take the beer Sam holds out for me. I guess he's forgiven me because he smiles as he takes the chips I pass over to him. It's a good night, I congratulate myself, looking at Fangli. She has gum. I have my Dior.

We're both happy.

July 2
STICKY-NOTE PLAN:
ONLY DO WHAT FITS ON THE STICKY NOTE.

MANDARIN PRACTICE

EXERCISE

LAUNDRY, SERIOUSLY

EPPY

FILM RESEARCH

EVENT PREP

Twenty

'm riding high on my success of the other night and muttering along to my Mandarin app as I sit on the couch drinking coffee. How I took this language in university for three years and not a thing has stuck in my memory, I don't understand. I was never close to fluent but now I even need to refresh my numbers. Yi. Er. San. Si. Wu. Liu. Qi, ba, jiu, shi. One to ten, then it's all very logical. Eleven is ten-one. Twenty is two-ten and twenty-one is two-ten-one. None of this *teen* stuff or adding *y*'s.

I think Malcolm Gladwell might have written about how its logic makes for easier math, and I'm about to do a Google search when I decide that's procrastination and return to learning the numbers instead of learning about them. I wish Mom had spoken Chinese to me at home, but she refused. Until her dementia hit, I'd rarely heard her speak it at all. The past in the past and all that.

Sam and I have an event tonight and I've already decided to divide my day between learning about the mainland Chinese film industry—background research, I should know the main players— and working on Eppy. Last night as I was falling asleep, Sam texted me a thought that launched a series of increasingly good ideas and I'm itching to get them organized.

That's right. Sam texted me about Eppy. He's been texting me off and on over the last few days and not only when he's worried about

Fangli. I do my best not to read into it but it's hard. Seeing a text from Sam makes my heart thump and I wish I could get past this reaction so I can be the neutral friend he's clearly decided I am. Friends is better than nothing, and far easier than adversaries.

My phone lights up with a message and again my heart bangs because it's from Sam.

I'm in the hall.

At least he didn't simply stroll in like usual. I need to get that key, though. I do an emotional check and am happy to note my heart rate has subsided and I don't have any quivers or interferingly strong feelings. I have accepted that this is a job. Good for me, very reasonable.

This lasts as long as it takes me to open the door and see Sam channeling casual dojo, with loose pants and slides matched with an oversize T-shirt. His outfit could cost anywhere from $100 to $10,000 and I wouldn't be surprised. I step aside and he comes in.

"I thought you were busy today."

"We're going for a walk," he says.

"No, we're not," I say. "Fangli is out at an appointment and I can't be seen with you at the same time." Even if I go with him without my Fangli disguise, I resemble her too much to not cause questions if caught by a photographer.

"Right." He goes to the window and stares out. "I want to see the city. My skin itches to get out of here."

Sam has changed toward me since our talk about Fangli, and it's a relief to be able to let down my guard around him. "We have a film premiere tonight." I already had to practice going from standing to sitting in the dress, which is a stunner.

He makes a rude gesture. "Being stuck in a theater."

"Aren't you busy?" I repeat the question since he hasn't answered.

"Finished early." He doesn't turn around but rolls his neck as if trying to get rid of a kink.

"Did something happen?"

"No."

I walk over to join him at the window. He smells good, that same chipped-stone fragrance. It's a cool, overcast day and the wind has whipped up small white-tipped waves on the surface of the lake. I open the sliding balcony door to let the breeze drift in and Sam closes his eyes.

His restlessness affects me as well. "What do you usually do to relax?"

"Work out. Watch YouTube. Play Candy Crush."

"What level?"

He glances at his phone. "Three hundred and eighty."

"I'm four ninety-two."

This makes him frown competitively. I get an idea. "What if we go to the arcade near the aquarium? You wear a hat and something less"—I wave my hand around—"fashionable." That might do the trick. No one will wonder who I am if they don't identify Sam.

He looks down at his outfit. "This is what I usually wear at home."

Other guys would wander around in boxers and a dirty undershirt. "You look like you walked out of a *Vogue* ad for casual wear. Average Toronto dudes don't wear flowy pants."

"Oh." He brightens. "Got it."

He disappears to his own suite as I run a hand through my hair. I look fine as me; no one will look twice.

Do I want them to look? I pull out the Dior. It's called Revelation and I wonder how I can get a job naming these things.

The first swipe goes on smooth like honey. Mei insists that I use a lip liner when I do the Fangli face, but this is for me and I don't mind the edges blurring. The color is as rich as I hoped and gives my entire face a more angular cast. I like it.

I like it a lot.

Sam reappears and does a double take. "That's a new look."

"I know." I don't ask what he thinks because I didn't wear it for him. Instead I check him over. This time he's got on tight black jeans, a ball cap, sunglasses, and a black medical face mask. I close my eyes. "Lose the mask or the sunglasses. And can I get my key back?"

"I usually wear them when I'm out," he says.

"One is fine. Both with the hat scream *Look at me, I'm famous.*"

"Fine." He whips off the shades. "Happy?"

I'm giving a master class in looking like a regular person. "Do you really never go unwatched?" I ask.

"I don't know. It's safer to assume I am so I can be on guard."

There's no answer I can give to this, so I grab my purse and we head out. He automatically moves to where the cars are so I take his arm and adjust course. "We're walking."

"Oh. Okay."

I drop his arm immediately because the feel of his muscled solidness is akin to touching a hot stove. "Keep looking straight ahead. Act like there's nothing to notice about you. You're a regular guy going outside, that's it. You drive a five-year-old Honda Civic and wonder if you have enough money for a down payment on a studio condo."

His body language gets more casual as he listens. "Got it."

It's a weekday and we're close enough to the Financial District that it swarms with office workers grabbing food or going about their day. No one takes a photo or asks for an autograph because most of them are on their phones or busy talking to each other, and Sam cheers up as he sees that no one recognizes us as Fangli and Sam. We're only two more faceless people in a faceless crowd.

"The CN Tower is so tall." He looks up as we pass.

"Do you want to go up?" I haven't been since an elementary-school class trip.

"Can we?" His smile is wistful. "There was a photo of it in a book when I was a kid. I thought if I went up that high, I would be able to see the whole world." He cranes his head back and I copy him. The spiky concrete structure looms over us, dwarfing everything around it.

Then he squints at the little red dots moving around the exterior of the main pod. "Are those people?"

"You can put on a harness and lean over the edge." I hold up my hand before he says a word. "You're on your own for that."

"I'll pass. Wirework is enough for me."

We buy tickets and yawn to pop our ears as we fly up the elevator to the observation deck. Although the day is overcast, it's not so cloudy that it completely obscures the view.

"You can't see the whole world, but that's Hamilton over there." I point out the city that edges the lake to the southwest.

He smiles and reaches out as if he's going to hold my hand. I freeze, then sag as he touches the window instead. "It's good enough."

I leave Sam dreaming by the window as I roam and take care to dance around the glass floor that gives a sickening view to the ground. That our relationship has shifted dramatically is unquestionable and I'm torn between accepting it and wanting to talk about it ad nauseam. A cool girl would take it all in stride.

I am not cool.

I stomp back to him before I lose my nerve. "Why are you being like this?"

His eyes turn down to take me in. "Like what?"

"Friendly. You started off rude as hell, and for the last little while, you're being nice to me, nicer than you need to be for this job. What's going on?" My voice shakes because I don't like confrontation, and although this isn't hostile, it's about feelings, which I also avoid. There's a lot I don't like about this situation, but if I get clarity on it at the end, I'll be happier.

"I'm sorry."

This is not what I thought he'd say. "For what?"

"Didn't we go through this the other night?" He looks out the window into the distance. "I told you I was worried about Fangli."

A chattering family approaches and we move to the other side of the deck.

"Right. That doesn't explain why you want to hang out with me instead of staying at the hotel playing Candy Crush right now."

Sam presses against the wall and crosses his arms. "Is it such a problem to be with me? You know there are people who would kill for this?"

"Name names."

"Fine, I was lonely," he snaps. "Happy? I was bored and you and Fangli came back glowing the other night and I wanted the same thing. I want to live for a couple hours with no expectations. I want to forget being me."

I understand the sentiment. "Okay," I say.

He eyes me. "Really?"

"Yeah, that's legitimate." I test myself. Am I hurt by this? In a way, it's refreshing to have it out in the open. He uses me to briefly feel like a normal person. I use Fangli for money and a voyeuristic glimpse into the world of the famous. Fangli uses me to save her mental health. I use Sam for... Fine. It's no real hardship to spend time with the Sexiest Man in the World. Shallow? Yes. True? Also yes.

"I'm sorry," he repeats. "We should go back."

I grab his sleeve as he goes past me. "No way. We said arcade."

"You sure?" He looks doubtful, then leans in as if ready to confide his life's secret. "Hey, Gracie?"

"What?"

"Do you know what kind of shoes ninjas wear?"

I do my best not to twist out my optic nerves while rolling my eyes. "Sneakers."

"Oh. You know it." His momentary disappointment is soon replaced by his game face. "Arcade time. Get ready to lose at an epic level."

Twenty-One

S am trounces me soundly at every game we try. Every fucking game. I do my best to keep my temper because having a tantrum like a child because you've lost at Plinko is not a good look, especially when your opponent is almost humming with contentment. I end up sublimating my resentment into a fight about who should buy the beer.

"A good winner is generous," I say.

"Loser always buys."

"You are a millionaire," I point out.

"A low but accurate blow." He holds out his fist. "How about we rock, paper, scissors?"

Three rounds later, Sam's at the bar putting his money down. I take my pint with a smug smile that makes him laugh.

I'm not surprised when Sam echoes the thought that's been revolving through my head for the last hour. "This has been fun," he says.

"Except for me losing all the games."

"As I said, fun." He sips his drink. "Cheered me up. How's Eppy?"

He remembered what it was called. I try not to beam. "Good. I think."

"Problems?"

"Not problems. Challenges."

"Thinking about how to layer in prioritization with time management?"

I gawk at him. "How did you know?"

"That's what I look for when I'm trying to organize a list."

I have a target market right here, and if Eppy can scale for a movie star, I figure it will work for the rest of us peasants. "What else do you look for?"

We spend a happy half hour—at least for me; Sam looks like he's about to fade after the first twelve questions—going through his ideal to-do list. Finally he coughs to relieve his dry throat and glances at my drink. "Want another?"

"Are you buying again?" I drain the glass and glance at the screens of notes I've taken on my phone. Sam was a gold mine of ideas. He even knew a few platforms I hadn't heard of.

"Only because I feel sorry for someone who couldn't even win a glorified version of Pong." He walks away before I can protest— that one game was way harder than Pong—and I do my best not to follow him with my eyes and fail miserably. The frazzled mom trying to corral three screaming kids does the same, and on her face, I see that fantasy that beautiful men create: *Please take me from this. Look at me. Be my prince. Be mine. Make me feel special. See me.*

By the time Sam returns, I'm pensive.

A woman to Sam's left had been watching him between sips of her white wine, but before I can warn him, she downs her drink and hops to her feet. I manage to get out "Uhh," and then she's on him.

"I'm sorry, but are you Kai's friend?" She looks up at him with big blue eyes under her heavy fringe of fake eyelashes. "I think we met the other day?"

"I'm not, sorry." He gives her a pleasant smile.

"Oh." She tilts her head and swings back her blown-out ombre hair. "I'm Lauren."

I reach out and take Sam's hand. "Nice to meet you!" I say, match- ing her smile with my own and throwing in a dash of *yo bitch, step off.*

I know she gets the message because her face squeezes when Sam lays his other hand over mine.

"I guess I had the wrong person." She retreats.

"Sorry," I apologize to Sam, quickly pulling my hand away.

He grins at me. "Nicely done."

"Do you get that a lot? No one ever tries to pick me up."

"I don't believe that," he says politely. "To answer your question, it happens occasionally. I'm not often alone when I'm out so I think that limits it to the most brave. They don't want me, though."

"What do you mean?"

"They're attracted to the concept of me, but it's a fantasy they've built. It doesn't matter if they know who I am or not. It's this." He waves his hand at his face, then shrugs. "The fame helps. At least she didn't recognize me. That would be a mess."

I peer into his glass. "Did you get the Massive Ego IPA?"

"I got the Realistic lager," he corrects. "My looks are an asset. Fully monetized."

I know he's right. It's Sam's public persona and the same as what Fangli said that first day about her fans. What kind of pressure does that create, to be on a pedestal that you never built and that is a by-product of doing a job to the best of your abilities?

"Huh." I beam at Lauren, who is glowering at me. "What's it like to be so good-looking?"

"You tell me."

"Whatever, Sexiest Man in the World."

To my surprise, Sam's ears go bright red. Then he says, "If I may point out, Fangli is considered one of the most beautiful women in film. You are acting as her double."

"No one ever thinks that about me," I say. "I've always been more weird-looking." It's only been the last few years that people have decided to make a fuss about how attractive multiracial people are, as if admiring our appearance makes up for their unnecessary need to talk about how we look at all. I poke at the ring my glass left on the table. Fangli and I look the same but we've had very different experiences of what our faces represent to other people. Hers can be considered on its aesthetic merits. Mine is still a social statement.

"No." Sam shakes his head.

Two pints means I have the courage to say what's been bothering me. "You said I was."

"What?" He puts his glass down and leans forward. "Never. Never would I even *think* such a thing."

"The other day you said I was only half. You said, 'If you weren't only half, I'd think you were a real Chinese.'" I remember each word.

Sam is silent. "That's not the same thing."

"It is, a bit." I pause and take my courage in hand again. "The same idea is there. Being different."

"There's nothing wrong with being different."

"There's nothing wrong with it if you want to be," I correct him.

He gives me a confused look. "Don't you want to? Why be ordinary when you have the choice to be so much more?"

"Because I don't want it to only be because of how I look! Or because my mom's from a different country."

To my shame, my throat swells and tears prick against my lids. I bite down hard on my tongue, not wanting him to see how upset I am. But this is Sam, who's trained to react to body language much more subtle than mine, and he takes my hand. "I'm sorry."

"Excuse me." I stand up to escape to the washroom, not wanting him to see me cry. Instead, Sam's hand comes down on my arm. It's a gentle touch, not controlling.

"Don't leave. We'll go outside," he says. "We'll talk."

————

We end up sitting on a bench at the train museum right in front of the arcade and staring at some little kids as they play hide-and-seek. Although me and my big mouth started this conversation, I have no desire to see it through. Why did I even bring it up?

"I upset you," he says quietly.

"Sorry. It's no big deal."

"You do that a lot," he says. "Say you're sorry when you have nothing to be sorry for."

"I'm Canadian. We're raised on apologies and maple syrup."

He ignores my weak joke.

"Gracie, I truly apologize for what I said. I won't make excuses as to what I meant, but let me say that I never want you to think you're less than who you are. I don't think of you as anyone but you, a whole and complete person."

"Okay." I look up. Sam's frowning at the shiny engine car in front of us as if weighing his next words.

"You are not limited by your appearance. When I meant that you could be more, that it's good to be different." He frowns. "How you look was the last thing on my mind."

A brief, disloyal, and guilt-inducing thought comes: Would I have the same perspective if I'd been raised by a Lu Lili, a woman who relished standing out rather than fearing it? Perhaps. It's too late now. I am who I am.

"I understand," I tell Sam. I do. I also know this conversation is now over because I don't want to talk about it anymore. "We should get going. I need time to get ready for tonight."

It looks like he wants to say more but Sam stands up and helps me to my feet. His grip is firm on my hand, and when he pulls me up, I lose my footing and stumble forward. Again, he sweeps me up, his hands warm on my back, and looks down in my face. My breath hitches and he releases me.

"That was like the time Fangli slipped and you caught her," I say to break the tension. "It was all over the clips Mei made me watch."

He nods. "Milan, I think. Two years ago. That got a good reaction."

"What?"

Sam rears back, astonished. "You thought that was real?"

Now it's my turn to be surprised. "You *planned* that?"

"The movie was about a doomed love affair." He thought back. "Was it my idea or Fangli's? Mine, I think."

"I had no idea. Do we need to do something like that for tonight?"

"That's more of a special occasion move. Tonight we go to see and be seen." He smiles. "It'll be a breeze."

I try not to think of how ominous that sounds as we return to the hotel. Not until we're back do I realize I'm hungry, so I call room service for a sandwich before I hop into the shower. The expensive shower gel cheers me in a way that only luxury products can, enveloping me in their fragrance, Chanel of course, thanks to Fangli. I come out with very soft skin and wrap my hair up in a towel to prepare for the spackling of my face that acts as a prelude to the makeup. I've applied the basics when I hear a knock. Must be room service.

I hunt around for a robe and open the door. There's no one there, so I step out to see if they've already left and are at the elevators. A movement down the hall catches my attention and I take another step out because I don't want that sandwich to escape.

Behind me comes a soft click as the door locks shut.

Then I stand there, wriggling the doorknob and refusing to accept reality. Shit. My phone is in there. I have no key. I go next door and knock on Fangli's door; no answer. At least Sam has my key, but when I knock, there's no answer there either. I go back and shake the door for a second time in case it's magically unlocked in the last thirty-four seconds. It hasn't.

I'll have to go down to the lobby in my towel and robe. I weigh the pros and cons. Pros: getting in the room. Cons: public shame. Photos of a half-naked me as Fangli going viral. I lean my head against the door and ask the universe for guidance.

It does not deliver.

As I try to recall the layout of the lobby and if there's any way I can sneak down a back stairwell and hiss at the concierge while hiding behind the downstairs door, a cart appears at the end of the hall. The universe has taken pity on me after all, because housekeeping can let me in. When I go over and find the woman cleaning the room, she looks me up and down with a bright smile.

"I'm sorry," I say. "I locked myself out of my room. Can you let me back in?"

The smile doesn't slip. "Do you have a key?"

"No, I locked myself out. I need to get back in."

"You need a key."

"Right," I agree. "It's in the room. That I locked myself out of."

"I can call security."

"Thanks." I know intellectually this makes sense, since you can't have people simply claiming they stay here, but I'm in the hall in a towel and my patience is limited. She calls down and I go back to my door. Maybe room service has arrived and they can let me in.

Room service has not arrived.

While normally I would file this under the "Welp, what can you do" category of mischance, the fact that I am in the hall in half makeup means my anxiety about this rebounding on Fangli is inching ever higher. Sam said cameras are everywhere. I don't need Fangli seeing footage of me-as-her looking like a drowned rat.

I pad barefoot down the hall, sticking to the walls as if I'm a mouse avoiding detection, looking down in hopes the security cameras are all near the ceiling and they'll only catch the twisted towel on my head. An exquisitely cut black suit comes my way. Excellent. It's Sam. I've never been so happy to see him.

He stops dead when he sees me, looking down at the robe. "What are you doing?" He looks as if he's prepared for any answer.

"I need the key to my room," I say. "I got locked out."

"I gave it to Mei. I realized I was infringing on your privacy."

"You had it this afternoon. You had it *two hours ago*."

"Because I forgot to give it to you when you asked and didn't want to make it worse."

I groan. "You had to be a gentleman? Right now? Mei's not answering her door."

"She left after I saw her to meet Fangli at an appointment. Why were you out in the hall like that anyway?"

"Got bored and thought I'd go exploring in my new fancy dress." I sweep a sarcastic curtsy that has the unfortunate result of swinging open my robe and revealing the towel underneath, which only reaches my upper thighs.

The elevator dings and Sam curses under his breath. "Let's get you inside my room before someone sees."

I glance back to see the front of the room-service cart appearing from the elevator. "I bet that's my sandwich."

Sam takes a deep breath. "I will collect your precious sandwich but right now, in this moment, I need you to get out of sight. Please."

It's reasonable. I nod and the towel drops off my head. I kneel to grab it but lose my balance after I twist the towel back on, forcing Sam to lean down and grab my shoulders to prevent me from toppling over. Awkward, but two seconds later, it's all sorted out. He ushers me into his suite, and as the door shuts, I hear him talking to someone in the hall. I listen at the door and hear another voice. Security. I caused quite a fuss.

While I wait, I try to stop myself from snooping around Sam's suite. It's the same as mine but with the rooms backward—where my bedroom is on the right, his is on the left. I will not go into his bedroom. I will not. To stifle my urge, I take a seat on the couch hunched up in my robe and rub at my hair to towel-dry it before wrapping it again. A good thing no one saw us in the hallway.

The door opens. "You're good," says Sam, doing his best to avert his eyes from my robed self. "Food's in your room. You have forty minutes."

I jump up like a jack-in-the-box, knocking the towel off my head again in the process. Sam digs his finger into his temple like he's warding off a headache and closes his eyes. That gesture will not make it onto the sizzling-hot-things-men-do list. I ignore him and wrap my hair back up again.

The security guard is waiting at my door, and I thank him with my face lowered so he can't get a good look before I go back in. Forty minutes. I inhale the sandwich and brush my teeth before drying my hair to prepare for the wig. I'm getting good at the makeup, and I manage a smooth smoky eye and a sharp red lip in no time.

This time, the dress code is Extra Fancy. I refused to have a pedicure because the thought of someone messing with my feet makes me cringe, so the shoes are closed-toed but so pretty I decide the torture of wearing them will be worth it. They're what a coworker called dinner and doma shoes—manageable only to take a taxi to the restaurant and back home.

After a brief but intense battle between my hips and the two pairs of Spanx that do their best to compress me like a sausage, I drop the dress over my head. It's a black cheongsam design with navy beaded embroidery that gives it a pleasing weight and a high collar cut to show off my shoulders. I add the earrings—simple studs with diamonds as big as peas and the multitude of thin gold bracelets Mei has put out. There are so many it takes actual minutes to get them all on, but once I'm fully decked out, I wave my arms around like Wonder Woman with her gauntlets. Assuming they are real, and it's much better for my stress levels to pretend they are not, I'm basically covered with money.

Once the wig is on, I glance in the mirror and do a double take.

Today I am indistinguishable from the real Fangli. This gives me confidence. I practiced her signature and her gestures and her smile. I can name her entire filmography and remember where she went to school and her favorite color, if any of those topics come up. More importantly, people are expecting to see Fangli and that's what they'll see. I decide to consider this my true debut in my alter ego.

I hear Fangli arrive back and tuck my lipstick, phone, and room key into the beaded clutch, which is much classier than stuffing them down my bra. When I knock on the connecting doors, I see Sam is already there and Fangli isn't.

"Ready?" I ask. When I see his face, I know there's trouble. "What?"

Mei murmurs and leaves as he passes over his phone. It's a post of a woman in a white robe kneeling on the floor in front of a man, his hands on her shoulders in a pose that looks unmistakably sexual. I know that carpet. I know that hallway. I know those people because one of them is definitely me.

"What the fuck?" I turn the phone sideways as if that will give me more information.

"Language. The guy delivering your sandwich took it," Sam says. "Fangli's team is dealing with it."

I can only stare. It looks bad, really bad. "Is it edited?" All I did was bend down to get a towel. The way it looks is terrible, as if I'm about to... My stomach churns. Poor Fangli. "What do you mean they'll deal with it?"

"It hasn't gone viral, so they'll get it pulled and scrubbed. That asshole will be fired, of course. The hotel is already on damage control because of the hit to their reputation. No one will want to stay here if their privacy can be so easily compromised."

I sit—very straight because of the dress—in a chair. "Fangli?"

"Doesn't know," he says. "She won't."

"Her team knows that can't be her," I argue. "She wasn't here."

"It's the perception. The photo names her as Fangli."

"What about you?" I go red as I look at the photo again. "I'm so sorry." For the first time, I understand what he means by always being vigilant. I thought I was being careful by keeping my face pointed down to avoid getting caught on the security cameras, but I now see that I have no idea of the real scope of damage that can be caused by a simple accident. Fangli can't have accidents, and by extension, neither can I.

But I did, and now I can only trust that Fangli's team can contain it. A fury builds in me at the man who took the photo. What was he hoping to accomplish? Some upvotes at the cost of other people's reputations.

Fangli's voice comes to me. *I'm a product, not a person.*

"It's not your fault." He kneels down so we're level and peers into my face. "I need you to know you didn't do anything wrong."

"Look at this." I shake the phone at him. "You told me to be careful."

"I did and you are. It was an accident."

My eyes go back to the photo and he gently takes the phone away.

"We're dealing with it." He holds out his arm. "Are you ready to go?"

"We're going?"

"This isn't our problem to solve. We have people for this. Your job right now is to make Fangli shine so no one will believe that garbage." He tilts his head. "Can you?"

Hell no, says interior me. I ignore that voice and lift my chin as I rise out of the chair. I've got a job to do. I turn to Sam. "Let's go."

Twenty-Two

"There will be cameras," Sam reminds me for the fourth time as the car pulls up to the theater on King Street. "Remember our signal."

We've decided Sam will take the lead, not in a draggy-caveman way, but an easy quarter-step ahead so I know where to stop and deliver a Fangli moment for the photographers.

He watches me fidget with the row of bracelets on my arm before laying a gentle hand on my fingers. "Are you ready?"

Seeing the photo has increased my anxiety but I try to dislodge the negativity and make space for the more imminent issue of the red carpet. "I was born ready."

This makes him shake his head—but he's smiling—before he gets out and leans back in to help me exit, providing cover as I do my best to keep from flashing the world because of the slit in my skirt. It's a good thing this absorbs most of my attention, because by the time I'm out with my smile on, I only have time to make out a blue carpet before it dissolves into a seizure-inducing barrage of camera flashes. It's not only the photographers who line the carpet, but every person there is calling my name and Sam's and taking photos.

Nothing Sam told me warned me for the physicality of this experience. The cameras aren't passive instruments used to capture moments in time; they're active and hostile participants.

I freeze, nonplussed but smile fixed, and Sam leans down slightly to slide his arm around my waist. He smells like sandalwood this time and I sniff, feeling the scent calm me. I'd picked Coromandel, a rich patchouli that boosts my confidence. Only bad bitches and hippies use patchouli, a fragrance that can go from distinctive to overwhelming in a moment. I've never had the nerve to wear it.

"You've got this," he murmurs.

It all becomes a blur. I smile and pose with my hand on my hip and my chin down and slightly to the right, which Mei reminded me multiple times is my best side. My face aches and my eyes tear up when I forget to blink. Earlier today I worked out a series of moves to casually change poses, and I work through them like a Beyoncé backup dancer.

I thought this would be the most thrilling thing that ever happened to me because walking the carpet is the epitome of movie-star glamour but the flashes and screams press up against me in the most maddening way. It's layered with the knowledge that a single wrong move—a stumble or frown or silly look—can be seen around the world before I even notice I've screwed up. Or that someone could point and yell, "That's an imposter!" emperor's-new-clothes style.

"Breathe," Sam murmurs and I take in a short gasp, then another longer wheeze. My chest feels cinched from fear and Spanx, but his hand grips my waist and I manage to get a real breath.

Sam guides me to the end of the carpet and into a main lobby filled with well-dressed people milling around giving air-kisses. Unlike at the art exhibit, the attendees range from formally gowned to downright eccentric. As Sam tucks his hand under my arm and I worry the sweat I feel beading on my upper lip is about to burst through my thick layer of foundation, a man walks by in a chartreuse polka-dotted shorts suit, panama hat tipped low over his eyes. Apparently both style and wealth are appreciated here.

Since I don't have much of either, it doesn't calm me.

"Ah, there he is." Sam waves at someone behind me.

"Sammy!" A short man with a high man-bun comes over, a huge grin on his face. I know who it is because this time I did my research and checked the IMDb for director Eddy Freedman before coming. "Your agent wouldn't confirm but I knew you wouldn't let me down."

"You'd never let me forget it."

"True. Wei Fangli, glad to see you." He nods and I remember the internet says he has a phobia about touching people. "It must be three years now. Four?"

"At least." I'm having a conversation with someone who knows Fangli.

"There's something different about you." He looks at me and cocks his head slightly to the side as I try not to freak out. "New hairstyle," he finally decides.

I passed the test. Sam touches my arm in a small celebratory gesture.

A harried woman in a gray dress and a headset tugs on Eddy's arm and mutters into his ear. He nods. "Right, I'll see you at the afterparty, Sam?"

"We have an early morning tomorrow but we'll come for a bit."

That's it. Eddy is swallowed by the crowd and Sam plucks two glasses of bubbly wine off a passing tray. I take it and resist tossing it back like a shot since Fangli doesn't drink.

The stars of the movie arrive and Sam and I drift back to the edges of the crowd. I make sure to keep on a small smile. "We'll greet them later," he says. "How are you?"

"Good," I say. Then I repeat it. "Good." I am. My smile hasn't slipped and I managed the Running of the Photographers, safer but somehow more intimidating than the bulls of Pamplona. "What's next?"

"Since we timed it to arrive a bit late, we can avoid most of the mingling. We'll be asked to go into the theater. We watch the movie. Clap. Follow everyone to a room. Decline a drink. Stay fifteen minutes and leave."

"Sounds like a hot date," I say.

"Only the best for you." He drops me a cheesy wink.

A low voice carries over an intercom. "Please take your seats. Ladies and gentlemen, please take your seats."

There's a slow turn of the crowd as they move to the open doors of the theater. I know from Sam the film is a comedy of errors loosely based on the Oscar Wilde play *Lady Windermere's Fan*. Sam sits beside me and we both smile at the people in our row, who seem to know who I am without saying they do. We engage in some light chatter about the weather and how hot it is in LA this time of year; they thank God they had the jet because it makes traveling so much more convenient when you don't have to wait for customs, and I thank God the lights dim before I need to continue this inane conversation.

In the dark, I am very aware of Sam sitting next to me. We've already done some polite elbow jujitsu over who gets the armrest between us but I end up ceding my hard-won territory to him when I realize the prison of women's clothes makes it more comfortable to sit with my hands primly clasped in my lap and my back straight as a ruler. I shift around to find a comfortable position, but to my dismay, the Spanx start slipping. Only a bit, but like when your socks inevitably come down your calves to land in wrinkled cups by your ankles, the edges roll and my stomach struggles for release. When I get up, I'm going to have a tube right around my hips. While I want to fight the good fight for body positivity, I do not have the courage to do it in front of an A-list crowd.

"What's the matter with you?" Sam hisses in my ear.

"My Spanx are falling down. If I stand up, they'll bind my legs together."

"Your what are falling down?"

"My underwear." It's the easiest way to describe them without getting into a discussion about women's foundation garments.

He doesn't even reply, merely covers his eyes with one hand as if attempting to gather his emotional strength.

"It's not my fault."

More silence.

"What do I do?"

He turns to me, stupefied. "How should I know? I don't wear women's underclothes. Surely by this age, you've mastered wearing them."

"I don't want to talk to you." This conversation has been conducted in whispers, as if we're sharing a private conversation that is absolutely not about my underwear.

"Good."

"Good."

The film starts right in without any trailers. I want to enjoy the movie, at least enough that I'll be able to talk about it in the party after, but my clothes make the experience endless. By the halfway point, my thighs are shaking with the effort of trying to keep myself upright and unmoving. It's no use. With every breath and tiny fidget, the Spanx continue their inexorable trip down my body and they're now cutting into my lower hips.

Sam puts a hand on my knee, and while at any other time in my life, I would have been left stunned at his touch, right now all I can think is that delicate pressure might bring the Spanx down another centimeter. I can't risk it and I knock his hand away.

"Then stop squirming around," he mutters.

"Can I go to the washroom?"

"No."

"Jesus fucking Christ, do rich people not pee?" This is a very not-Fangli thing to say and the dark look Sam shoots me confirms it.

"I'm sure it's not as bad as you think," he whispers.

There's some solace in knowing he's probably right. The chances of anyone looking at my stomach for the three minutes it will take me to get to the washroom for some adjustments are minimal. That is, as long as the Spanx don't fall down completely. I take a few deeper breaths and wince as the elastic cuts into the fleshy part of my hips. That's going to leave a mark.

What I need is distraction, like when you're trying to get through the last ten seconds of a plank pose. The movie is good but not good enough, so my mind sorts through all my current issues: looking for a job, worrying about Mom, getting caught as a fake Fangli. Then it lands on the one that looms largest because he's physically right beside me.

Sam.

There's always an intimacy in a dark movie theater, and having him so near and in that suit is enough to send my imagination into overdrive. Sam taking my hand and pulling me close. Sam, his arm wrapped around me as he laughs in my ear at an excellent joke I've made. Sam watching me get ready before he pulls me back on the bed, his black hair and tanned skin a striking contrast to the white sheet. Sam giving me that same look as the first time in Fangli's suite, but this time meaning it. Sam seeing me and not Fangli's double.

The images on the screen pass by without me noticing what's occurring because I'm thinking about Sam. Just for this little while, I promise myself. Only for the amount of time it takes for this movie to run will I let myself dive into the fantasy of what it would be like to be wanted by Sam, to be one of the few to know the man beneath that public exterior. To have him only want me.

I stifle a heavy sigh. It's sweet that he and Fangli are such good friends but I'm even jealous of that. Not of Fangli specifically, but of the strength of their relationship. There's a level of trust between them that can only have been forged through supporting each other in the hard times, when the work is difficult and you're going to collapse because every muscle aches from fatigue. They know they can turn to each other.

The movie ends too soon and I reluctantly bid my dreams goodbye. I'm back to being fake Fangli with her Spanx cutting off her circulation.

"Beautiful tones," approves the man beside me. "That palette was perfect."

"Gorgeous," I agree. Sam stands, and when I do, my Spanx slip down further. Sam senses my sudden grab because he glances back and then down. His eyes widen slightly.

Ah, so it is as bad as I thought. I can't decide if this means vindication or humiliation.

I hobble out of the row after him and he puts his arm around my waist with his palm flat and spread against my hip. His touch is firm because he's trying to keep up the damn elastic. We walk as if we're in a three-legged race to the washroom, Sam with his dazzling social smile and me beside him. He leaves me at the door.

There's a *line.* I can't believe it. The men are probably swanning up to the urinals without a care in the world. Between my underwear, hunger, and this stupid aching yearning for Sam that I did to myself, I'm so done with tonight.

Sam is talking to a strange woman when I come out with my precarious undergarments now under control. Our gazes catch as I head toward him. He doesn't stop his conversation but the eye contact lingers about two seconds longer than it should and I try to avoid stumbling over my own feet.

Don't read into this. All that happened is that he looked at me as I approached. He's looked at me before. He will look at me again and see me as part of a job.

I don't want to be his job. I want to think he was looking at me, Gracie, the person who loves a generously poured glass of wine and thinks way too much about organizational planners, and not an alternate Fangli. This isn't safe.

Then someone grabs me by the arm, hard, squealing into my ear.

"I can't believe it's really you!" A wide-eyed blond woman leans close, too close, and her grip on my arm doesn't soften. "Can I get a selfie?"

This is what Fangli meant by people acting as if she's nothing more than a robot. Sam's at my side in a moment, but she doesn't take her eyes off me.

If I humor her, it will end faster. "Of course," I say politely.

"Your face is so cute! I loved you in *Sin Eater*."

I stare at her, racking my brain for Fangli's movies. I know that's not on the list but it's familiar. Comprehension hits Sam and me at the same moment.

Ellen Gao is the only Chinese actor in *Sin Eater*. She thinks I'm another person.

Deciding discretion is the better part of valor, I pose and smile as expected. She disappears almost as quickly as she appeared and Sam reaches for my arm. His smile fades and he glances around and makes a hand signal. In seconds, there's a man in a black suit and earpiece beside him. Sam has a hushed conversation and the man nods once, looks at my arm, and leaves.

"She thought I was Ellen Gao," I say, almost laughing. It's not a funny laugh. I'm a little breathless and my adrenaline is up.

"That shouldn't have happened. She snuck in and security will get her out." Sam gestures to my arm, and I raise it to see the livid marks from her fingers. He strokes the skin gently, his expression hard. "Does that hurt? Do you want to leave?"

"No." I steady my voice. "You said fifteen minutes at the party?"

"Only if you're up to it."

"I'm up to it." I said I'd take this job seriously and I'm going to. This time, I lead Sam.

———

"I didn't get a chance to eat," I tell Fangli when I arrive back. She came over to my suite after I had peeled off my layers, and now my body flaps around like a crab that's rid itself of a too-small shell.

She shoves over a container of celery that she's been nibbling on and a tub of hummus that she hasn't touched. "Here."

I scoop a huge glob and stuff it into my mouth. "How was your day?" Please let her not mention how I nearly trashed her reputation by dropping a towel and making it look like she was going to give Sam head in the hallway. Sam has assured me it was taken care of without Fangli even knowing, which gives me some confidence in the ability of their people to deal with the tabloids if news of what I'm doing for Fangli ever gets out—but I hate thinking about what might have happened.

She makes a face and drinks her seltzer. "My father called."

The light in the suite is dim and in the background, some music I don't recognize is playing on her phone. It makes me think of nostalgia. "Sounds like it wasn't a great conversation."

"He disapproves of me working out of the country," she says. "He thinks I should stay in China."

"Parents."

"I know. I always wish I had a sibling to take off some of the pressure. I wanted a sister. My stepmother was not amenable."

"I wanted a sister, too."

"Why didn't you?" she asks. "For us, it was the one-child policy. I was born after it started."

"I don't know," I say. "I never asked my mother. I suppose I always assumed she thought I was enough."

Fangli leans over and touches my hand. "You were. I would have loved to have known my mother."

We sit quietly for a moment. Then she speaks again. "Would you like to come to the show tomorrow?" she asks. "It may be an experience for you to see what it's like."

I nearly jump out of my chair. "One hundred percent. Am I going as a regular guest or your makeup artist?"

"Guest." She tilts her head as she assesses me. "Mei will get you a ticket and we'll go separately so we're not seen together but it should work."

"I haven't seen a play in ages," I say.

Fangli pulls the celery toward her. "Your dossier said you acted in school."

"I did and I went to shows all the time." I trace my finger around the table. "When Mom started getting sicker, it got harder for me to go out."

"Physically leave the house, or find the energy to do it?"

"Energy. I had to decide on the show, get the tickets... I was so overwhelmed that it was too much." I shake my head. "That sounds dumb when I say it out loud, that it was too hard for me to buy a ticket off a website."

But Fangli is beside me, nodding. "It happens to me," she says. "There's too much choice, and since all of them have merit, it's exhausting to choose. At least I have Mei to help me whittle them down."

"Outsourcing decisions." I take back the celery from her and start eating. "I like it."

"Most of my days are managed for me," she says. "I'm told where to go and someone else gets me there. I wonder if it's made it hard for me to think for myself."

Fangli's face drops with a sudden blank expression, as if introspection has taken over. I gave a little wave. "Hey. Earth to Fangli."

"I was trying to think of the last time I made a big choice," she says. Then she grins. "It was when I decided to come after you."

"Not even acting in this play?"

"I wouldn't have considered doing it without Sam. He was the one they approached first and he thought it would be fun for both of us. They agreed, and so did I." She wipes her fingers on a napkin. "Sam usually gets what he wants. I think it's the streak of Lu Lili in him."

"His mother."

Fangli's huge eyes say it all. "She's an über-diva. Absolutely in a class of her own."

"Have you ever worked with her?"

"Once." Fangli pulls her robe closer around her shoulders and speaks in the hushed tones you'd use to describe a force of nature. "Lili was magnificent. She never raised her voice, not once, but you knew exactly when you made a mistake. She knew how every scene should be shot, the best angles and lighting. And she was right, every time. Poor Sam."

"Why poor Sam?"

"She doesn't run her personal life any differently than her professional one. She's tried to push him into countless projects, and even if he says no to most, he has to agree to some for the sake of family peace." She glances at the clock. "I should be going. I'll make sure Mei gets you a ticket for the matinee. We don't have an evening show tomorrow. Sleep well."

She leaves and I go through my nighttime cleansing ritual. I instinctively hid the marks on my arm from Ellen Gao's one-woman fan club but now I examine them closely. She grabbed me hard enough to leave little half-moons from her nails. I shudder. Fame and money would be nice, but at what expense? That was a minor incident. This fame thing is nothing like what I thought it would be.

July 3

GOING TO A PLAY!

EVENT NIGHT
PREPARATION
(AT LEAST ONE HOUR)

Twenty-Three

The theater is within walking distance of the hotel, and I leave a bit early to take in the sun on my way there. It's a beautiful day, with a sky blue enough to be in postcards.

It takes my eyes a minute to adjust to the dim theater lobby after the summer sun's bone-white gleam. I've been here before, but even if I hadn't, it's exactly what you'd expect a theater to look like, with dark wood, red carpeting, and gilt fixtures. Mei set me up with a great ticket in the middle of the orchestra section and strict instructions to keep on the fake eyeglasses she's provided. An usher hands me a program as I make my way to the red velvet seat and I tilt the booklet at an awkward angle to catch enough light to read before the play starts. I've read the script so I skip the synopsis to spend an extra minute checking the bios. Sam's wearing a black collared shirt and a huge grin, while Fangli has a sly expression and her hair tumbling around her shoulders.

The seats fill up rapidly, and after the warnings to turn off phones and that filming is prohibited, followed by the Indigenous land acknowledgment, the lights dim and the curtain rises to thunderous applause.

The first act takes place in a Chinese restaurant, with white-draped tables and black cane-backed chairs. Fangli appears wearing a blue dress with a tight waist, and her waved hair makes her look like a 1940s pinup. She is perfection as she moves around the chairs. Even silent, she manages to keep my attention with her sheer presence.

Then Sam comes onto the stage. I do my best to not stare at him, but it's like trying to avoid gazing at the sun during an eclipse. I know I shouldn't and that it will be bad for me, but I can't resist a little peek because surely that can't do any damage.

He's dressed in a dark-gray suit, and they've styled his hair to reveal his face instead of his usual tousled look. When he tugs on the bottom of the vest, I add it immediately to the hot-things-hot-men-do list, which I fully recognize is a hot-things-Sam-does list.

Together, the two of them weave a story with more than their words. Their every action adds layers. I watch with avid eyes as they build their relationship around a multitude of secrets—his upcoming secret mission in Southeast Asia, her absent and despised fiancé.

Before the intermission, their chemistry has become a tangible thing, drawing in the audience. Fangli-as-Lin is powerfully attracted to Sam-as-Jimmy, although she knows he's hiding something from her. Jimmy feels the same and is finding it difficult to resist her. I watch him, barely breathing, as Lin reaches out to touch his lapel and he moves from her with a quick step to lean against the wall.

Then the lights come up and the crowd relaxes in their seats with a collective sigh. The people around me file out in search of wine and washrooms, and I check my phone to distract myself from visions of a gray-suited Sam dancing in my eyes.

There's a text from Mei. Change to tonight's event. Attending children's hospital for a meet and greet before gala. Leave one hour early.

Got it, I send back. Thanks for the ticket, the seat is great.

Silence. I'm left with the uncomfortable sense that I've offended her, even over text. I don't see how—I've been faithful about doing my best, which I thought made her life easier. I'll try to do better; that might help soften her.

The woman beside me sits back down with a sippy cup of white wine and turns to her friend, who is also holding a clear lidded plastic cup. They're loud enough that I suspect those aren't the first they've had.

"Beautiful story," says the one next to me as she adjusts her polo shirt.

"A bit unrealistic." Her friend downs at least a third of the glass in a gulp. "All the Asians were put in camps during the war, so there's no way they could volunteer to fight."

"Really? I had no idea. You learn something every day."

My eyes shift over to them as if magnetized. I can't believe anyone is this ignorant of history but I guess you care less if you don't consider it your story.

"I knew a Chinese girl from book club." The woman nods confidently as if this has given her the equivalent of a PhD in East Asian studies.

I have to interrupt despite Mei's caution to keep a low profile. "Sorry, but that's not true." I settle the glasses more firmly on my face and lean over. "There's a historical note in the program."

Their faces freeze. "Why, thank you, dear," says the one woman. That's it. They turn back to each other, politely ignoring me, and chat quietly. Then I hear "The lead is quite attractive for an Oriental man."

"He sure is. I wasn't sure about these last-minute tickets instead of a musical but I suppose it's quite cultural."

They're beyond redemption. I let them go back to their wine.

The curtain rises and the action blasts the two women right out of my mind. Much like when I watched *The Pearl Lotus*, I find it hard to stop watching Sam. He's utterly compelling, and I remember what he said about navigating through an environment instead of simply getting from A to B. He's not fluid like a dancer but so controlled his every movement is poetry. The Sam I watch on that stage is not like the Sam I know, and I wonder how he channels his energy. I'm awed at his ability to physically conjure emotions, and I force myself to stay away from thoughts of what he's like in bed. It's hopeless because when he reaches for Fangli and moves her against the wall, capturing her with his arms on each side of her head, Sam is so convincing I believe he'll do anything to get Fangli to submit body and soul.

No, Jimmy. Jimmy and Lin, not Sam and Fangli.

When the show ends, there's a standing ovation when the actors come out to bow, and I go out at the other end of the row so I can avoid the two women.

I leave the theater in a pensive mood. That I'm harboring these emotions toward Sam is unwelcome, and I need the steady beat of my steps to get my thoughts in order. The first and most obvious reason is that I don't have a thing for Sam at all but for what he represents. Put any rich, handsome, and famous man in his place and I'd have the same skin prickles, like getting in an overly hot bath when you're cold.

Except I was at a premiere last night with several rich, handsome, and famous men in attendance and I barely noticed. Apparently Chris Evans was there. Normally, Chris Evans being within a kilometer radius of me would have been enough to trigger a DEFCON level status change in my hormones but I didn't know until I checked the celebrity gossip pages this morning. This is *Captain America* we're talking about, the best Chris.

If I accept it *is* Sam, then what is it about him? I pause to think this through and then duck into a little park to stop getting jostled by the crowd and take a sunny seat on a peeling wooden bench. Being with Sam, despite his many faults and failings, makes me feel alive. That strange low-level yearning for something different, something more, quiets when I'm with him. I'm alert.

More unwelcome news because if there's one thing I've been taught, it's that you find meaning and value from life through yourself, not a man or anyone. Independence is the pinnacle, and while a man can be a companion, it's a grave mistake to think he can be your center. You should never be a satellite orbiting your own life. Mom drilled this in me from childhood but did she live that philosophy? She was bereft when Dad died.

I jump up and stride away as if to physically leave these thoughts on the seat next to me. I'm exaggerating all this. Sam is in my life for another six weeks, maximum, and so far there have been zero signs of him reciprocating any interest, as I saw firsthand the other day. I need to redirect those energies into a more positive project, like my Eppy planner.

On my way back to the Xanadu, my phone buzzes with a text from Anjali. Hey.

Yo yo yo, I write back.

Anjali: Are you kidding?

Me: All the cool kids say it. What's up?

Anjali: Rough day, she writes.

That's not usually like her. I hesitate. Can I call you?

Anjali: Yeah.

She picks up on the first ring. "What's going on?" I ask.

"Work stuff." She sounds down. "This life coach. I'm trying to integrate what he says into my work style."

"Is it not working?"

"I get what he's doing," she says. "I need to tone it down to get shit done, give people space to make mistakes."

"I hear a but."

"I feel like an imposter," she says, each word dragged out. "It doesn't feel like me. Do you think I was such a jerk before?"

"No. It's not bad to be assertive, confident, and open about your feelings. I thought you liked the coach."

"I did at first, but now I don't know." She sounds discouraged. "At work, they keep second-guessing me. That's never happened before."

"You're a project manager. It's your job to make decisions and get the work done."

"I know."

"Anjali, you know you can stop, right?"

"What?"

"This life coach. He's not, like, a god. You can thank him kindly for his time and stop seeing him."

There's a long silence. "He was so helpful. It made me think more deeply about things."

"You've gotten what you can, and now you can leave."

"I can, can't I?" She sounds a bit happier.

"Yup."

"I've got two more sessions prepaid," she says practically.

"Tell the guy it's not working and to change his approach, then. You're paying him."

"Thanks, Gracie." Anjali sounds relieved. "I needed to talk this out."

"No problem."

We talk a bit more and hang up. Then it dawns on me that was the first time we've talked on the phone. We always text or meet up. I feel like I've unlocked a friendship achievement.

The rest of the day passes peacefully. I go for a run, and the physical activity, which I've been missing, does wonders for my mood. Could this whole Sam crush thing be the result of not getting enough exercise?

I see Sam in the hallway as I come back up, and there's no disguising my sweaty and matted-haired self. He's in a black ball cap pulled low and his hair covers his eyes.

"We should talk about the event tonight," he says as a greeting. He follows me in and grabs a drink out of my fridge as I pour a glass of water. If I don't drink at least two, I'll get a brutal dehydration headache.

"Is Fangli out?"

"She'll be back before we need to leave." He takes off the cap and runs his hand through his hair. "What did you think of today?"

"It was amazing. Were you channeling that detective in *Gold Road* deliberately?"

He puts the bottle down with a clink on the table. "What do you mean?"

"The scene with Fangli, when you moved her against the wall."

"Yes, I know it." He makes an impatient gesture. Is this a big deal? I guess it is.

"It was the same thing you did in *Gold Road.*"

"That movie is eight years old."

"Well, I only saw it the other day," I defend myself.

"What else did you see?"

"Nothing. It's not like I studied you." Although, since I've seen enough of his movies to pick up his tells, I feel I'm well on my way to a graduate degree in Samonomics.

He's about to press me when the phone rings and I grab it. One of the nurses from Mom's home tells me that she's been agitated all day. "I know how busy you are, but it might soothe her if you came by, even if you can only manage a few minutes."

"Of course."

I hang up and check the time. It's already four, so I do some quick calculations. If I take a cab...but rush hour's starting. The TTC will be faster. "I need to see my mom," I tell Sam. "I can get ready there and meet you at the hospital."

"There's no way you'll make it," he says. "I'll come with you."

"What? No."

"It's easiest and the most effective use of our time."

"Think this through. Why would Sam Yao, celebrity, be visiting my mom? With me as Fangli?"

"Well, and what would Fangli be doing taking the subway in full gala dress?" He grins and those dimples appear like magic. "I bet you dinner no one will notice. Do your makeup and put on your Fangli clothes for when we leave the hotel."

"You're sure you want to go? We might get rumbled."

"As I said, this will be more efficient so it makes practical sense." He gives me a look. "Trust me. I'm not reckless."

He must be confident if he's willing to risk blowing my Fangli cover, so I don't back down from the bet. "You're on."

"Pack a hat and change of clothes." He raises his eyebrows. "I'll start thinking about where you'll take me for dinner."

Twenty-Four

S am leaves and I turn to the dress sector of the closet to find one I can easily change in and out of while in the car. It's hard to focus, because although this isn't the first time the home has called about coming to calm Mom down, it feels odd, more urgent. I bite down hard when it occurs to me that her Alzheimer's might be getting worse. The doctors warned me to watch for mood and personality changes and I thought I had. Had I been so concerned with this Fangli plan that I hadn't noticed?

When I finally find a dress, I have to wipe my clammy palms on my thighs before touching the delicate material. I pull it out and check it quickly, eager to get going. It has a tight waist and full skirt but the real draw is that it zips up the side, so I don't need Sam's help to change. The makeup and wig go on quickly. I'm getting used to it.

Sam arrives—with his key, which I had him get back from Mei in case of future emergencies—as I'm stuffing a skirt and tank into a backpack.

He gives my bag an incredulous look.

"You can't seriously think you can walk out wearing that evening dress with a nylon backpack slung over your shoulder," he says.

"How else do I pack my clothes?"

Like a magician, he displays a plain leather tote large enough to transport a small farm animal.

"Hermès," he says as he puts in my clothes, as if this explains the gargantuan size. Maybe it does. "Where's the hat? You'll need that to try to cover your face when we get to your mother because you're fully made up."

I give it to him. "What about you?"

"I'm fine. Fangli came back about fifteen minutes ago, so we're good to go. Luckily she was early." He looks me over and I wonder what Fangli appearance checklist he runs over before he gives a single approving nod.

We head down to the car and this time I'm able to simply move through the lobby without obsessing about my walk. I'm too worried about Mom to care—why's she so upset? Sam hands me into the car and I give the driver the address.

Then I turn to Sam. "Since I'm changing in the car, won't the driver notice that I'm not Fangli when we get to the home?"

"I've known Gregor a long time," Sam says. "He can keep a secret."

"Good." I pull off the wig and ruffle up my hair. "I need some privacy."

He turns to look out the window, which is luckily tinted.

"Can you cover your eyes?"

"Really?"

"Please just do it."

He shoots me a glance but then covers his face like a child playing hide-and-seek. I get changed in stages to maximize the coverage, like at a badly designed gym where the door to the change room could open any moment and reveal you to the world. On goes the skirt, pulled up under the dress. I unzip the top, turn to face the other way and pull on the tank top. I take off the dress, yank on my hat, and I'm Gracie again, or Gracie with fantastic contour.

"Your turn," I say.

He turns around and peers at me. "You smeared your lipstick."

"I did?"

"Here." He reaches out with his thumb and rubs under my lip.

Oh. My. His touch is gone almost as soon as it happens, but the echo of it thrums through my body.

"It's gone now," he says, looking at my lip.

"Good?" I clear my throat. "What about you?"

He shrugs off the blazer and the collared shirt to reveal a white T-shirt that he untucks, then pulls out a smaller bag from his huge bag. Inside are a pair of sneakers. He bends over to put them on, swears as his seat belt ricochets him back, manages his shoes, and then pulls his own hat down to shade his eyes. Transformation complete, he lifts his hands as if to invite comment and I have to laugh.

"You honestly think no one will recognize you?"

"You need to see your mother, don't you? It's the only way we can do that and get to the gala. The risk is negligible."

"Is it?"

"How many Asians will we see?"

I think about the home. "My mom."

"Yeah. I think it'll be fine." He smiles.

"I'll introduce you as a friend from work who gave me a ride," I say. "She doesn't know I was fired, so keep that quiet. In fact, best if you don't talk at all."

"Why didn't you tell her?"

"I don't want to upset her." I look out the window, feeling the worry rise and dip as I tell myself that her mood might have passed by the time I arrive, then convince myself that she's in serious distress and the home is downplaying it so as not to worry me and her Alzheimer's is getting worse and I'll need to find her more help and...

Catastrophizing is such a bitch.

Sam touches my hand briefly and begins humming quietly as he repacks his bag. I start humming along with him to cover the rotating thoughts in my head, getting distracted by knowing the song but being unable to put a name to it. Soon we're in a humming war, each of us trying to hum louder than the other until I slap my leg in triumph, letting out a small yelp.

"'Girls & Boys' by Blur," I announce.

"Took you long enough." He grins.

"There used to be a club that did Brit pop nights and they played this every time," I say. "Had dollar shots, too."

"Not sure if that sounds appealing or dangerous."

"Little bit of A, little bit of B." I sigh with nostalgia. "It was such a dingy club and they had those blacklights so if you wore a white bra it would show through your shirt."

Sam's eyes drift down but then snap up to my face. "I never had to worry about that."

"Yeah." I shrug. "Not like I go to those places anymore."

"I never went."

I frown. "Are there no clubs in China?"

"Of course there are but I always had to go to ones that were good for my image." He looks out the window.

"Then no dollar shots. Bummer."

"Definitely not."

"I was kidding about it being a bummer," I assure him. "I mean, at the time, it was fun to get drunk and grind on the dance floor with random people you'd never see again, but cheap booze hangovers are a real pain."

He groans. "Not helping."

I know he's trying to make me laugh and it helps get me through the drive, even though my knee is jiggling as I try to chill out. Mom's not hurt. She's upset. The doctors said this can happen. It's not good but it's not unusual.

We turn the corner and the dread returns. "We're here."

He catches the change in my tone and nods. He gives my hand a soft touch and holds the door open for me as we enter the home. I try to keep from running in the hall.

"You said my mother was agitated?" I ask when I arrive breathless at the desk.

"It's been a bad day for her," says the nurse. She glances at Sam and then ignores him. "Is it an anniversary? Something that would trigger her?"

"No, I don't..." I stop, appalled. It's the anniversary of my dad's death. "I'll go see her," I whisper.

How could I have forgotten? Guilt sickens me. Sam waits until we've cleared the desk to touch my shoulder. "What's wrong?"

With her dementia, I can't believe Mom remembers what today is, but I suppose some dates are seared on your mind forever. Or, in my case, not. "My father died ten years ago today. It's why she's upset. I should have been with her."

"Gracie." This time he takes my hand in his. "You're here now. That's what matters."

I want to believe him, but I can't. He keeps my hand in his as we go to Mom's room, where he releases it. "Work colleagues," he murmurs.

With a brief nod, I poke my face around the door. Mom is up and wandering around the room, arms clasped close to her chest. I must have made a noise because she looks up as Sam runs his hand down my back.

"Mom?"

She greets me with a burst of Chinese that I can't understand. "Mom, it's Gracie. You need to speak English, okay? Shuo Yingyu."

Mom sees Sam behind me and her eyes widen. "Xiao He?"

This I understand. "No." I nearly lunge forward. "This is Sam, a friend. From work. He's a friend from work. Work friend."

To Sam, I say, "She thinks you're her little brother."

Sam comes into the room and reaches his hand out. "Ni hao. Wo jiao Sam. Wo shi ni nu'er de tong shi." I bless the app because Sam spoke slow enough to let me understand what he said.

Mom blinks again. "Ni hao?" She glances at me. "Gracie? Sweetie?"

"Sam dropped me off. It was on his way," I say.

"He's a friend? Chinese?" She sizes him up. "Married?"

"Mom!"

Sam laughs. "Only to my work."

She clucks at him. "Do you like my Gracie's hair? She cut it the other day. So short."

"Gracie is lovely." He says it simply as he looks at me. "You are lucky to have her as a daughter."

She nods, satisfied with this polite answer because what else can the poor guy say, and reverts to Mandarin. Sam listens before he turns to me. "Your mother wants to show me a photo of her brother."

I go to the cabinet and pull out the tattered photo album. Before Mom came into the home, I made digital copies of all the photos and have another identical album ready if something happens to this one. I wait until she sits down and wave Sam to the seat across from her before I pass over the album and sit down on the bed.

Mom's crooked finger jabs down at a photo, and I lean over to see a man who looks like Sam only because they're both Chinese men. Sam gives her the same smile as her brother does in the photo, and she slaps his leg and laughs.

"Gracie is much like Xiao He." Mom reaches over and pats my hand like she did when I was small. "Much integrity. True to himself, with a core of rectitude."

Such an old-fashioned word and my face flames because in thirty minutes, Rectitude Gracie is going to leave and put on a wig in a car so she can trick a bunch of kids into believing she's a film star.

"Tell me more about him," says Sam.

"Ah, he was an engineer. Smart, smart. We were all very proud of him."

"Does he live in China?"

Her smile fades. "He died in an industrial accident after Gracie was born. She was named after him."

"I didn't know that." How could I not know that?

"He, for harmony, and there must be harmony to have grace. I owed him much." She shakes her head. "The past remains in the past."

The bell rings in the hall and Mom perks up. At the home, meals are what tether her and she gets upset if she needs to wait, so I tell Sam I'll be back in a minute. Dinner has wiped thoughts of Sam's singledom status out of Mom's mind and she walks eagerly to the dining hall after giving him only a cursory farewell nod.

I decide not to mention Dad as she's better now and instead give her a kiss and greet the dinner ladies at her table. They all fuss over each other, making sure they have forks and water.

Sam is flipping through the album when I return. "I don't understand how you can look so much like Fangli when this is your father."

The page is open to a classic picture of Dad from the early 1990s. His reddish hair is permed and he wears a turtleneck and fanny pack, arm slung around a young and happy Agatha who only reaches to his shoulder. Mom's wearing bike shorts and an oversize sweatshirt. What an era.

"He always said he was happy I took after my mother instead of him because she was the most beautiful woman in the world."

Sam smiles and hands me the closed album to tuck away. "They were very much in love."

"They were." My voice catches as I hug the album. It's silly but I'm loath to hide the album back in the dark drawer, like I'm tucking away Dad's memory. "The money from this job for Fangli... I want it for Mom, to move her into a better place. It's not because I'm greedy."

Sam comes over and pulls me into his chest. "Gracie." His voice is low, and for a brief moment, I let my eyes close and simply feel. On the day he died, Dad held me fiercely, as if he couldn't bear to let me go. He'd lost so much weight from the treatment that his bones almost creaked as he gripped my shoulders.

"Ten years ago when Dad hugged me, I didn't know that was the last time I'd have his arms around me," I say into Sam's chest. "I didn't *know*." Why didn't I know? I should have sensed it, I should have acknowledged that I'd never feel his touch again. It passed me by and I'd never get that chance back. There's no redo for that moment.

"Gracie." Sam brings his hand up and rests it on my hair but doesn't say more than my name.

I can't cry. I cried so much for Dad over the years that right now my dry eyes are burning. My breath goes hot against Sam's shirt and I turn my head slightly to the side. I'm not panting but my heart is racing and he runs his hand over my head with slow and deliberate strokes to calm me. I look at the wall but I can't see a thing. I'm only existing.

I don't know how long it is before I break away from him. "We should go," I say, rubbing my cheek. "Oh God, my makeup."

Sam's shirt is stained with a perfect imprint of my face. He looks down, and when he meets my eyes, his are lit with gentle laughter. "This is more than I wear on the stage."

"That's my special occasion face," I say. "Or was."

I don't look at the album as I put it away. "Thank you," I say to the doorway instead of Sam. I don't want to look at him. I'm embarrassed for him to have seen me like that.

"You're welcome." That's all he says, and I decide to leave it at that and walk out the door.

Twenty-Five

Gregor is down the street where I insisted he wait with the car so the nurses don't see us get in and become suspicious. It's a little too fancy even for an Uber Black, that great democratizer of swish rides. Once we're in the car, my composure returns.

"I brought an extra shirt in case," Sam says. He picks up the collared shirt he'd worn down to the car and puts it aside.

Then he strips his T-shirt off. Right there in front of me, Sam Yao is shirtless and he doesn't even care. Half-naked, he rummages in that gigantic tote before murmuring in triumph and pulling out a folded black shirt that he shakes out with a snap. I know it's rude but I have to stare because I have never seen a body like this in real life. He's sculpted, his arms firm with muscle and his shoulders wide. Little muscles, I don't even know what they're called, ripple down his ribs. After he pulls on the shirt, he lifts up his hips to tuck it in—my mouth might have dropped open here—and then runs his hand through his hair.

"Shouldn't you get ready?" he asks.

I close my eyes to relive the memory of his chest. "Turn away."

He does and I reverse my technique of earlier, taking off the tank and pulling down the dress and patting it into place before I remove the skirt. The car seems too small and Sam very close.

I pull on the zipper but it sticks. "Damn."

"What?" Sam starts to turn around but I stop him.

"Don't look!"

"All that shifting around and you're not decent?"

I lift up my arm and crane my neck to see the zipper. I'm scared to pull too hard, in case I break it or rip the dress. There's only one choice. "I need a hand."

He gives a furtive look over his shoulder, as if he's not quite sure what level of undress I'm at. Confirming everything of importance is covered, he says, "Zipper?"

It's unfortunate that, unlike a zipper at the back, which would only show...my back, this zipper reveals my entire side between armpit and waist. He comes to sit beside me. "Raise your arm."

When he fiddles with the zipper, his fingers brush along my ribs, causing my skin to goose bump. *Please, please let him not notice. Please.* I gaze out the window as we go down University Avenue toward Hospital Row. "Some of the material is caught in the zipper," he mutters. "Give me a second."

He reaches one hand down inside the dress to try to wrestle it up. Now I have Sam's entire hand pressed against me and his head leaning so close his breath moves against the bare skin of my chest. Never have I been so glad to have put on deodorant.

"Got it," he says proudly. He tugs the zipper closed. My arm is held high where I had it out of the way as he worked, but since the blood's been running out of it, I lower it faster than I intend and end up with my arm landing over his shoulder, partially embracing him.

Although I expect him to move away, he doesn't. He doesn't do anything but look at me and I freeze.

"Sorry." I lurch back and scramble for my wig, which I jam on. "Better fix my makeup. Where are my shoes?" I'm rambling.

"Hold on." He stills me with a touch on my knee. "The wig is crooked."

He reaches up to tuck some of my hair under and then rearranges the haphazard hair helmet, his eyebrows angled down as he concentrates. Now he's definitely close enough to kiss and again, for a crazy moment, I wonder what would happen if I did.

It would be bad. I'm overthinking this the same way I did at the art gallery, seeing romantic opportunities only because I'm wishing them into being. He finishes with the wig and moves to his side of the car while I apply lipstick, blot it, and reapply it before powdering my face.

Finally, I push the hair so some stays in front of my shoulders as the rest hangs behind my back. Mei says it frames my face better. "Am I good?" I ask.

He shifts over and pulls the hair all behind my shoulders before moving to his original seat. "This is better," he says. "I can see your face."

I raise my eyebrows. "Since I'm trying to not have people focus on my face, don't you think the first one is preferable?"

"I like it this way."

Oh. *Oh.*

"Also," he adds, "you owe me dinner."

"What?"

"As I promised, no one recognized me today." He gives a pleased nod.

"Give it twelve hours, and if it hasn't shown up on social media, I'll concede."

Gregor pulls up to the hospital entrance where we're met by a tall woman with a cell phone and a clipboard who introduces herself as Jessica. "The kids are excited to see you, Mr. Yao," she says in a warm voice. "I can't tell you how much we appreciate you doing this, especially so last minute. As requested, there are no media but we'd like to take a few photos for the kids."

"That's fine," he says. Sam, for his part, is legitimately excited at the idea of meeting kids and peppers the PR woman with questions. How many kids? What ages? What should he be aware of? Is he allowed to touch them or should he only wave? He pauses at the entrance to sanitize his hands at the dispenser and I follow suit. It's a hospital, after all, and the kids don't need our germs.

I've never been in a children's hospital before so I let the two of them go ahead of me and chat as I examine the atrium, which is painted with murals and has cartoon characters on the signs. Two people pass holding hands and a woman hugs a little baby wearing a helmet to her chest. I'm harboring a lot of emotions from earlier and look carefully at people's faces. Some are interested in the two people in dressy clothes walking through—Jessica's attitude screams *famous people alert*—but mostly the people we pass are involved in their own worlds and their own families. We take an elevator up to a windowed room packed with kids and parents as well as foosball tables and games.

"This is where the older kids can come and hang out," says Jessica.

One of the kids has an IV pole draped with lines and lines of brightly colored beads. "Are those significant?" I ask.

"They're called bravery beads. The kids earn them, one for every procedure or event they undergo."

Sam and I both stop dead. "That child has many," he says. "Hundreds."

"They're tough kids," Jessica says simply. "Are you ready?"

I hold back because this is Sam's show, and the kids are here to meet a real-live action hero, not a fake movie star. He stands outside to wait for his entrance, his entire face lit up. One of the kids has been nominated as the MC, and he makes the introduction better than any UFC promoter could; we can hear his booming voice in the hallway. By the time he's described one of Sam's fight scenes in comprehensive detail, complete with sound effects, the entire room is laughing and cheering.

"Please welcome Sam Yao!"

Sam leaps into the room and lands in a fighting stance, causing chaos to ensue. I can't stop smiling and laughing, and Jessica grins from ear to ear. "They told me he wouldn't have time to come, but I knew he would," she confided, her dark eyes glowing.

"How did you know?"

"Laurence, the boy who did the introduction, wrote him a letter that we sent to a contact at the theater. I cried when I read it. There was no way Mr. Yao could have said no, not if he read it." She nods into the room. "These kids miss so much of life. Come on in."

Sam is determined to meet every person in the room, and instead of surrounding him, the crowd guides him so he can spend a private moment with all the kids. One girl, sitting in a wheelchair, covers her face with shyness and Sam kneels beside her. Whatever he whispers into her ear causes her to giggle hysterically, which makes him laugh, a big open thing that I'd never heard before.

"Are you Wei Fangli?" I look down to see a small blond boy with big glasses staring at me. I crouch down, blessing the full skirt, so we're the same height.

I can't bring myself to say I am, so instead I say, "What's your name?"

"Laurence."

"Laurence! I was impressed with your introduction. You're a big fan of Sam's." I lean in. "Me, too." That's true enough.

"I didn't know you would come." His blue eyes behind the glasses are huge and his skin so translucent I can see the veins tracing beneath.

"I hope it's okay that I did."

"Wo hen kaixin."

Thank God I understand that and can say, "Ni de Zhongwen shuo de hen hao."

"I'm learning so I don't have to read the subtitles of Sam's movies," he says with pride. "I have a lot of time here at the hospital."

"What about his movies is appealing?" My thighs ache and I lower myself to my knees.

"He's real, don't you think?" He bites his lips as he considers his words. "And good. Even when he beats people up, it's to protect others. Not to be mean or show off."

"A very decent trait."

"I think you're the same in your movies. When you sent Sam on that mission in that movie to die, you didn't want to. Why did you?"

"In *The Pearl Lotus*." I think about how to describe it to this child and then decide what he thinks is more important. "Why do you think the empress did that?"

"Well, you loved Sam," he says promptly. "He loved you, too."

"The characters did in the movie," I clarify. "Yes."

"I don't think you should have," he says earnestly. "You didn't even talk to him about it. He might have had more ideas."

"That would have been smarter," I say. "You should write your own movie."

He frowns. "What do you mean?"

"You can write a movie. A screenplay of your own, telling the story you want. Or a play if you want actors to do it on a stage at a theater, like Sam is doing now."

Laurence's eyes are huge. "People do that?"

"Sure they do. It takes a lot of work, but you can do it."

The boy looks down at the floor. A woman comes up and smiles at me. "Mom," he says, adjusting his glasses. "Wei Fangli says I can write a screenplay. Is that true? I can do that? She's in the movies, so it must be true, right? Is it? She wouldn't lie to me, would she?"

I'm about to explain to the woman but she's busy nodding. "Sure you can, baby."

"Will you show me how?" Laurence turns to me with huge eyes.

"I've never written one," I say. That at least isn't lying to the kid. "An actor's job is to act out what you write. I can tell you one thing that might help. Do you want to hear it?"

He nods.

"No one else can be you. No one else can tell your story like you. You are unique, so write the movie you want to see."

"No one can tell my story," he repeats with wonder.

"Only you."

He beams at me. "I'm going to start right away. I already have an idea about a dragon. Do you think Sam will star in it?"

"Will I star in what?" Sam comes up beside me and Laurence's eyes go so big they engulf his little face.

"The movie I'm going to write. Fangli says I should. Do you think I should?"

"Yes." There's no hesitation. "You do it and then send it to me."

Behind Laurence, his mom ducks her head as the boy screeches in joy. I see the tears on her cheeks.

"We need to head out but can I give you a hug?" asks Sam. "Thank you for inviting me."

Both Sam and I hug Laurence, who is so fragile I'm scared to hold him too tightly. He's like a tiny bird. His mother walks us out. "Thank you for coming," she says quickly.

"I hope I didn't overstep by suggesting he write his own work," I say. I'm filled with regret that I said something wrong.

She shakes her head. "To have a project to absorb him will be wonderful."

The mom disappears and Jessica leads Sam and me back out to the entrance. She's thrilled with how it went, and I let Sam deal with the small talk because I'm racked with guilt about Laurence. He thought I was Fangli. It didn't matter that a bunch of rich art collectors or movie industry people or randoms on the street think I'm Fangli, but this does. *She wouldn't lie to me, would she?*

We thank the woman and get into the car for the gala. Unlike me, Sam is jazzed by meeting the kids and can't stop smiling. The event is down near the water at an art gallery/event space, and I pray there's no art I need to have intellectual opinions about. This day has drained me, and I press my forehead against the window.

"Are you ill?" asks Sam.

"Thinking," I say. "About the kids."

"They were great." He fixes his collar and smiles so big his dimples appear. "You did well to suggest writing to that boy. Laurence.

I could see in his face that it was like a door in his mind had been opened."

"He wanted to do it because Wei Fangli told him he could," I burst out. "I'm not Fangli. It was a fraud."

Sam's dimples vanish. "The trigger is irrelevant. Once the idea you can do something occurs to you, that's all that matters. Who cares who twists the handle for Laurence as long as he can walk through the door?"

"It's not right," I say, digging in. "The ends don't justify the means."

"I disagree," he says. "A positive outcome can come from a negative path."

Deciding this conversation is about to devolve into an unwinnable *does not, does so* argument, I grit my teeth and let it go, in part because this is a deep philosophical debate and I need time to organize my points. I need an Eppy for that as well, a way to neatly categorize the swirl in my brain and formulate the mess of impressions and reflections into clear and arguable ideas.

Sam has already moved on to remind me who we'll be meeting at the gala and I try to focus on him. We're there to represent the *Operation Oblivion* cast since the director couldn't make it, and Mei had confirmed that none of Fangli's personal contacts are on the guest list. If arriving at the movie premiere was a solid eight on the stress scale, this hovers near a three.

"Gracie?" Sam peers at me. "Are you listening?"

"Yes." I wasn't. Maybe Fangli was right. Laurence and other fans want the idea of Fangli, what they project on her.

"What was I talking about?"

I take a guess. "The guest list."

Sam looks suspicious but we arrive before he can reply. He helps me out of the car, and I make sure my smile is calibrated to show how happy I am to be here. There's a photographer—I now understand that every event hires their own photographer—and this one is stunned silent when Sam looks at her, her camera lowering so she can see him without a filter.

We walk into the event space, which has been decorated with huge floral garlands woven with dyed daisies that sweep across the ceiling and are draped down the walls, interspersed with long fringes hanging from the ceiling and lit from within to look like they glow. There are pastel neon lights along the floor. The art direction must have been to make it look like a unicorn is hosting a wedding at club night, and I wonder why they didn't give the money they spent on those decorations directly to the hospital. We wander up to the silent auction tables, covered with tablets to enter bids. I try not to choke when I see that minimum bids are in the thousands or tens of thousands, for everything from a cruise (be the private guest of a bank CEO) to a spa week for the winning bidder and three guests.

It's a lot. It's too much. I need to take a breath.

"Excuse me," I say to Sam. "I'll be right back."

He follows my glance to the washroom and nods. A minute later, I'm alone in a stall and breathing in the light lavender scent of the diffusers on the counters. I can't stop thinking about Laurence's expression. In the car, Sam asked who cared how the handle was twisted.

Me. I care.

Mom said my uncle He had rectitude. I pull out my phone and quickly google to confirm it's what I think: moral righteousness. A sense of right and wrong and the willingness to act on it. I did not show rectitude today. I have not been showing rectitude since I took the job with Fangli. Is this the person I wanted to be? I need the money for Mom, but I know if I told her what I was doing to get it, she would be horrified.

Worse, she would be disappointed in me.

The door opens and I realize that if my university years have taught me anything, it's that although bar washrooms have witnessed many an existential/love crisis, they aren't great places to have them. I check my face in my phone and go out to wash my hands. I might not have shown any ethical morals earlier, but my business morals know that I made a deal to pretend to be Fangli and being present at this event is part of the job. I can have my meltdown later, I tell myself as I push my hair behind my shoulders.

Once I force myself into the right headspace, the gala goes surprisingly well. Despite my dark night of the soul, I'm able to channel Fangli so smoothly that Sam feels confident enough to leave me now and then so we can stop our codependent orbiting. A few people speak to me in Mandarin, but when I answer in English with my explanation, they take it in good humor. No one touches me. Todd's not there. No one asks for an autograph or a photo. The food is tasty and I leave the carrots on the side. The speeches are even good because they're about the kids. I don't drink, but holy God, do I want to. I decide to empty that minibar when I get home.

So I do.

Twenty-Six

My close friend hangxiety visits with a vengeance at five in the morning, yanking me into total wakefulness with its grabby hands. What did I do? What did I say? At least I had the foresight to hide my phone before I opened that first tiny vodka bottle so I don't need to worry about discovering humiliating and misspelled drunken texts.

I groan into the pillow and try to ignore the parade of images that trot through my mind. But I can't. It's not what I did while I was drinking that's affecting me; it's what led up to me opening that fridge in the first place. I can still feel Dad's phantom arms around me, but when he looks at me, it's with Laurence's huge eyes, sparkling with excitement at the prospect of writing a movie for his favorite actor. I pull the pillow over my face and nearly hyperventilate from stress and lack of oxygen.

I need to tell Fangli that I can't do this anymore.

There's more than a month left on this contract but seeing it through to the end feels wrong, or at least wrong for the person I want to be. I wish it was more straightforward because I don't want to lie to people but I hate having to tell Fangli I'm breaking my promise.

Then there's the money. What Fangli offered is more than two years' salary and a lot to walk away from without a damn good reason. That's Mom's ticket out of Glen Lake.

Curling up on my side, I wrap my arms around a pillow. I want someone to talk to, but I can't tell Mom and Anjali made it clear from the beginning this was a bad idea. Sam and Fangli and Mei are obviously not good candidates for a heart-to-heart.

Like always, I'm on my own.

I turn over and hit the pillow with an impotent fist. I'm always on my own. In movies and books, women seem to have a "you go, girl" squad-posse of personal cheerleaders but that's not how my life turned out. Most of the time, it's not an issue but today all I want is a person, my person, who I can call and who will drop everything to be by my side. Anjali and I are getting closer but we're not at that level and I don't want to be a nuisance. I see it with Fangli and Sam and I want the same bond because if I had that person, I could ask them for advice. I could tell them that I was tired of blending in but that I don't want to stand out the way Fangli does. I'd ask them how I can be my best Gracie.

And they'd let me talk and soothe me and then probably tell me this isn't the way to do it.

What should I do, then?

I think of what Anjali would say. *You know what you need to do.*

I need to break the contract. I need to give up that money and the freedom it represents. I roll on my back. I don't want to do that at all but I can't feel like this anymore. I don't want to lie. I want to be like the man I was named after, a man who had principles and stuck to them. I want to start living my own life and stop putting it on hold for others.

That's enough to get me out of bed. I drink some water, pull on a robe, and go sit outside on the balcony, the early morning cool acting as a balm for the slight nausea remaining from my hangover. I watch the sunrise with my notebook on my lap, but my contentment with watching the waves on the lake only lasts a minute before I need to do something, anything.

I open the notebook to a fresh page and start to work. Of course, it goes well because life is like one of those stars you make by drawing a line up, down and to the sides. Love, health, wealth, family, and work sit on the angles, and if one goes well, it pulls to the side and the lines contract. Love and family life great? Bet you get fired. Excellent new job? Guess who's getting dumped. Everything hovering in equilibrium? Things are boring. It's like life doesn't have enough space to expand those lines so you can experience all you want all at once.

Once I'm happy with what I have, I put the notebook away and get a mint tea. Right now, my work—Eppy—is going well and contracting everything else, so I'll focus on that. So far I have the basic idea of it set out in spreadsheet form. It's basically a day calendar but with columns for different areas of your life, so you can see at a glance all the things you have to do and when you have time to complete tasks. I tap my finger on the table, thinking hard and glancing over the notes I made after talking to Sam. At least I can be grateful I have this. One thing is working.

When a pale light breaks across the horizon, I decide to go for a walk to clear my mind. The tension about Fangli is gone now because I know what I need to do. I'll tell her I'm sorry but I can't work for her anymore. Then I'll suggest a therapist. I won't hint; I'll tell her straight out the way I should have the other day.

I pull on a sweater and stuff my feet into a pair of sandals and my phone into my pocket. In the hallway, the only sound is my soles scuffling across the carpet and the ding of the elevator when it arrives. The concierge is busy making notes in a binder so I slip out without him seeing me.

I love walking around a city as it wakes up, the doors and windows winking open as if they're the eyes of the street. A few people are out even at this early hour, yawning over cups of coffee clutched in lazy hands. A woman walks down the middle of the sidewalk wearing last night's dress and a satisfied smile. She's limping a bit in her high heels and then she pauses, balances herself against the wall and unstraps them. When she passes me, she's walking barefoot and swinging her shoes as she hums this summer's Drake song.

"Gracie?" A man dressed all in black with a ball cap stops and pulls out his earbuds. It's Sam, sweaty from a morning run. "You're up early," he says.

"I couldn't sleep."

He peers at me and takes off his hat as if that will help him see better. "Are you well?"

Now. I should tell him right now so he can prepare Fangli. "Sam, I need to talk to you."

"What about?" He looks apprehensive, probably since nothing good ever comes after *we need to talk*.

A happy bop bursts from his hand and he lifts his phone. "Mei," he says. "Strange, she usually texts. Do you mind if I answer?"

I wave permission; I'm curious as well and this will give me time to think of how to phrase what I want to say. I need to get it out before I can feel bad about leaving them in the lurch. The key is to make it clear there's no changing my mind, that it's very unfortunate but there's simply nothing to be done about it. Sympathetic to the situation but matter-of-fact in how it's going to end.

Sam's expression darkens and I can hear a faint echo of Mei's voice. "Hao," he says. They talk for another minute and he disconnects.

"We have a problem," he says. "Fangli is sick."

"Like with the flu or something?"

He moves his phone from one hand to the other as he inspects the street. "Were you going back soon?"

I turn around and we start walking north back to the Xanadu. When the sun appears in a ball of orange-yellow at the cross street, I raise my hand to shadow my eyes. Sam fishes around in his pocket and hands me a pair of painfully stylish aviators. "Here."

They're gigantic on my face, which is exactly how I like them. He glances over and nods. "Nice," he approves.

"Why do you have sunglasses stuffed in your pocket when you're running?"

"In case it gets too sunny." He looks at me as if this should be obvious and coughs. "You look good. Keep them."

"I can get my own but thanks for the loan." I wriggle them up my nose until my eyelashes brush the lenses before pointing to a convenience store. "Let's grab some orange juice if she's sick."

He holds me back. "It's not that kind of sick."

There's a sinking feeling in my gut. "What do you mean?"

"Mei says she won't get out of bed. She won't answer besides saying she's too tired to work."

"Has she done this before?"

"Once during a movie but she wasn't due on set for a few days and she was better by then."

"What happened to make her better?"

He looks puzzled. "She said she needed sleep. That's it."

I'm so angry on Fangli's behalf I can barely breathe. I know Sam is doing the best he can, or says he is, but it's not enough and I think he knows it. That I'm complicit is not making me feel better.

He checks for traffic and steps into the street. "We need you to help us."

"No." I don't need to get any deeper into this. I made my decision.

"Please. You don't need to take her place onstage. We have an understudy and there's no show today."

I goggle at him. "Oh, good." Like that was ever going to happen.

"We were due to film a promo spot for the play for the second phase of the marketing campaign. It has to be done today."

"Why can't they use a clip like everyone else?"

He makes a face. "They want it live. It's part of a segment they do that has good social media reach. We're committed. There's not a lot of dialogue and you're quick enough to get it."

He might think I'm quick but I'm slow right now. "Are you saying you want me to pretend I'm Fangli to promote her own play?" This is too much. This is more chutzpah, cojones, and big bitch energy than I can conceive of, let alone muster.

"Yes."

"There's no way."

"You can do it. I've been watching you with people at the events."

"Sam, it's the dumbest idea I've ever heard."

"Fangli needs time." He hesitates. "Please. I need your help."

That activates my inner people pleaser, a practiced muscle that can flex stronger and faster than my fledgling vow to be better. God fucking damn it. My plans to give up my contract disintegrate but I grasp onto something I can do that might mitigate some of my dismay at being a lying liar who lies. This is it, I promise myself. Once this is over, I'll tell them I need to break the contract.

"On one condition."

"What?" Even in his desperation, he's cautious.

"You get Fangli help. A therapist."

His face clouds. "I've tried."

"You need to try harder," I say. "Look at her. She needs help."

"I can't force her."

I stop so I can turn, take off the sunglasses, and glare at him with full force. "Weren't you the one to tell me you were a great actor? Figure it out and convince her. Otherwise you can film this thing by yourself."

We walk another block before Sam turns to me. "It's a deal."

"Good."

We walk another block. "Sam, there's no way I can do this."

"We'll run it through a few times when we get back." He glances around, then reaches out to tug me close in a friendly hug. "There's no one I'd trust more to do this."

"What?" His arm feels like home.

He turns me around. "Gracie, you've managed to impersonate Fangli within days of studying her. You have a natural talent. I have faith in you."

"That's not what you said a month ago."

Sam sighs. "What do you want from me?"

"Oh, you know. An apology?"

"I apologize."

I think about this. "More specifically I'd like you to say you were wrong to judge me like that."

"I was absolutely wrong. I apologize."

"Because you didn't know me."

"Right, but before you get too far down this path, I should point out you thought I was an arrogant asshole."

I frown. "What's your point?"

"Judgment goes both ways, Gracie."

I give him a big smile. "But you see, *you* were wrong."

He bows his head. "You win. Now, will you please help me?"

"I'll try but I reiterate that I think this is a bad idea."

"It will be fine." He raises his eyebrow. "Plus, I can carry you."

"Okay."

"You know I have an Oscar."

"I know."

"Best Actor. First Chinese man to win one. Historic moment."

"Sam."

"So. I'm that good."

I only sigh.

Twenty-Seven

S am tells me not to go in to see Fangli and for this, at least, I
agree. During my bad days, the last thing I wanted was to have
someone hovering around me and I don't want to make things worse.
Instead I send her a text of heart emojis and hugs and then a video of
me blowing a kiss so she knows I'm thinking about her. After I send
it, the *Operation Oblivion* script arrives in my email.

Start at page 47, says Sam's message.

Luckily, I've already read it and seen the play. I close my eyes to
remember what happened in the scene. Fangli didn't say much, but
there was a lot of looking. A lot of very sensual looking that appears
extraordinarily stupid when I experiment in the mirror. I grab my
phone and google "acting basics." The first hit tells me how important
it is to learn my craft.

Checking the time confirms I am capital-S Screwed. I can't learn
the craft of acting to a professional level in ninety minutes.

I throw myself down on the couch and topple over so I'm lying
on my side. I'm about to humiliate myself in front of an entire film
crew with no hope of it being kept a secret because the point of this
fucking endeavor is to capture it for public viewing on a citywide and
potentially global scale.

Why is it so hard to say no to everyone except myself? No,
Fangli, I'm not going to pretend to be you. No, Sam, I'm not going to

try to act in your promo. No, Todd, I'm not going to let you intimidate me. Why am I so worried about what these people, all of whom are or were using me for their own ends without a care, think about me? I no longer live on the plains where ostracism from the group will cause me to starve. None of them care what I think about them.

My phone buzzes. It's Sam. **Here.**

I answer the door. "Isn't it easier to knock? Also, this is a bad idea."

"Texting is equally easy and then you don't need to look through the peephole. If you don't like the plan, I'm happy to hear an idea that results in us getting this shot today with Fangli or an appropriate designate." He points to the connecting door. "I went in to see her."

"And?"

"After some begging and threats, neither of which felt good or comfortable to do, Fangli agreed to see someone who makes emergency house calls. She'll be here in two hours."

"You did the right thing."

He closes his eyes and leans down to rest his cheek on my head as if I'm a pillow. I freeze. "I hope so."

When he straightens up, I leap across to the sink to fill a glass of water with the eagerness of someone escaping a desert. *Be normal, Gracie.* I grip the glass with numb fingers, hearing Sam speak in the disembodied, unintelligible voice of a Charlie Brown adult.

"And that should be it," concludes Sam. I haven't heard a thing.

At least Fangli will get help, which means I can stop being worried for her and transfer my full distress back onto me.

"Sam, I can't act."

"You've been acting for over two weeks, as I pointed out before. Are you listening? You're not even listening."

I'm spiraling. "That's not acting. I'm mimicking."

"Semantics and if you can do it there, then do it here."

"It won't work," I say immediately. "The makeup people will know I'm not her. They have to see my face up close."

"Luckily, Mei has a new woman in for today who's never met you. Nor has anyone on this crew."

That's convenient, but still. "It's a bad idea," I repeat. "It won't work."

"Why not?" He asks this as though earnestly interested in my answer.

Why not? *Just because* doesn't seem like the best answer but I also can't think of another one. Thinking an option won't work is the default mode of the Defeatists, which I've always considered to be my people. What if for once I thought it might?

I can copy Fangli. I can pretend to be her because I have been. If I can do that in real life, I can pretend to act as her acting, couldn't I? These mental gymnastics are exhausting and it's not made any better when I suddenly understand why I haven't dismissed Sam out of hand. It's because deep down, I want to try, the same way I wanted to try to be Fangli's double. I want to see if I can do it. The denials are mostly face-saving, so if I screw it up, I can point back as an *I told you so.*

I'm so tired of lying to myself.

I look at the script and back at Sam. "Tell me what to expect."

He's a good teacher and coaches me through the process. First we read it through, only the lines. Then the lines with the feeling. I channel my inner Fangli to do this. The final step is the acting. Sam stops me almost immediately.

"You're thinking too hard about how to be *like* the character," he tells me. "You need to feel it, to *be* the character. Close your eyes."

I close them but not all the way.

He makes an impatient sound. "Close them."

Then he comes behind me and puts his hands over my eyes, blocking out the light. His voice comes close to my ear. "Right now, you're not Gracie. You're not Fangli. You're Lin, a waitress in a run-down restaurant who wanted better things. You're in love with a man who you know will leave but you want him, even though you're supposed to marry someone else—a cruel man your family chose. Jimmy is an escape, even if it's only for the day. You're conflicted but here, in this moment: All. You. Want. Is. Him."

He takes away his hands, and when I look at him, he's Jimmy, my salvation.

"Why are you here?" I know Fangli's voice and I pitch mine the same as she would, light but low.

"I can't leave this unfinished."

We finish the scene and Sam steps back, hands on hips. "That was good," he approves. "Good enough."

Good enough for Sam is fantastic for me, and I can't stop grinning. That was satisfying to do. I had such a rush, like being in total flow.

"The next scene you're safe from dialogue." He coughs. "We need to kiss."

I rear back as if a cobra dropped down from the ceiling. "Sorry, I think I misheard." A kiss was not on page 47 of the script.

"It's a later scene," he explains as if it's the time continuity I'm stuck on. "We've both accepted we're in love."

"We need to kiss." I cross my arms. "Tenderly? Passionately? With sweet regret?" I think I know the exact scene but I want it confirmed.

"Passionately."

"I am not prepared for this."

To my surprise, he bursts out laughing. "No one is, ever. It's the most awkward thing in the world. I use about a bottle of mouthwash."

Jesus, I hadn't even thought about my breath. Another worry. "Do we have to?"

"Is it better to know I'm self-conscious as well?"

"Yes?" Not really, because he's Sam fucking Yao and of course I want him desperate to kiss me but in private and because he wants to, not because of a script direction. "There's no way to get out of this?"

"I'm sorry." He sounds genuinely regretful. "I tried."

I take a deep breath. This may be my last time helping them, so I might as well go out with a bang. "Okay."

"We can practice."

"Great."

Either he doesn't sense the sarcasm or decides to ignore it. He comes up to me and he's so close.

Mouthwash. All I've had this morning is coffee. "Excuse me." I duck under his arm and run to the bathroom where I proceed to eradicate most of the skin from my tongue and the top layer of enamel from my teeth. I even brush my inner cheeks.

"Better?" he asks when I come out.

"Yes."

"Are you ready?"

"Yes." *No.*

He leans in again, one arm dropping down to my waist to bring me close as the other hand lifts my chin. Dazed by his face so close to mine, I overstep and promptly stomp on his foot.

"Ow!" He drops me and leans to grab his toes, knocking his forehead against my chin in the process.

"Sam, watch it!" I rub my face as he glares at me.

"That hurt," he says.

"You came at me too fast. I was unprepared."

"Did I or did I not say the words *Are you ready?*" He straightens up.

"You did," I admit.

"You said you were. You said yes."

"I thought I was!"

He looks at me, suddenly more serious. "If you truly don't want to kiss me, I won't force you. This is up to you."

C'mon, Gracie. I rub my arms to ground myself while staring at his lips.

"I kiss Fangli like this almost every day onstage," he offers. "Try thinking of it like kissing a mannequin."

"That's not helpful but thanks for trying." A mannequin. That might work. I motion him forward.

The moment his face comes close to mine, I see the issue. Mannequins are not people with warm lips and eyes that flicker across your face to see how you're reacting. I burst out with nervous giggles. "Sorry."

Sam has the long-suffering expression of a man who simply wants to get to work. "I see the mannequin idea was a bust. Glad you find this funny. We have an hour."

"Right." I try to wipe the smile off my face but when he gets close again, I have to squish my lips together to try to physically stop the cackling.

This time, Sam doesn't give me time to recover. He takes my face in his hands and covers my mouth with his.

There is no action he could have taken to make me stop laughing faster. One hand traces down to my neck, and then around the back of my head in that move that looks so sexy when I see it on the screen but in real life always felt like being trapped. Not with Sam. With Sam, it feels as good as I always thought it would, possessive but gentle. He's claiming me.

How can you not respond when a man kisses you like that? I stop thinking that this is a character named Jimmy fake kissing a character named Lin for a fake scene for the marketing team because *Sam is kissing me*. Instead, I step in closer, my hands running up his arms. His muscles tense under my touch.

How long does it last? I don't even know because I've never been so lost. Finally, he pulls back but then leans his forehead against mine for a brief moment, eyes closed as if he's thinking of the kiss that only just passed.

I'm wrecked. My knees are weak. I have never been kissed like that before, and I know that my eyes are huge and they are broadcasting all the feelings I have but wish I didn't.

"Ah, is that... Does that work?" Even my voice is hoarse.

Sam gives his head a little shake. "I think so. I forgot to record it."

"What?" It comes out as a squeak.

"To check the angles." He rubs his chin. "You need to keep your head tilted for the camera. It's a bit different than on the stage." He sounds unaffected, because we are *acting*.

Have I ever deflated so quickly? While I was lost in the moment, he was thinking about how it would look on-screen. *Because this is a job to him, idiot.* How many times do I forget this? Too many.

"Are you ready?" Sam is now standing near the mirror. "Come here."

"What?"

"I want you to watch us so you can decide how you want to look."

This time when I laugh, I can barely stand up. "This is the most unsexy thing ever."

He points at the mirror. "It's supposed to be unsexy. You have lights on you. People are watching. Thank God it's not a sex scene."

I think my eyes might fall out of my head. "I couldn't."

"Luckily, passionate kissing is as far as we get in this one." His frown forms a crease between his brows. "Too much exercising involved if I have to take my shirt off."

I join him at the mirror and decide to take this as coolly as he is. He's not Sam, minty-mouthed intriguing man. He's my colleague and kissing him happens to be part of the job. How does Fangli do this every day?

This time when he kisses me, I keep my eyes open and cranked toward the mirror. My body language is stiff but his is...my goodness. Sam's entire body is leaning over me and every inch of him screams unquenchable thirst. He wants me and no one but me. I can't help it. I close my eyes and let myself feel the kiss, knowing I'm never going to have this sensation again. I'm almost drowning in this intoxicating sea of feeling destined for someone mixed with the impression of being caught up in a tidal wave I can't control.

I end the kiss this time but he pulls me back. My arm is caught between us, and I snake it around his neck to bury my fingers in his hair. This time, I lead the kiss and he lets me.

Neither of us are smiling when we break apart.

"I think you have it," he says. "Practice that script and be ready to go in forty-five minutes."

He's gone before I can answer and I sink into a chair, not knowing how to feel.

Then I bite on my fist and grin so hard my smile touches my ears.

Holy *shit*, I kissed Sam Yao.

Twenty-Eight

I need a drink."

We're back in my suite and I'm curled over the table mumbling into my outstretched arms. Sam is on the couch behind me. "That wasn't bad."

"I survived. Do you think anyone knew?" I lift my head with great effort to look at him. "That it was me and not Fangli?"

Sam's eyes are closed and he's sitting with his arms spread along the back of the couch, his head tilted to reveal his throat. I try not to remember that several hours ago my lips were tracing a line down that very spot. It's been a weird day.

"I think they bought it. You two are almost twins." He cracks open one eye. "It's unbelievable but a good deal of it is how well you can channel her. I can hardly believe you're not a professional actor."

Never has "acceptable" been something to celebrate. I did it. There go all of Mom's injunctions to stay under the radar and not be noticed. I blew them out of the water. And I *liked* it.

"How's Fangli?"

"The psychiatrist came by." He hesitates. "Fangli agreed to the medications but they'll take a while to work. She's started therapy with her and gave her meditation exercises. Fangli says she wants to work tomorrow. She has an understudy if she can't, so that will give her more time if she needs it."

"Did you tell her what happened today?"

"She says thank you." Sam leans forward. "She's up to talking, if you want to see her?"

"Thanks."

"Did I hear you mention a drink?" Sam asks.

"Or more than one. I'm open to suggestions."

"We're supposed to eat at Honsen's tonight."

I don't know that place. "Is it fancy?"

"Probably."

"Will people recognize you and think I'm Fangli?"

"Probably."

"Will I need to dress up?"

"Probably."

"Will people be watching us?"

"Why are you asking when you know the answer?"

I can't deal with that. I need comfort. "How about I buy you that dinner I owe you? At a place I choose."

"Fine." His quick acquiescence tells me he's not into being on display tonight either. A relief since I don't have the energy to deal with his caution about been seen with me in public.

"I'm going to talk to Fangli and then we'll go. You get ready and look like a regular person."

He doesn't even argue but gets up and leaves. He must be exhausted to not give me a hard time on principle.

I scrub my face, put on my new Revelation lipstick and throw on a black tank dress and sneakers. Summer hit with a vengeance today and the deep humidity makes it too hot for jeans.

Then I tap on the connecting door to Fangli's room. Mei opens it and looks me over.

"I'm about to go out with Sam but I wanted to talk to Fangli. Can I?"

Her cheeks hollow and I think she's chewing them. She's so protective of Fangli. I wonder if she's about to refuse when Fangli's voice drifts out. "Gracie?"

Mei steps aside.

I walk through the suite to Fangli's room. It's a larger mirror-image of mine, and Fangli sits curled up on a couch by the window. She's in silken lounge pajamas, bare feet poking out from a cashmere blanket draped over her bent knees. Steam from the cup of tea in her hand drifts up to veil her features.

"Hey," I say.

She doesn't smile but the tightness around her mouth relaxes. "How was the filming?"

"Sam was happy with it."

Fangli rests her head on her hand, exhaustion in every line of her body. I take the tea from her and place it on the table, then hesitate. I don't know what to say but I can't stand here listening to the silence build.

"Can I hug you?" I say. I'm not a hugger and always tried to dodge them by standing far enough away to make it inconvenient for someone to grab me. But Fangli looks weary beyond belief and in need of comfort.

She doesn't answer for a minute, then dips her head down in a nod. I sit on the couch beside her and place a tentative arm around her narrow shoulders. We stay like that for a minute until Fangli sighs, a deep and ragged sound.

"I'm tired," she says in a low voice. "I want to be better. Why can't I get better?"

I commit to the embrace, pulling her up and over so I can get both arms around her. "It takes time," I say.

"That's what the therapist said. I don't have time. I need to be fixed now. Now." Her voice rises.

"I know." I wanted the same thing. She curls against me, not crying but breathing with shallow pants. "You should sleep," I tell her.

"Don't want to."

Don't want to go to bed, don't want to wake up. Don't want to do anything. Been there. "I'll wait with you until you do. Come on."

I urge her to her feet and she walks over to the bed, where she lets me pull the covers over her. I settle down beside her. "Want me to tell you a story?"

Fangli gives a watery laugh. "Like a kid?"

"There's a reason bedtime stories work," I say. "You want to hear it or not? It's one my mom told me."

She sniffles. "Yes."

"It's called the balloon hotel. You know when a kid lets a balloon go and freaks out? This is where the balloons all go when they escape into the sky."

I draw the story out, speaking slow and soft until Fangli's eyes flutter shut. Soon she's asleep. I stop the story and wait for a moment, feeling my courage ebb away at the thought of telling Fangli I'm done. I can't leave her like this. How can I turn my back on her because I feel bad that some people think I'm her? Fangli is flesh and blood. The others are abstract. They're *people* but Fangli is a *person*.

Even Laurence. It made him happy to meet who he thought was Fangli, and can't that be enough?

I have to stay.

I stand up from the bed. I'm not perfectly happy with my choice but it's only for another few weeks. I'll learn from this. I have learned from it.

Mei isn't there when I leave. I head back to my room and take a few minutes to compose myself. When I've splashed some water on my face, I text Sam and tuck the power trio into my bag—card, key, and lipstick. Sam arrives in black pants that hit at his ankles and a light gray shirt. I'd have huge sweat stains under the arms of a shirt that color within seconds.

He looks into my face. "Gracie?"

"Fangli was fine."

"I'm more concerned about you." He comes into my room and shuts the door. "Was that difficult for you?"

"I'm fine," I assure him.

"Fangli likes you," he says. "She hasn't had a friend in a long time apart from me."

"Poor woman."

"Yeah, you're okay." He smiles. "You still want to go out?"

"You bet." More than before. I want to be surrounded by noise and people and eat greasy things so I don't have to think for a couple hours.

"Where are we going?" He falls into step beside me as we leave.

"Surprise. Meet me outside the lobby." It's safer to go down separately since I'm dressed as myself.

Although I expect him to press me for details, Sam seems happy enough to follow me outside and onto the subway.

"I can tell you our stop if you want to sit alone," I say before the train arrives.

He rubs the back of his neck. "Why would I do that?"

"So we're not seen together?" Obviously?

Sam glances down the platform. We're the only people waiting. "Seen by whom, exactly?"

I nudge him with my shoulder. "Funny. I mean on the train."

"I'm sure a car will be empty."

"Up to you." An interesting change from the man who is paranoid about everything. He hasn't even mentioned the security cameras, although the chance of being recognized from grainy black-and-white footage is probably slim. It's nice that he's loosening up about it.

He's quiet as we wait for the train to arrive. As he predicts, we find seats that are relatively isolated.

"I like trains," he says as we sit down on the stained red velour seats.

"I thought you took cars everywhere."

"Mostly," he agrees. "When I think it's safe, I like to use public transit. More people to watch."

"Safe?"

"If I think no one will recognize me."

"People watching is that important to you?"

He glances down the subway cars. We're on one of the interconnected trains so we can see all the way down to the end. "I can't get
ideas for how to play characters from being alone inside my house.
Look there."

I know exactly who he's referring to because a few rows away
is a man in a full tuxedo and a dotted bow tie carved of wood with
polished combat boots who's reading a Georgette Heyer Regency
romance. The questions ask themselves. Who is he? Where is he
going? Is this his usual look or a special occasion look? Why that
book?

We have the manners to not talk about the man right in front of
him, but the moment we get out, we compete for who gets to tell the
man's backstory first. I win and regale Sam with my narrative—that
he's a modern Miss Havisham pining for his lost cat and the bow tie
used to be Lady Fluff's—for the block it takes us to get to the bar. It's
one of my local places and I'm one hundred percent confident that not
a single person there will recognize or care who Sam is.

We take a booth in the corner. Sam sits facing the wall, which is
decorated with framed black-and-white photos. "Mugshots?"

"It's called the Mugshot Tavern."

"Of course it is. I see James Brown and Robert Downey Jr."

I point down the line. "Paris Hilton. Bonnie and Clyde. Lindsay
Lohan. Macaulay Culkin."

Sam nods. "What I'm hearing is that if I get arrested, I can look
forward to being on this wall of infamy."

"Are you planning on a new career in crime?"

He sucks in his cheeks as though considering it. "Never say
never." Then he smirks at me.

The server slaps down a couple of menus and we order wine. I'm
not Fangli tonight, so I have no qualms about drinking. I look at the
menu. "I want fries."

"As long as they're not sweet potato."

"Those are a travesty."

Because Sam has a photo shoot the next day, he doesn't want to order anything with a lot of sodium, which will make his face puff up. That limits his choices to a green salad, and he finally sighs and orders a burger. "I'll drink a glass of milk before bed."

We sit in a companionable silence with our wine. The bar is about half-full and I casually eavesdrop on the conversations around me. Everyday person things: gossip, work complaints, and a bumpy first date.

"Weren't you going to tell me something?" Sam asks. "Before Mei called?"

"Can't remember," I lie. No point going into my concerns now that I've decided to stick with the contract.

"You did well today." Sam finishes his glass, sees I'm almost done, and orders two more.

"You were patient."

Now that it's over, I can barely recall the day. Like most crisis situations, it comes to me in flashes of perfect recall among a background of vaguely acknowledged impressions.

"Was the kissing as bad as you thought it would be?" He glances at me over his wineglass and his tone is more curious than mocking.

I choke. "It was fine."

"Gracie."

I rub my nose. "It was strange, that's it."

"Do you want some advice?" Sam looks at me intently under the low brim of his hat.

"On my kissing technique?" I ask with utter dismay. "No. Of course not. Jesus. What is it?"

"Your kissing was fine," he assures me. "It's your face."

"My face," I echo. The problem Sam has with kissing me is my face, excellent news. I'm going to melt from shame but this is like watching a horror movie. I need to know. "Weren't your eyes closed?"

"Before you kissed me, you looked away."

"I didn't." Surely I would have known that, plus how could I have looked away from Sam about to plant one on me?

"You did it when we were practicing, too. When I'm about here," and he holds his hand about fifteen centimeters from his face, "your eyes go to the left as if you were looking for an escape."

I clutch my wine and hunch into the red leather back of the booth. "It's probably because of the context. I think with a real kiss I wouldn't."

"That's why I told you to look at me."

"I thought it was part of the scene that I forgot."

"Ad-lib."

"What does your girlfriend think about you kissing Fangli?" I've been trying to find a way to confirm what Mei said, and the internet was no help. This is as smooth as I can make it.

"What?" He drops his burger and swears when it falls apart. Not so smooth, then. "My *what*?"

"Mei said you had a girlfriend, or hinted at it."

"I don't. But if I did, we'd talk about it. I wouldn't do anything to make her uncomfortable." He mashes his burger back together. "Why do you ask?"

"I think it would be hard if that happened," I say thoughtfully, trying to pretend that my goal was a deep dive into relationship maintenance instead of nosiness.

"It can be. All jobs have their pitfalls."

"Not like that, though."

"I've heard actuaries can get fairly wild." He starts eating again.

I share my fries and he shares his onion rings and we don't say much more until we're done eating and have a third glass of wine in front of us. It's a cozy silence. Sam pours a glass of water and pushes it across the table to me. I drink it down because I want to work on Eppy and see Mom tomorrow as well as do my Fangli practice, and although I deserve a damn break after today, I don't want to do any of that with a hangover.

"What happened at your last job?" Sam asks, breaking into my relaxation with his unerring ability to home in on uncomfortable subjects.

I already have an answer ready for job interviews so I trot it out. "It wasn't a good culture fit for me. I wanted a place open to testing out new ideas."

"If you're going to give that answer, don't scrunch up your body," Sam says. "They'll sense you're lying."

I look down and see both my arms and legs are crossed. "I wasn't lying."

"How many times do we need to have this fight? For a woman who's currently pretending to be someone else, you're a very bad liar."

"I don't like lies because I always forget what I've said."

"Yet here we are. What really happened?"

"I hated my manager, the one you saw at the art gallery." It comes out in a burst. "He was a weasel and then he fired me when he saw that photo of me in the coffee shop."

Shit, I've said too much. I forgot I was hiding that. Stupid wine.

Sam puts his glass down. "He saw what?"

Time to come clean. "I called in sick the day that was taken and told him it wasn't me but he knew it was because it looks like me. My hair, my bag."

"Did he threaten you?"

"Not in a way that would affect Fangli."

"You're lying again."

I uncross my arms. "I have a lawyer, okay? It was handled."

"There's more you're not telling me."

"Can we not talk about it? I assure you I have it under control." This time I keep my body open and look him in the eye.

After a long beat, he sighs. "I can't force you into talking, but between you and Fangli, I'm drowning in secrets."

I have no answer to this because it's true. We drink quietly, pay up—my treat since I owe him dinner, even though he protests—and leave to go back to the hotel without saying much else.

Fucking Todd spoils the party again.

————————

Fangli is able to get to work the next day. She pops her head through my door to give me a hug before she leaves, and though she's pale, her shoulders and gaze are straight. "Thank you," she says.

"It got better for me," I blurt out. "Once I got help. It was hard though. I felt weak, like I couldn't handle my own problems. Talking to someone about how I felt...yeah. Hard." Of course it was. I can barely bring myself to talk to people I like about my issues, let alone a stranger.

Her gaze flickers down. "Hard. Also easier?"

"Because you don't feel like you're burdening someone with your problems."

"Yes."

"It's not going to happen all at once," I say. "Slow but steady."

"The turtle, not the hare." She pulls her hair around her shoulder and looks at the ceiling. "That's what the therapist said to me yesterday."

I raise my fist high. "To turtles. Long may we prosper."

This has her smiling—only a small lift to her mouth but I'll take it—as she leaves, Mei muttering into her phone beside her. I'm in a better mood after talking to her. I like Fangli. Sam said she considered me a friend. I want that, although I also know she'll be back in China soon and I have trouble enough maintaining friendships with people in my own city. I consider this. It's also possible that our short but intense relationship, much like people get on cruises, is fooling me into seeing more than there is. I hope not. I'd like to keep her in my life.

I push all these worries away and pull out Eppy. Today is the day that I've decided to test it out, and I happily log all the things on my mind into the neat columns. It takes about twenty minutes for my total brain download and then another ten to check my calendar to make sure I've logged in all my events and appointments. I need a calendar sync feature and jot that down in the "App" column.

Then I manufacture a coffee from the pods and simply smile at my laptop. It's there. My idea is there, in front of me. It might be dumb to be proud of creating a to-do list, but I am. This isn't like anything else out there.

Time to start. First thing is to pull together what sets my app apart because I'm going to need money to hire a coder and launch it. I'm building the plane as I'm flying but I feel good.

By lunch, I've found a few problems, and after I make notes, it's time for a walk to get the blood flowing. No one can be creative stuck at a table for hours. It's a bright and sunny day and my steps are light as I wander around without a destination. I text Anjali, who wants to know if Sam continues to be hot and I continue to be alive.

Yes. We kissed, I reply.

Anjali: Sorry WUT and why do you always tell me this shit when I'm in a meeting OMFG was it awesome how why when.

Me: For a promo. Fangli couldn't make it so I had to play her.

Anjali: I repeat was it awesome

I stare at the phone for a minute before I write back, Yeah.

She sends back seven eggplant emojis.

I wish Anjali was in the city to talk to but she's off on a work trip. Stop that.

More eggplants. I need details when I'm back.

I send a thumbs-up emoji because my feelings about Sam are too complicated for me to deconstruct, let alone summarize on text. How do I try to explain kissing Sam over and over? The film crew took multiple takes and each time he moved us a bit differently, touched me a new way so that I forgot about everything in the world but him.

I suppose my feelings aren't complicated at all. I know what the issue is. I'm falling in love with Sam. In the most clichéd of clichés, I've got a thing for a movie star who is going to bye-bye out of my life in weeks.

The least I can do is keep it to myself, so he doesn't know. That's a risk that I'm not willing to take, not even at my bravest. The shame of rejection would be too much. Sam said he was surprised that I could act at all. Well, let's keep that going.

Twenty-Nine

The next two weeks pass in a fairly predictable routine. Sam and Fangli work. I half-assedly job search and whole-assedly refine Eppy. Every few days, I visit Mom. At night, Sam and I go out to smile and be seen, and I am careful to keep conversation light and my hands to myself.

Thus ends the first month of me pretending to be a movie star. This is what I've learned.

Eppy is super amazing and I'm going to be a millionaire and maybe in *Vanity Fair* to talk about how it changed my life in a very inspirational but humble profile story. I have put this out to the universe multiple times.

Being a movie star has become easier now that I have the hang of it.

Fangli is cool and I like her very much.

Mei is professional and I take it at that. She considers me staff.

Mom doesn't do much but look out the window every time I visit, and I call Xin Guang every two days in a polite and cheerful not-pushy way to say "I remain very interested."

Sam...is killing me. Killing me simply by existing. Even when he's not near me, I think about him and I don't like it. Agatha Wu Reed always warned me against letting a man take up too much space in my thoughts, and Sam consumes an inordinate amount of my waking time, partly because he's around so often. My suite has become a bit of a gathering place for the three of us late at night—Fangli, Sam, and me—where we watch movies, go online to check out the world's weirdest houses or grossest recipes, do quizzes to see what Disney princess we are, or play cards. That's the most fun because although Sam might have crushed me at video games, he's atrocious at cards and Fangli and I take great pleasure in his inability to hide how much it bothers him to lose.

"War?" I ask one night in disbelief as Fangli checks over the deck to see how he messed up yet again. "You even lose at War?"

"I had bad cards," he sulks.

"Five times in a row?"

It's this side of Sam that has me stuck. He's unguarded and that makes him more real and unbearably attractive. He doesn't change from when he speaks to me or Fangli and me together. I know it's genuine but it's as friends. Sometimes the two of them lapse into Mandarin but my app has only gotten me to eating in a restaurant (Wo yao chao fan, I can now order fried rice) so there's a lot I miss. Occasionally he shoots me a look from the corner of his eye paired with a sly smile, and my heart stops. He doesn't mean anything by it. He's not a professional flirt but he's aware of his visual power and I think it's become second nature.

Messes me up every time, though. *Every time.* What also ruins me is that he wants updates about Eppy. That he takes it so seriously thrills me.

"Tell me the changes you made on it," he says as we attend another soiree. Toronto's big film festival is coming in September, and since Fangli's management wants her to be seen and Sam has a movie premiering at it, we're on a bit of a circuit.

I hold my gradually warming glass of white wine that I'm forbidden to drink as we stand at a table in the corner taking a quick break from schmoozing. "It's going well," I say.

"When do I get to try it?"

"Later." Why am I dreaming about *Vanity Fair* and morning shows but I immediately say no to Sam trying it out? The whole point is to have people use it.

"You're going to need testers, and you already promised me I could beta test," he says reasonably. "It has to scale and I gave you a bunch of ideas."

"Why do you want to try it?"

He grins. "You make it sound exciting, like it's going to turn my life around. I could use that."

"You. Sam Yao, movie star."

His smile doesn't drop. "Who only has limited time in a day and on this world to get things done."

"You can try it once I write up how-to instructions," I say. He's right, I do need to test it.

By the time our next big engagement comes around, I'm more confident, which is good because it's for Chanel and is an all-eyes-on-me situation. Fangli was going to do it but begged off last minute. She's come down with a cold and truly does look like hell.

"Claudie can't make it, so it will be easy," she coaches me. "She's the only one who has met me in person. You'll go with Sam and watch a mini-fashion show and that's it."

I stand in a robe inside the closet as Fangli hovers beside me. Obviously I have to wear Chanel, but I don't know which of the outfits I have are Chanel. I think they're known for little boxy suit things with rough knobbly fabric. Pearls? I have distinct memory of seeing models wearing lots of pearls.

Fangli reaches around me to pluck out a little pair of shorts with a matching tube top and a sleeveless blazer. I wrinkle my nose. "I only shaved my legs to the knees."

She sighs but exchanges the shorts for a long, flowy skirt. "This will do."

"What do I need to talk about?"

"How much you enjoy working with Claudie is good, but ask

them questions. People love to talk about themselves. This is a special VIP pop-up, so it will be a mix of people, not only fashion. They usually ask their local premium-client list."

I pull on the wig and swipe on a final touch of lipstick before kissing a tissue to blot it. Fangli blows her nose and pops a lozenge in her mouth. She reeks of eucalyptus and lemon. "You saw your mother today, didn't you?" she asks.

"This morning. She's the same." I sigh and Fangli's hand squeezes my shoulder.

"You never told me how she came to Canada," she says.

"She never talks about the past," I say. "All she would ever say is that she wanted a fresh start."

"Aren't you curious?"

"You have no idea. I used to ask my dad but he only said it was her story to tell and now I might never hear it. I have family there I'll never know."

"Does it bother you?"

"In the abstract, sometimes, but what would we have in common? They'd be related but strangers."

"That's sad. Perhaps she felt safer keeping silent."

I stop, pressed powder compact in my hand. Safe? I never even considered the idea that Mom would be running from something or someone. I always assumed that she only wanted a new start in Canada for a job or money. She had a whole life in China, over twenty years, and I know nothing about it. I didn't know it was possible for me to feel more regret over not asking Mom more about her life, but I guess, like all children, I thought that her life only began after my arrival.

Fangli sniffles into a tissue. "I imagine if she was married to a man like my father, she'd want to make sure he couldn't find her again."

"A man like your father?"

Fangli sees from my face that I'm imagining the worst, and she holds up her hands as if to stop me. "No, no. He's a good man and tries but he's in love with his work and with rules."

That actually seems like a man Mom would appreciate, although Brad Reed was more of a free spirit.

Fangli continues. "It's having a clean break and all that. I often wish I could take a similar action."

"You can't?"

"I love him and although we have different philosophies, he's my father." She shrugs. "He's difficult, but how can I cut him out of my life when he's my only family?"

There's no answer to that. Fangli hands me an adorable purse and approves when I sling it over a single shoulder rather than as a cross-body.

Then Sam and I are in the car headed to the event space. It's on the top floor of an office building in the East End but I gasp out loud when I see the view. The entire city lays itself out in front of us, the lake to the south, the skyscrapers to the west, and residences and trees to the north and east.

"Ms. Wei, what a pleasure." A tall woman approaches us. "Mr. Yao."

She's smiling and I have no idea who she is, so I murmur a suitable greeting and follow her into the main room. A long walkway splits the space in two, and there are rows of chairs lining the sides. Black-clad servers walk around with food and wine, and I decline both when they come in my direction. I can't eat and be Fangli and save my lipstick all at once.

The woman points out our seats and leaves. A nasal voice comes from behind me. "I'm only here because of Angelica," a woman says. "The Chinese have absolutely wrecked Chanel with their fakes everywhere. Really it's quite terrible, but you know Angelica. Once she finds a style, she never changes."

A booming voice cuts her off.

"Too many Chinese, that's the problem. Driving all the prices up. Real estate's the worst. Never know what they're thinking. There's too many of them, all look the same. We're going to be overwhelmed. It's a numbers game."

Sam's face has stilled into neutral but he touches my arm when I go to turn around.

"Forget it," he says softly.

"Like hell." I glance behind to see who the asshole is and have no trouble locating him. He's older, in his fifties, wearing a baggy black suit. I take a long look so I can recognize him later, watching as he shoves his empty glass at a passing server and jabs his finger in her face until she gives him a fresh drink from her tray.

Sam and I mingle but the man's comments have soured my mood. Sam must notice because he leads me onto the balcony that provides a view out over the black lake. Thanks to an unseasonably cold night, we're the only people out here.

"You need to let it go," he says. "You're not going to accidentally spill a drink on him or beat him in rational debate, so quit thinking about it."

"How did you know I was going to spill on him?"

He gives me a look out of the corner of his eyes. Against the night, his face is starkly outlined. "There are many like him here."

"At least you can go back home and not have to deal with people like him. I'm stuck."

"There are always people like him, everywhere." Sam leans his forearms on the balcony rail. Tonight he's in slacks and with the sleeves of the dress shirt rolled up, he exudes coolly confident style. I've already seen two men glance over and fix their own sleeves. "He's scared and he feels inferior and he doesn't like it."

"Or maybe he's not scared but just a class-A dick who needs to be snapped into place. I bet he lords his money over everyone around him." I look back into the room. "Oh my God."

"What?" He stands in front of me as if to block whatever it is. I pull him out of the way gently.

"That's Robin Banerjee."

Sam waves his hand. "Some context, please?"

"A venture capitalist based in the city who only funds local business and has a focus on lifehacking ventures." I've done my research.

Understanding dawns. "Like Eppy."

"Like Eppy."

"Now's the time to get him," Sam urges. "Pitch him."

"I can't." I want to stomp my feet in rage. "I'm Fangli, not Gracie."

"Right." He gives a brisk nod. "I'll go talk to him."

"What do you mean?"

"I'll go over, introduce myself, and tell him I have a friend with a great idea and will he meet with her."

"Just like that?"

"Well, he might say no."

"You'd do that for me?"

Sam looks down at me. "Of course. Why wouldn't I?"

"I feel weird."

"It's called networking."

"I've always managed by myself."

He doesn't say anything but I can hear his voice as loudly as if he had. *How's that working for you?*

How is it working for me? I look back at Robin Banerjee. Networking was always for people who had connections and I never did. Sam's casual offer, that he could simply walk over and ask this stranger a favor—and have a good expectation of receiving it by dint of who he is—speaks to a level of confidence I envy.

I don't want Sam to do this for me. I want to be able to do it for myself.

"I think I'd rather..." The words die in my mouth. Because Todd is strutting through the crowd.

Thirty

He's here.

Todd the asshole boss. Todd who somehow continues to make my life hell. I don't understand why he's here until I see his blond friend from the art gallery smiling and air-kissing the hell out of the room.

"You'd rather what?" Sam sees me shiver. "You're cold. The wind's picking up. Shall we go in?"

"I like it out here." I can't stay on the balcony all night but I need a few minutes to collect myself. Dealing with Todd will require a plan. A solid plan that I currently do not have.

Sam runs his hand down the goose bumps on my arm but says, "Whatever you want."

The balcony is separated from the main event space by a wall of windows, but it's darker outside than in, so I know I'm not visible to the crowd. I keep my breath controlled and even, forcing my body to calm itself even though my palms are so damp that Sam makes a face when he touches my hand. "About Robin," he says before he squints through the windows. "Oh, can you give me a moment? That's my old friend Dmitri. I haven't seen him in years." He gestures to a man inside wearing a bow tie.

I nod to Sam to show he can go off and talk with his friend—and regret it instantly.

Because Todd comes out to the balcony seconds after Sam exits to check the space for someone worthy to talk to. I've no place to hide.

He recognizes me instantly and strides over. "Gracie, all alone out here. You're looking good." How did I never notice he looked like a wolf with his shaggy hair and the wide mouth filled with big teeth? He's a wolf and I'm a lamb. "That long hair. I approve."

He knows that under this perfect makeup and styled hair and expensive Chanel getup, I'm only Gracie.

"You should have dressed like this for work," he says.

He shifts closer, too quick for me to back up. So I don't. I stand my ground even though it means he's near. I don't grant him the power to make me move, and that small, unintended gesture reminds that I'm not a lamb at all. I won't be the same vulnerable Gracie who left his office a month ago. That distance has given me enough space that I can keep my head even though my teeth are about to start chattering.

I channel Fangli, with no smile and astonishment he would be so rude as to approach me. "Excuse me. Who are you?"

His fingers slip down to encircle my wrist tightly enough to press the bracelets into my skin. "Come off it, Gracie. I don't know what game you're playing but I always knew there was a bad girl under those thick sweaters and submissive look."

He's so fucking gross. Why didn't I see this before? How did I let this piece of shit beat me down so badly? I feel the weight of the wig on my head, the delicate straps of the leather heels cutting into my ankles. He might treat me like Gracie, but I'm Fangli here.

"I'm talking to you, Gracie." Todd gives me a little tug when I don't answer, and I shift my gaze down to where his hand encircles my wrist. Fangli wouldn't put up with this treatment. Neither would Anjali, although she'd probably opt for breaking Todd's nose.

I won't put up with it either.

I flick his hand off. "I don't care," I say. It comes out in a scalpel-sharp voice I recognize from one of Fangli's dramatic roles.

"What did you say?" He leans in too close but I don't move. Instead I keep silent and stare him down.

And I see what I missed for so long.

Standing in front of me on the dim balcony, Todd is nothing but an empty man-shaped shadow surrounded by the lights shining from thousands of windows in the city skyline. With the filter of fear stripped away, I recognize him for what he is: a mediocre and blustering bully who I despise. I take a deep breath and let all my fear go, because he's not worth it.

I don't need to answer him.

I turn to leave Todd stewing in his impotent rage on the pretty balcony but although I'm done with him, Todd doesn't think he's done with me. I feel a heavy hand land on my shoulder just as I spot Sam stepping through the doorway, a frown growing between his brows.

Twisting back sharply enough to knock his hand aside, I give Todd my most unimpressed look. Sam's beside me now and his presence bolsters my confidence. I can almost feel the strain he's under to keep cool but he waits for me to handle the situation.

Todd glares at me. "I don't know what you're trying to pull here, but it doesn't matter how you dress yourself up—you're the same boring girl you always were. You should be grateful I even bothered to look at you."

"No." I glare back. "No, that's not something to be grateful for at all."

God, that feels good. Over his shoulder, I see the woman who welcomed us watching with a dark look on her face. She's speaking into her walkie-talkie. A security guard materializes beside her seconds later and they both walk over to us, expressions hard and eyes trained on Todd.

Todd sees her and glances over at me with a look of almost hilariously misplaced triumph. "Get her out of here," he says, pointing at me as they approach. "She doesn't belong here."

The security guard doesn't even hesitate. "Let's go, sir."

I take in that beautiful moment as Todd smirks at me, right before he understands what's going on. Then he looks between me and the guard. "What?"

"Time to go, sir." The guard looks at me. "Ma'am, do you want us to call the police so you can press an assault charge?"

It's like Todd really doesn't get it until he looks at the event woman, her lip curled in disgust. He turns back to look at me and... crumples. It's like watching a bag deflate in slow motion.

I pretend to consider what the guard said, although I know that I can't. Fangli's image needs to be considered. "Banning him from all events will do."

Todd's face goes red as I refuse to move or look away.

I've won.

I turn away first, giving him my back. He's not worth my time.

"He's gone," Sam says after a moment. I nod but I'm listening to the people around me as the crowd spills out to the balcony. The moment with security has not gone unnoticed.

"What was that about?"

"The nerve of that guy."

"That's Wei Fangli. I heard she's a real bitch."

"For what, not wanting to be pawed by that pig?"

"Did you see that?"

Sam's touch on my arm reminds me to straighten my back and keep my expression neutral. Todd's gone but my triumph is dampened by the knowledge that this might rebound on Fangli.

Sam quells the murmuring with a frown that makes me tense, and it's not even directed at me. He takes me to the side, out of sight of others on the balcony, and wraps his arm around me. "What happened? Do we need to go?"

"I'm fine."

"No, you're not. You're shaking. That was your old boss, wasn't it?"

"Yes."

Sam's expression hardens. "Tell me the whole story. All of it."

The sordid tale spills out. "I don't know why I couldn't stand up to him, but I couldn't. I couldn't. I couldn't lose my job and I didn't want to accept it was happening."

Sam tucks my head under his chin. "Gracie. It's all on him. Not you." He pauses. "Can I tell you a story?"

"Yes." I want to get my mind off this mess.

"I told you about my mother and how she wants me to take over the production business."

"You did."

"She also tried to get me my first job. I said no, I was going to change my name and do it myself." He leans us against the railing, the wind lifting up our hair. "She warned me against a certain acting coach and I was sure, because I was a teenager, that she was lying to me so I'd fail and have to come back to her."

"What happened?"

"I went to meet the coach. She was famous and everyone knew if she agreed to take you on, you were special. It was her and me." He sighs. "Then she told me to sit down and she put a hand on my thigh. High on my thigh."

"How old were you?"

"Eighteen."

"What did you do?"

He laughs and it's the same tone that I have when I think of Todd. "Nothing at first. Maybe it was in my head. I didn't want to make a fuss. I didn't want her to think I was a little kid."

"Did she stop?"

Sam looks at me, mouth turned down. "Do you think she would? Did your boss?"

"No."

"What I realized later was it's not only sex. It's power. She saw a vulnerability in me and took advantage."

"I'm weak, is what you're saying." I move further around the side of the balcony and Sam follows. We're now completely hidden from the crowd.

"I think Todd saw you care about people and you avoid calling attention to yourself. He saw a chance."

This is too true for me to debate. "Did the acting coach... I'm sorry." I suddenly realize I'm prying.

"I managed to drop the script, and when I bent to pick it up, I pretended to fall off the chair, muttered my apologies, and ran out."

"Smart."

"I felt like an overreacting idiot until I went back and told Fangli and Chen. We knew there was no point in telling the instructors so they helped me talk it through, process it. That was that."

"What about the coach?"

"Faded into obscurity after she got caught misreporting her taxes." He smiles broadly. "I might have been the one to report her."

"They say revenge doesn't make you feel better."

"Do they? Felt pretty great to me."

Sam's story encourages me about the situation but I still feel like past me was gutless. "I should have..."

He puts a finger on my lips. "Fuck shoulds."

"But..."

"Gracie, you are perfect as you are. It's not a bad thing to want to keep peace in your life and care for the people in it. That a bad person can manipulate it doesn't mean it's wrong. To be kind and generous is a gift."

"Please take your seats." I hear an usher politely herding people into the main room. "We're about to begin."

In our secluded side alcove, Sam and I ignore him.

"Todd knows I'm Gracie when I'm dressed like this, as Fangli." I point to the tube top.

"Did you admit it?"

I think. "No."

"Then forget Todd." He puts his finger under my chin to lift my face. "You're beautiful inside and out. Don't let a person like him extinguish any of you. You should be proud of yourself."

"Thank you." My reply is barely a whisper.

"Gracie." He's so close. The breeze from the lake licks my skin where he pushes my hair back behind my shoulder.

"Sam?" I don't move for two reasons. The first is that my knees are so shaky that if I move, I might fall over. The second is that I want him to make the choice. I want Sam to close the distance between us.

He doesn't make me wait long before he presses his lips to mine, butterfly soft and so fleeting I wonder if it happened. Then he pulls back, only a bit, as if to gauge my reaction. "Gracie?" he asks. "Is this...this is good?"

"God, yes." I wrap one arm around his neck and grab his arm with the other as I rise up on my toes. I can feel the smile on his lips disappear as I lean into him for a proper kiss, the one I've been craving ever since I saw him on that stupid magazine cover. His mouth slots perfectly into mine and this time, it's real. Sam is kissing me, Gracie. Not Fangli. His arms are wrapped around me, and he kisses me again. Hidden on a balcony overlooking a dark lake, he kisses me until all I can think of is Sam.

This is all real. I can feel it's real. I know it's real. It has to be.

Thirty-One

I'm not sure how I make it through the rest of the Chanel party. Angular women strut in front of me in thousands of dollars' worth of clothes and I react with smiles and appreciative nods for the cameras and eyes trained on my face. All this happens on the periphery of my mind because all I can think about is Sam's leg brushing me when he moves and thanking every god in existence that the lipstick I wore tonight is layered with a varnish that would withstand a hurricane. Our balcony make-out session didn't even smudge it, let alone leave the two of us with clown mouths. That's a quality product worthy of a five-star Amazon review.

I can't tell if the show ends too soon or too late, but at some point, we clap politely, stand, and go. Sam ushers me silently into our waiting car and sits beside me. Very close beside me.

He takes off the wig and brushes his hand over my short hair, which is sweaty and mussed from being under the equivalent of an insulated winter hat. "Gracie," he says, his fingers tracing along my ear and pushing the wisps back.

I want this. How could I not? The man who's burrowed himself in my mind is about to kiss me again. Luckily, there is no moment too romantic and no experience too wondrous that my brain cannot ruin.

"We need to talk about this," I say, pushing him back.

The slashed brows almost meet in the middle. "About me kissing you?"

"More about why."

He blinks. "Did you want the entire thought process or shall I summarize the highlights? I can probably manage a quick slide deck on my phone if you give me a few minutes. There's a template I like."

"There's no need to be a jerk."

He captures my hand in his and kisses my fingers, his lips warm on my skin. "I want to kiss you because I want to kiss you. I don't know how to break it down. I can't tell you that it's twenty percent the way you smile at me when I help you out of the car, or sixteen percent the way you laugh at your own jokes."

"Not that I look like Fangli?"

Sam grimaces. "I've had to kiss Fangli for weeks onstage and it's like kissing my sister. You are not Fangli and I want you."

His conviction is a bit ruinous to my self-restraint. "It's that this is a very strange situation," I explain.

"I like to think we've grown on each other."

"Like a moss?"

"Or a mold."

"You tell me you're a good actor. I don't know what to believe, if this is real or not."

He thinks about this. "What would be the point of acting like I want you if I don't? If I didn't, there would be no need to fake that I did."

This makes sense when he lays it out like that. "You could be pretending to like me because you want to get laid."

His entire face creases in disgust. "Please. If meaningless sex was the only thing on my mind, I wouldn't have a problem acquiring it."

True enough. Sexiest Man in the World and all that.

"However," he adds, "I'm excited to know you're considering the possibility."

"Sam."

He sighs. "We agreed that we started off on the wrong foot, correct?"

"Correct."

"We agreed we would begin fresh. We signed a contract."

"We agreed, yes."

He opens his hands wide as if that says it all.

"I'm a nobody."

Sam glares at me. "Enough with that."

"It's true, though. Look at you. Rich, famous, and so on."

He moves a bit away. "Is that all I am? That's it?"

Shit, I put my foot in it. "That's not what I mean."

"Sure sounds like it." His voice is wry.

"All I'm saying is that, given the society in which we live, which prioritizes fame and wealth and makes that desirable, being born in that perfect Punnett square of life means you can get whoever you want."

"Why do you talk like this is a competition? I don't want to *get* anyone. I like you, Gracie Reed. I like the Gracie who stood up for Fangli and made sure she got help when the rest of us were tiptoeing around it. I like the woman who is obsessed with time management techniques and whose towels fall off on a recurring basis."

My face heats. "I was hoping you'd forget that happened."

He snorts. "Me be able to forget you standing there with no towel? Never."

"It was an accident."

"That's what made it great." He smiles. "That's the woman I want, the one who picks up the towel like it's no big deal and doesn't fuss about it. I want the one who, when asked to take part in the most idiotic plan I'd ever heard, decides to give it a go because she has enough confidence to pull off being Wei Fangli."

No one has ever described me as confident but hearing it from Sam makes me realize maybe I am more than I thought. I mull this over as I try to tamp down the fireworks going off in my chest. "This is a short-term contract," I say. "I'm going to be out of your life in a month."

"A lot can happen in a month." He moves back. "Gracie, you have no idea of the risks I take to be with you. Going for walks? Visiting your mom?"

"Those are not high-stakes activities. Lots of people walk around."

"I am not lots of people. I know this plays into your need to see me as shallow and egotistical but my image is important. I'm cautious."

I wiggle my eyebrows at him. "Making out on a balcony when anyone could have come around the corner?"

"This is exactly what I mean. You make me..." He throws himself back in the seat and runs his hands through his hair. "It's like everything I thought was serious becomes less so when you're around."

"Am I offended at that? I think I might be."

"I'm saying, obviously poorly, that you give me perspective. I'm grateful. I like it." He shrugs, looking at the roof. "I like you."

I want to quiz him on this a bit. Like as in the way I like hot showers? Like as in appreciates my company? Or, he *like* likes me? But I chicken out because I'm not sure I'm ready for the answer. It's an emotional roller coaster of a night, to be frank, and part of me just wants to put off all talk of feelings until tomorrow.

Sam straightens up and looks at me, hands pressed flat against the seat. "Gracie, I've never forced a moment. I'm going to sit here. What happens next is up to you."

He doesn't even have time to finish before I'm on him. His hands come up to catch me around the waist, turning us to lean against the back of the seats. Kissing Sam is like nothing I've experienced. When Riley kissed me, it was always as if it was preparation for the main event. Sam kisses me as if it's the destination, not the journey. He's teasing, layering tiny kisses on the corners of my mouth before he captures my lower lip with his. Then he lets me go.

"Gracie?"

"Yes?" I give my head a shake to get my brain back in order. "What's wrong?"

"You seem a little... Ahh." He wriggles and I slowly grasp that I've been stiff-arming his shoulders.

"Sorry." This time, he lets me take the lead and I can feel how his mouth melts under mine. Releasing his shoulders, I card my fingers through his hair and he groans against me. "Keep doing that," he says.

A minute later, we push apart and he grins. "By the way, you looked to the left again," he says.

"Should we stop?"

He runs his hand over my leg. "No, I think maybe we should practice."

We do for the rest of the drive.

I don't have sex with Sam, but only because I'm not that spontaneous and I want to shave above my knees first. Not even passion can get past my mental gatekeeper, the Dread Lady Overthinker.

The moment we arrive at the hotel, I rearrange my wig so we look like we've done nothing in the car but chat platonically and check our phones. My lipstick continues to be tonight's real MVP, and I don't need to touch it up at all.

Conscious of the security cameras, we don't make out in the elevator, although Sam's hair is disheveled and his lips are even fuller from kissing in the car. He leaves me chastely outside my suite, where I manage to lock the door and take a single step before I sink down on the wooden floor and curl up in a rictus of unbelieving happiness.

Which immediately turns to total terror. What have I done? We had a good thing going, a collegial thing, and I've blown that right out the window. What if he regrets this in the morning and it's weird? What if Fangli is mad? What if I turn into a jealous shrew of a woman, furious this has to be kept secret from the world?

What if I get hurt? I haven't been with a man since Riley. I should have at least taken a ride on the merry-go-round before I buckled in for the roller coaster.

There's no one I can talk to. Fangli is asleep and so is Anjali. I don't know what to say because I don't know how I feel, exactly. It's almost like the first time I had sex, where I wanted to tell everyone and also hug the secret to myself to savor it.

Too wired to do anything as banal as sleep, I putter around my suite tidying and thinking. Fretting. Sam put Todd out of my mind but now that I'm alone, I'm worried about what he's going to do. My severance from work is safe but what if he comes looking for me? What if he tries to contact me or threaten us? He's vindictive; I know that from how he treated people at work, how he treated me. I hate that the amount of real estate he should take up in my head should be the size of a hovel, a subcloset, but instead he's living rent-free in a sprawling mansion.

A knock comes at the connecting door that leads to Fangli's room. "Are you awake?" she asks through the door.

I open it. "Yeah."

"I can't sleep and I saw the light under your door." Fangli rubs her eyes. "Can I come in for a bit?"

"Let's sit on the balcony." It would be nice to have the company and take my mind off worrying about Todd. But now that there's another human near me, I'm almost bursting with my Sam news. That gets diverted almost immediately when Fangli touches my hand.

"You were the one who had Sam make me agree to talk to someone," she says. "Thank you."

"The decision was yours," I say. "I think you were ready."

"Sam's been trying to get me help for years." She takes her hand back, and the chair leg scratches as she shifts it along the concrete balcony. "I didn't realize how heavily it weighed on him."

"He was worried about you."

"I know, but I didn't want to admit it." Fangli raises her face to watch the full moon flooding the sky. "I thought it would be death for my career. That's what my manager said. He told me to cure myself because it wasn't that bad."

"Cure yourself?"

She glances at me out of the corner of her eye and gives me a small smile. "It didn't work."

"No, I imagine not. It didn't for me."

"You tried, too?"

"Failed the same way I wouldn't be able to cure my own

pneumonia or cancer through willpower."

"I never thought of it like that."

I think over what I want to say. "You said it would be bad for your career."

"My manager said if it was known I had problems, no one would hire me. They would think I was unpredictable."

"When was this?"

She thinks. "Five or six years ago."

I make up my mind. "You're more established now. Other people feel like us. It might help them to know they're not alone, if you think that's something you can do."

The long silence makes me worry I've gone too far. Then her soft voice rises. "I think so, too. But I don't have the courage."

"You?" I twist in my chair. "Did you know one of the most common fears is speaking in public? You do it all the time. You put yourself out there with your art in front of a critical world. I could never do what you do. I don't have the guts."

She bursts out laughing and grabs my shoulder. "You don't? What do you think you've been doing for a month? You're the one who took a chance when I asked you to pretend to be me. Do you think most people would have the courage to do that?"

"I think it was the money."

"No, you're braver than you want to believe," she says. She eyes me. "You like to pretend you're not bold because it's an excuse to not stretch yourself."

I wince. "Harsh."

"You helped me. This is me helping you. Sam told me about Eppy and how well you did filming with him. You can do whatever you set your mind to, Gracie. I've seen this in you but you need to see it in yourself. I believe in you."

Have I ever had a pep talk like this? Mom loves me but she was more about setting realistic expectations to avoid disappointment and failure. I never had anyone tell me to dream. I'm not even sure I've ever had a talk with a friend like this before, at least not sober.

Fangli fetches a blanket from inside. "Cashmere or wool?" she asks as she spreads it over our knees.

"For what?"

She twitches the corner of the blanket. "What material do you prefer?"

"Neither. I like that synthetic stuff they make into stuffed animals. It's so soft you can barely feel it on your fingertips."

"I like cashmere," she says in the comfortable tone of a woman who owns a lot of it. "Yak is good, too."

"Yak?" I turn to see her face, pale in the moonlight. "Isn't that, you know...yakky? Coarse?"

"Oh, no. The inner coat is very soft."

I file that information away and we sit in the dark for a while longer, idly quizzing each other.

Pasta or rice?

Train or plane?

Dramas or comedies?

Despite our disagreement about the best blanket fiber, we are eerily in sync for the rest of our choices. Finally we both yawn in unison.

"Back to bed," I say, happy to have distracted myself back to exhaustion.

Fangli leans over to give me a hug before she stands up to go. "I'll see you tomorrow."

I drag myself into the bathroom to shower. The water washes away some of my unease and after towel-drying my hair, I collapse into bed. Todd crosses my mind and I force his nasty face away with a physical gesture.

Tomorrow I can worry about this.

Tonight, I'm going to dream about what I want. Eppy. A job. Freedom. Mom safe and happy.

And maybe a bit about kissing Sam.

JULY 20

DONE IT

(ACT AS IF TASK IS ALREADY COMPLETE)

✓ Researched and downloaded a more
interesting Mandarin app.

✓ Reduced coffee intake to 3 cups.

✓ Decided best platform for Eppy mock-up.

✓ Brushed wig.

Thirty-Two

S am throws his tablet to the side and stretches on the couch where he's ostensibly been reviewing scripts. For the last twenty minutes, he's been shooting little glances in my direction as if hoping to casually catch me looking up from my laptop.

The last time I did, he'd smiled and I'd blown him an over-the-top kiss, which he had pretended to catch out of midair and tuck into his pocket. Then he'd gone back to work as if nothing had happened, ignoring me as I groaned.

He gets up and begins pacing. I wait until he's made multiple circuits of the room but he doesn't say a word.

"You're going to wear a path into that floor," I observe finally.

"Are you done working?"

"Do you have something more interesting for me to do?" I glance up and see the wicked expression on his face. "Never mind."

He assumes a look of extreme innocence. "I was going to suggest a sedate game of cards but what did you have in mind?"

I roll my eyes and close my laptop. "You hate cards because you suck at them."

"True. I was lying about playing cards." He nods out the window. "What are those?"

"Toronto Islands."

"Real islands?" Sam looks at them with new interest.

"Sand spits they dumped a bunch of landfill on to make bigger." I join him. It's raining so the islands look mysterious under a thin fog. I haven't been over there in years.

"Where's the bridge to drive over?"

"You take a ferry." I point to a little ship chugging across the water. "There's one."

"A ferry?" He looks at it longingly.

"You like ferries?"

He turns to me with a face that expresses his disbelief that anyone could not. "Of course. When I was in Hong Kong, I always took the Star Ferry to cross the harbor." He tugs at his ear. "My mother hated me doing that."

He goes over to the fridge and pokes around before coming back empty-handed to stare out the window again. His eyes follow the ferry as he rocks back on his heels, lost in thought. Sam looks trapped in this fancy hotel room, and I want to take that blank expression from his face.

"Let's go out on an adventure," I say impulsively. "You and me."

Sam raises his eyebrows. "I am somewhat frightened."

"I'm hurt by your skepticism. All my ideas are good ideas." He opens his mouth and I steamroll over him. "Get your things."

"You want to go now? In the rain?" He acts like it's acid falling from the sky.

"Are you a witch that you'll melt if you get wet?" I move past him to open the balcony door and stick a hand out. "It's barely spitting."

"I might be seen." I can hear the waver in his voice and want him to say yes. It would be fun to go out. On a date? It's not a date. Is it? What constitutes a date anyway?

"In this weather?" I shakes my head. "I don't think so. The islands are busy in the summer but less so in bad weather."

"An adventure, huh?"

I slide the balcony door back shut. "It'll be good, I promise."

He mulls it over and then grins and gives me a light, quick kiss that makes me blink with surprise at how natural it feels. "It will, with you."

Sam goes to get ready and I first press my fingers against my lips because, wow, kissing Sam never gets old. Then I wonder if I'm a complete dumbass to be dragging Sam out in the rain for an outdoor adventure when I could have suggested we have indoor ones.

Maybe later.

Finally, I check for the umbrella that must come with the room because I know rich people don't have to remember to bring things like that when they travel. I only have one so I knock on Fangli's door. Mei answers and waits for me to speak.

"Do you have any umbrellas?" I ask. "Sam and I are going on a date so I need two."

Her face freezes. "Pardon?"

"Not a date," I rush to explain. "A walk. It's not a date-date. Do you think Fangli will be mad?" I can't ask if she and Mei want to come because we can't be together.

"Excuse me."

She shuts the door in my face. I stand there, shocked. Mei is never rude. Cold, yes, even abrupt, but never rude. Then the door opens and Mei hands out an umbrella.

"Oh, thanks," I say. "Uh, everything good?"

"Have a nice day." This time she waits until I turn to shut the door.

I let it go—Mei is an eternal mystery to me—and go to meet Sam.

"Where are we going?" He takes the umbrella I hand him. I realize Sam doesn't have many surprises in his life—everything is scheduled—and decide to make him wait to know.

"You'll see."

It's a twenty-minute walk, and Sam badgers me about our destination the entire way, laughing when I give him increasingly silly locations.

"The elevator at the end of the world?" he repeats. "You just said it was the invisible shopping center."

"Could be the pioneer village near the underpass." He gives me a doubtful look, since this could be a real place. "Kidding, the pioneer village is further north. We're here."

"The ferry terminal? We're taking a ferry?" He lights up.

Sam is as excited to get on the ferry as I've ever seen him or any person. As predicted, hardly anyone is going over to the islands in this weather, and Sam relaxes a bit under his umbrella, holding it high to read the signs.

"Do we want Centre Island, Ward's Island, or Hanlan's Point?" he asks.

"Hanlan's has the nudist beach."

He wiggles his eyebrows at me. "I'm game if you are."

"You're wearing a face mask and a hat so low you look like the invisible man in disguise," I say. "You expect me to believe you'd go to a nudist beach? Where the entire point is to be naked?"

"Well, I doubt they'd be looking at my face."

Don't look down. Don't look down. I keep my eyes straight. "We're going to Centre Island."

The ferry arrives in a few minutes. Sam climbs the staircase to the upper level and leans over the side, breathing in deeply. "I love the smell of water," he says.

"Ocean or lake?"

"Ocean but lake will do. I have properties on both." He catches my glance. "Grossly overindulgent to have multiple homes?"

"You know it is."

"They're investments. I rent them out."

"Slightly better."

The ferry starts moving and Sam grins into the wind, his capitalist spirit silenced by the beauty of the view. Sam stands at the front of the ferry, watching the island as it approaches, then moves to the back. The city shrinks in the distance until it transforms into a graph, the CN Tower the western outlier to the normal distribution of downtown business towers. A few intrepid boaters are out, and one dude on a Jet Ski zooms by. I often forget that Toronto is a lake city and there are people who own things like kayaks and actively enjoy being on the water.

When we arrive, Sam's content to let me play tour guide. Even though it's been years since I've been to the islands and it's rarely been while sober, I do a good job of getting us to the beach on the other side of the island. The rain has stopped but it's deserted. We pull off our shoes and make our way across sand that's been dappled by the raindrops, taking selfies and digging in our toes.

"Canada geese," Sam says, pointing as if I can miss the flock ten meters away. "Pretty."

"Don't go near them," I warn. "Geese are mean."

He's already approaching them and looks over his shoulder with scorn. "I can handle a goose, Gracie."

I swipe the water off a picnic bench and sit down to enjoy the show. Sam is determined to get the perfect close-up of one of the geese, as if the zoom feature doesn't exist for a reason, and he creeps closer. I pull out my phone and start the video to show Fangli later.

He's already off-balance in a stealthy attempt to get to the goose without spooking it when it attacks, thrusting out its beak as if to give him a nip. Sam leaps back, phone flying off to the side. The goose hisses and advances on him and Sam—action star Sam Yao, hero of the silver screen Sam Yao—falls back on his butt and does some weird commando roll to get away from it.

I'm laughing too hard to film properly so I don't capture Sam's indignant expression when he pops back to his feet.

"It's not funny."

"I'm sorry."

"Go ahead." He dusts the wet sand off his knees.

"What?"

"Say it, Gracie. I know you want to."

"I told you. I *told* you so." I hop off the bench to find his phone, which I hand over.

"You did." He opens his phone and we check the photo. Sam captured the goose in attack mode and the entire image is a wide-open hissing beak, slightly blurred, with open wings in the background.

That sends me into another laughing fit. Sam groans. "All that for nothing."

"Nothing? That's a classic goose shot. It's gorgeous."

"Like you."

Does he mean that as a real compliment or a quick tease? I don't want to say "thank you" if it's the latter because that would be embarrassing. I decide to treat it like a joke. "I think the goose has better feathers."

Sam reaches out to touch my hair, then realizes he's covered with sand when a clod drops on my shoulder. "You're much prettier than a goose, feathers or not," he assures me as he rubs his hands on his thighs.

Is it still a joke? It's safer to act as though it is. "High bar."

I grab my shoes and keep going down the beach. Sam comes up from behind and almost hesitantly laces his fingers with mine, his hand wet from the rain and rough from the sand. I do my best to be casual but holding hands is almost more intimate than kissing. When I glance up, Sam smiles and kisses my temple.

Ugh, why is he like this? My heart can't deal.

We walk like that for a bit, matching our steps to each other until the rain begins again and we let go to open our umbrellas as the wind picks up. I gasp as it catches my umbrella and promptly turns it inside out.

Sam keeps us dry as I check my umbrella over. "Broken," I say.

He wraps his arm around me, heavy but warm on my shoulders, and holds the umbrella over both of us. "Shall we keep walking or do you want to go?" he asks. The rain has beaded on his hat and his mask is tucked under his chin, ready to pull on if someone comes.

"Keep going."

I move but he tugs me back. "I forgive you for laughing," he says.

"I forgive you for not listening to me about the goose."

"Fair enough." He bends down and kisses me, lips cool from the damp day. The rain patters against the umbrella as my hands come up to wrap around his biceps, bringing him even closer. The kisses meld together and the sound of the lake fades and Sam is all there is around me. He's warm in the cool day, and his hands smooth down the droplets on my hair. When he presses tiny kisses on me, he leaves a longer pause between each one, making me chase after him.

His last kiss makes me shiver and I'm not sure if it's from the chill or his touch. In any case, he pulls back, rubbing my arms. "Let's walk to warm up," he says.

We turn east to the walkway that traces the edge of the lake. The rain comes in fits and starts, the same as our conversation.

"You know what's weird?" I ask.

"That the largest living thing on earth is a fungus?"

"What? No." I hop over a puddle. "Seriously? Not a whale or a tree?"

"The humongous fungus in Oregon."

"That is fascinating but not what I was thinking. Why would I be thinking of that?"

He picks up a rock lying on the boardwalk and tosses it out to the lake. "I was."

"I might delve into that later but I was wondering about why interviewers don't ask you or Fangli about politics or human rights in China. It's strange. It's in the news all the time."

"That's not strange. Reporters are more interested in Fangli's manicure and how I get in shape for action roles. Generally fans want us to stick to our lane and reporters give them what they want."

"Oh."

"I don't need to share all my personal thoughts with the world." He eyes me with amusement. "Do Canadian actors speak out against your own country's abuses?"

"Not often," I admit after I think about it.

"Did you ever think to ask why we're responsible for answering for our government when they're not responsible for yours?"

"A good point."

"Obviously, there are problems with my home," he says. "Those are issues for us to solve, the same as yours are for you to solve."

We walk along in the misty rain for a few more minutes, thinking.

"Do you come here a lot?" he asks. "This is a calming place."

"Not as much as I should," I say.

"Where do you usually go? Say you have a Saturday free. Your ideal Saturday."

I tug at a branch as I pass, letting the wet leaf drag along my palm. The entire left side of the path is treed. "It would be summer, but not too hot. I'd take a book and go to a café I like in Kensington Market. They have those Parisian-style seats on the sidewalk and I'd get a Mexican hot chocolate and sit and read and watch the people pass."

"All day?"

"Two hours." After that I'd need to pee, and when you're alone, you can't leave your bag, so I'd might as well head out. "Then I'd wander through the market and look in some stores to buy things I don't need, like a hat."

"Would you see a show? Go to a movie?"

"Nope. I'd go see Mom. How about you?"

"My perfect day? Sleeping. I'd sleep in and turn off my phone and then sit on the couch and do nothing. I wouldn't leave the apartment. Get food delivered."

"What if you had to leave the house?"

"I wouldn't."

"It's on fire. You have to."

"If my apartment is on fire, then it's not my perfect day."

"It's a thought exercise, Sam."

He gives me a shy glance out of the corner of his eye. "You won't laugh?"

"Cross my heart."

"It's not very exciting."

"My day involved reading and drinking hot chocolate," I remind him.

"I'd go for a walk in a park. There's one at home called Beihai Park. The amahs weren't allowed to take me because my parents were worried about security so I've never been." He rolls his shoulders. "I'd see the water lilies. I heard they're beautiful."

Poor Sam. His life mixes extreme privilege with such a poverty of normal experience. He doesn't wait for me to speak but says, "Your day. You'd spend it mostly alone?"

I consider this. "I might meet a friend for a drink in the evening but yeah, I guess. Same as you."

"I'd meet you after I sleep in," he offers. "You could come to the park with me."

I bop his shoulder with my head. "I'd like that."

We head back to the ferry, doing tandem silly walks as we try to stay under the umbrella. The ferry will be a few minutes so I go into the café to grab hot chocolate as Sam stays under a tree, keeping his face down.

When I hand over his paper cup, I notice his right arm is soaked. "What happened?"

He gives me a look over the top of his cup. "It's raining."

"I'm dry, though." I shake my arms at him and immediately spill a bit of my drink.

"Good," he says, glancing up. "There's the ferry. Can we sit on the top again?" When I nod, he kisses me on the nose and his lips warm me all the way through. "I changed my mind," he says. "About my perfect day."

"No park?"

He shakes his head. "I'd do this again."

Yeah, I think it was a date.

Thirty-Three

The day after our maybe date is not weird but also *isn't* not weird. Sam warned me he'd be busy but texts me little thoughts throughout the day, and I find myself carrying my phone around with me in case I miss one. It's not productive and I finally text Anjali after getting ready for bed.

jfc it was totally a date, she writes.

I stare at the screen. My phone rings.

"You know it was a date," Anjali says.

I wrap the plush robe closer around me and adjust the pearl-infused sheet mask Mei left out for me to get it out of my eye. "It was, right?"

"Kissing? Hot chocolate? Holding hands?"

"What does it mean, though?"

Anjali snorts. "That you enjoy each other's company and are getting to know each other. And want to bang."

"Probably."

"You mispronounced 'definitely' as 'probably.'"

"I don't know if that's a good idea." The mask slips again and I try not to move my mouth too much when I speak.

"None of this is a good idea."

"I don't need to compound it."

"You don't need to do anything you don't want to," she reminds me. "The question is if you want to."

"I don't know."

"Then figure it out before you go further."

Easy for her to say—she doesn't have to deal with the dreamboat that is Sam Yao up close and personal. I give a noncommittal response and change the topic. "How's work?"

"I had to reprimand a guy on my team," she says. "He thought it was a good idea to use a photo of Miley Cyrus on the wrecking ball as his laptop background."

"Why?"

"Said it was a cultural meme. I walked him through how it was a bad idea, and he took it better than I expected. Not Todd level."

"Still irritating."

"I'll say. Speaking of Todd, has he acted up like the immature man-child that he is?" I'd told her what happened at the Chanel show.

"Nope."

"Good. Bullies like that back down when they're challenged."

"Let's not waste breath talking about him anymore." Todd is out of my life. "Did you finish with the life coach?"

She doesn't hesitate. "Canceled the last two sessions. I'm in control here. Not him."

"You tell him."

"I run my life, and if that means I remain moderately dictatorial, so be it."

"No one tells you what to do, within reason."

"No one's the boss of me, except my boss."

We both slap the phone in a virtual high five.

———

The next morning I wake to a text from Sam. **Breakfast? When do I get to test Eppy?**

Yes and soon, I text back.

We meet out on the street and Sam's in his usual disguise of ball cap, black jeans, and black T-shirt. He has a coffee that he hands to me—a latte, exactly as I like it—and a paper bag with what I suspect are pastries.

We stroll down to the lake and take a seat on one of the benches where he hands me a croissant and takes a bite of his own. It's peaceful with him, watching the sun glisten on the lake, alone except for a stream of panting joggers who speed by.

I've been thinking about what Anjali said about Todd acting out and how I'd deal with it. Todd is a wound that's currently stanched and I want completely cauterized.

"Then we called the company and had her reinstated." Sam finishes his story about a colleague and I suddenly turn to look at him, croissant halfway to my mouth.

I don't have to deal with Todd by myself, because he's no longer only a me problem. There are people better equipped to deal with Todd than I am, and all I have to do is ask.

"I need to ask you a favor," I say.

"Sure." No hesitation.

"It's about Todd."

Sam only nods when I tell him I'm concerned Todd might try to get back at me, and as usual, the siren call of Fangli's name spurs him into action. "I'll take care of it," he says.

"What are you going to do?"

He looks thoughtful. "Hire some goons to break his legs?"

I hesitate, unsure if he's kidding.

He lifts the brim of his hat to look me better in the eyes. "I'm going to talk to my lawyer, Gracie. No kneecaps will be broken."

"Good."

"Unless the lawyer recommends it, and then what can I do?"

I nod seriously. "It's a law if a lawyer says it."

There it is. The end of Todd in my life, not with a bang but with a lawyer's dry language.

Very satisfying.

Sam's phone rings. He looks at it, silences it, and then eats the rest of his croissant.

"Your mom?" He only gets that tight look around his mouth when it's Lu Lili.

"She's stepped up her campaign." He glances at the phone, then flips it over so the screen is covered.

"How so?"

He sighs. "She called Denis."

"The director for your next movie?" After this, Sam is due to start filming on a corporate spy action movie that I haven't been thinking about because it reminds me how finite our time together is.

"He told me yesterday. She didn't threaten him—Lili doesn't do anything so crass—but she said she wanted his advice on how to get me to see reason."

"Wow."

"I know," he says. I look left and right to confirm we're the only ones on the boardwalk, then pull him in to lean against me. The faint thump of his heart sounds against my arm and I trace little circles on his shoulder, feeling the muscles slowly relax. I have a moment of unreality, that I'm sitting here with Sam Yao, but he's only Sam, a guy I like who happens to be talking about problems with his iconic mother and his new action movie—normal person stuff. "Luckily Denis took it well."

"Is she trying to sabotage you?" What kind of a mother does this?

"She would say she's looking out for my future."

"What did you do?"

"Nothing." His shrug shifts against me. "What can I do? It's impossible to make her see reason."

"That's a bit defeatist."

"You don't know my mother," he says darkly. The phone vibrates between us and we ignore it.

"Aren't you the one who told me there are enough people in the world ready to pull me down and that I didn't need to join them? Same goes for you."

"Hardly the same thing." He stands, then turns away, tugging his hat down to hide his face as a pod of runners approaches en masse. "Can we walk for a bit?"

We go west to the Music Garden and wander the paths through the landscaped plants. The sun is already hot but the garden retains some of the coolness from the night.

"What will you do when Fangli goes back home?" he asks as he balances on the edge of a grass-covered step. I reach out to grab him as he tilts back, but he only winks at me.

"Find a job, I guess." I'm not enthusiastic.

"Not Eppy?"

A warm flush comes over me; he believes in it enough to think I can make it a business. "I'll have to do that on the side. Need to pay the bills."

He hands me a card. "Robin Banerjee."

I gaze at it. "What?"

"Didn't get a chance to talk to him the other night, so I asked around. Apparently he's a nice guy." He nods at the card. "That's his personal cell."

"You did this for me?" I take the card. There it is, black font on matte card stock. Robin Banerjee's cell number. At the Chanel party, I'd been torn between wanting Sam to intercede and needing to do it myself. That's faded. Help isn't anything to be ashamed of and it doesn't take away from my independence.

"I want one thing in return."

"What?"

"You let me use Eppy right away. With Deng gone, I'm desperate to keep my life in order."

I take my phone out and send him the hidden URL right then and there. Then I pause. "You got me this number and you have no idea if Eppy works or not."

"I believe in you," he says. "You haven't failed at anything I've seen you try yet."

When was the last time someone had this blind faith in me, even more than I have in myself? Combined with what Fangli said the other night, it makes my vision go a little blurry. "Thank you."

"Except for faking laryngitis at the art gallery," he adds. "That was bad."

"Silence, you."

The phone vibrates in his pocket again and this time he pulls it out with a muffled curse. "My mother again."

"Answer it."

He stares at the screen and doesn't move.

"Sam, take the call."

"For you." With a sigh, he answers. "Wei?" There's a long silence that stretches. I try to read Sam's expression, but all he does is squint into the middle distance like an old-time pirate scoping out the horizon for land.

Then comes a burst of Mandarin and more silence. I walk over to the water's edge to give him some privacy, because whatever the two of them are talking about is causing Sam so much tension his entire body is clenched tight. Sam, worldwide star, has mega-mother issues. I never would have thought his life was anything but charmed.

Instantly, I'm ashamed at how shallow I am. This is what Sam was telling me in the car, that I had trouble seeing beyond all the trappings of fame. No matter what, money will help smooth over whatever problems Sam and Fangli experience—that's not even up for debate—but the more I see of them, the more they become people rather than characters. The more I care about them.

I glance back. Sam's frowning at the sky as he listens and he doesn't need me spying on him. When he looks over, I make a gesture that I hope will be correctly interpreted as *Take your time; to give you space, I am going to go for a quick walk.* At his nod, I head down toward the tall ship moored at the end of a pier about fifty meters away.

He's waiting for me when I get back. "That was interesting," he says, tossing his phone from one hand to another. He doesn't use a cell-phone cover so I need to turn away because all I can picture is the screen shattered on the ground when it drops.

We walk along the water and I thump the palm of my hand on the thick pedestals that line the edge of the path, which apart from more runners in the distance, is empty at this early morning hour. "Were you honest with her?"

"I was."

"Not a success?"

He kisses the top of my head and I do my best not to melt. "You can say that."

"She won't get off your back about joining your father's company?"

"Lili only mentioned it once." He pauses. "She has a new goal now."

"What's that?"

"She decided I'm going to marry Fangli."

"What?" I twist around to see him laughing, but not in a happy, life is good way.

"She mentioned it before but I headed her off. Now she's determined because she saw clips of us in Toronto and knows we'd be a successful match because of how we looked at each other. Except, in those clips, I was with you."

"She didn't see that I wasn't Fangli?"

"I told you, you're good. Also, the image she sent me as proof of this predestined love wasn't a close-up." He pinches the bridge of his nose. "I'd better warn Fangli." He takes out his phone and frowns. "Too late. Her father called her."

"Your mom and her dad know each other?"

"Fangli's father is very influential, which means Lili absolutely knows him." His expression is less a smile than a line formed by his lips pulling tight.

I shrug. "Well, what if they do want you to get married? You're thirty. They can't make you."

"I wouldn't put it past them to announce it on our behalf," he says grimly. "My mother would see it as helping the family business, given Fangli's father's role in government."

"Does she live in the Victorian age?"

He raises his eyebrows. "You think these marriages don't happen all the time?"

"I never had to think about it."

"Lili does." He looks at the sky. Clouds have swept in with a heavy wind. "We should head back. Looks like rain."

He doesn't move, though, and drops his gaze to the harbor in front of us. The boats bob on the water as they strain against their moorings.

"Hey, Sam?"

"What?"

I lean over so my shoulder grazes his arm. "It's okay to not want all that."

"I know." He speaks quickly and gives a harsh laugh that almost hurts to hear.

"No, Sam." I tug on his arm so he looks at me. "I mean it."

"I owe her," he says. "I've had an easy ride because of my parents. Their names, the connections. I'd be nowhere if it wasn't for them."

I can't argue that because it's definitely true being the treasured son of a film star will give you the most head start of head starts so I focus on the real matter. "You owe them love," I say. "Not some outdated sense of filial loyalty where you abase yourself to their orders."

"You don't understand."

"Probably not." I shrug. "Tell me. Would it be so bad to be CEO?"

"I'd never escape her then." The words spill out and Sam looks astonished. "Holy shit," he says. "I'm a terrible son."

"No." I step around so I'm between him and the water. "You can want to live your life, Sam. Lu Lili has her own life. She doesn't need yours as well."

He rubs the side of his cheek and I hear the slight scrape of his stubble as he works his fingers nervously back and forth while his eyes move between my face and over my shoulder. Then his hand drops back to his side and he stops moving completely. "Okay."

What a wonderfully fluid word that is, depending on the tone. Give it an emphasis at the end and you have joyful triumph (o-KAY!). Draw out the beginning for a nice dose of doubtful hesitation (ooo-kay?). Then there's the way Sam says it now, hushed and vulnerable as if the O is a window through which he can see a road he never knew existed.

"Okay," I say back. Used to ease this time.

"Okay." Firm and decisive. End of conversation.

He gives the water a final look before he bends down and captures my mouth under his. This time he moves slowly enough for me to feel the shape of his lips against mine before he shifts the tempo and pulls me tight as the kiss deepens. His big hands slide from my shoulders until he holds both my hands in his and the kiss changes to soft flutters against my mouth.

It's only him and me, standing by a wind-blown lake.

I can never tire of this.

———

"I can't believe she called my father." Fangli gives Sam a tired look across the table. The three of us assemble after Fangli and Sam get off from work. Fangli picks at the sashimi in front of her, her brows knit together.

"What did he say?" asks Sam.

"My father thinks it's a good idea. He's been after me to marry because he wants a grandchild." She pulls her hair back into a ponytail and lets it drop down. "Why now? We've known each other for years."

"Lili says we look happy together."

Fangli groans. "That's Gracie, not me."

"Sorry," I say weakly. "I can dial it back."

Sam puts his hand on mine. Fangli notices and her eyes widen. "Oh my God," she says. "How long has this been going on?"

"What?" we ask in unison.

She stares pointedly at our hands, because Sam hasn't moved. "No wonder they think we should get married." Then she laughs and I can tell she's not upset but more bemused at the situation.

Then she shoots me a look. "You didn't say a word the other night." Another frown, this one at Sam as she points at him with a dramatic gesture. "Neither did you!"

He snorts. "You took that right out of *January February*."

"When I was accusing my mother-in-law of murder." She nods. "It's a powerful movement."

"Very good," he compliments her.

"But not an appropriate reflection on the situation." Fangli winks. "Unlike when I unleashed it on my killer mother-in-law, I'm happy for you."

He tightens his hand on mine as Mei comes into the room. Her immobile face stiffens even more and I assume she's put off by PDA. She turns to Fangli and speaks quickly.

"My therapist is here," Fangli says. She wiggles her eyebrows at me and leaves, Mei closing the connecting door firmly behind them.

"She said that more openly than I would have thought," I say.

He nods proudly. "She's trying hard." Then he gets up to clear the dishes. "Do you have plans for tonight?"

I play it casual. "Not really."

He sits back down. "Want to come here, then?"

I go over and sit on his lap. Sam takes my leg and pulls me over until I'm straddling him and we're face-to-face. He's warm and the flutters that start in my stomach take only moments to ripple out over every inch of my skin. Sam runs his hands along my back, and when I bend to kiss him, I make sure my eyes stay on him.

Two hours later, I'm very glad I shaved above my knees.

Thirty-Four

When the phone wakes me up, I want to ignore it because I'm curled against Sam and he's warm.

"Forget it," I mumble.

"It might be important." He gropes around the night table and hands me the phone.

He's right because the nurse on the line tells me Mom's distressed again. "It's been a few days since your last visit," says the nurse. "It might cheer her up."

I hang up and Sam leans over to cover my body with his. Last night was... I can't think about it because I need to be out the door in a few minutes.

"Everything okay?" he asks. He brushes my hair back from my face and nuzzles into my neck.

"I need to see Mom."

"Want company?"

I do, I realize. Sam gives me a kiss on the forehead, which is good because the idea of kissing anyone, even Sam, with morning breath is not a pleasant one. "Give me twenty minutes," he says.

He disappears and I get out of bed rejoicing. The morning after is always a crapshoot, filled with worries about making things weird. But it wasn't; Sam is as attentive in the light of morning as he was in the dark last night.

Which was very attentive indeed.

I almost skip over to the shower, where I wince when the water hits the burn on my skin left from Sam's stubble. Towel-dry my hair, minimal makeup, a dress, and I'm out the door. Sam's waiting by the elevators.

We take public transit and don't talk much. Sam sits close to me, lazily watching the people around us from under the brim of his hat. The fact that no one has noticed us on previous outings must have made him more confident about coming out with me.

I want to curl up into his shoulder. It would be so nice to keep going on this bus and never look back, but guilt hits the minute I think it. What kind of a daughter thinks such selfish thoughts? Sam tucks my hand in his and an ache goes through me when I remember Dad picking up Mom in those bear hugs or planting raspberry kisses on her cheeks as she laughed.

It hurts. I pretend I need to check my phone and take back my hand. When he doesn't reach out again, it's almost as if I have proof that he doesn't care. Why am I doing this to myself? We had a great night and he's here with me now, on the bus, to see Mom. That's what matters. He wants to be here and I'm not forcing him.

When we sign in at the home, the smell of bleach is almost unbearable and it stings my nose. Mom's in her room, the album of photos open in front of her. Her eyes skate over me to land on Sam. "Xiao He," she says, her fingers stroking the page in front of her. Tears stream down her face and I don't know what to do. I've seen my mother cry exactly once in my life, when we came home from the hospital after Dad died and she tripped over a shoe he'd left by the door. She'd picked it up and hugged it and sobbed as I held her. She hadn't even cried at the funeral.

She's crying now for her dead brother and talking in fast Mandarin.

"She's back in China and begging him for help," whispers Sam. "I think she's reliving a memory."

"Xiao He," calls my mother.

"She thinks I'm her brother again," Sam says.

I grab Mom's hand as if my touch can yank her back from the past. "Mom?"

She mutters in Mandarin but Sam shakes his head in confusion when I look at him for a translation.

"Xiao He?" Now her voice is tremulous and pleading.

I say the idea before I think it through. It makes sense. It might work. "Can you be her brother?"

He turns to me, perplexed. "What are you asking, Gracie?"

I don't think, just whisper so Mom can't hear. "Please, pretend to be Xiao He to calm her down. Only for a minute."

Sam steps back. "I can't do that."

"You're an *actor* for fuck's sake." I stand up and work my hand out of Mom's grip to motion Sam to the far side of the room. "You do this all the time."

"Not this," he says in a quiet voice. "I won't do it."

He won't do it, when I know he wouldn't hesitate if it was Fangli who asked? If he cared about me at all, he would. "Please."

"Gracie, no. It's wrong."

The pettiness of his refusal is like a match lighting up my stressed mind. "It's wrong?"

"To fool your mother like this, yes." A muscle twitches in his jaw.

"This is wrong. You helping me out with my mother is wrong. Me pretending to be Fangli isn't? Where were your high morals when I was tricking that kid at the hospital? When we were lying to him? How come the ends justified the means then?"

His face goes still. "It's not the same."

"It's absolutely the same and you know it." I glare at him. "Fangli wanted it. That's what makes the difference. Fangli was the one asking."

"That's not fair, Gracie." His voice is hard. "Your uncle is real and your mother is real. Fans have an idea of Fangli—they don't know the real person and they don't want to. They want the fairy tale."

"I'm asking you to do this." I don't add *because I've done a lot for you and Fangli* but the silent words hang between us, unsaid but not unheard.

He turns abruptly as if to walk away.

"Fine, leave," I say. "If you're not going to help me, get out. You hypocrite."

Mom starts to call for her brother again. I'm about to go to her when Sam turns around and starts to speak in Mandarin, a soft and assuring tone with no trace of his earlier reluctance. I have no idea what he says, but Mom calms almost immediately, eating him up with hungry eyes.

It only takes a few minutes for Mom to begin to drift, her face relaxed. She's having more trouble staying awake, and the violence of her emotions would have tired her out more. Sam speaks in a lower tone that takes on the feel of a lullaby and soon Mom's fast asleep.

He waits until her chin is buried against her chest before he looks at me with a grim expression. "I want to talk to you."

We move into the doorway because I want to stay near Mom but also don't want to stand in the middle of the corridor for all to see.

"What did she say?" I ask. "What did she talk about?" I know Sam's mad but I'm desperate to know what could have upset her so much.

"She said she was sorry and she did as he asked. She said she wished she could have seen him again and that he needs to be at peace." He reports on their conversation without comment on what it could mean.

"Thank you."

Sam leans against the door and crosses his arms, the image of a man taking his ease. "I don't want your thanks. I wanted you to not make me do that."

"I didn't make you," I say. "I asked and you agreed."

"You knew I would do what you asked, Gracie, and you took advantage of it."

Fuck. He sounds resigned, like he should have expected it. "I didn't assume you would, if that's what you're saying."

"No?" His expression is unreadable. "Making it a ranking between you and Fangli wasn't a deliberate choice?"

I can feel the prickling heat of shame. "It was an emergency, Sam. You saw how she was."

"Would she have calmed down if you tried a bit harder to talk to her?" He runs his hand through his hair in what I now know is his habit whenever he feels uncomfortable. It falls back over his eyes. "Without making her believe her dead brother was talking to her? Without making me do that? It was wrong."

"So?" I turn on him. "Maybe I'd take a bit of wrong to give her some peace."

"She said she admired your integrity," he snaps back. "Do you think she wants truth or peace?"

"I think you don't know her, so you can keep your speeches to yourself."

"You could be right. I don't know her but I know you."

"You don't know me," I say. "We've known each other a month. You don't know a fucking thing about me and I don't know anything about you, okay?"

Even as I say the words, I want to grab them back. Sam's face goes hard. "Is that what you think?"

"Forget it," I mutter.

"How am I supposed to forget it?"

"I didn't mean it." Now that the flush of my anger is gone, I'm mortified. I was in the wrong to ask Sam. The nasty motivation that made me push him would be as obvious to even the worst Psych 101 student as it was to Sam. I wanted him to show me he cared by making him do what I wanted. I feel nauseous that I stooped so low. This is not cool. Not remotely cool.

Mom stirs and I glance over at her. "We can talk about this later. Are you staying?"

"I think I should leave." He hesitates, then looks over my shoulder. Someone's coming down the hall. Sam tilts his head down and jams on his hat, then leaves without saying another word.

"Gracie?" The brief rest has brought Mom some clarity. I walk over. Damn, I should have taken the photo album away while she was sleeping.

I'm so upset with what's happened that my hands shake when I reach out to close the photo book. Mom's hand lands with surprising strength on mine. "Tell Xiao He I kept my promise," she says in English, looking at me. "I kept the past in the past and lived my future."

"I will." I soothe her with gentle pets on her hands. I don't know who she thinks I am. "It's time to relax now."

It takes me about an hour to relax her enough to get the album away. I hold it in my hands, wondering if it would be better for me to take it home, when a sheet falls out, the edge jagged from where it's been ripped out of a magazine. It's a photo of Sam and Fangli, a publicity shot from one of their movies. I guess Mom took it because it reminded her of Xiao He. I can't bring myself to deprive her of the memories, even if they cause her pain, and I put the album back in its drawer.

Finally I see residents walking by on their way to the morning coffee break. "It's time for a cookie," I tell Mom. "Let's see if they have chocolate chip."

She follows me like an obedient child, and after she's had two cookies and a cup of tea, she seems to be back to her old self. "You're a good girl to visit, but go back to work," she says. "You are hired to do a job and shouldn't disappoint them." Her tone brooks no argument and I give in the same as I always did growing up.

Sam isn't outside waiting for me and the taste of disappointment comes up hard and sour. I told him to leave. Why would he stick around after what I pulled? I was worried about Mom but it wasn't the choice I should have made.

I blink back the tears as I turn the corner and head for the bus stop. It's a long ride home, made even more depressing by the lack of texts from Sam. I take my phone out to check again and my finger hovers over his contact. I need to apologize.

He said I knew he would do what I asked. I want to ask him exactly what he meant.

On autopilot, I go from the bus to the subway, the subway to the hotel, the hotel to my room. I get a glass of water and sit down on the couch to decide my next and hopefully less disastrous step when the phone rings.

Sam or Anjali would text and the home is the only one who phones so I answer without checking who's calling. "Hello?"

"Is this Gracie Reed?" It's a woman.

"Yes." I stare hard out the window at the lake without focusing. Definitely the home and please let Mom be okay.

"This is Miranda calling from ZZTV. We'd like a comment from you."

ZZTV? My heart slams into my throat but I try to play it cool. "From me? About what?"

"We have a tip that you're impersonating Wei Fangli and want to give you a chance to tell your side of the story. We pay well and it would play in your favor to get ahead of the story."

I hang up without saying another word. Shit. How could they have found out? Who gave them the tip? Then I know. Todd, of course. Sam had only told me he took care of it, not what he did. I'd trusted Sam, through his lawyer, to take care of this but it's becoming clear Todd is a Terminator—always coming back when I think he's out of my life.

I put the glass of water carefully on the coffee table because my arm is shaking so hard I can't control my hand.

The secret is out. I check online immediately and sag with relief when nothing comes up, then take a deep and shuddering breath before sitting on the couch and mentally running through my options, which are very few. Obviously the best one is to tell Sam and Fangli what's going on and let them deal with it because I'm no PR shark to try to make deals with ZZTV. I'd make a bad situation worse.

I pick up my phone but hesitate, not wanting to commit the words to a screen. Maybe ZZTV is hacking my phone and that's how they know. I put the device down on the table beside the water and eye it like a loaded gun before staring up at the ceiling. Could the room be bugged?

God, what about Mom? If they know who I am, they'll go digging. What if they call the home and ask about her? I should call them. I stop again. For all that Glen Lake isn't Xin Guang, I do trust them to keep their patients' privacy. Plus, if my phone is hacked, I don't want to give any clues. I don't know if I'm being paranoid or realistic.

The luxury Xanadu suite feels like a cage, the walls closing in over my head. I jump off the couch and go out to the balcony, where I grip the rail so hard my knuckles go white. This is the exact situation Anjali warned me about. Now that it's here in front of me, what do I do? That sensation of powerlessness binds me—the same feeling I felt going in to work for Todd, which makes sense because here he is ruining my life again.

I never want to feel this again.

With a quick shove, I push away from the rail and check the time.

I need to talk to Fangli and Sam to get a solution. I won't let this happen to me as if I have nothing to do or say about it. For the first time, it dawns on me that I need to give myself the same consideration I do Mom, or Fangli or Sam. I need to matter.

I go back into the suite and over to the connecting door. Better to do this in person than by phone, even though I'm not sure what to say. I know Sam's very rightfully angry with me but this is urgent enough a problem for him to put aside his personal feelings, at least until it's fixed.

I'm about to knock when I hear voices—Sam and Fangli are both in.

"She told ZZTV?" It's Sam's voice, colder than I've ever heard him. "You have to let her go."

Are they talking about me?

"I trusted her." Fangli sounds sad. "I thought she was paid enough. How could she?"

Shit, it *is* me. They think it's me who ratted them out. My hand hasn't moved but now it's frozen. All I need to do is walk in there and tell them the truth.

What if they don't believe me? Miranda had my name. What has she told them?

I'm desperate to know more before I go bumbling in. I've learned my lesson that there are no clear-cut answers in the world, no unilaterally good actions. I can't help my mom without hurting Sam. I can't help Fangli without lying. What I can do is get all the facts before I open my mouth and embarrass myself yet again.

"Keep your voice down," Fangli says. "She can't hear this, not yet."

Sam answers in rapid Mandarin, no doubt to hide what they're saying about me *from me*, and I'm lost.

No, I'm not.

I grab my phone and tap the new language app I found, the real-time audio translator. My conscience hits as I hold it up to the crack in the door but it quickly disappears as I read the translated text. I know it's not going to be one hundred percent accurate but it will at least give me the gist of their conversation so I can go in prepared.

"What benefit was there from the suitcase?" This is Fangli. This stupid translator. What the hell is the suitcase?

"Greed." Sam's voice comes through clear enough. I stare at the words appearing on the screen so hard they blur. "Envy."

"There was enough."

"For some people, there's never enough. I should have traveled sooner." He sounds furious. "That argument caused this."

"You heat lamp have known."

"We can't trust coffee."

"It must have been the mackerel." This is Fangli. "I'll talk to her. I hate it."

"I'll do it for cheese."

"Sam, it's my responsibility. I hired her."

That's me Fangli is worried about firing. And Sam offered to do it for her. Their voices dip too low for the translator, and I back away from the door until I bump the table with my hip. I look down without seeing it, my attention held by the conversation going on behind that door between two people I had come to consider friends and, in Sam's case, more than friends.

Then I creep back and slowly twist the bolt to lock my side of the door. I act on impulse, only knowing that I need to stop any chance of either of them coming in. I need to think this through logically but my mind jumps from one idea to another without lingering long enough for me to process. I need to think. I can't think. It's too much.

There's an aura around my sight, almost like tunnel vision. My eyes light on a jar of poppies on the table before they travel to my phone, which I don't remember putting down. The chairs are all tidily tucked under the wooden table and I see a pen near the edge. My hand combs over my hair, short and stiff with product, before giving my earring a slight tug and running the hem of my shirt through my fingers. I grab the back of a chair. My thoughts begin to slow. A siren wails from the street outside and the refrigerator hums in the corner. In the hall, I hear someone laugh. The room smells of the candles I lit last night, a rich lavender, mixed with the purple hyacinth scent from the perfume drawer of wonders. Finally, I run my tongue over my lip and taste the synthetic fruit of my lip balm.

My chest hitches a bit as I inhale, like my body is trying not to cry but I force the air in again and again. I'm not okay but I can function, which is the best I can ask for right now.

Sam might have liked me but not enough. It's only slightly less painful than if he didn't have feelings for me at all. Whatever he felt, it wasn't sufficient for him to default to my side when he thought I sold them out and called ZZTV. Fangli is the one who mattered.

I can't prevent the wave of self-disgust. I should have known this would end in disaster because that's what happens when you reach too high. I forgot that this little bubble I'm in isn't real.

The best thing for me to do would be to unlock that door, explain that I did not call ZZTV, thank them for their time, and leave.

I want to. I know I should.

I don't have the guts.

I'm done, but I can do Fangli the favor of not forcing her to fire me in a painful and stress-inducing conversation. I can help her one last time by clearing out with enough class to leave us all with some dignity and without hostility.

It doesn't take me long to pack.

Then I write an email to Fangli.

> *You probably know that ZZTV called me to get my side of the story. I hung up on them. I know I signed the NDA, but even if I hadn't, I never would have told them. I overheard you and Sam but I swear it wasn't me who told ZZTV.*
>
> *I wish I could spend more time with you. I'll miss you. Thank you for everything.*

I hesitate, weighed down by the thirty grand sitting in my bank account. Should I keep it? The money might be tainted but I did earn it. I decide to keep it but tell her I understand if she wants me to return it and of course I waive all rights to the rest of the money.

I read it over a few times before I decide it will do.

Sam, though, Sam's another story. He knew I needed the money for Mom, not out of greed or ego. Refusing the rest of the pay seems like a message to Sam as well, at least in my head. I walk out the door, and right before I enter the subway, I click Send and then block both their numbers from my phone. It's better this way.

Just like that, it's all done. I'm back to being Gracie Reed, sad, jobless loser.

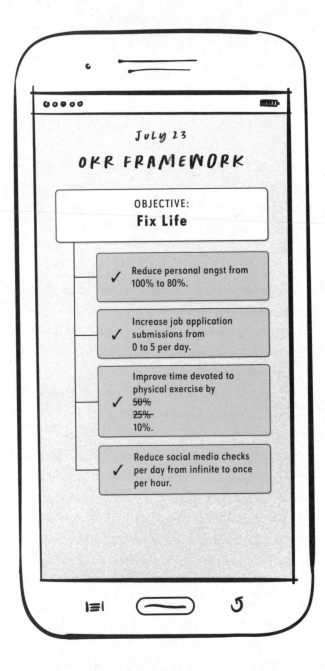

Thirty-Five

It almost feels like getting fired all over again, but with more heartache and in a less comfortable environment since I decided to get an Airbnb for a few days. Thanks to their detective's dossier, Sam and Fangli know where I live. I don't want to talk to either of them because it would be too painful to have to recount what I said in the letter in person. A clean break is the best break for both bones and relationships.

It's no Xanadu, but it's cute, a small sunny apartment in a low-rise on the other side of town. The central design element in the living room is a hard couch that I sit on for hours, staring at my phone, half expecting and half dreading what could happen and refreshing my browser every three minutes to see if I've been publicly shamed. Thank God my social media is under the generic @gracie_graceTO, so I don't need to worry about that getting flooded. I can watch cat videos in peace even if I need to go into hiding from the world.

For the twentieth time, I almost check to see if Sam or Fangli have shown up in my voicemail for blocked callers. I toss the phone aside. That experience is over and whether they try to contact me or not doesn't matter. It's done. I'm done.

Rectitude. If I'd acted with rectitude, I wouldn't be in this position now. I wouldn't have a thing to be ashamed about.

I call Anjali and tell her I left and that ZZTV called. I leave out the part about eavesdropping. That hurts too much to talk about.

"I'm sorry, Gracie." Her voice is gentle and holds none of the smugness she's entitled to as a result of being correct that this would end in tears. She's in Vancouver for work, but physical distance has not prevented her from taking on the role of cheerleader with a vengeance.

Anjali lets me talk, not interrupting at all, which is so unlike her that I know I must be a more pitiful mess than I thought. Finally, once I peter out, she says, "You have to stop blaming yourself. You have nothing to be ashamed of."

"It was dumb. You told me this was a dumb thing to do."

"I did," she agrees. "But you keep acting like this is some moral failure on your part."

"Didn't you hear what I said? About tricking people?"

"Do you think Fangli is ethically lacking? That she's a bad person?"

"No."

"Then give yourself the same consideration."

"Is this life coach advice from the good days?"

"Saw it on an online advice column but it remains valid."

"Maybe." Easier said than done.

"What are you going to do now?"

"Wait for ZZTV to drag my name through the mud and move to Tierra del Fuego?"

"It's cold there. Damp, too."

"I'll bring a coat," I say morosely.

Her sigh gusts into the phone. "Do you have a plan B? What about Eppy?"

"I'm working on it."

"Are you working on it or sitting on your ass checking your phone to see if ZZTV released your name?"

I pause. "The latter."

"When this started, you said Fangli's team could handle any scandals."

"I did."

"Nothing has happened yet."

"Not *yet*."

There's a bang, then Anjali's voice comes back on. "That was me hitting the phone in frustration," she says. "Here's what you're going to do."

Despite myself I grin. Anjali's back in fighting form. "What am I going to do?"

"I'm going to set up a Google alert for your name and I'll tell you if anything happens. You're going to turn off your Wi-Fi and work on Eppy."

"I might need to research something."

"Save everything you need to search and send it to me. I'll copy and paste the web pages."

"This is ridiculous. You don't have time for this."

"I've been on the phone with you for an hour. Trust me that I have the four minutes to set an alert. Plus it's a scientific fact I made up that 98.9 percent of internet searches are only mindless surfing."

"Anjali..."

"Two days. Try for two days. Give yourself a break, Gracie. Leave your phone at home. See your mom. Work on a project you love. Let me help."

I lie back on the couch and nod before I remember she can't see. "Thanks."

"Now turn off your damn phone and get some rest."

———

Over the next two days, Anjali texts me updates every few hours that only say "None" so I know she's checking for me. It feels good to have her on my side. I think she and Fangli would have liked each other.

It's not so bad being myself full-time again. It's a relief to not have to be a person I'm not, and I was never able to take full advantage of the wine or food as Fangli anyway. I miss talking with Fangli more than I expected and a few times find myself thinking of things to tell her before I remember that part of my life is done.

I also, because I'm a bit materialistic, miss that expensive perfume collection. I left it all there, every little bottle, so they couldn't accuse me of stealing. I even left that gorgeous jumpsuit but mostly because it reminded me of Sam.

I refuse to think about Sam at all.

It's particularly hard at night. I never realized how empty my life had become until I no longer had Fangli and Sam there to talk with at the end of the day. Finally, driven by a need for human connection, I head to Cheri's coffee shop. I want a friendly face if only for a few minutes of surface-level in-person conversation.

"Hey, babe, long time." Cheri automatically starts making a latte for me but I stop her.

"Just a coffee today."

"Got it. What you been up to?"

"Ah, you know." Pretending to be a movie star, falling in love with another movie star, worrying about worldwide humiliation, as one will.

"Right, right." She glances over. "I got chocolate."

"Double chocolate scone."

"You can have the last one." She plucks it out with the tongs and hands it over. "Loni's preggers again and can't stand the smell of it, so her kid's stuck eating the lemon ones."

We chat about nothing for a few minutes, and as she's about to hand me the cup, Cheri says, "Hey, some dude was in looking for you day before yesterday."

Please not ZZTV. "Me, by name?"

"Yeah, superhot Asian guy." Then her dark eyes narrow. "There he is now. You need to go out the back?"

I turn.

It's Sam.

Cheri's voice fades out behind me as my body kicks into fight-or-flight, adrenaline making my ears hum and the muscles in my stomach clench so hard I almost hunch over. I didn't expect this. Sam came looking for me. Why?

He looks tired but when our eyes meet, his shoulders drop slightly, as if in relief.

"I'm good," I tell Cheri.

Something in my voice makes her eyebrows rise. "Hey, I got your back here. No one gets hassled in my shop."

"Thanks, Cheri. He's a..." I hesitate. "He's a friend."

My heart is high in my throat and part of me wants to talk to him more than anything. With Sam, I felt alive, complete. Too bad that was based on a lie, too, and I don't want any more of that in my life. I can't trust someone who doesn't trust me.

Sam hasn't moved from the door and I point to a table against the wall. He joins me after a slight hesitation.

"You left without saying goodbye." He speaks even before he sits down. "You blocked my number. I didn't know where you were, if you were safe."

A little glow lights deep down. Sam was worried about me. He cared, even though he thought I sold them out.

"How did you know I was here?" The flowered plate clinks as I set it on the table. I'm too nervous to eat now.

"I checked your apartment and your mom's place. This was where Mikey took the photo so I thought it was worth a shot."

The glow expands at the work he put into finding me. "I sent an email to Fangli."

"Fangli is not me. Why did you leave?"

"ZZTV knows what I was doing." I adjust my hat, thankful I wore it instead of walking out the door with my bedhead on full display. At least I put on lipstick.

"We know." He looks straight at me. "We've taken care of it."

"I overheard you and Fangli," I say. "You think I was the one to leak to the reporters."

He looks astonished. "I never said such a thing."

"Really? You're such a fucking actor." I poke viciously at the scone. "You never thought I was in it for the money? You never pointed out that I was doing it because I lost my job?"

"That was before I knew you." He hasn't stopped looking at me. "Gracie, I promise I trusted you. I know you wouldn't have done such a thing."

That glow roars back, heating me from my bones.

"I came to find you to help smooth things over with Fangli. Your letter hurt her."

Fangli. Fangli again. The glow disappears under a wave of sheer disappointment. I thought he was here for me, finally, but even now, he's her friend before my...whatever we were. I want him to care about me with the same openness. I won't cry but the restrained tears knot up in my throat and make it hard to breathe.

Click. *Click-click-click.* We look up, startled. The flashes come through the window thanks to the photographer, Mikey, resplendent in his trench coat.

Sam swears under his breath but rallies lightning fast to slip into his part. He smiles at me, that same look he gave me at every gala and event, the practiced easy smile of a leading man. Enough of my Fangli training comes through that now I can at least stay seated instead of hiding under the table, but there's no way I can look happy. Not right now.

Cheri comes over, scowling. "This dude again?" She stands in the window, arms akimbo and calls over her shoulder. "Out the back. Same as before."

"Gracie, listen," Sam says. "We need you to come back."

We. Not him. Always for Fangli. I thought he wanted me, but the truth is bare in front of me. He admitted he tried hard to find me but it was to get me to be her double again. I can't even be envious that she holds such a place in his heart. The bells on the door jangle and I abandon my scone to head for the back door. I glance behind me to see Sam and Cheri acting as if to prevent the photographer from following me.

"Sorry," I say.

Then I'm out the door and alone in the alley.

Cheri's is where this whole mess began. It's fitting that it ends there.

July 27

EPPY: SORTING BY TIME
(PROOF OF CONCEPT)

DAY TASKS

○ Check job ads.

○ Tidy house.

○ Work on Eppy. (Use Pomodoro timer to get motivated.)

○ Do not check social media, not even once per hour.

Q: should these auto-populate month-to-month?

MONTH TASKS

○ Update budget.

○ Laundry (twice minimum).

○ Meditate

Thirty-Six

I wander over to the fridge and open it to reveal a collection of condiments and no food. I don't want to eat, anyway; I'm only looking for a way to distract myself.

It's been three days since I saw Sam. True to her word to keep me informed, Anjali sent me Mikey's photo from some stupid gossip rag, and the way it's framed makes Sam appear in full bodyguard hero mode protecting Fangli. "Fangli's hat looks familiar," Anjali wrote.

It looks like I can be pulled back into being Fangli even when I try to avoid it. I tuck my hands behind my head. What would a moral Gracie have done in the first place? She would have said no to Fangli, even for the money. She would have squashed that little fame worm in her mind and told it we'd find our own way. Todd...I acted as best as I could have there, and I won't blame myself for his actions.

Then what does a moral and slightly more daring Gracie do now? I look at my laptop, where despite Anjali's nagging, Eppy has sat neglected for most of the week. That Gracie follows her dreams and listens to her gut.

The phone rings and my heart leaps before I remember I blocked Sam. It's an unknown number but I have to answer. It might be a response to one of my job applications and I need one now, badly. I pick up.

"Hello?"

"Is this Gracie Reed?" The man's voice is brisk.

"Yes."

"This is Ken from the Xin Guang nursing home. I'm pleased to tell you we have a space open for Agatha Wu Reed. I know you've been on the list for a while."

I have to stop myself from whipping the phone at the wall. Of course they do. A beep comes on the line and I glance at the screen.

Incoming call from ZZTV. I didn't block them.

We pay well.

"We would need an immediate deposit to save the spot," Ken says.

We pay well.

"How much?"

He tells me and my heart drops. I can pay it but there's no way I can make the ongoing payments, and I can't move Mom there only to take her back out again. "Is there a way I can pay in installments?" I ask.

"I'm sorry," he says and he really does sound apologetic. "We offer premium care for our residents."

I know they do, which is why I want Mom in there. "Can you give me some time?"

"We have a standard six-hour grace period before we go to the next person on the list."

We pay well.

This time, I act the way I know I should.

The phone screen pulses one last time and ZZTV fades from it. Mom would kill me if I went into debt for this, and six hours isn't long enough to get a loan. I should have thought of that earlier and guilt pulses through my blood but I let it fade. I'm only human and I'm doing my best.

"I'm afraid I don't have the fees right now," I say finally. "I'm going to have to pass."

"I understand," he says. "Would you like to be added back onto the wait list?"

"Please."

We hang up and I lie back on the couch with the phone clutched against my chest. *Rectitude.* I roll the word around in my mind. I thought doing the right thing would make me feel good but instead I'm empty. I did the right thing—I said no to ZZTV—but who did I help? Not me. Not Mom. Maybe Fangli by not selling her secrets. Shouldn't I have a deep satisfaction in doing the right thing?

I don't, but as I lie there, quietly breathing, something happens. It's not happiness, but it's not guilt. There's no shame. The decision I made was based on what I could do—me, not depending on anyone else or lying, not trying to ease someone else's way at the expense of my own. It's a small start, but it *is* a start.

Mom said I had integrity, and even if I don't, I want to live up to her ideal. I couldn't get her into that home this time, but I will and I'll do it on my terms.

I pull my laptop close and start working.

BETA TEST
MOBILE VERSION

EPPY

DAY TASKS | MONTH TASKS

EVENTS
None

LIFE
○ Visit Mom

WORK
○ Check job opportunities
○ Fix Eppy ranking system.
(Figure out how to weight urgency and time required.)

FUN
○ Make plans with Anjali.

EVERYDAY
○ Do Mandarin module.
○ Take multivitamin.

DON'T THINK.
None

Thirty-Seven

Mom smiles over at me. It's cool for early August so I've tucked a blanket she knit twenty years ago around her knees. The zigzag orange-and-green pattern hasn't faded since it was first folded over the couch in our old living room to Dad's thunderous congratulatory applause.

Although I moved back to my apartment, I've made an effort to work from her room since I left the Xanadu and my life of luxury, and I think it's worked out well for both of us. My productivity has been through the roof—Eppy now has an official website—and I asked Anjali and a couple of old work colleagues to test it. It's a real thing in the real world now. Not wanting to put all my eggs in the entrepreneurial basket, which I guess is itself not very entrepreneurial, I keep applying for jobs and have an interview next week at a small nonprofit agency doing interesting work with newly immigrated Canadians. Baby steps.

Keeping busy stops me from thinking about Sam. I saw on a gossip site that a Canadian actor took on his *Operation Oblivion* role but that he's due back in Toronto for the September film festival, so I assume he's left the city. Knowing he's gone left me confused because although I don't want to talk to him, I gathered obscure comfort knowing he was on my soil. I assume they made a deal with ZZTV because nothing has appeared and my fear has decreased exponentially. Anjali

has made me promise not to google myself and sends me daily itera-
tions of "no," "nyet," and "nopeity nope nope" to assure me her alerts
haven't caught anything.

"Gracie, sweetie, will you get me a glass of water?" Mom holds
out her cup and I take it to the sink. Mom has been talkative the last
few days and moves fluidly between the now and the past. Today has
been a mix. She remembers me, but she places me in her youth. Right
now, I am Gracie but I am also with her back home in Beijing.

I hand her the water and she sips at it a few times before setting
it down. "Bring me my album."

This has been her comfort for the last few days as well, so I fetch
it. She opens it to Xiao He and her waxy fingers stroke the page. I
move to the other side of the bed to tidy her nightstand, and when I
check on her after getting out a new box of tissues and rinsing out her
water bottle, it's to find Mom's fingers still tapping gently on the page.
Is this one of the symptoms the doctor told me to watch for? Heart
hammering, I walk over to look at the page.

I've never looked too closely at the details in the photos, much
as you do with anything that's familiar. The one she's looking at is of
Mom and Xiao He, taken before she came to Canada. The two are
standing near a set of stairs, both looking at the camera with passport-
serious expressions. But Mom's fingers aren't connecting with the face
of her brother, as I would expect given the amount she's been talking
about him. Instead they're touching one specific spot on the page—
her abdomen. When her fingers move away, I lean forward, wondering what has Mom's rapt attention.

She's wearing a cotton navy dress with a little ruffle around the
wide neck, cinched in at the waist and falling to her knees. The wind
is pushing the skirt back a bit and giving her stomach a strange, almost
rounded shadow.

I want to examine it further but she turns the page. Now the
photos change to Canada. Mom in front of the CN Tower. Mom with
friends at Niagara Falls. Then Mom with Dad. There's a series of

now-pregnant Mom rocking bangs in front of those same standbys, the CN Tower and Niagara Falls, a page later.

Her fingers fall from the page, and I take the album off her lap to scrutinize the earlier photo.

That's not a shadow on her stomach. Is she pregnant?

I look so close I almost go cross-eyed. Holy shitballs, she's definitely pregnant. I suddenly realize the photo's been trimmed. Xiao He is to Mom's right and there's the edge of a shoulder to her left. There was enough space between Mom and whoever it was that it wasn't obvious at first that there was someone there.

"Mom." My voice is louder than I intend and her brown eyes fly open.

"Gracie?" She focuses on me and I know she sees me, really me.

"What aren't you telling me about Xiao He? What happened that you came to Canada?"

"He said to leave the past in the past. To live my future." She closes her eyes and I nearly shout in frustration. I let it be and look back at the photos. The photo of Sam and Fangli slips out again.

This time, Mom catches it with a quickness I would never have thought her capable of. "She grew so beautiful. I knew she would." Her voice cracks.

"Her? Don't you mean Sam?" I thought she kept it because Sam reminded her of her brother.

"Fangli. She didn't change her name. Nor did he."

I'm confused but know I'm walking through a minefield. I use my words like a stick, prodding for bombs to find a safe path. "Why would anyone change her name?" I keep my voice soft and soothing, trying to coax out the story.

"Her father was furious. A good but haughty man, so sure he's right. That's why my brother helped me. I wanted the baby."

I look at the album. There's a photo of a man and a child Mom said were relatives who owned a farm she used to go to. I always liked it because the girl looked so much like me that I used to pretend it was my sister. I hesitate, then go for it. "Mom, are you saying this is Wei Fangli?"

Her eyes fill with tears. "I knew her father would take care of her. Then I lost the other baby when I arrived alone in Canada. I had no one. It was my punishment. I couldn't go home but I had nothing."

I look at the album and then back at Mom. Then back at the album, which has somehow become impossibly weighty in my hands. The edge of it dips dangerously, and I catch it right before it tumbles out of my numb fingers to the floor.

"Mom." There's no way I understood her correctly. "This girl is Fangli?"

She reaches out and grabs my arm with a surprisingly strong grip. "Fangli. Yes."

"The actor." I pull out the magazine photo. "This woman here." I jab it so hard that the page crumples under my finger.

"My Fangli."

Is it the dementia? I try to remember what the doctors have told me. They said she would be confused...but like this? Making up a daughter? Mom fumbles for the gold chain around her neck that I've never seen her without. On the end dangles a jade coin, the empty center filled with gold and inscribed with the character for love. Her hands shake as she tries to take it off her neck and she finally gestures me closer, turning the pendant so I can see the reverse side.

I know those tiny characters because I practiced them until I could fake them at a moment's notice. Fang. Li.

It's true. My knees weaken and I half sit, half collapse on the bed, the album thumping against my thighs as I stare into Mom's face, seeing that connection between the three of us in the slope of her nose and the shape of her eyes. She blinks and smiles at me uncertainly and that's Fangli's expression, right there.

My mouth is so dry that it takes me two tries to get the words out. "Mom, it's okay." I take her hand. My heart breaks at what she's endured in silence all these years. No wonder she was so adamant about only living for the future.

She squeezes my hands. "Xiao He said the same thing. He said I had to think about what I wanted, that rules weren't the only thing in life. My husband wanted the baby, too, but would never admit it. Not when the Party said one child was enough."

I need the final confirmation. "This was your husband?"

"Wei Rong. My first. I was so scared he would find me. It was better she thought I was dead."

Always stay under the radar. Don't call attention to yourself. Temper your expectations. Mom must have used all her daring to take that step into the unknown to keep her baby. I look down to see my hand shaking on the edge of the album. Mom is staring out the window again, her face empty.

That photo from the magazine. I'd assumed she kept it because she thought Sam resembled her brother, but it was for Fangli. The agitation at *The Pearl Lotus*; that wasn't for the acting. There's no way I can ignore this. It's not chance that Fangli and I look alike—we both take after our mother. We're half sisters.

I have a sister.

I have a famous movie-star sister who thinks I don't ever want to see her again.

———

Mom eventually goes to sleep, leaving me to deal with this info bomb.

I'm not doing well with it.

I managed to wait a few minutes after the initial revelation to press for more but she simply stopped talking and looked out the window with tears tracing down her cheeks. I used all my self-control to not take the album and quiz her about the details of every person in it while simultaneously kicking myself for not showing more inter-est in my family history sooner. Mom had always been so adamant about ignoring the past that I'd simply not asked, as if it was taboo. I want to demand more information, I *need* more data, but I don't have the courage to force her back through memories that painful. I rub my shoulders, feeling the anger and regret at what she'd hidden deep in my bones.

I think I understand the basics. She'd been married to Fangli's father in China and they had one child, Fangli. Then she got pregnant again, and although they both wanted the baby, the one-child policy made it impossible. According to Fangli, her dad was a Party official, and even if he wasn't, a quick Google search showed enough benefits would be pulled from urban dwellers who had a second child to make it unfeasible.

Mom had wanted the baby, so her brother, Xiao He, had helped her leave her family and come to Canada. Obviously a big part of the story was missing, and I feared it would never get filled in. Once here, she had a miscarriage, eventually met Brad Reed, and had me. Did Dad know about the first marriage? The baby? Her other daughter? I want to shake her awake and ask but I restrain myself. This is part of my story but not all of it. I might never get all of it.

How do I tell Fangli? Then I hesitate. Is it a good idea to say anything? Maybe I'd be better to keep the secret as quiet as it has been for the last thirty years. It's not like Fangli and I meant that much to each other—she needed someone to do a job and I needed money. A transactional relationship at best.

Right. Tell yourself that. I like Fangli, and though I don't believe in fate, we were very comfortable with each other. We fit as if our pheromones matched.

We fit like sisters.

I turn on my laptop and press my thumb into the bruise on my heart by searching for images of Sam and Fangli. There are pages of them but I catch my breath because the first one isn't of Fangli. It's me, at the Chanel show. Sam is tilting toward me, a small smile playing on his face and his eyes fixed on me. I click to the page and check the comments.

🔥🔥🔥🔥🔥

if sam looked at me like that, my panties would combust

get you a man who looks at you like sam looks at fangli

samli forever

so hot

that lucky b

just missing the lip bite

exhibit A in Samli in love

I click through a few more images. Some are of us at the Xanadu. There's a blurry shot from the first time we went out and I slipped, with Sam's arm around me. There I am getting out at the premiere, Sam holding his hand out to take mine. Then on the red carpet, Sam a step ahead of me and looking back with admiration as I pose with one leg displayed, my hand on my hip and my head thrown back.

In each one, he's looking at me and only me.

I'm a very good actor.

He's not smiling at me. He's smiling at the woman who's supposed to be Fangli.

This is too much to think about right now. I keep watch over Mom and work on Eppy. Mom and work are the constants in my life right now, and that's what I'll focus on.

BETA TEST
MOBILE VERSION

EPPY

DAY TASKS | MONTH TASKS

LIFE
- ○ Laundry
- ○ Gym

WORK
- ○ *[autofilled since incomplete]* **Fix Eppy ranking system.** (Figure out how to weight urgency and time required.)
- ○ Get Eppy social media handles.
- ○ Research app developers.

FUN
- ○ Meet Anjali for drinks.

EVERYDAY
- ○ Do Mandarin module.
- ○ Take multivitamin.
- ○ Check job opportunities.

DON'T THINK. DO.
- ○ Call Robin Banerjee.
- ○ Tell Fangli her mother is not dead but alive in Toronto and we are sisters.
- ○ Work on how to word above point.

Thirty-Eight

I love this thing." Anjali and I are out for drinks and she has Eppy open in front of her. "I use it for work and everything. All together. You need an app, though."

"I know." Right now it's only available as a web version that I built myself, thanks to online tutorials.

"It keeps me so on track. Do you know how much time I've saved this week? Six hours. Six! I binge-watched Netflix without shame."

I beam at her. Eppy is good. I know it. "Thanks."

"I don't know how you came up with this." She shakes her head. "It's the thing I didn't know I needed but I can't live without. What's next?"

"I need to sell it. Promote it. Get the funding for the app." I have a business plan and my list of people to call. Robin is right on the top but I haven't had the courage to make the call, not after what happened with Sam. Now that I've put it in my Don't Think, Do column—saved for the tasks that you'll do anything to avoid—it's going to happen.

"You're the Marie Kondo of time management," Anjali says. "I already have people at work using it."

We get new drinks and then Anjali leans forward. "Spill."

"What?" I empty about half my drink in a single gulp and have a coughing fit that Anjali sits through with an impassive face.

"Sam Yao." It's a soft name with smooth, rounded sounds but she enunciates it crisply.

"What about him?"

"That's what I'm asking. I saw a lot of footage of you guys together. You looked great, by the way."

"Makeup and hair."

She snorts. "Bull. You glowed whenever you looked at him and he... Whew, girl." She shakes her head. "That man was *into* you. I don't know why you two are over just because you didn't want to be Fangli anymore."

I trace circles on the table with my fingertip.

"Gracie."

"They thought I called ZZTV." I sigh. "I thought they did anyway. That's the main reason I left."

"How did you get that idea?" Her eyebrows pull down to a point between her eyes.

"I listened to their conversation." I fill her in on what I overheard and she sighs, then looks around the bar for a moment before letting her gaze rest on me.

"Did you think, possibly, an app wasn't the most authoritative way to get a translation?"

"I do now," I mutter. "I was wrong. Sam said so when he came to find me."

"He did what?"

"Only to get me back to help Fangli."

Compassion softens her face. "That sucks."

"Yeah."

We sit in silence for a moment. "Are you sure that's why he came after you?"

"That's what he said. So yes."

"Or is that what you expected to hear? You never trusted his feelings."

"I did." Didn't I? Or was I always nervous, as if I was getting played? That there was no reason that Sam would be interested in a nobody like me? Doubt. Always that little seed of doubt no matter what he did.

"I don't think you did. I think you think he's some big-ass movie star and you're not, so why would he care about you."

I go bright red because having these thoughts laid out is as embarrassing as being stripped in public. "What if I did?"

"God, have some pride, woman. Look at you. You're smart and driven enough to create a new productivity plan like you run a fucking Toyota manufacturing line. You managed to trick the world in thinking you were a movie star. You're attractive enough that it was believable." She pauses, gripped by feminist regret. "Not that looks are important."

"Right."

"You doubt yourself too much, Gracie." She reaches out across the table and grabs my hands, which startles me because she's not a big toucher. Now she looks into my eyes. "You need to believe in yourself."

Fangli said the same thing. Fangli, my sister. I'm bursting to tell Anjali but it seems wrong to share Fangli's story before she knows herself. I must have started and deleted a dozen emails to Fangli, each one a master class in graceless phrasing.

"Refill, ladies?" The server comes by and the moment is broken, but I'm a little shaken. Why don't I believe in myself? It's why I say yes instead of no. Why I let the Todds of the world walk over me.

All those things Anjali said are right. I did do those things. I take care of my mom. I do my best.

As if she knows she's hit a sore spot, Anjali backs off and we have a final glass of wine and talk about her trip to New York and a new spa we both want to try but don't want to spend the money on. When we leave, Anjali surprises me again with a hug. "Call if you need me," she says. "You're not going to bother me."

I get on the subway with her words in my ears. I do worry about bothering people. I worry about taking too much space, too much time, too much attention. Maybe I shouldn't. Maybe it's possible to take up the perfect amount.

A Gracie-sized amount.

———

I'm a little hungover the next morning but a glass of water does the trick. I check my Eppy and see I have enough time to doze before I start my day but it's not a comfortable rest.

Two choices lie in front of me. I can contact Sam and Fangli, apologize, and explain my side of the story and hear theirs. Or I can pretend this entire month never happened. I didn't meet Fangli and Sam. I didn't find my sister. I didn't fall in love.

How can I turn my back on that, even if I risk getting hurt?

I need to think so I jump out of bed, grab my head when I realize the hangover isn't completely gone, and then throw on my clothes and sunscreen before steeling myself to swim through the heavy summer humidity. I swing open the door and stop dead.

Mei stands there. She looks the same as always, cool and collected, her hair in a perfect center part that doesn't cowlick to the side at the rear. She's not even sweating.

"Hi?" I step back, a silent invitation for her to come into the house. She must be here on a mission from Fangli, and I'd prefer to have the conversation in the air-conditioned living room rather than on my steaming steps.

Mei follows me in, leaving her black flats tidily at the door. Her gaze flits from the mess of blankets on the couch, where I'd been nesting yesterday, to the half-empty cans of diet root beer scattered on the floor. My laptop is precariously balanced on the edge of the table.

She sits on the yellow quilted chair, a garage sale find from two years ago, and doesn't say a damn word.

Now that the sun's not in my eyes, I can make out a few more details. Her shirt is a bit wrinkled and her eyes look swollen. "Is there a problem?" I ask, anxiety climbing fast at this unusual Mei behavior. "Is it Fangli?"

"I was the one who called ZZTV." Her shoulders are straight as she delivers this news.

"Huh?"' Not the most articulate response but honestly? It's been a hell of a week for bombshells.

Mei's dark eyes meet mine. "You heard me."

I suppose I did. "Fangli knows? Sam?"

She looks down. "Yes."

"You called ZZTV." I let the words settle. "Why?" A thin rush of anger starts to trace through my veins. "Why the hell would you do such a thing? Did you hate us so much?" Because Fangli wouldn't come out of this undamaged. I should kick Mei out of my house but her body folds in on itself before I can act.

"I'm sorry." Her voice is so feather soft it barely reaches me across the room.

I can tell she is, that she's sorry for something, but I can't tell if it's for what she did or because she got caught. "But why?" I repeat.

"I'm sorry. I wasn't thinking clearly."

"Wasn't thinking clearly about *what*?"

She looks me right in the eye. "I wanted you gone."

Oh. Not what I expected. I knew she never liked me but this level of sabotage is beyond the pale. "Got your wish, then." That was sharper than I wanted, and I don't like the satisfaction I get from making Mei wince.

She doesn't say anything and again I'm stuck in the role of having to force conversation with this woman. "How did Fangli find out?" And Sam, who tried to tell me in the café but I was too stubborn and sad to listen.

"I told her."

I have grudging respect for that. "I thought it was Todd."

She shakes her head. "He went away after Sam sent him a copy of the dossier he had the detective collect on his behavior. Sam also warned him that he would be watching to see if he treated other women poorly."

Some good news at least. The final bit of tension that had sat under my skin about Todd loosens. I don't have to worry about him anymore. He's a repulsive little worm but at least he won't be taking his inadequacies out on other women.

I suddenly see that I'd stood up without noticing and sit down because I need all my energy to process what she's saying. "I don't understand why you did this. Why did you want me gone?"

Mei is silent. We never had a close relationship but don't I deserve a reason why she hated me? I think back over our interactions. I did my best to be good to work with, eventually. I tried to be polite and friendly. Had I overstepped when I asked her for help?

Then I remember the way she shut the door when she gave me the umbrella for my date with Sam. When she saw us holding hands. Even before that, her face, watching Sam as he entered a room. I should have recognized it, because it was so close to how mine must have looked.

Dear God, it wasn't me at all. She was in love with Sam? It's on the tip of my tongue to ask her but I freeze. Despite what she's done, the question is too intrusive for me to say out loud and it's too egotistical to ask, *Did you try to wreck my life because you thought I was a rival for Sam?*

"What did Fangli say?" I say instead.

Her eyes fill with tears. "She said she understood but I'd have to leave."

Makes sense. "Did she forgive you?"

Mei nods.

Of course she did, damn her generous heart. If Fangli can forgive that kind of betrayal from someone she trusted, so can I. Deep down, I'm tired. I don't have the strength to be angry at Mei. It happened. I can't reverse time and make her not pick up the phone. She's going back to China and we'll never see each other again. I want to be free of all the negative parts of this experience, and topping that list is ZZTV and all things ZZTV-adjacent.

"Thank you. For telling me." I take a breath. "It's fine." It's not, but saying *I forgive you* is so ponderous, like a crime boss excusing a subordinate confessing a massive cock-up.

Mei bows her head and stands, and I do as well. Now that she's had the pleasure of unburdening her sins, I want her out of my house. I pity her but I don't want her around me in case she adds more to my emotional dogpile.

She's gone quickly and I collapse on the couch, walk forgotten.

It was Mei. I text Anjali.

Anjali: I'm in a meeting but is she in the games room with the dagger?

Me: nice. She told ZZTV. It was Fangli's assistant. I think she did it because she was in love with Sam.

Anjali: That is seriously messed up. Toxic. Dudes aren't worth that shit.

Me: Said she was sorry. Came to my house.

Anjali: Oh that takes guts. What's your move.

Anjali: No answer?

Anjali: Radio silence cool cool. I'm up to present at this meeting and when I'm back I want to hear some Eppy-level planning

I don't reply because I've pulled over my computer to look at Eppy. I highlight **CALL FANGLI AND TELL HER ABOUT MOM.** This might have been one of my Don't Think, Do tasks but I've been Think, *Don't* Doing. Then I add another: **TELL SAM I MIGHT HAVE JUMPED TO CONCLUSIONS.** My chest clenches at the idea that the Sam ship has sailed and my ticket lies in tatters on the pier.

Eppy is a great planner but I wish it had a module for how to approach this kind of emotional obstacle course.

I pull out my phone and my newsfeed comes on my screen before I can tap for the texting app. I want to give Fangli time to decide her response and a call puts her on the spot. "Exclusive wedding news," the headline blares.

Fangli and Sam smile out at the camera.

I click on the story before I can help myself, and it's what the headline promises. Actors Wei Fangli and Sam Yao will be married before the end of the year. Quotes from sources about how they've been in love since drama school punctuate long paragraphs about Sam's film royalty lineage. Another photo features the two of them, except it's me in a black dress smiling at Sam, not Fangli.

My body chills as I stare at the photo. Marriage? It makes sense, I tell myself. Lili's interference obviously only hastened the inevitable. After all, neither of them had absolutely rejected the idea of getting married, and Sam had seemed fatalistic about his mother's plans. Obviously they've known each other for a long time and Sam would do anything for Fangli and...what a mess this is. I curl up on the chair. What a fucking mess but I can't run away from it. Despite this update about their relationship status, I need to contact them.

Don't think, do.

I grab the notepad and move over to the kitchen table.

Fangli is first and easiest because talking to her was always comfortable. I decide that even with the news about the marriage, I can't keep what I've learned about Mom a secret. She can decide what to do with the information, whether she wants to believe me or not. The text I send to her now unblocked number is simple and to the point—an apology for leaving her and that I know the truth about ZZTV from Mei. I tell her I might have some information about her mother, if she'd like to know. That I miss her.

I'm not usually this open with feelings but I want to restart on the right foot if she'll let me. I decide to not mention her engagement because every time I write it out, the sentence sounds painfully passive-aggressive. I'll do that in person if she wants to meet.

I read this block of text over about twelve times and then send it.

The second one is harder, and I decide to send a hello to commit myself before I get into the nitty-gritty.

Hi, Sam.

It bounces back.

I stare at the message in disbelief. Not in service? Here I am, about to take an emotional leap into the unknown, and the number doesn't work. Even if I had been tentative before, now I'm desperate to get Sam this message, if only to get it done with.

I don't have his email. Do I? I open up my email to look and find an interview request from the *South China Morning Post*.

As I'm reading it, the notification bar drops down to announce a message from the BBC. CNN Asia pops up a moment later.

They're not about my impersonating Fangli. They're about Eppy.

Now almost frantic, I grab my laptop and check my website and check it again. Yesterday, my downloads were exactly twenty-six. Now it's been downloaded over twenty thousand times.

What the hell happened?

It's too much for me to take in and time slows to a crawl. I need to get back to these people but what do I say? Is this all a big accident? It must be. A great joke on Gracie.

You don't believe in yourself.

I open my laptop and read the emails carefully. They all say the same thing, that Sam Yao swears by this method and it's now a trend in China. They want to talk to me about my philosophy and what I want to achieve. They want me to walk through why Eppy is different.

Sam plugged Eppy. Why?

Because it works and it's good. I might not believe in myself yet, but I believe in Eppy.

I'm not ready but I can do this.

The first thing I do is try to find what Sam's said. It takes some digging but I eventually find a tweet translated from Weibo, the Chinese microblog.

> *No way I could keep organized without Eppy. Swear by it to keep productive.*

It links to my website. That's it, but I guess when you're Sam Yao with millions of followers, that's enough. The retweets on Twitter alone are over forty thousand, and I have to do some breathing practices to keep calm. This is what I wanted, after all. I believe in this.

I jazz-hand my fingers to get them to stop shaking and email the *South China Morning Post* to set up an interview. Then the BBC and CNN Asia. When the *Guardian* and Bloomberg requests roll in, I accept those, too.

The interview requests arrive all afternoon, and after I do the first two, I notice the questions are similar. I get more comfortable each time I talk about how Eppy is designed to help you organize your whole life, since we're all busy and multifaceted. I give examples of some of my tasks and why I add items immediately because I have the memory of a goldfish. When they ask how Sam Yao heard about a planner that's only in beta, I laugh and say they'll have to ask him but I'm glad it works for him and do my best to not let my voice shake.

The hardest are the TV interviews but the producers are kind and walk me through what to expect, since I suppose me freezing in fear doesn't do them any good either. In between, I check my downloads.

The number keeps ticking up.

It's almost midnight by the time I'm done, and I'm so wired I pace my apartment in circles. Anjali sends me an emoji-laden text with a link to the CNN interview. I knew you could do it, she says.

I did but it's all thanks to Sam, who I can't get in touch with. Can

I email his agency? Agent? There has to be a way to contact him if Fangli doesn't call.

I go to bed exhausted and my dreams are filled with Sam using my planner. Second sexiest night I've ever had.

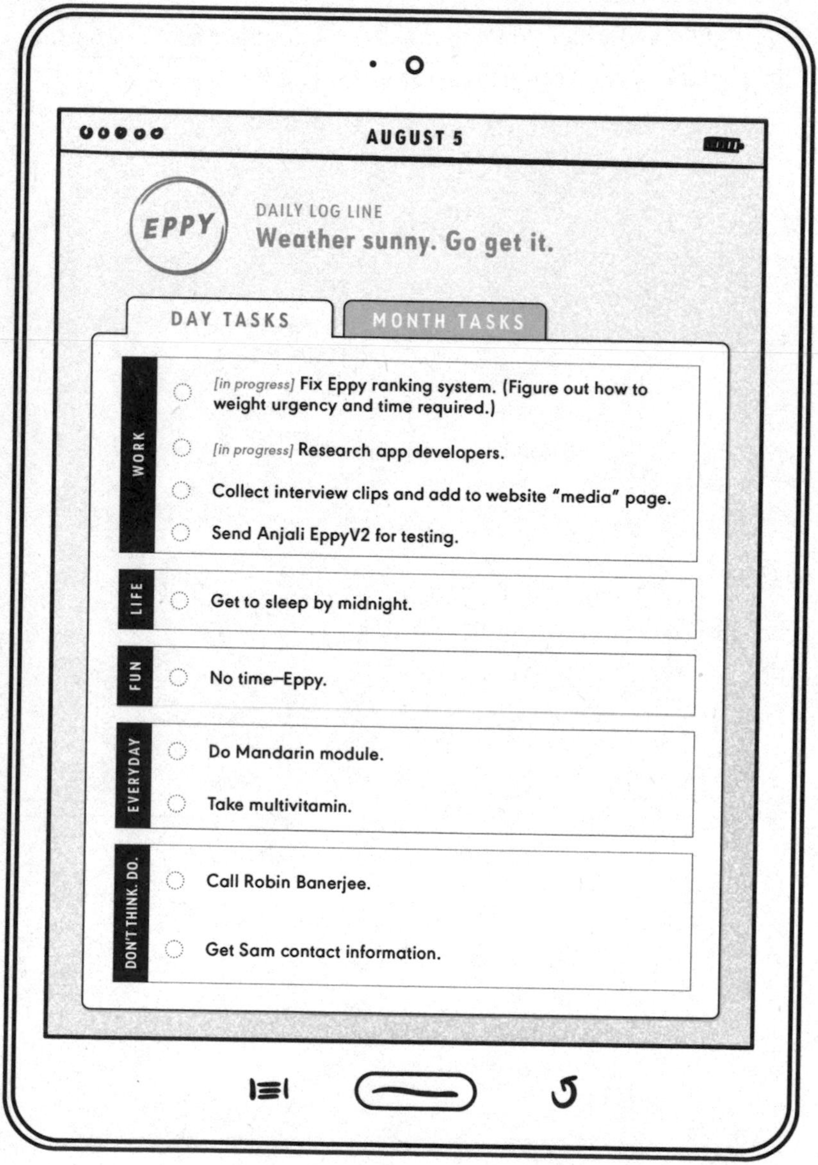

Thirty-Nine

I t takes me a couple of days to come down from my interview high. The downloads on Eppy keep going up, and even better, people like it. They really like it. I take careful note of the suggestions that come through on the Twitter feed I hastily set up and already have a rough version 2.0 ready. I send the link to Anjali to test.

Anjali: That fast?

Me: Maybe I didn't sleep.

She answers with a GIF of a disappointed Dolly Parton.

I'm on the couch debating the merits of having a nap when the doorbell rings. Was I expecting a delivery? I can't remember, but I like packages so I yawn and stumble over to the door to check.

Fangli stands there.

I freeze. I might have sent that text but I'm not ready to talk to her face-to-face. I thought she'd call me. Or text or email back, but that it would be a distance communication that would give me enough time to script out my response or at least think.

"Open the door, Gracie." She closes one eye to peer through the peephole. "I can hear you."

It takes me two tries to open the door because my palm is so sweaty.

Then we stare at each other. Fangli looks like, well, she looks like me. Her hair is pulled back in a neat, low ponytail that comes over her shoulder, and a ball cap shades her face, bare except for some gloss on her lips. She looks a bit tired and a lot nervous.

"You got my message," I say.

She waves to herself as if to say, *obviously*.

"Sorry." I move away. "Come in."

Like Mei did, she takes off her shoes and pads barefoot into my place. Then she smiles. "It's nice here," she says. "Homey."

"Would you like a drink?"

She snorts, a delicate sound as if from a small animal. "I would like to know what information you have about my mother. And why you left me like that. I would like a lot of things, Gracie, so I think we can skip the drink for now."

"Fair." I take a deep breath. "Give me a second."

I go into my room and grab the duplicate photo album. When I get back to the living room, Fangli's sitting stiffly on the couch, knees pressed together and hands folded in her lap. She looks small and a bit scared, and I feel like an asshole. I must have worried her with that message when I was doing my best to be sensitive.

Nice one, Gracie.

I open the album to the photo of Fangli and Wei Rong. She glances down, then brings the album closer as if to see better. "This looks like my father. With you?"

"No. With you."

She flips the page as if to check to see if there's more information about the photo on the other side. "Why do you have a photo of the two of us?"

As gently as I can, I tell her what I learned from Mom. Her escape from China, the secret baby who died, the deserted elder daughter who became a global superstar.

Who looks almost identical to her younger Canadian half sister.

"We're sisters?" she repeats, hands splayed over the photo.

"It looks like we are."

Fangli turns the pages until she gets to the one of Mom and Dad. "That's her?"

"Yes, Agatha Wu Reed. Her Chinese name is Wu Miaoling."

"She's not dead? My father said she was dead."

"Not dead," I assure her. "Her Alzheimer's means she drifts in and out so it was hard to get the whole story. I might have misunderstood parts, and we should get a DNA test to confirm it."

"How sure are you that we're sisters?"

I don't hesitate. "Almost one hundred percent."

Fangli slams the album shut and sets it down with trembling hands. I don't know what to say or if I should reach out. I know how difficult it was for me to understand and Fangli is coping not only with a new sister but a living mother.

I shift on the edge of my seat, silent for fear of saying the wrong thing when Fangli opens the book again. She analyzes every page, her eyes fixed on the mother who left her. Her hands run up and down the pages and I watch them. I have Dad's broader hands but Fangli's are like Mom's, with long, smooth fingers. She even wears the clear polish Mom always favored.

"Tell me again what she said," Fangli says, flipping another page.

I go through the story again, right from Mom thinking Sam was her brother. She doesn't look up from the book but I can tell she's listening to each word, testing it for truth.

I finish the story as Fangli reaches the last page. Finally she looks up. Her eyes are bright with unshed tears.

"She left me?" Her voice breaks. Then she repeats it, changes the tone. "She *left* me."

"I'm sorry." This isn't a trauma I can help with because I imagine it wounds Fangli to her core. I can only sense the edges around my own pain of all the things Mom stole from me when she decided to keep her secret. I also can't fault Mom for trying to do the best she could, but I won't blame Fangli if she can't do the same. She's just heard what must be one of the most painful rejections a child can know. No matter how much Mom might have loved Fangli, she chose to leave.

Fangli stands and then sits again. "My father kept this from me as well." Her laugh is more of a bark. "Everyone lied to me."

"Should I have told you?" Now I'm uncertain I made the right decision.

"Yes." She's sure. "This isn't your fault."

"I know. I guess I feel…" I hesitate, trying to name the emotion. "Guilty?"

She puts the album down on the coffee table. "Is that drink offer on?"

"Fuck, yes." She follows me to the kitchen, where I skip the beer and wine and grab a bottle of gin from the cupboard. I pour us two very generous drinks, dump in some ice and soda, and we toss them down like water.

"Guilty." She says it slowly. "Why?"

I shrug but when I go to pour myself another drink, she puts her hand on the bottle. "Later," she says. "After we talk."

She's right. "I feel bad I had time with Mom that you didn't."

When she laughs this time, it sounds more like Fangli. "Not much you could do about that."

"I'm mad at her, too," I burst out. "I'm mad and I can't be because I know she tried and she's sick and what she did to me is nothing to what she did to you and I don't understand why no one told me and—"

My big sister steps forward to enfold me in a tight hug. I clutch onto her, feeling her warmth under my hands as she simply lets me be safe in her arms. As we stand there, I feel her shake and she exhales, thin and unsteady.

"It's okay," I tell her and feel her nod hard against me. "We'll be good."

"Right," she says, laying her head on my shoulder. "Fine."

When we untangle, we look at each other. Fangli's a mess, with a red nose and swollen eyes and creases along her cheek from pressing into the seam of my shirt. I assume I look as bad. This time, she doesn't stop me from pouring another shot and edges her glass forward when it looks like I'm going to stop pouring.

"You don't drink," I remember when she refuses more ice. "I was never allowed to drink wine when I was out as you."

She takes a sip. "Because it's too hard to control my words when I drink. No filter. This, however, is a special occasion and a time for honesty if I've ever seen one."

We go back to the living room. Now that we've reached the first base camp on Mount Reconciliation, I'm not sure if I need a break or want to power on.

Fangli paces around my space. "I have so much to say and I don't know where to start." She sits down and drains her glass before clinking it down on the table. "No. I'm going to say it. Next topic is Sam."

We're climbing again.

"Right." I hold up my hand. "I need to..." *Congratulate you on your engagement.* I can't get the words out.

"Did you see the announcement? That we're getting married?"

"I did. Congratulations." There, I managed it with a smile.

"A lie," she says vehemently. "That snake Lu Lili told that story."

My eyes go wide. "What?"

"Sam isn't in love with me, nor I him. We are friends only." She narrows her eyes. "You knew that. He made it clear enough."

I avoid that. "Why would she say that?"

"Sam went home and told her to stay out of his life." She smiles proudly. "He's never done that before. Lili is a power and he finally had it out with her."

"Then where did the announcement come from?"

"Lili tried to force his hand. Sam was furious, as was my father. She overstepped."

I thump back into the chair. "What are you going to do?"

"Say we broke it off and hope it plays well for Sam's movie release." She adjusts her sleeves. "We have to let Lili save some face, but this is enough for her to know her limits. At least there was a gold lining because she'll never try to do that again. Sam feels free."

"Do you mean silver lining?"

She laughs. "Gold. Lu Lili would have nothing less than the best."

To know they're not engaged buoys me up and I can't stop grinning, even though it doesn't mean anything for Sam and me. "About Sam..." I don't know how to finish the sentence.

"I've never seen him more miserable," Fangli says. "It's hard for him to connect with people."

"Sam?" I raise my eyebrows.

"His mother is a monster, as you know. She kept him on display and he grew up quite the little emperor, petted and spoiled. She sees him as an extension of herself and sometimes he does, too."

"He told me about her."

"It's hard for him to trust that people like him for himself, not for his family or his money. Or his looks."

I take a deep breath. "I never knew if he was with me or you. Whether he'd prefer to be with you." That's hard to say.

"We are *friends*." She claps her hands for emphasis. "Long-time friends who love each other, but what I have with Sam isn't what you have with him. I never saw him so relaxed as with you. You brought out the best of him. It was like being with the old Sam, the one who used to laugh with me and Chen." Her expression looks wistful.

I run my finger around the edge of my glass. "I screwed it all up."

"He told me he tried to talk to you."

"I overheard you speaking and thought it was about me." I tell her about the translator, and her face is an exact replica of the mixed disbelief and pity Anjali had displayed. "Mei came and apologized."

"We knew as soon as ZZTV called who the leak was." Her expression is grim. "I couldn't see what was in front of me. I didn't know she had feelings for Sam and what she would do. She wanted him. You were in the way."

I shake my head. "Unbelievable."

"I trusted her," says Fangli, her voice breathy. Then she shakes her head. "She felt terrible after. She said it was like being in a fog. I had to let her go, but we didn't press charges."

I'm glad. Mei wasn't a friend, but I understand the regret of bad decisions. "I didn't see the story."

"Mei told them it was a lie. They decided not to run with it because they couldn't corroborate and we threatened to sue. She said it was the least she could do."

Poor Mei, even though she could have caused much damage.

Fangli grimaces. "My manager was furious, rightfully so, but once I explained, it was better."

"That's good."

"He hadn't realized how bad things had become for me. He's listening now." She smiles. "Another thing I have to thank you for."

"Thank me?"

Fangli pauses to look at me carefully. "Do you not know?"

"Know what?" I can see my expression reflected in hers, pursed lips, tilted head.

"Gracie. You changed my life." She says it so simply, like it's a fact. "I was exhausted and you brought me rest. Confused and you brought help. Now you bring me a mother I thought was dead? A sister I never knew I had? How can that not change me?"

"We have each other." When I say the words, it's a revelation. I thought when Mom died, I would be alone.

I have Fangli.

She smiles as if she knows what I'm thinking and says, "We have *each other.*"

"We do," I say. Wow. I mean, *wow.* "What does this mean?"

This makes her laugh and it's toned with delighted excitement. "I don't know. I never had a sister. I think we'll fight and make up and do sheet masks with each other. I see that happen in American movies." She comes over and gives me a spine-cracking hug. For a small woman, she's strong.

"This is a lot for you," I say.

"I need to talk about this with my therapist." Fangli sees my look and goes red. "It's hard to say that."

"You should be proud you're helping yourself," I say gently.

"I can't talk about it at home, not yet. I can't help others. I will, one day."

"First get yourself in order."

"I'm trying." She hesitates. "About our mother. Should I visit?"

"She might not recognize you. I know she thinks of you." I smile. "She always wears a pendant. Your name is engraved on it."

Fangli squeezes her eyes shut for a moment. "Is she well treated?"

"I hate the home Mom's in. I want to get her into the Chinese home with private care." I say it without thinking but realize what I've laid on Fangli when it comes out of my mouth. "I mean, it's good enough," I hasten to clarify. "She's safe."

"Safe isn't happy. We'll get her in. I'll have my manager make some calls and I can pay."

I'm too grateful to argue. "Thank you."

"She's my mother, too, although I have a lot of feelings. I need to process what to do."

"When you decide, I can bring you to her. If you want. Only if you want."

"Do you think she wants it?" Her lids flutter to keep back the tears.

"Yes." I don't elaborate or explain. I don't want to pressure Fangli but she needs to know that Mom wants her.

Fangli curls in a ball. "I need to think."

"I know."

"It's too much." She looks apologetic.

"She's stable," I say. "Nothing's urgent."

That seems to reassure her because she lifts her chin and then gives me her old small smile. "I should go. I need some time before the show tonight. I'll see you soon? Promise?"

Her eagerness sets aside any anxiety I had that I'll be intruding on her life. "Yes, soon."

"I can't convince you to be my double for a very boring party tomorrow?" she teases.

"Not a chance in hell."

She tucks her hands between her knees. "I'm sorry I made you do that when you weren't comfortable with it. I shouldn't joke."

"I did it because I wanted to," I tell her. "I stopped when I had to. It was my choice." It was my decision and I know now there's more power in owning my own decisions than pretending I had no alternative.

"Before I forget." She sends me a text and I check my phone.

"Did you change your number?"

"No." She stands up. "It's Sam's."

Sam. I look at the daunting gray text bubble. "Do you think he wants to talk to me? What do I say?"

She's already in the hall and looks at me over her shoulder in the pose I've also mastered. "I think the globally trending creator of the hottest planner on the planet can figure it out." She winks. "Good luck, Sister."

AUGUST 7

TAKE DEEP
BREATHS.

Forty

angli's faith in me is sorely misplaced because it takes me two days to text Sam. Part of it is that I keep hoping he'll text me. I mean, in a movie, I give the hint to his friend, his friend tells him, and he gets in touch with me. But Sam doesn't.

Who does call, literally as I'm picking up the business card to act on the first of my Don't Think, Do tasks (Sam being the second), is Robin Banerjee's executive assistant, who invites me to his office to talk about funding.

"He knows about Eppy?"

"Sure does." Marcus, the executive assistant, laughs. "Everyone at the office has been using it. I finally got the thank-you notes for my wedding in the mail because of Eppy. We were married eight months ago."

I beam at the phone as we sort out the appointment time, and when I disconnect, I hug the phone to my chest and dance an uncoordinated jig.

Robin Banerjee wants to know more about Eppy. He asked *me*.

Nerves take over but this time, I'm not alone. Fangli and Anjali are both there to coach me through. I check through the simultaneous text conversations and feel my courage grow.

Anjali: You're doing him a favor by meeting. It's popular and he knows more people will be after you.

Fangli: I met with my futurist. She's using Eppy. This is a winner and you did it.

Anjali: Do that thing where you lift up your arms Rocky-style to build physical confidence before you go in if you need it. Saw it on a TED Talk.

Fangli: I believe in you.

Anjali: [Rocky montage GIF]

An hour before the meeting, I put on a green dress, paint my lips oxblood, and tell my mirror reflection *You got this* until I feel it in my very trembly bones.

Then I gather my laptop and my notes, and I go in ready to impress Robin Banerjee enough to get the money I need for my app. It's not a favor, I remind myself. The investment will make both of us successful. Eppy is valuable.

The office is in an industrial part of the city that's been taken over by tech start-ups and circus arts schools. Marcus greets me with a smile and sets me up with water in Robin's office, which is walled with whiteboards and littered with Rubik's cubes and building blocks. A jar of tall, pink hollyhocks provides a spot of color.

I don't even wait a minute before Robin comes in. He gives me a warm smile and a wave.

"Saw the tweet from Sam Yao and gave Eppy a go," he says by way of introduction. Robin is my height and bald and has a smile that covers his face. Unlike the suit at the Chanel party, today he's wearing a black hoodie and cargo pants and huge gleaming basketball shoes you would never wear to play any sport. "Good stuff. I like your story."

He gestures me to the leather chair and sits on the couch. Because his office is in a reclaimed warehouse, the only view is the worn brick of another warehouse. "Tell me your plans."

I've prepped this—Anjali suggested I treat this like a job interview so I spent three hours creating smart answers to every question he might have—and I'm ready.

I tell him my goals: the app, the analog planners, the eventual community of people helping each other reach their goals by providing tips and encouragement. He listens and doesn't interrupt me once. I pull out my business plan and he pages through, asking questions I have ready answers for and a few that make me think.

"Sounds good," he says when I finish. "I want in."

Then he names an amount of money that shorts out my brain and gives me the contacts of people who can help, including an app developer who was on my short list. His lawyer will be in touch.

When I get outside, my teeth chatter in stress-citement. It's all happening so fast that I can't take it in. I send Anjali a quick text and get a blast of emojis back and a promise that she needs the whole story once she's out of her meeting. Fangli sends a video of her blowing a kiss.

Sam sends nothing because I'm too gutless to contact him.

I check my website—downloads slowing but going strong. I email all the contacts Robin gave me, right there on the street. Then I stand there, filled with restless energy. I want to yell into a forest and dance around a fountain until I exhaust myself.

Mom. I'll go see Mom and tell her what's going on. That will soothe me.

There's a bus coming and within the hour, I sign in at Glen Lake. When I get to Mom's room, I stop. She's speaking to someone in a soft voice so I decide to give them a moment to finish; it must be one of the aides or a nurse.

As I stare at the framed picture of the sweet white kitten, I pull out my phone. I haven't been able to get Sam out of my mind and I can't put it off any longer. This is my true Don't Think, Do task. I send the text to the number Fangli gave me and I do it fast, before I can think about it anymore. The same message as before.

Hi, Sam.

A ping comes from inside Mom's room.

Forty-One

What? I stare at my phone, then at the door. When I reach out to open it, I note clinically that my fingers are trembling.

Sam is sitting next to my mother, holding her hands. They both look up at me, twin expressions of surprise on their faces.

"Sam?"

This is weird. This is very weird because Sam is supposed to be in China doing movie-star things, not here in my mom's long-term care home, dressed in jeans and a white shirt.

I want to rush across the room but my feet step backward into the hall as I frown at them. Why is he here, alone with Mom?

Sam's eyes track my progress, and he must think I'm about to make a run for it because he gives Mom's hands a squeeze before crossing the room to stand in front of me. "Gracie."

I don't know what to say. I don't even know where to look because I can't focus through my newly blurry eyes. Shit. I'm crying. Sam reaches out to run his thumb across my cheekbone, and when I don't move, he comes in a bit closer.

"I'm sorry," I whisper. He ducks down to hear me. "Sam, I'm so sorry."

"Why?" Sam looks astonished. "I should apologize to you. I gave up after you left in the café because I'm a stubborn fool."

"I don't think I was in a mood to listen."

"Maybe not but I should have tried harder."

This is not a productive discussion so I turn to the more salient point. "I don't understand why you're here. In my mom's room?"

He takes such a deep breath that it whooshes out when he exhales and he closes his eyes.

"Sam?" I don't know how many more butterflies will fit in my chest before they burst out *Alien*-style.

"Jiayou," he whispers, opening his eyes. "Come on, Sam. You can do it."

"What?"

Sam takes my face in his hands and silences me with a kiss that travels down to my toes. "I think I'm falling in love with you," he says in a rush. "No, I know I am. I should have told you sooner."

I feel the blood rush to my face under his touch.

"I'm here because I missed you. I needed to see you." He runs his hands down my arms. "Fangli told me about her visit and that you had my number but you never called. I couldn't stand it. I thought I might see you here, to talk in person."

"Here?" I echo.

"I wanted to see your mother as well. I can't be her brother, but I can be a friend."

Mom's voice calls out from behind him. "Sammy knows my old neighborhood. He remembers the noodle house." Mom watches us with huge eyes and a grin that says maybe she understands what Sam is to me.

Sam wraps his arms around me. "It's the best I can do for her."

"Thank you." All I do is thank him.

"Maybe you two should go and talk." Another voice comes from the corridor. It's Fangli, wearing a determined expression and holding a bouquet of daylilies.

"Fangli?"

She looks over my shoulder to Mom. "I talked to Dad today. Just now." Her voice wavers. "It's true, what you said. He won't tell me the whole story but I don't want to lose any more time with my mother."

"I understand."

"I should have told you before I came but..." Her voice trails off. "I wasn't thinking."

I give her a hug. "She's your mother, too."

Mom has already risen out of her chair, her arms outstretched and her face alight. Both of us go and embrace her. "You look like my little girl," she whispers. Then she begins to speak in Mandarin. Thanks to my app, I'm getting better but Sam has to translate because although Fangli opens her mouth, no words come out.

"She thinks Fangli simply looks like her daughter," he whispers. "She doesn't know."

Even as he speaks, Mom's expression changes and she opens her eyes wide, her gaze fluttering between me and Fangli. "My girl?" she whispers.

"It's me," Fangli whispers. "Me."

Mom looks at me, and I give Fangli a hug. "It's her, Mom. We found each other," I say. "And now she's found you."

"My baby." Mom's shaking, groping at her neck for her pendant, which she clutches in her hand. "I'm sorry, my baby. Qing yuan liang wo."

"Forgive me," Sam murmurs in my ear.

My new sister doesn't take her hungry eyes off our mother. "Please, let me have some time alone with her," Fangli says. Mom looks happy so I only hesitate for a moment. Sam tugs my hand to lead me out into the hallway and then outside.

"I don't want to go too far," I say. Not with my family there.

"We can stay right here." He brings me to a small, empty play-ground to the side of the home, a place for visiting grandchildren to play.

Now that I'm with him, I don't know what to say. He saves me.

"I never thought it was you who called ZZTV," he says.

"I know now." I rub my cheek. Sam managed to tell me about his feelings. I can be as brave. "I was hurt you thought it was me, even though it was only in my head."

"I'm sorry." Sam sits down on the bottom of the wide slide and I join him. "I knew how I felt about you was different, but I never made it clear enough."

"I never knew where I stood with you, whether you were acting or not."

"Tell me what I can do to make you trust me. I'll do it."

I bump my head into his shoulders. "You already did when you came here today."

He wraps his arms around me. "I missed you. Missed talking to you." He runs a finger over my lower lip. "Missed kissing you." A small kiss drops on my temple.

"It's been a while."

"Seventeen days," he says promptly, then goes red when I look at him. "I mean, about that."

"Give or take?"

"I was counting each day. Sue me." Another kiss, this time on my hair.

"You were supposed to be in China."

"I went to talk to my mother."

"Fangli mentioned it."

He leans against me. "It was quite the event and, as you know, culminated with her telling the media I was marrying Fangli."

I know it's not true but the memory of the feelings I had when I thought it was remain and they sting.

He twists around to look at me. "We're not. I love Fangli, but as one of my truest friends."

"I know," I assure him. Although Fangli told me the same thing, hearing it from Sam hits deeper and releases the last bit of doubt I didn't know I had.

We sit in silence for a moment, watching as a gray squirrel runs by, fluffy tail undulating. "Cute," he murmurs.

It is, especially when it stops to look at us, but I'm not here to admire tree rodents. "How are you doing?" I ask.

"Good," he says with some surprise. "It was...frightening." He goes red. "A stupid thing to say."

"No, I get it." I did, too. Lili is no Todd, but there can be people in our lives who take on more of a presence and influence than they deserve. "How is she now?"

"She won't speak with me, but my father agreed with me. She's furious at us both." His dimples show in a wry smile. "She'll understand one day. I hope."

I tuck myself under his arm. "You did good."

"Not as good as you with Eppy."

"Thanks to you."

He shrugs. "No one would have cared if it didn't work. It does. You were great on the interviews."

"You saw them?"

"Of course. In part because I couldn't miss them. You were everywhere."

I grin. "I know." There goes keeping under the radar and not taking risks. "Robin Banerjee called. I don't have to find a job. I can work on Eppy because he's funding me."

Sam whoops. "I knew he would. That's my Gracie."

His Gracie. I probably like the sound of that more than I should.

"You'll be busier." He runs his hand over my hair.

"You're one to talk," I point out. "Don't you leave to shoot a movie soon?"

"Yeah." He coughs. "Hey. Do you think you can add one more task into your Eppy list?"

"Like what?"

"A relationship? I'm thinking in the long-term plans section."

I look at him.

"I want to give us a chance," he says. "Sam and Gracie."

"You're a movie star."

"Sure am."

"Surrounded by beautiful people."

"Like the woman I'm with now. Should I point out you're a CEO, surrounded by brilliant people?" He shrugs. "I trust you, Gracie. Do you trust me? Trust that what I feel for you is real?"

He pulls back completely like he doesn't want to sway my answer. I grab him because I know. "I trust you."

"Plus, I like that you're a CEO." He puffs out his chest. "A good ego boost for me." He catches my eyes. "Don't say it," he warns.

"Not like you need it."

"You said it." He shakes his head.

I want this. His chest is pressed against me and I can feel his heart pound against my skin. It's fast.

Despite the light tone, he's nervous, too.

I take a chance. "I think I want to try. You and me. Let's do it."

"A ringing endorsement." He leans in. "I'll take what I can get from you."

My lips capture his and I feel him smile against my mouth.

He pulls back. "I'm so glad you walked into that coffee shop."

"Me, too, even though that muffin was terrible."

He laughs and strokes my hair. This time, when he kisses me, I know it's absolutely all for me.

NOVEMBER 1

EPPY

DAILY LOG LINE
Dream Bigger

NOVEMBER EYES ON
THE PRIZE GOAL:
EPPY APP LAUNCH!

DAY TASKS   MONTH TASKS

WORK
- ○ Meet with PR firm.
- ○ Return call to app developer re beta test.
- ○ *[in progress]* Hire website/social media coordinator.

LIFE
- ○ Book spa day for Anjali, Fangli, and me as Fangli's birthday gift.
- ○ Tour Mom's new room at Xin Guang.

FUN
- ○ Lunch with Robin Banerjee.

EVERYDAY
- ○ Do Mandarin module.
- ○ Take multivitamin.

DON'T THINK. DO.
- ○ Tell Sam I love him, too.

THE END

Reading Group Guide

1. Gracie is biracial and at times struggles with other people's perception of what that means. What preconceptions do you think you have about biracial identity, or what do you see in the media? How do you react when people discuss experiences that may not be familiar to you?

2. The author is also biracial. How much of an author's experience do you think is incorporated into a book? Would you feel different about a book if the author is writing about an experience they have not had first-hand?

3. Gracie has a particular fondness for lists and organizational methods. Is this something you find useful in your own life? Which of the various methods Gracie explores would you most be interested in trying?

4. Gracie and Sam's mothers have different philosophical approaches to life: one cautious and one assertive. How has this impacted Gracie and Sam?

5. Why do you think it was so important for Gracie to get her mother into Xin Guang? What would you be willing to do in Gracie's place?

6. Gracie finds a moment of empowerment when she ditches her attempts to blend in and chooses her own specific power red lipstick—a shade distinct from Fangli's. Is there a personal token (whether it's makeup or some other item) that makes you feel powerful? What do you think it is that gives you that feeling?

7. If you were going to be mistaken for a celebrity—and then step into their life for a week—who would you want it to be? Why? Who would you *least* like to trade lives with?

8. Fangli reveals that she was discouraged from seeking help for her depression. Why was that? What do you think would have happened if she'd sought help anyway? Can you think of any moments in your or others' lives where mental health stigma kept you/others from seeking help?

9. Gracie is thrust into a far more glamorous life than she's ever known before. If you found yourself in her situation, what's the #1 luxury you'd most enjoy?

10. Gracie initially felt powerless in the face of her boss, Todd. What do you think was keeping her from facing him down? What did you think of their final confrontation and the realization that he didn't have any power over her?

11. Sam clearly envies Gracie's ability to live a normal life without the eyes of the world on her. How do you think you would handle being famous? Would the trade-off of luxury vs. loss of privacy be worth it?

12. Everyone assumes Sam and Fangli are either a couple or certain to become one someday. If you were in Gracie's position, would you feel jealous knowing so many people considered them endgame?

13. Gracie has to go through a lot of training and research to become Fangli. Do you think you would be able to convincingly pretend to be someone else for a few months?

14. Gracie and Fangli discover that the reason they look so alike is because they are sisters. Would you be able to forgive your parents for hiding a secret like that from you? If you were in Fangli's situation, would you be able to forgive your mother for leaving?

15. Gracie and Fangli's mother was put in an impossible situation when she realized she was pregnant with her second child, thanks to the one-child policy. Women's reproductive choices have often been politicized and controlled. This has put women around the world in impossible positions. What do you think the impact has been and how can women resist?

16. Why do you think Mei did what she did? Would you have been able to forgive her?

17. Gracie long wished for an organizational method that actually met her needs and, finally, decided to create one herself—becoming a huge success in the process. Is there a similar kind of problem in your life that needs solving, and what steps do you think you'd need to take to create your own kind of Eppy?

18. The future looks bright for Gracie, Sam, and Fangli, but there's a long road ahead of them. What do you think is in store for them? How will Sam's complicated relationship with his parents play into their future?

A Conversation with the Author

What was the inspiration for *The Stand-In*? What did you draw on as you developed the story?

I wanted to write a book featuring a biracial main character who has similar experiences as I have. I also wanted to address issues that I think are important, namely questions of identity, love and friendship, and mental health.

On the lighter side, I wanted to create a fun, entertaining story as an escape for readers, like an emotional spa day. *The Stand-In* was written in the early months of the pandemic, so this became increasingly significant as I looked for a place to retreat from reality.

What comes first for you: the plot or the characters? Why?

I usually get a plot idea based on a what-if scenario, and it evolves from there. In this case, I wondered: What if a woman was approached to be a celebrity double? What would she do? What kind of woman would say yes, and what would motivate her to agree? I then create the plot and characters at the same time, which means I go back often to check to see if my characters have had fundamental changes that need to be rethreaded through the draft.

Did anything about the story (characters, plot, etc.) significantly change from your first draft?

Many things changed! I first planned *The Stand-In* with chapters that alternated between Sam and Gracie. The first chapter had Sam on a movie set dealing with his overbearing mother, when a very clueless Gracie walked through as they film. But that didn't feel right because I wanted more intimacy between the reader and the story. The next version was all from Gracie's point of view, but Fangli and Sam were there to film a corporate action spy movie instead of acting in a play. But in every draft, the characters remained who they are. They're the core of the story.

What is the most valuable piece of writing advice you've received?

Of the very many pieces of writing advice I've heard over the years, the one that I come back to the most is that there is no such thing as perfect—there's only the best you can do right now. It's important to recognize that as you grow and learn, your writing will (hopefully) improve. I try to apply this to my non-writing life as well. Oh, and don't read reviews. That's solid advice.

What are some of your favorite moments in the book? Are there any particular characters or situations that you most identify with or that were the most fun to write?

I'm a huge fan of makeover moments, particularly if it's a montage set to a classic 1980s song. Although it doesn't have a soundtrack in the book, the most fun scenes to write were the ones where Gracie is exploring her new luxurious world. Even though I dress for comfort (read: sweatpants) I'd kill to have a walk-in closet filled with designer clothes like Gracie has in her hotel room. I'd just stand in the closet and admire them.

What was the hardest scene to write?

Spoiler alert, but I'm going to assume if you're reading this, you've finished the book. The hardest scene to write was Gracie's confrontation with Todd on the balcony. I personally wanted Todd to get a really brutal comeuppance, like a total knock-out. I also needed it to be realistic to Gracie's character. Balancing the two to make it emotionally satisfying took multiple rewrites.

On its release as an audio original, there was an amazing response from listeners. What are some things fans of the story enjoyed that you were excited to see?

I was thrilled at the response from readers. I was moved to see how many people resonated with the mental health themes of the book, and how the characters deal with it in their individual ways.

Mental health issues are still stigmatized, hidden or endured in isolation because people are ashamed to ask for help or scared to express their feelings. I'd love to see mental health discussions normalized and as a writer, the way I do this is through my characters. I wanted Gracie, Fangli, and Sam to represent how some people might approach those often incredibly important but difficult conversations.

What was it like to first hear Phillipa Soo narrate the audiobook?

It was extraordinary. A performance like Phillipa's brings an additional layer of brightness and depth to the characters. I have a huge amount of respect for her performance and gratitude for how careful she was in her interpretation of the text.

You balanced social issues in this novel with humor and heart. Why did you feel it was important to push the boundaries of the traditional love story to include more complexity and nuance?

Good characters have multi-faceted lives. They work, they have friends. They get overwhelmed by big problems and aggravated by small ones. It makes sense to me to reflect that in the story as well, since when we fall in love, we fall in love as whole people, bringing with us all of the intertwined joy and pain and confusion of our lives. Characters should, too.

How did your own experience as a bicultural author inform your characters' stories? How else has your background and lived experience influenced your work? Are there any scenes that you pulled from real life?

Experiences of racialized people depend on so many factors: family, gender, geography, dominant culture, and ethnic background being only a few. But at the same time, I think there are common moments for many of us. Straddling two cultures shapes how we perceive our identity, the world, and our place in it. There are definitely some elements of real-life reflected in Gracie's story. Her attempt to learn Chinese is identical to my own. I use an app, too!

What are you hoping readers will walk away from your book thinking about or talking about?

I hope there are enough elements that will resonate with different readers. Some may wish there's a real Eppy app available (I do) or come away finally feeling seen in a book that features characters like them. My overall goal was that people could lose themselves in a different world for a few enjoyable hours. If I achieved that, I'm happy.

There is a lot about family and how that is defined in the book. Why did you want to tackle that issue?

I like to write multi-dimensional characters and family is a huge component of who we are and how we're shaped as people. To have a story without family, or that didn't incorporate the impacts of family, both good and bad, would be like having a sandwich without bread.

What do you think are the most important elements of good writing/storytelling?

When I look back at stories I've enjoyed versus stories I've adored, the main difference is that the enjoyable stories have had strong plot or strong character elements. The incredible ones have had both. Having that mix, and then layering on themes and threading through motifs build stories that people want to keep reading.

If you were to write a spin-off about a secondary character, who would it be?

Wei Fangli. We're not all movie stars, but I think most people can relate to her longing for connection, her battle with balancing her professional and personal lives, and her struggles with coping with her mental health. She's a very rich character who I could see going in many different directions.

What can we expect from you next?

My next book is another rom-com that tells the story of an ambitious lawyer who falls in love with a K-pop idol. It was a huge amount of fun to write, and I had the best time researching K-pop boy bands.

Acknowledgments

Thank you to my incredible agent, Carrie Pestritto, who said I should definitely and totally write this book. Allison Carroll from Audible and Mary Altman from Sourcebooks were editors extraordinaire. Go, team!

Candice Rogers Louazel is always my first and best reader. Allison Temple, Farah Heron, Jackie Lau, and Rosanna Leo were spot-on in their gently worded advice.

A thank-you goes to those who generously took the time to answer my emails that started "Weird question, but...": Lydia Jin, Natasha Mytnowych, Denise Tay, and Michele Yuen-McDonald.

Most of all, thank you to Elliott and Nyla, who gave me the space to write and didn't make me play board games with them even though we were in lockdown.

About the Author

Lily Chu lives in Toronto, Canada, and loves ordering the second-cheapest wine, wearing perfume all the time, and staying up far too late reading a good book. She writes romantic comedies with strong Asian characters.

You can learn more at lilychuauthor.com and @lilychuauthor.

A TO-DO LIST
FOR EVERY MOOD.

DATE:

DREAMS LIST

ULTIMATE GOAL

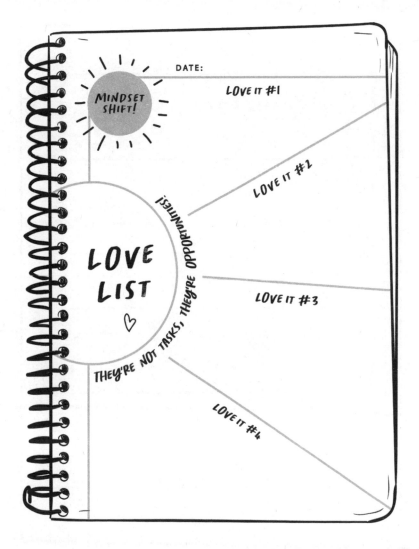

DATE: _____

THREE TASKS A DAY:

☐ _____

☐ _____

☐ _____

DATE: _____

THREE TASKS A DAY:

☐ _____

☐ _____

☐ _____

DATE:

BILLABLE HOURS TEMPLATE			
DATE	TIME	TASK	HOURS

DAILY LOG LINE

THE STAND-IN
BY LILY CHU

DAY TASKS | MONTH TASKS

WORK
○
○
○

LIFE
○
○

FUN
○

EVERYDAY
○
○

DON'T THINK. DO.
○
○